# A GIRL
# MADE OF AIR

# A GIRL
# MADE OF AIR

## NYDIA
## HETHERINGTON

Quercus

First published in Great Britain in 2020 by

Quercus Editions Ltd
Carmelite House
50 Victoria Embankment
London EC4Y 0DZ

An Hachette UK company

A CIP catalogue record for this book is available
from the British Library

HB ISBN 978 1 52940 887 4
TPB ISBN 978 1 52940 888 1

10 9 8 7 6 5 4 3 2

Typeset by Jouve (UK), Milton Keynes

Printed and bound in Great Britain by Clays Ltd, Elcograf S.p.A.

MIX
Paper from
responsible sources
FSC® C104740

FSC
www.fsc.org

Papers used by Quercus are from well-managed forests and
other responsible sources.

For Andy

What potions have I drunk of Siren tears,
Distill'd from limbecks foul as hell within,
Applying fears to hopes and hopes to fears,
Still losing when I saw myself to win!

William Shakespeare


We travel along the thread of narrative like
high-wire artistes. That is our life.

Angela Carter

# A Dream? A Falsehood? A Memory?

## *An unanswered question*

First, there are no pictures. I see only darkness. My nose is keen, my brain sharp as a pin.

There are smells.

The burning of wood and earth for heat, or light, or both. Damp ground: soil mixed with animal dung and urine. Wool: clammy with sweat and rain that has dried and dampened and dried, almost to a crust. Sugar: fragrant yet repellent, like the sweet-tasting, treacle-coated strips of cloth hung up in summer for catching flies. Engine oil. Dusty hay bales that release their musky whiff as the all-pervading smell of oiled canvas from the big top, that great yawning beast, wafts its sour aroma over my face.

That is not all.

There are other smells. Paint, wood shavings, bottled scent and hair pomade. These are the familiar stinks of life, of hope. I am not afraid, neither am I calm.

Next, comes feeling.

Knees. Shins. The tops of my feet. The flats of my hands. These bits of me, scraping along compacted sod, scratching on loose hay and litter. Warm snot, running from nose to upper lip. Cold saliva on my chin, chafing as I duck down and graze my face on the ground. My fingers, small and searching, feeling with soft pads hardened by cold, skilfully avoid the crunch of a heel, the kick of a toe cap. Smooth leather brushes my fat cheeks that, in turn, catch on metal eyelets and the treacherous ends of shoelaces, forcing me to keep my eyes closed until the show starts.

Then, there is noise.

In fact, although I only notice it now, I am in a sea of sound. There is a loud hum-thrum of voices. Shouting; laughing; chattering. They mingle together, creating a veritable roaring ocean of din. I cover my ears with my hands and the sound is muted. If I cup my hand, the sound changes again, and now it really does sound like the sea, like waves crashing, like the wind in a storm. I let out a short giggle, adding my own tiny expulsions to the symphony. I imagine myself floating happily on waves, singing to passing rocks. Until the boom-boom of a drum snaps me from my daydream, quenches the humming of voices, turning them first to a murmur, then to a hiss – with my eyes still closed, I now imagine the big top to be a nest of snakes – and then, silence.

Opening my eyes, I crawl through a hushed wreckage of ankles. Woollen socks, dress hems, stockings and trouser bottoms struggle, like the iron hulls of sunken ships, to bar my way. At times a hand comes down to slap me, a face bends close, tuts, and I smell the different bouquets of warm, salty breaths. Another hand; a shove; a whisper: *It's a child, look, a child*. Still, I am not to be put off. I inch forwards. I know my way. This is my territory, and I am an expert in its terrain. It does not take long before I surface. One final push through the tangle of knees and bags, and my efforts are fully and wonderfully rewarded.

Light and colour flood before me, as if I am emerging from the blackest cave, out into a valley of pure gold. Everything is transformed. I have stepped from the world of normal existence into another, more real, immeasurably more touchable, more believable place. I sit, eyes wide, mouth agape, fingers entwined and twisting. Up to this moment I have lived in sepia, my muddy life devoid of meaning. That is how it always feels, until I see her, once again, bathed in colour and light.

My mother is standing in the centre of the ring.

Ropes sway above her, lights blaze. Her hands are on her hips. Her mouth is large and red. She is smiling, nodding to grateful strangers (how I wish I was one of them). Bending one leg, her hip moves up and down in a perfect jiggle. She keeps one hand resting on the moving hip as the other reaches above her head, giving her sweeping salutations to the crowd, who explode into a chorus of happy applause. Her costume shimmers. Colours seem to pour from her body. She is all the colours of the world. She laughs at the warm reception, as if every person in the big top is her very best friend. All the while, waiting patiently behind her, the silent water shivers in its tank.

Blowing kisses to her, the way she does to the crowd, I set off in the direction of my mother. Sliding my body from the darkness of the audience and onto the slippery, bright tarpaulin of the ring, I edge and inch towards the water tank. She turns away, starts to scale its glass walls by way of rope and siren strength. A splash, and my mother is in. Still, I push on. If I try hard enough, she will see me.

There is movement above me now, and weight upon my shoulders. Although I do not wish to make a fuss, I scream out. I am lifted. Colours dance in rapid succession. My head cranes around, my neck bends and I am fighting a force much larger than myself. Yet, I must struggle, I must fight because I am afraid to lose sight of her. It is too late. I am ushered away by big hands. Wriggling and shrieking get me nowhere.

The big top spins. The colours fade.

Returned to darkness, I listen to the distant sounds: music, laughter, applause. I do not cry. One day, I will reach her. She will drip her colours over me, and we will swim together in her tank. For now, my head rests on the hard ground. Rocking from side to side, I sigh, and try to summon sleep. I whisper her name, crossing my fingers, first one way, then the other, counting the times I say it, to give gravity to ritual, power to the magic spell: *Marina [one]. Marina [two]. Marina [three]* . . .

# 1

# Rabbits' Feet and Hokum

**World on a Wire: The Fallen Star**
**Ellie Macveigh, the *New York Times***

June 14, 1983 / Manhattan / 10.30 a.m. / Transcription:
Tape 1 of 1

*Can you tell me who you are?*

I've been called the Greatest Funambulist Who Ever Lived.

*You smile when you say it. Don't you believe it?*

Sometimes.

[Pause.]

Sorry, I don't like being recorded very much. I've never been
good at talking. I'd rather write things down. My voice is awful,
isn't it? I don't recognize it sometimes. I never should've started
smoking. I mean, once you're hooked . . . It's a lived-in voice,
I suppose.

*The recording's only for me. No need to worry. And your voice is great.*

Was I babbling? I'll try to relax. You're the first person I've spoken to publicly, or privately for that matter, since my, I don't know what to call it, my retirement? That makes me sound old. Since my last performance. Yes, that's a decent description. There've been offers of interviews, appearances and all kinds of things. To be honest, I couldn't face them. But I'm ready now. You came along at the right time. It's not that I care about being out of the public eye, you understand. I'm done with that. I'm babbling again, aren't I? Sorry. Please, do go on.

*What makes you the greatest, sometimes?*

[Pause.]

Fearlessness, I suppose. I'm not afraid.

*Of falling?*

It's not the falling one must fear, it's the landing.

*Ah yes. And are you afraid of landing?*

Never. I have protection. See?

*You're showing me a piece of jewellery. It's lovely. Amber?*

Thank you. I saw you looking at it as I came in. It's okay, you can touch it, if you like.

*Yes, it had caught my eye. It's very bright. Unusually so.*

It keeps me safe.

*You're superstitious?*

[Pause. A cigarette is lit. The crackle of burning paper. A deep exhale.]

I've never thought of it like that before. I suppose I must be. I mean, it's a talisman, of sorts, like a rabbit's foot.

*Like, some actors wear certain clothes, you know, the 'lucky socks' or something, before going on stage. Is that how it works?*

Honestly? I'm not sure. When I climb the wire, my fingers search my throat for the pendant. I admit, there's a certain amount of theatre to it. I'm prone to the poetic, I'm afraid. But there's comfort in it, too.

*You say it's amber. Was it a gift?*

You asked if it was amber and I do refer to it as an *amber pendant.* Only it's not. It's a glass locket containing a snip of tightly bound orange hair. Probably worthless to anyone else, but priceless to me. It wasn't really a gift either. I'm ashamed to say I took it, the hair I mean, not the pendant. I bought that.

*It's human hair?*

I've always supposed so.

*Extraordinary. Who did you take it from?*

It was a long time ago.

[Pause. Sigh.]

I mean, there's a story to it, if you'd like to hear it. It's just hard to unpack. I don't know where to start.

*I'd love to hear it. Why don't you start at the beginning? There's no rush.*

Okay, let's see. I took the hair from Serendipity Wilson. But, that's already much later in the story.

*That's a very unusual name. Who was she?*

She was a performer. My teacher, and closest friend. I suppose she still is, in a way. Some people have a lasting effect. They stay with you. If you know what I mean?

*Indeed, I do. How did you meet her?*

I was in my mother's womb when Serendipity Wilson joined the circus. That didn't mean her arrival was lost on me. Even now, if I close my eyes, I see her, walking into the circus encampment, her head a shining orange beacon, her heart full of hope.

[Pause.]

Are you sure we've time for this? I mean, I know how far-fetched it sounds, and it doesn't get any less like a fairy story as it goes on.

8

*Go on. Please. I love fairy stories.*

I thought you might, somehow.

[A cough and clearing of the throat.]

Let me see then. Oh, yes: the light from Serendipity Wilson's hair shone with such ferocity it flooded the circus encampment. It burrowed through the thick skin of my mother's belly, bathing me, womb-bound as I was, in its glow. Most circus folk have seen many improbable things in their time. So, a human flame, in the shape of a skinny girl with overly large feet, merely confirmed that such curiosities still had the power to impress. A spark of excitement shot through the encampment as soon as she arrived, growing in wildfire whispers, until everyone came to the big top to see the fabulous young thing whose gift might save their circus.

*To be clear, you weren't there, this was before you were born?*

I was there in a manner of speaking, *in utero*. My mother was there.

*But you speak as though you remember her arrival first-hand?*

This is difficult to explain, and you might think me mad, but I do. It's a question of belief, I suppose. Can you believe that Serendipity Wilson's hair shone so brightly it cast a light upon my darkened nest? Of course, this could all be hokum. The ramblings of someone who lives alone and is out of the habit of talking to people. I can't make you believe the story. My performances on the wire have all been stories, really. Each one with its own narrative and world. Its own truth. I suppose I've always been a storyteller.

*Do you want me to believe you?*

Oh yes. You have such a sparkle in your eye. I bet you believed in fairy stories as a kid? I did. I mean, yes. Everyone wants to be believed, right?

*Well, I'd love to hear more of your memories.*

I'm not entirely sure where my memory begins. Truth is, even though I've kept quiet about my past, I've always wanted to tell these stories, but only to the right person.

*I think lots of people would enjoy them. Let's tease out the important bits, then. Get your stories out there. When and where were you born?*

Can't say for sure. I know that when I emerged, I was unremarkable. My mother showed no interest in me. I was, at best, an inconvenience.

[Pause. The crunching out of a cigarette in an ashtray, the lighting of another. A window is opened. The hum of traffic mingles with the inhalation of smoke into lungs.]

As I grew up, I took to hiding in dark places. I was far too dull and quiet a child to be enveloped in the perpetual cacophony of a circus, with its trumpet blowers, painted faces, glittering ladies, roaring animals, the whooshing of derring-do, the never-ending drone of a distant accordion and the constant yell of all-encompassing egos. That was the landscape of my young life. And all snug beneath the blue-and-white stripes of an ominously joyful big top. I'd walk around the encampment, eyes closed, fingers shoved in my ears, longing for a grey calm to match my grey spirit.

*Grey? Yet you were the darling of the New York cabaret scene. One article called you 'a kaleidoscope of colour in a dull world'. So where and when did you find your colour?*

I suppose I learned it. By quietly watching, by taking notes. And maybe I inherited it, from my mother. They do say these things are in the blood. I believe in bloodlines.

*Your mother. Was she a circus performer?*

Oh yes. My mother was a great beauty, the first big star of our show. She swam around a glass tank, waved, smiled, and sparkled for the crowds. She was an artist of the finest degree. Her name was Marina. Or rather, that's what she called herself. Her costumes were hand-sewn with tiny gold and silver patches that caught the light and glistened like the scales of a trout, and she wore a tight-fitting hat, tied neatly under her chin. The men in the crowd whistled as she swam around her tank, but the ladies scowled. Then the ladies' scorn turned to fear, then to sheer admiration, when the crocodiles slid in.

*An exciting act!*

I never saw it. At least, that's what I was always told. Apparently, she was too far gone by the time I was born, too full of gin and self-pity. I know it by heart, though. An act like that is nothing short of legendary. She seemed to belong in the water. There were even claims she was an actual mermaid, found by the ringmaster on a jaunt to the seaside, captured and taught to do tricks by an animal trainer.

*The wonderful fantasy world of the circus.*

Absolutely. The world was at war. The human race needed to believe in another reality, and circus people have vivid imaginations, it's their stock-in-trade. By the way, the animal tamer was Manu, my father.

*Not an English name.*

French. Manu grew up on his family's farm in rural Brittany. He was brought to England through poverty, fear and – fuelled by a childhood fixation with Sherlock Holmes – a thirst for adventure. This was not quenched by selling onions in London street markets to rude old men who called him a filthy Frog and spat at him. So, Manu became an ardent and adventurous lover.

*The French lover. A nice cliché.*

Yes. One he enthusiastically propagated. His dark eyes and Celtic charm, along with his tight muscles from pushing ancient ploughs through hard Breton ground, made him an instant hit with the giggling English girls. Still, he wanted more from life. So, when a circus came to town, he threw himself on the mercy of the Italian ringmaster.

*This is real storybook stuff.*

I've never spoken about my childhood. I hope I don't sound too eccentric. I know that's how I come across sometimes. Most journalists would want to hear about the New York club scene, my wild escapades as a nightclub darling, before moving on to my retreat from public life. You seem different though. You've got soft edges.

*Soft edges? I'm not sure what that means, but thank you. Honestly, I don't care about the sensationalist stuff. I'm interested in where you came from and how you ended up living on the Lower East Side of Manhattan. Please, go on. The Italian ringmaster?*

Ah, Fausto.

[Pause as she pulls on her cigarette.]

Fausto Flavio was a miserly one-time lion tamer, whose circus, bulging waistline and ageing figure had all seen better days. He was looking for an apprentice and a bargain, just as Manu fetched up. He put my father on contract – on half wages, of course, due to the unfortunate situation of his being French.

*It's quite a jump, from onion seller to lion tamer.*

Fortunately, Manu found he was as gifted with the circus animals as he was with women. Using his carefully honed skills
in the art of romance, he wooed wild beasts into compliance,
putting aside the animal trainer's whip, coaxing them with a
soft voice and outstretched hands. He turned great lions into
cavorting kittens, forced tigers to lie down at his feet as obedient as any lap-dog; over time he became more compelling
than ever. It was a well-known fact that women wept when the
circus left town. Then he met Marina.

*Your mother.*

The story of Marina and Manu's first joining became circus
legend. Show people love to make legends of their stars. There
was no escaping the stories of my mother and father's
love-making.

*Every child's idea of a horror story.*

There are many horrors to be had, yet. This one's not so
bad, really.

*Would you mind telling it now?*

Happy to. It's a love story, after all. Everyone loves to love.

[Cigarette. Heavy exhale.]

Marina was like no other creature. Everyone saw how her
beauty and grace left Manu troubled. For the first time in his

life, when confronted with a possible conquest, my father's palms began to sweat, his mouth went dry. In the confusion, he couldn't remember the English words to entice her, clumsily substituting them with his own language. He needn't have worried. At their first meeting, in the shadows of tent poles and flags, Marina felt a fierce heat rush through her frozen veins. She took his hands and brought them up to her face, kissed the ends of his fingers, then, closing her eyes, placed them under her clothes. Manu didn't stand a chance. He felt her breathing, a fluttering of tiny birds beneath hot liquid flesh, the cage of her ribs, bone-brittle under his hands. *It is all for you*, she said, as they slid under a trailer, discarding their damp clothes, writhing together in the dirt.

*You say you're not used to talking about it, yet you rattled that off as if you'd told it a thousand times. You certainly know all the details.*

Everyone in the circus knew.

*It's great. There's more?*

On their wedding day, Manu gave Marina the greatest gift: two juvenile crocodiles. He taught her to train and tame them. She learned to stroke and coo at them so that they looked up at her with the tenderness of children in their dreadful eyes. In turn, she loved and cared for the animals. You'd think she'd actually given birth to them. They were the ultimate proof of Manu's love, and they made her a sensation.

*Yes, of course, the crocodiles.*

Two years after they married, Marina was a huge star of the circus. Pictures of her shimmering beautifully with her reptilious beasts, rippling in their underwater tank, appeared on the cover of magazines. Manu devoted himself to her, creating ever more impressive routines.

*Routines? Were they dangerous?*

All routines are dangerous. You must master them. For example, Manu taught the crocodiles to retrieve peaches and other soft-skinned fruits from the hand of a smiling Marina, who stood, magnificent, on the bottom of the water tank. The crocodiles held the fruit gently in their mouths, crawled out of the water to slink their way down the side of the tank and place the fruit, intact and unblemished, on the dry ground, in a gruesome game of fetch. Manu then replaced the fruit with larger objects such as baby dolls and teddy bears, giving the crocodiles the macabre aspect of monstrous children. Eventually those objects were also replaced, by Marina herself. The final routine was breathtaking.

*You never actually saw it, though.*

I'm told that's the case; yet, I have memories. I can't explain it. I believe I was there, that I watched my mother swim with her crocodiles. The circus folk insisted that Marina refused to continue after I was born. That I was the cause of her descent into oblivion. I'm not entirely sure what's true and what's not.

When I was born, the axis had to shift. I was nothing. No, I was less than nothing. I was invisible. And yet, my birth changed everything, forever. All I can tell you are the basics, the story as it was told to me, and if I can, I will embellish it with my own memories. I have an excellent memory.

*So it seems. I'm all ears.*

At the very pinnacle of her art and fame, or so legend would have it, Marina realized she was pregnant. The constant vomiting made it impossible for her to continue her act without the risk of disgracing herself. She took to shouting at the other circus people, furious with her body for letting her down in such an abhorrent way. Manu tried to comfort her. Having his constant attention seemed to ease her distress, a bit. But as her belly grew fat and full of me, my mother would scream out in despair at her hideous disfigurement. Everyone, it seems, went to my parents' caravan during the days of my mother's self-confinement, so worried were they for their dear Marina. They brought gifts of cakes and biscuits made with parental care. Cutting the sugary treats into crocodile shapes, feeding them to her with tumblers of homemade lemonade, laced with gin, for the pain. Meanwhile, the show had to go on, whether my mother liked it or not. In the absence of The Great Marina, the circus was forced to look for a new main attraction, a temporary necessity. Luckily, only days before Marina found out the terrible news of her condition – or so the story goes – a young girl with freakishly luminous orange hair was brought to the circus by her father.

*Serendipity Wilson!*

Yes! She was a most unusual-looking person. Long-limbed so that she looked somehow stretched, entirely flat-chested, green eyes like those of a cat rather than a person, large feet and an elegant pointy nose. And with a gentleness of spirit that shone almost as much as her astonishing mane. She wanted to be an artist, to twist and glide and spin. Fausto, overlord of the circus, decided that Serendipity Wilson, with her head full of fire and strong, thin young body, would become the circus's first female funambulist. In her excitement, Serendipity Wilson forgot to mention she suffered from a terrible fear of heights.

*Oh dear, a problem indeed. I can't help but notice that every time you mention Serendipity Wilson you touch your pendant. As if the act of saying her name causes you to check it's still there. It's a link to her, right? Would you like to tell me about it?*

[Pause.]

*Or are you reluctant to tell that tale?*

I don't mean to be. I want to be open with you. But it's difficult to find words for things you've spent a lifetime trying to . . . not forget exactly – we can never do that – but live with. Plus, it's a difficult tale to spin. I'm not sure where to begin, other than at the very beginning. But then that feels like we're going backwards.

*Okay. Let's go back. You were born in England, in a circus . . .*

Yes. My birth was unspectacular. Marina squatted naked in the caravan. Manu sat behind her, holding her up by wrapping his knees around her hips and crossing his arms over her breasts. Marina yelped and barked, swore revenge on the gods of pain who racked her beautiful body with such evil. I was brought to my mother by one of the dancing girls, a faceless, makeshift midwife who, hearing Marina's screams, had rushed in at the last minute to help. Soft, squashy and new, my eyes blinking in the strange light and a belly still full of my mother's bile, I cried for flesh and warmth. Marina leaned forwards, stunned sweat running down her face, breathless and uncompromising. *Yes, it's a baby*, she said, and fell back, exhausted, onto the bed.

*Your birth became another circus legend, then? No one can remember their own birth, so I guess this was told to you, as a child?*

My memory doesn't seem to work like other people's. Sometimes I fill in the gaps, but there's always an echo of truth in there. It's the only way I can find the words: by seeing the whole picture, the whole truth.

*All right. I can go with that. Please, carry on.*

Manu stroked Marina's head and soothed her as best he could. My unwilling nurse put me into a wooden-crate cot and tiptoed away. I lay kicking my legs, arms groping the alien air. There was no one to pick up my tiny frame. No comfort on this cold new earth. So yes, there we have it, another legendary beginning: the heroic, beautiful mother, the desperate father and me, the wretched child.

*And?*

And, I soon learned crying didn't bring me love, or food. Any attempt to gain my parents' admiration or attention fell on deaf ears and blind eyes. So, I was a silent child, standing in the shadows of my glorious parents, the pocket audience for the lives of my progenitors. As I grew, I became withdrawn from the physical world. I locked myself deep inside the confines of my mind, where I could pretend to be a spirit, a girl made of air and clouds. If anyone touched me, even accidentally brushed against me as they passed by, I'd shrink away, whimpering like a wounded dog. People were amazed that the snivelling infant who cowered in corners came from Marina's magnificent body.

*You had a home, a family. You weren't completely abandoned?*

The circus was my family and my home, but I was more like a pet than a beloved child. My parents couldn't spare me love, attention, or time. So, I would roam the encampment. Some of the other artistes would feed me every now and then, teach me my numbers or tell me stories, and generally be good Samaritans to a poor unloved thing. They'd stroke me, look at me with big watery eyes like I was a friendly feral cat, then send me on my way to play in the dirt under the trailers. When it wasn't possible to squeeze my little life into our caravan at the end of the day, I'd sleep where I could, in the beds of other people's children or, on warm nights, in the place I liked best: with the animals.

*No one took care of you?*

The circus people were kind enough, but I was quiet, easily forgotten. For most of my early childhood I was invisible. I was even thought to be a halfwit. Then, when I was around six years old, everything changed. That was the day Serendipity Wilson took my hand, kissed me on the forehead, and pushed me up a ladder. That was the day I became a funambulist.

*And another story begins.*

And another and another. All the way up to the crashing end of my career, and me sitting here today.

*It's been extraordinary meeting you. I wish we had more time. This will be great in print. I'm sure all your stories are equally fascinating.*

That depends on who's reading them, I suppose.

[End of tape.]

# 2

# Beginnings

This is not the beginning.

I've already written two pages. They lie crumpled in the raffia basket under my desk, a sarcophagus bought expressly for this purpose.

I hope you don't think it odd, to receive this correspondence. Perhaps you'll think me half mad? Perhaps I am. Since our meeting I've not been able to banish you from my thoughts. Your questioning had a marvellous effect on me, and although my introspections are sometimes a torture, I feel I must write them down, share them with you. I could see you wanted to know more. You said as much yourself. Our meeting was too brief. My mind has been on fire since our conversation. You found me at the right time.

There was a thread of understanding between us. I believe you felt it, the strength of our connection? It's something I've rarely experienced. Certainly, never with someone introducing themselves as a stranger. Still, I realize this letter is a presumption, and one I hope you will forgive. I fear it's more than a mere missive, so I urge you to settle down, be comfortable, be warm and at ease as you read on.

This is my life; my search.

Through my terrible carelessness, a child was lost from the circus. It's been a heavy burden to carry. I denied someone her true name and heritage, denied her the love of her mother. A lifetime has tumbled by since I first vowed to get her back. I admit I've sometimes been lazy, even turned away from my search. Yet I've lived in hope and do so again. Which brings me to you.

Above everything, this correspondence is a cry for help. You seemed so alive to my stories. Even if you can't publish everything I write here, even if it's a long shot, will you help me?

I've little to offer in return, only the story of my life, and the promise of truth.

Let's begin with hope, then. My words are a labyrinth into which we can wander. As I write these tales, I can follow each path, each fallen leaf, in the hope they might take me to the person I seek. I'm grateful to have a companion, again.

Many of these stories were jotted down in notebooks over the course of my lifetime. I will copy them out for you, as best I can, onto clean sheets of white paper. Some are diary entries, or snippets, some remembrances from faded photographs which have lain forgotten for decades, their images bleaching into yellowing pages. Others are letters or taken from notes secreted in pockets and bags over the years. Some are just memories. I came late to the world of words, but once it was shown to me, I learned quickly. Hardly a moment went by when I couldn't be seen scribbling away.

It was (unsurprisingly) Serendipity Wilson who taught me how to shape letters and read the words on the posters around our encampment. Big Gen, the circus bookkeeper and one of the last stars of the English sideshow circuit, was a hoarder. Her trailer was said to be like a museum; full of cabinets bursting with knick-knacks and moth-eaten stuffed creatures with bulging glass eyes. Amongst her precious treasure, she kept a book. Big Gen wasn't ungenerous. She didn't mind sharing her book with us. It was full of old photographs depicting people the book called *living curiosities*. I thought it was a storybook, about a mysterious island called Coney, where the curiosities lived. *Coney's the old English word for rabbit,* Serendipity Wilson told me. I imagined a desert island inhabited by bearded ladies, four-legged women, and millions of bunny rabbits.

*If we lived there, could I have one, as a pet?* I asked.

*One what?*

*A bunny rabbit?*

*My goodness, Mouse. If we lived there, you could have anything you wanted. That's why they call it Dreamland.*

At bedtime I'd climb in beside Serendipity Wilson, her hair loose over her shoulders, shedding orange light onto the pages, and we'd sit up, late into the night. She would point at words, making me say them out loud, and help me to copy them out with a pencil. The first word I learned to write was *dipygus*. I have a lot to thank Serendipity Wilson for.

I want you to picture me here, as I write. This is a new place for me. Another rented room. I haven't been here long. There's a bed against the wall. It's large but single; the sheets covering it are red velvet. They are my own. The furniture isn't. There's a heavy, ancient-looking oak wardrobe in the corner. It holds a handful of my costumes. They're a feast for moths. My everyday clothes lie neatly folded in a brown leather suitcase under the bed, which I cannot see from where I sit.

The room is the smallest in the building. I didn't want anything fancy, though I could afford it. I'm done with fancy. On the wall above my bed is a print of a rather beautifully painted portrait. The sitter perches on the edge of a glass water tank. She wears a golden swimsuit with matching swim hat, her legs long and waxy. She is unbelievably glamorous. My mother twinkles at the painter as crocodiles swim behind her, contained by the tank and the water in a smudge of green – a clever imitation of movement. Her head is thrown back. She is smiling, radiating a warmth I only ever saw her give to others, as a halo of lights proclaim her greatness. It's just one of my old circus posters, well painted, albeit with an over-sentimental hand, as was the style of the time. It's carefully preserved and elegantly framed. The frame is silver and polished. I polish it regularly. I'm not a sloven. Other than this the walls are bare. Eggshell, I think they call it. It's clean, like a hospital. There's a large window by the desk, behind which the sound of traffic rises to meet me. Even at this hour, people are living out their dreams, or pretending to do so. Their costumes are amazing. This is undeniably Manhattan and I am undeniably a person in exile. But it's the same wherever I go. Everyone is the star of their own show, performing for the passing, faceless crowds. We are all clowns.

I think I should begin with a memory, from a time before the documents which lie in front of me, from before I could write it all down. Take this oversized, somewhat unattractive yellow jumper I'm wearing. It was made for me many years ago by Serendipity Wilson. The jumper is misshapen (it always was) and full of holes. It's what I wear when I feel cold, or when the gloom descends, like a child with its blanket or favourite knitted toy. Every now and again I catch a tiny bright flare from deep within its weft, like light bouncing off a prism. This is because, even now, there are strands of Serendipity Wilson's hair deep within the fibres, tangled and knotted into the very structure of the garment at its making, armour-plating it, and me. These are flashes from long ago, from a time when Serendipity Wilson joyfully sat through the night, knitting for my warmth and comfort. I can picture her as she clicked the wooden needles together, the warm glow from her hair lighting up our wigwam. Once in a while she stopped, stared at me with her impossibly green eyes, plucked a hair from her magnificent head and knitted it into the jumper.

*For protection, my Mouse*, she said.

I giggled, sipped cinnamon tea and did not let my own stare fall away from hers, scared to blink in case I missed a precious moment of that precious time.

With the jumper I wear my red tartan pyjama pants, made from soft brushed cotton. As always, my amber pendant sits snug around my neck. The single orange tear is bright enough to cast light upon the words I now write. Between it, and the city lights shining into my window (will they ever stop?), I don't need a lamp. Whenever I sit at this desk to write my stories for you, I will be wearing these same things, sitting in this same place. The desk itself is old, more a table really, made of dark wood. Documents, from which I'm about to copy, lie scattered all over it. The wastepaper basket sits under the desk by my left foot.

My typewriter is not electronic. Imagine the sound it makes as I hit the keys and the hammers snap at the paper. The L sticks, so I stop every now and then to lift it back into place. It's heavy work. I can feel the words as I write them with my Challenger Portable Typewriter (the word Challenger is written on the right-hand side, above where the ribbon sits). The whole thing is grey and plastic; my fingers tingle from the effort of striking the keys, and I can smell the ink from the ribbon as each key strikes. Maybe you can imagine the sounds and smell of this action, this putting down of my stories, as you read them? I want you to feel the sensations I feel as I sit here writing, putting together a comprehensive picture of everything I've known, or thought, or felt, for you, a virtual stranger, a woman of words, and now, my confidante and helper.

So, to begin.

★

I am approximately seven years old. I'm not sure where we are. We move so often, and the encampment rarely changes. Except when we're at the seaside. Things taste different then. This memory does not have a salty, fishy taste. Nor is its air scrubbed clean by ocean spray. It's full of earthy, dirty smells: mud and the mess of stray dogs. Even the ammonia pong of our animals is cleansing compared with that.

This is yet another muddy common, surrounded on three sides by rows of scruffy back yards with brick walls and wooden privies. The ground is thick with sloppy muck, or tough as concrete where it has hardened to a crust. The dominant colour is brown, with thin mucky-green patches. As always, the bigger trailers are parked in a semicircle around the encampment, top to tail, giving the circus folk a degree of privacy. The animal enclosure is on the periphery of the encampment, cordoned off with chicken wire and bits of broken wooden fencing. We dig our privy next to the animals and put the caravans and tents on the opposite side, away from the smell. If you're caught short in the night you either piss in a pot or have to run across and risk disturbing the animals.

The big top is at the centre of everything. A colossus, dwarfing our meagre dwellings, it's always at the forefront of the encampment, facing the nearest road, surrounded by bunting and flags: yellow and red triangles that beat out time in the wind, and Union Jacks waving a friendly hello. In all probability we're somewhere in the north of England, but we could be anywhere.

I have been living in the colourful wigwam with Serendipity Wilson for a couple of weeks now. We've been friends
forever. When I was very small, she would smile at me
across the encampment, stop to ask me questions, or point
out clouds, birds, insects and other interesting things. Once,
she gave me two sugar mice, wrapped in greasy paper. They
melted on my tongue and I cried because I'd never tasted
such pure sweetness. As soon as I was big enough, she
showed me her wire, started to teach me how to balance,
said I was a natural. How happy she was to discover my hidden gift (so hidden I didn't know about it until she helped
me find it). Then, two weeks ago, she came across me sitting
in the llama enclosure. I was eating rotten apples meant for
the horses because I'd had nothing to eat for a day. She
picked me up and, striding at pace on her long legs, carried
me back to the colourful wigwam (though I was quite capable of walking).

*You'll be living here with me, from now on*, she said. And that
was that.

Most of the caravans and tents, the abodes, are huddled
together on one side of the encampment. But the colourful
wigwam is a little way off, towards the animals. Serendipity
Wilson says she'd rather sleep with the smell of animals and
shit than be surrounded by the sweat and snoring of circus
folk. I'm happy. I've never felt this emotion before.

Each day Serendipity Wilson teaches me how to be a
funambulist. We rig the practice wire up behind the big
top, ensuring protection against the wind. This wire is only

six feet from the ground but runs the length of the big top. It feels hard under my feet. There are burns and bruises on them right up to the ankles because they are still too soft, and I have to fight against the wire. It tries to rotate as I move along its rounded surface, forcing me to pull it steady with each step, twisting and turning my feet and toes as I go, in an unseen battle of wills. The soreness makes it difficult to walk when back on the ground. But there's no pain when I'm on the wire because I'm not thinking about it. I'm holding my muscles tight in my chest and across my middle, so that no matter how hard my feet are working, my legs can feel free, and no one will ever see how hard it is to keep my thighs pulling and straining against my knee sockets.

*Keep down! Lower your centre of gravity!* Serendipity Wilson shouts. *The lower you are, the easier you'll balance and move across the wire. Don't bend at the waist! Do you want to fall? Use your knees.*

After a while my muscles ache and cramp. So I listen to my breath as I pull it into my body and count how long I hold it there – *one potato, two potato, three potato, four* – high in my chest cavity. Then, I count again. As I take a step, I let the air go in a steady stream, my mouth pursed in a smiling O shape, so that my breath is leading my movement. Any cramps or bad thoughts glide away on that outwards breath, making me confident and strong for the next step, and the next, and the next.

If I do feel sore afterwards, I don't care. When Serendipity Wilson tells me how well I'm doing, when she holds me to her and says how proud she is, or when we're on the wire together and she turns and smiles at me, it's like I am flying.

My parents, Manu and Marina, have not noticed I have a new abode and a happy life. Maybe they believe I'm still sleeping with the llamas? Maybe this is why they haven't come to visit?

Two weeks and three days ago Manu spoke to me. I was in the animal enclosure playing with a baby llama (I've called him Solomon, although no one knows this. Maybe I'll tell Serendipity Wilson, or maybe I'll keep it to myself). Manu half-smiled at me. He ruffled my hair, put two fingers under my chin and lifted my head so I had to look directly into his face.

*Tu pues, ma puce*, he said, and marched away towards the cat enclosure.

I gave myself a hard sniff. My nostrils filled with the smell of soiled straw and animal grease so that my eyes filled with water and stung as I blinked.

Now, I am sitting head down in the wigwam, pondering all that has befallen me, as Serendipity Wilson knits. I look up. A gentle breeze outside touches the fabric of our shelter. The colourful scarves and scraps of cloth, sewn together with invisible stitches by Serendipity Wilson, seem to throb and breathe around us. The night is dark, but my friend's hair is uncovered, giving off a warm light. Colours flicker like flames from a bonfire, and thoughts, like moving pictures, start creeping through my mind. I close my eyes and imagine that Manu and Marina come to the wigwam. I make them cinnamon tea. We sit laughing and telling each other about the day. Marina looks healthy, like on the posters. Manu is strong and bold. He lifts me onto his shoulders, gambols around the tent like a horse, bending slightly because he is taller than Serendipity Wilson and the wigwam cannot accommodate his height. We fall in a heap and laugh until tears appear on our cheeks. When I become conscious of smiling, the moving pictures stop.

I open my eyes.

The colours from the wigwam dance back into view. It's all right that I'm smiling because Serendipity Wilson is smiling too. She often smiles. I sometimes find it hard to fathom why someone would smile so much. The big top is filled with smiles, the audience awash with them. To reward their glee, everyone in the ring smiles back. Dancing girls, horse riders, trapeze artists and acrobats, to mention but a few, all smile their lovely heads off. Until they run through the curtain and out of the ring. Then the smiles stop. Then there's snarling, and biting, and *whore, bitch, slut.*

Most likely Marina and Manu have heard of my new situation; the circus isn't an easy home for secrets – although I do well keeping mine. Not that there's anything secretive or underhand about my new life. Yes, they probably know, but have not been so touched by the information to bother enquiring how I'm settling in. They are across the encampment now; past the big top, past the boards of colourful circus posters, behind the other tents and dwellings, surrounded by their orange canvas awning with the frilly trim. They are a perfect, solid unit, nestling inside the caravan of my birth. I always know where they are. When I am not practising on the wire with Serendipity Wilson, I spend my time hiding under trailers and wagons, watching them. But this is not why I know where they are, especially Marina. Even when I cannot see her with my eyes, I can tell you her whereabouts. This is to do with magnetics. It's because of the blood.

Serendipity Wilson hates the stories about my mother, especially the ones about how Marina and I have seawater running through our veins. *Utter bile*, she says. *Ridiculous myth-making to bring in the slobbering crowds.* Serendipity Wilson doesn't like me talking about it, in fact, she won't stand for it. If she so much as hears a whisper about it, she gives the whisperer what for, and no mistake. I know better than to cross Serendipity Wilson, so I keep quiet.

The story of how my mother came to the circus, together with her strange accent, are all the proof some people need to believe that Marina is half – or maybe whole (who would know?) – mermaid. Or perhaps pure selkie. In any case, some creature born of the sea, come to show us that the ugliness of war cannot kill true beauty. Big Gen told me about it when I was very young. She didn't mean to pass on any great knowledge, I'm sure of that. She would not purpose-fully have shared her secrets with me, not even when I was a helpless infant. She was merely idling away her time while Marina slept in a haze of gin-soaked desperation, as she often did after my birth.

Big Gen is not a bad person. She at least tried to keep an eye on me when I was an innocent babe, as much as she was able. I never look upon her with spite. She loves Marina dearly. She cannot give me the time or consideration she might wish to because she's too busy caring for Marina, and Gen cares with every piece of her enormous body, like a great blanket of love.

When I am watching from my secret places, I often see Gen holding my sobbing mother; her gigantic arms moving in ripples as she strokes Marina's hair, cooing comfort in a low voice. I like Gen's voice. It's dark and grainy from smoking pipes and Woodbine cigarettes. She's a Yorkshire lass, and although she left that county while still in her girlhood, her accent is as strong as anyone's I ever met. Full of dull, flat sounds that give the impression of warmth.

On the day she told me about my mother's arrival at the circus, she obviously presumed I wouldn't understand because I was too little. I was lying in my crate-cot, busy playing with my toes and shitting out the llama milk deemed a fit enough – and free enough – replacement for the nourishment I needed from my mother. (The vile substitute turned my guts inside out, sometimes making me scream so loud, eventually someone would come to put me under a trailer on the other side of the encampment.) But on that particular day, I quietly listened as Big Gen spoke.

*Now then, you poor little mite, let me tell you a story that will guard you against the demon of constant sorrow. I'll have me a drinky first.*

34

*What? A lady needs some golden drip-drops when telling such tales to young 'uns. That's better.*

*It was a dirty, bitter day. The wind whipped around the big top and the sea gnashed its jaws into the land. All who were left on the encampment — for many had gone to war — swaddled themselves in blankets, getting their comfort from bottles and the skin of whoever could be persuaded to share their beds. We'd been forced out into the hell of it early doors, battening down flaps and boarding up animals with sand swarming around us like disease, mixing with the air and settling in our mouths and eyes and gullets. But we got the work done and ourselves back indoors before the worst of it hit. Fausto — dear Fausto — well, he spent the rest of the morning wrapped in the corpulent pleasures of my glorious thighs. His small but supple fingers working between the folds of my heaven — What's south of heaven, the boys used to say; Big Gen's knees! And how we laughed — his quick tongue darting and tasting as I sighed and supped on golden drip-drops from the bottle. I don't mind telling you that I'd pray for the wickedness of bad weather back then, for the gods to grant me mercy and fill up the aching emptiness of the hours. Though my Fausto — dear man — he never needed no prayers, nor excuses for that matter, if you see what I mean. That's what it was like before Marina came, when the war with Germany was everything and everything was as nothing. You're lucky, little 'un, you'll never truly know such badness. Lucky you was born in England, for it was luck that birthed you on these shores and you should thank the gods for it. But we must not think on that now, best to leave such sorrows behind and not look back. That's what I tell your poor mother. Don't look back, lovely, I say, there's nothing to come of it — but how she weeps.*

*And when she looks at your sorry little nut — and those chubby hands always wanting and grabbing at her and her unable to give because she sees the badness right there in your innocent eyes, blinking up at her — bad bad bad. It's a sorry business, little 'un. I'm sorry for your part in it.*

*The afternoon grew dark as the wind settled itself down along the Kent coast, for that was where we stopped for much of the time back then — down in Kent. There wasn't much moving to be done. Fausto said it was not viable to be moving around in such times — viable, he said. But us girls could put on a good show, mind, you can be sure of that. And I told him so — told him many a time — but they were bleak days and Fausto suffered like the rest of us, in his own way, though he never let on.*

*Having sated himself fully that afternoon with yours truly — and me with him — Fausto dressed quickly and off he went for his daily jaunt along the beach. The wind had all but disappeared and a silence fell hard on the encampment. There was a strange stillness as he made his way over the dunes. What a lonely figure he cut, all woollen overcoat and boots, trudging through the damp and early darkness.*

*Dear Fausto walked along the beach sweeping the sands, looking for saleable wreckage or bits of treasure — treasure, he called it — blown in from who knows where, anything that could be sold for a pretty penny, for Fausto loves his pretty pennies more even than he loves his Gen. But I'll weep no tears over it as such is the way of things and all good men have their weaknesses. You'll do well to remember that, little 'un.*

*The moon was out and at her best — bright and full she was — as*

*Fausto crouched on the sands, digging his fat fingers into the wet slop in search of hidden coins or lost jewels. When he looked up he could see along the entire beach — stretched out it was, like polished glass before him — all the way over to the distant cliffs. He breathed it all in and wondered how there could be such loveliness on the earth and yet such badness in the very souls of men. It's what he's often said and he says it still. Each time he claps eyes on your poor mother he shakes his head and wonders at it all.*

*As he was doing his pondering, his fingers still deep in the sand, he saw something move in the distance ahead of him. It seemed to tumble away from the sea edge, or was it just his eyes playing tricks, for these were funny times and could do funny things to a man. This thing — it was merely a thing for the moment — shone white under the moonlight like a clustering of opals or pearls, but it was soft, he was sure of that, for it moved again and its undulations were more flesh than stone. A wounded animal, perhaps. But from what shore could such a beast have come? He saw, even from where he was, far along the beach, that it trembled terribly. Fausto was certain whatever it was it was still alive — though only just — and his dear, sweet heart filled with pity for the creature. He ran — as best he could in boots — across the slapping sands, hoping to give some comfort to the poor dying beast. But as he reached the thing he suddenly stopped — frozen completely he was — because of the magnificent sight before him. You see, the creature on the ground, lying at his feet, was a young woman.*

*She was not a wretched thing, like those who sometimes wander the beaches at night, having been spat out of some boat by sailors searching for a good time in return for the promised jangle of their pockets. No. She was something quite apart from such earthly lusts. Fausto thought he'd never seen such perfection in a human body – in man nor woman neither. She quivered, as if the fine downy hairs covering her beautiful frame suffered at the very touch of the air. For a moment Fausto was incapable of movement or even breath. Your body is made of stars, he whispered as he bent down to the drowned girl. The light bounced from the young woman's flesh and Fausto, blinded by her nakedness, wanted to touch her and maybe, for the briefest of moments, even to taste her – after all, he is only a man. But when her fingers lifted from the sand and she began to shake even more violently than before, dear old Fausto forgot his appetite – or so he says – and took off his stale overcoat to cover her. It seemed unfitting somehow to cover her with such rags, but he feared the cold and, having nothing else, it would have to do. She sunk her hands back into the mushy sand, pushed her breasts towards the moon – letting the overcoat slip like butter from her skin – and began filling her lungs at last with cold air. Her mouth opened. But when it did there came such a terrible sound as you never heard. Such a song of suffering and pain from deep within the very tissue of her flesh. It was a siren song, said Fausto, high-pitched and ripping her asunder from within, like no earthly cry. And the cry was so terrible that Fausto said it broke the very heart of him and didn't he just stand there beside her, blubbering like a babe himself.*

*Fausto wrapped the girl up as best he could in his overcoat. Although a small man and no longer a youth, he's mighty strong. Then he carried her all the way back along the beach, screaming my name as he went – and with a desperate urgent voice such as I'd never heard.*

*She stayed in my trailer for many a week. I slept next to her each night, warming her and holding her close, stroking her when the terrors struck, as often they did. I made her soup. Fed her up and made her strong and soon she began to smile, even laugh, but she would not speak. That would take a while longer yet. Fausto gave her the name Marina, because she came from the sea. Our princess from the sea, he said, and she nodded and smiled in agreement. So it was that The Great Marina was born.*

*Soon enough Fausto had the water tank built and Marina took to it with surprising eagerness. We were worried at first that it might frighten her, being back in the water an' all. But Fausto said that was where she'd come from so that was where she belonged. Oh, how graceful and beautiful she was, swimming and dancing in the water. It was like she'd come to life at last, like the water was giving her the gift to forget – or maybe to remember, I could not say – but we knew, Fausto and me, that we could open up a show with what we'd got in her. That she'd pay her way, all right – and what a good and clever thing it was to have saved her. Oh yes. We could help the world become beautiful again – for the simple price of a pretty penny – through the grace of our beautiful Marina and her siren show.*

*And so there it is, little 'un. This is the story of how your mother came to the circus and it is the story you had best carry with you. Not a bit of it is a lie. I'm sure many will tell you the tale again – as a fine tale indeed it is – but not me. No, I shan't speak of it again. The past is best left to those who remember it. Look at you, poor little mite, I can do nowt for you. Gen has done her bit. May this story always protect you.*

★

39

Serendipity Wilson has fallen asleep. There are knitting needles, scissors and short offcuts of yarn beside her pillow. She is still smiling. Across her sleeping figure is a large yellow jumper with all its seams neatly sewn. I crawl over to her and try to pick it up, but it's heavy. Serendipity Wilson stirs.

*Do you like it, Mouse?*

*It's far too big for me.*

*That's the best thing about being small: the world is so big.*

Once again, her eyes close and she is asleep. Sliding the jumper under my own bedcovers to quash its gentle glow, I begin to wrap Serendipity Wilson's hair, still shining, incandescent and fire-like through the dark, in the blanket laid out for the purpose. Like everything else in the wigwam, the blanket is made of knitted squares; they are dark blue, like a midnight sky. At last the light is all but extinguished. A few strands of hair poke out from the turban-blanket, giving the effect of a single guttering candle. My hands seem to move without my bidding. They hover for a moment over the scissors as my heart rings heavy through my chest. I gather my courage, and in one quick move, snip off the offending light.

The hair is soft and thick between my fingers. I hold it to my face, brush it against my skin, drink in its perfect odour of spice, cedar and wool. And although there's no one now to see it, I am smiling. I place the lock of hair under my pillow, lay my cheek upon the fabric cover and feel the brightness under my head, burning, protecting. I shall keep this lock of hair forever, I shall wear it in a pouch around my neck so that she, my dearest friend, is always with me.

My sleep is sound and deep. For the first time in my life I am sure that nothing bad can happen to me. I know I am saved.

# 3

# A Photograph. A Costume.
# A Portal into the Past

*It's a girl.*

*How do you know?*

*She told me.*

*You can hear her?*

*She's quite the chatterbox when she wants to be.*

*What's her name?*

*I don't know. I haven't asked.*

*Do you want to know?*

*Of course. But maybe you should ask her?*

Serendipity Wilson bubbles with delight, her hair shining so brightly I must squint to look at her.

*I don't know how.*

*Put your mouth close to my belly and whisper the words clearly but softly, so only she can hear. Such things should only be asked in private conversations. I won't listen, I promise. Then wait. And listen carefully, see if she answers.*

Serendipity Wilson lifts up her cotton dress. Her belly, revealed, is small, round and tight. It makes me think of a helium balloon, like the ones Big Gen and the Joey clowns sell. I place my cheek lightly on her bulge, scared in case I press too hard and she might pop. But she's solid, and full, and warm. I feel the electric intensity of my skin touching hers where it never has before. My breath is hot and wet against her flesh. There's only this barrier of thin skin between myself and the new life within. I am suddenly lost, unable even to think or speak. Serendipity Wilson strokes my hair, untangling knots between her fingers, breathing softly.

*Don't be afraid, Mouse. The baby is our friend.*

But I'm not listening to her voice anymore. My ears are channelling deep into her, to a place beyond sound, burrowing through wires of blood vessels and the pulsating mass at her core, listening for the slightest movement, perhaps a sigh, from somewhere within. I wonder what it's like to be on the inside, unseen and warm and protected. If it were me, I'd never come out.

*What's your name?* I say.

*Bunny*, says the baby.


I am smoking too much.

I've been sitting here for hours, staring into the void, watching daylight ebb away, holding this old photograph as if it were made of glass. I shouldn't be writing about Bunny, not yet. It's too soon. No matter that with her came the start of my search, my reason for writing all this. But that's later, she's not yet lost; indeed, she's yet to be born. There are other things to get through first. Still, she hovers in the background, her large, baby face like a whisper of smoke or a cloud that never goes away.

Everything in this room is inert. I might not be here. All life could be extinguished, and I am seeing through a camera eye, a cold automaton's view. It's a feeling I know well, and one which, in normal circumstances, I feel entirely at home with – long for, even. Not today. I can almost hear my inner workings; the machinery moving under my skin; the whirring of wheels in place of muscle and blood. It sounds like celluloid rushing over metal: tick, tick, tick. Maybe it's just the clock on the landing outside my room, the sound of time passing? And yet, it does not pass. The light may diminish but time hangs, unmoving, repeating the same memory, as insistent as a dripping tap. So I repent, let the dam burst, and watch as the froth of words appear on the paper: Bunny. Bunny. Bunny.

Pulling hard on each cigarette, I try to fill myself with smoke. Anything to ignite the embers of self in my brain. Moments ago, I was resting on the window ledge. The traffic is loud with the window ajar, my old jumper no protection from the chill air. At least I feel it, which is some reassurance. I am made of flesh, after all.

I realize I have need of company (an unusual state of mind these days), which is why I opened the window in the first place. The sirens and horns, the shouting, whistles and engines, all the noise that clambers through this window wraps me in the familiar cacophony of other people's lives. Tonight, I'm grateful for it.

It's only a few hours since my fingers rummaged through papers, excitedly searching notebooks and documents for the next chapter. I was finally ready to tell my tales. Then the photograph . . . and I am in stasis. I should not have looked at it. It was foolish to jump ahead like that. *The egg is not ready to hatch yet, Mouse.* But the words are on the page now. I won't resign them to the basket. They tell of the missing child. She won't be still, it seems. She's begging for our attention.

Let me describe the photograph.

It's much smaller than modern-day snaps. I'm no good with measurements and the like, but it could quite easily fit into a pocketbook or wallet. There's a white border around the edge (artistic detailing, sadly lost to modern cameras), which makes the picture somehow less real; somehow illusory. The top right-hand corner is torn off, injuring only the border. And there's a teacup stain around the top on the same side – the offending cup probably being the cause of the missing corner. The image itself is faded. A series of washed-out greys and whites, although I can still make it out quite well. It shows two smiling figures. The first is me. I am approximately thirteen years old and wearing a tutu made some years previously by Serendipity Wilson, for my first public performance on the high wire. The tutu is small for me, so I've taken the straps off, leaving my shoulders bare, exposed. I am sat in front of the wigwam on a short, three-legged stool, normally used for milking llamas. The tulle of my costume sticks up and out around me, making me look like a giant flower. On my knee sits a baby. She is fat and bald-headed with full, squeaky cheeks. Her arms stretch towards the camera, her fists clenched, grabbing for the person behind the lens. The baby wears a knitted dress, made for her by her mother. The dress looks grey and muddy, but I know it's made of red squares. The baby is one year old. Her name is Bunny.

I see now why I started down this path, why the photograph showed itself to me in an apparently premature fashion (do objects have their own way of doing things?). It's because of my costume and has nothing to do with the baby. I must tell you the story of how it came about that I, the invisible child, was able to prove my worth as a true circus star. It is, after all, perhaps the most important event of my life, and well documented in my notebooks. Without it, I wouldn't be writing this, because nothing written hereafter would've happened, and you would never have wanted to meet me. My thoughts are running at lightning speed.

Combined with copying from my notebook, I will write down everything I remember from the day of my first performance. I will transcribe the whole episode, if it means sitting at my desk all night. I'd sooner write than dream.

I've grown tall like my mother, limbs stretched and long, but I'm ungainly. I don't know how to manage my body, which, at now eleven years old (or thereabouts), has outgrown me. My walk is clumsy, off-kilter; my hands great shovels that swing hopelessly about, propelled seemingly without my instruction by over-long arms. I am, in every respect, big for my age. My breasts are already pushing outwards, heavy and fleshy like burdensome fruit. They force my spine to curve forwards in an unconscious effort to disguise a precocious end to childhood, for which I'm not ready. Nobody on the circus encampment seems to have noticed this metamorphosis. Even now, as my body turns me into a lumbering freak, they don't see me. I shuffle on, invisible, dragging my feet, head folded to my chest, thick brown hair falling like a messy veil over my face, covering and concealing my thoughts.

Unusually, I have no training today. Serendipity Wilson left a note under my pillow as I slept in the wigwam, informing me she will be busy with some private thing, so all practice is cancelled. I'm not to rig up the wire alone, as it's *far too dangerous* and I am *not ready* for it. She knows very well I'm perfectly capable of doing so. I can erect the rigging, fix the metal cross bars onto the wooden base and bolt it down. I know how much padding to use so the wire doesn't slip from its bindings. I've done it lots of times. And I've made the slings and attached the ropes so often I could do it in my sleep. Serendipity Wilson believes she knows best, but she doesn't. She treats me like a baby. In truth, I'm much stronger than she is for tightening bolts and buckles and getting the tension right. I wanted to tell her this, force her to show more faith in me, if it meant screaming and pulling at my hair. But she was already gone when I awoke.

As I'd not planned to hide under the big wagon with my

notebook, or to sit with the animals today, I have nothing to do. I'm not at my best if my day is not fully planned out. I'm grumpy and unsettled. Anyway, what can I do? I've rarely spoken to anyone other than Serendipity Wilson in my whole life. And no one has ever bothered talking to me. These days, if someone does try to speak with me, I panic. I cover my face, run away, hide from the attention, so I cannot even imagine how it would be to join in with the chatter of other circus folk, or jolly along in their games. They think I'm not all there, up top. So I stumble around the encampment in search of entertainment.

My disorientation, as I wander about, passing dancing girls and acrobats who sit in front of tents and caravans playing cards or cat's cradle, or who lie on blankets on the ground, sunning themselves, means I do not notice Marina's approach.

I'm ambling around between the big top and the animal enclosure, pushing dusty dirt through my toes, when she nudges past me, thrusting hard into my shoulder, shoving me aside and almost knocking me to the ground. I catch my breath and turn to watch her float into the distance. She is barefoot in the dust, giving off the usual flurry of chiffon, smelling of lavender-water and gin. I am also barefoot. I prefer it this way.

Marina smells entirely different to Serendipity Wilson. There's nothing musky about my mother's smell. Her odour is strong and synthetic. She's all fake flowers, all cake and sugar. I never want to smell like Marina, she is vanilla pudding to Serendipity Wilson's woody glen. If there was a heaven and a God, I'd pray hard, ask to be changed into the very flesh of Serendipity Wilson. I'd learn to use the magical mists passed down to her from the ancestors (it can't be that difficult, but oh, how she struggles to control them). I certainly wouldn't try to hide them as she does, pretend to be normal, like any old Johnny or Joanna. I'd relish such a gift. My hair would shine too, just like hers, and everyone would smile at me. Instead, I am locked inside this fleshy pod, all animal dung and stale spun sugar. Marina's monster child.

These days I perceive a slight wobble to Marina's walk. I'm sure nobody else notices. One must know her utterly in movement and rest to see it. In any case, her movements remain fluid and easy enough, even in her pickled state. She's making her way to the animal enclosure now, no doubt to drape herself around Manu, distract him from his work and let the animals go hungry. I'll go over there later when no one is around, make sure the work is done, the animals cleaned and fed. They should not be made to suffer from her neglect.

Marina doesn't look at me or acknowledge me in any way as she shoves past. If a stranger was looking in on this scene, they'd see nothing to betray that we are mother and daughter, or even casual acquaintances. The keenest eye might notice our naked feet. But this is not unusual around the encampment. It reveals nothing.

In truth, I spend as little time in the caravan as possible. Daylight and early evening are for training (and watching from my hidey-holes), and nights are spent with Serendipity Wilson in the wigwam (where I have my bed, my glory-box and all my special things exactly the way I want them). There's rarely any complaint about this. If my absence is ever noted – usually in some drunken fit when my mother craves extra attention – Marina causes a stink about how neglected she is by her own child. This isn't aimed at me. It's to give Gen and others a chance to run to her and make sounds like concerned vermin. I know how to appease matters. I wait until dark, go quietly to the caravan, lie down by the stove and cover myself with my second-best knitted blanket (the one possession I keep there). Sometimes I have to close my ears as well as my eyes, to block out the noises coming from behind the curtain separating the cramped living space from Marina and Manu's bedroom. In the morning, one of them inevitably trips over me and everyone is satisfied that I have not deserted the familial tin-can of ecstasy. Once again it's made clear that life is better when I'm not there, that there's not enough space, food, or air for three in the caravan. Gen and Fausto are called in, and it's agreed I should go back to the wigwam and to the care of Serendipity Wilson. I've learned how to play their games. I could win prizes.

Someone calls to me from outside the big top.

*Quick, where have you been?*

I stop for a moment, close my eyes, take a breath, try to orientate myself. Opening my eyes against the morning sun, I turn to face the big top, and wince. Serendipity Wilson is not wearing her turban, she's unkempt, her head ablaze with light. I look away, close my eyes and wish I was invisible.

The unexpected meeting with my mother has left me unsteady, and Serendipity Wilson, having told me specifically not to look for her, stands beckoning me. Such contradiction makes me dizzy. She waves frantically with one long-fingered hand, cradling a bundle of white fabric in the other. Standing completely still, feeling the dirt settle under my toes, I try to gain control of myself. When finally I open my eyes, I do so in glimpses, giving myself time to take in the situation: Serendipity Wilson is still waving, calling. Shielding my eyes, I start to walk over to her. My mother wafts past again. The edge of Marina's housecoat brushes my leg, the almost imperceptible hiss of nylon on skin makes me lose my balance. I stumble, this time hitting the dry, compacted ground with a slap.

There's grit in my mouth. I spit and watch as frothy saliva deepens the colour of the earth under my face. Wishing with all my heart that I could disappear, I manage to get to my feet and shuffle over to where Serendipity Wilson stands, alone, in the open mouth of the big top, in a fever of light and movement.

*Look at you, covered in muck. I don't know what you look like. Don't worry about Marina, Mouse. Ignore her. You've got bigger fish to skin. Now, quickly.*

She grabs me by the shoulders, pats and brushes at my clothes, smiling – always smiling – as she tuts and scolds.

*There now. Better*, she says, pushing the bundle of fabric at me. *You'll need to try it on. I'm sure it will fit. I'm usually right about these things.*

The fresh white cloth looks wrong in my hands. My fingernails are lined with black. I hide them in the folds of the lovely fabric.

*A costume?* I say. *For me?*

*Perfect, isn't it?*

Serendipity Wilson is clapping her hands, bouncing on her toes like an excited child. For some reason, this makes me angry. She doesn't seem to care, or even notice my flushing cheeks, my uneven breathing, as I stand bewildered, like a sweating, panting dog. She doesn't see me at all. I wonder what I must do for her to consider me a real person, rather than her puppet. A shot of pain runs along my jaw as I clench my teeth. I realize then, with horror and confusion, that at this exact moment, I might even hate her.

*Do you like it?* She kisses me on the nose.

The costume has layers of white tulle under its floating satin skirt. The bodice is also satin; simple, with a line of criss-cross pink ribbon down the back, ending in a fine bow. The ribbon matches the trim of the skirt, and the thin, elegant straps also have tiny pink bows on them. The dress has a sheen that catches the light, but not in a glaring way. Everything about it is soft. I relax my jaw, feel the tension slide from my neck. Serendipity Wilson is right (she always is). It's perfect. Nevertheless, I can't help wishing it wasn't, and she'd made an error in the design or construction.

*It's time, Mouse.* Her arms slip around my shoulders. She pushes me forwards and although I want to resist, I do not.

I am standing on the edge of the ring. Seats are folded and stacked around me, hay bales scattered untidily about, spilling pale straws onto hard ground. The ring is a shiny red and yellow tarpaulin edged with wooden blocks, some of which have become displaced. I step slowly over the blocks, knocking one against another with my big toe, and freeze. Other than Fausto standing in the centre, there's no one around. He looks smaller than usual. He's unshaven and sleepy, wearing ill-fitting trousers and a collarless shirt.

Familiar smells (oilcloth mixed with greasepaint, damp earth and straw), combined with the noise, heat and petrol fumes from the generator, not to mention my confusion, make me reel slightly. My stomach lurches, hot sweat turns icy cold on my skin, and I'm taken with a sudden, desperate need to run to the privy. I do not move.

The big top is a sacred place. You must earn your time there. There are guidelines, training schedules to be followed. Everyone has their turn to rehearse in the ring. The bigger acts get the longer slots. These are jealously guarded. Any deviating from the schedule can cause rifts that last a lifetime. But if your act is deemed important enough (lucrative enough), this is taken into consideration and changes can be made, even at the last minute – with the blessing of dear old Fausto, our lord and ringmaster (pray to Fausto for pity and pennies). I wonder how we can be here, and why. Whose place are we taking, who is standing scowling behind tent poles, hating us for usurping their precious rehearsal time?

Fausto Flavio has never looked directly at me before. Maybe he did when I was a baby, but I've no memory of it. Now, he's staring at me through drowsy, porcine eyes. I look around. Serendipity Wilson has disappeared. I am the focus of his weary attention.

Not knowing, but believing the thing to do is approach the man, I move forwards. The tarpaulin floor is cold and slippery. I want to curl each foot from heel to toe across the shiny surface, experience it fully on the soles of my feet. I look up. Ropes sway gently above me under the shadow of striped canvas, and a pigeon has found its way up to the tent top, quietly perching on a wooden board in the rigging. It moves its head in quick, curious motions, and blinks. Without thinking, I half-close my eyes. *There's magic here*, I whisper.

*At last!*

Fausto's voice, as loud as a gun, hits me in the gut. My legs falter. I judder to a halt, clench everything and hope to avoid embarrassing myself.

*Come, girl. I do not have all the day. This it?*

He snatches the costume from my hands, uncovering shameful, dirty fingers. Fausto flicks them a look. Tears prickle my eyes. Something unseen tightens around my neck; it feels like an invisible rope made of ice. It grabs at my throat. Waves of boiling and freezing blood seem to flood my head, my hands, my guts, consuming me. I wish I was hidden under the big wagon; I wish I was anywhere but here; I wish I was Serendipity Wilson, so I could summon the fogs of my forefathers and vanish forever into them.

Fausto's enormous face is staring into mine. I look down, forcing my weeping eyes to examine the waxy ground under what I now see are my extremely grubby feet. My shame is complete.

*You got two hours*, he calls to Serendipity Wilson, who, timid as a kitten, peeps out from behind the entrance flap, and smiles.

*If she's good as you say, then fine and dandies. She don't come up with the goods, I dock you one week's wages, and she goes back to hiding in dirty places. I've not time for wasting.*

Fausto Flavio sweeps out of the big top, his overhanging belly hampering the majesty of his exit. He leaves a darkness behind. It fills every part of me. The rope of ice, until now the only thing holding me up, releases its grip, and I fall.

I am on the ground now, drenched in sweat, cold and not sure how long I've been lying here. Serendipity Wilson is touching my face with her long, warm fingers. My breathing becomes lighter, calmer. I am pulled to my feet, steadied, and kissed on the forehead.

Serendipity Wilson holds me up by the waist, looks into my eyes, and says nothing. She picks up the tutu, lying like a dead thing on the tarpaulin, shakes it once, and smiles. At her side is a bucket and a slab of green soap. Her fingers brush through my hair. She helps me out of my soiled clothes, washes me with the cold water and strong soap, and helps me into my bright new costume.

*Once they see you up there, no one will be able to touch you, Mouse.*

*What do you mean?*

*Don't you know? You'll be the star, the greatest funambulist who ever lived.*

# 4

# The Birth and Origins of
# Serendipity Wilson

Serendipity Wilson was from a sort of fairyland. She was
born (so it seemed) and raised on the Isle of Man. Her father,
Ned, was a kipperman who caught herring in orange nets
and smoked them in a brick furnace. He was a simple man
who the locals affectionately christened Kipper Wilson. Her
mother cleaned hotel rooms for holiday visitors, and the
houses of polite English ladies before the days of intern-
ment. She was a small woman with a loud laugh and devilish
eyes. She, like Ned, had been born on the island and knew
nothing much of anything outside island life. Ever since she
could remember she'd been called Little Lou, which baffled
her because her name was Sarah-Jane.

Kipper and Lou Wilson did not share the same blood as
their daughter. Lou could not have children due to an almost
fatal childhood illness, which had left her with her life, but
condemned it to be childless. Or so she thought. This is also
how Serendipity Wilson got her name, as it was just that which
brought her to be the child of the smiling Kipper-Wilsons.

As they took a walk, as the Wilsons often did on early

spring mornings, the mist seemed thicker than usual. They snuggled into each other as they strolled through the foggy glen at the foot of Bradda Head. A bittersweet, woody odour hung in the air and on their clothes. This, along with the smell of cooked kippers and salty sea water, is the smell of the island. But it seemed sharper, more vivid than the day before, as if heightened by the dense haze. They weren't concerned. It's what happens when the season changes, when life begins to shoot and bud again in the glens and sidings. The locals called this place 'The Fairy Glen', due to its Celtic beauty, and mischievously told holidaymakers that if they listened carefully enough, the little people could be heard cavorting in the bushes.

As the couple wandered through the deepening fog, they saw a bright light through the mist. The light was shining with such ferocity from under a tangle of thick heather and bracken that they could not help but stop to investigate its source. They pulled back the scratchy branches and saw a baby. It was newborn, wrapped in newspaper, like a cod. It would have been for all the world a perfectly normal sort of baby had it not been for its astonishing head, from which sprouted a shining beacon of glowing orange hair.

On seeing the child, Lou Wilson's heart leapt and banged against her bones. Convinced this was a gift, maybe not from the fairies, but certainly from providence, they took the baby girl home and began their family life. The islanders agreed it was the right thing to do, and the proper cogs were set in motion to make the child legally their own.

The older island dwellers, whose Norse-Celt blood made them a superstitious breed, guessed the truth about the baby immediately, or at least their version of it. Her thick luminous hair, and the unseasonal fog that day, confirmed their suspicions. They knew the fog was a magical thing. This legendary cloak of mists, they said, was a gift from the baby's true ancestors. She would carry it with her at all times in case of trouble, as a place to hide. The old-timers took it upon themselves to ensure Serendipity Wilson grew up knowing her true identity, or rather, what they heartily believed it to be.

Serendipity Wilson never quite got the hang of the mists. Every time she climbed the rope to the high wire, a slight haze whispered around the big top. In truth, she couldn't always be bothered to fight the fogs, and on occasions she would go missing. Nobody noticed the connection between the mysterious mists and Serendipity Wilson's occasional vanishing. Nobody, except me.

*Keep it under your hat now, with the nits and the bugs*, she'd say.

Serendipity Wilson was, the old Manxmen told her, a direct descendant of Manannán mac Lir, a one-time sea god who became mortal and founded the Isle of Man back in ancient times. She came from the line of his daughter, Niamh of the Golden Hair.

Serendipity Wilson had a deep dislike for the old people. She told me, *They smelled of cabbage, boiled beef and piss. Stupid people, full of mystical ideas, selling them to honeymooning couples, or anyone who'd listen, for bags of chips and mugs of beer.*

She detested their fading pale eyes, *glassy and grey like used dishwater.*

*They watched me,* she said. *Those eyes followed me. I could feel them, with their twisted old bodies, staring at me. They made the fogs appear with their pointing and whispering.* Like all young people, she wanted to hide from the ugliness of age.

Once, on a stormy wigwam evening, when the sound of our flapping fabric shelter was louder even than the thunder outside, Serendipity Wilson told me of the biggest storm that ever was, and how the old islanders had almost destroyed her.

The winds had been battering the island for a week. The lighthouse, which was built even before the old-timers were born, could not withstand such a beating and crumbled to the dust and sand of the beach. Two fishing boats from the local area were known to be out at sea and would surely be trying to battle through the storm, to get home before the worst of it hit.

When the skies began to break, Serendipity Wilson was in the kitchen with her mother. They were baking bread to take their minds off the weather when the back door was flung open. At first, they thought it just the violence of the storm, but standing at the door, pushing into the kitchen, soaked by the rain and the night, were twenty elder Islanders. They shielded their eyes from the brightness of Serendipity Wilson's hair and crowded into the kitchen, causing such confusion that the girl somehow became separated from her mother. The old men surrounded Serendipity Wilson, grabbed her by the arms and wrists. *You must come with us*, they snarled. *This is your chance to do good, this is why the fairies left you. It is your duty.*

And without even a coat they pulled her out of her home, away from her screaming mother, and into the cruelty of the storm. They pulled her across the beach and through the glen. Two of the strongest men began pushing her up the three hundred and eighty-two feet of the great Bradda Head. Up, ever up, until they reached the top. At the summit, teetering on the headland, reaching into the angry clouds, was the folly of Milner's Tower. They pushed her up further still. Up the stone stairs, up to the viewing platform, vanishing way up into the clouds.

*It was so high*, she said, *I thought the angels would come and take me. I was shaking and sweating and screaming, but they wouldn't let me go. They held on to me with their awful hands.*

One of the old men, who was staring at the burning wonder of Serendipity Wilson's head as she pleaded with him to let her go home, took rope and string from his pockets and tied her by the wrists and ankles to iron mounts in the wall. She screamed and sobbed after the old men, who ran quickly down the tower and away, back to the warmth of their homes.

Serendipity Wilson was stuck fast. Her fantastic light could be seen all over the island and all over the sea; a bright orange warning to the fishermen of Bradda's terrible rocks.

*I was terrified, plunged high up into the clouds like that. I was dizzy and felt sick in my belly. The cloak of mists took over. I had no control over the descending fog. I was cold and wet and very frightened. All I could do was scream and cry. I didn't want any harm to come to the boats out on the sea, I just wanted to go home. I thought I was going to die up there.*

As Serendipity Wilson's tears fell into that dreadful night, a great fog, as thick as cotton wool, covered the whole island. It shrouded everything, including the sea around the headlands. The two fishing boats had no chance in the Manannán fog. They were dashed against the rocks; all men were lost.

The next thing Serendipity Wilson remembered was waking up in her own bed, her mother and father sitting beside her, her beacon mane wrapped in seven yards of thick yellow fabric.

The cloth was heavy and made her head itch, but she kept it in place, not even allowing her parents to see her without it, until the day her father took her to the circus encampment. Then at last the breeze lifted her hair. Serendipity Wilson knew that for her, the price of freedom was spectacle. She embraced it with vigour. But she never loved it. Not in the way she loved her beautiful island home.

# 5

# Stella the Harlot, Bubbles, and the Big Change

I am light today. Filled to the top of my head with bubbles. My fingers tingle with them. Still, no one other than Serendipity Wilson dare look at me. So, I hide under the wagon.

We're moving. The encampment is all bluster and noise; tent poles clanging, chains and trolleys scraping along the ground. I cannot bear the shouting, the shoving around of people and things, the fake attempts at being *first for the off*, in the hope of impressing Fausto (who is never impressed and doesn't care who's first, as long as everything is packed and ready to go before the time written on his precious contract, otherwise all hell breaks loose and everyone's wages are docked).

The Flying Frazer Family follow his fatness around like obedient dogs. They're a sight; a second-rate trapeze act of little merit and ugly children, who swing around the big top like shrieking monkeys, always at Fausto's boot heels on moving day. The two boys, Nathan [Cain], and Donald [Abel], squabble and slap each other whenever their dear mother turns her broad back. How she strides about, linking arms with Fausto as if she were the star of the show. I've seen Joey clowns do better routines on the trapeze, big boots, baggy trousers an' all. Of course, Old Man Frazer trails behind, as she, Lady Muck, warbles on. Look at him: head down, limping, smoking, looking for all the world like he'd rather be somewhere else, but playing the game, putting on the show, winning Fausto's favour. Everything's a competition. Someone must always be best. Pathetic.

There are three girls from the dance troupe standing on the edge of the encampment by the road. They wave at men and boys who pass. If the men wave back, the girls giggle and huddle together in a coven of peroxide and lipstick. Some men are shameless, indecent. They whistle, shout obscenities, make the girls laugh even louder and shout back in shrill, mocking voices. These girls look like harlots. They probably are. All three are gift-wrapped; perfectly packaged in identical costumes of white shorts and matching shirts, fringed with red streamers, and white cowboy hats that glint with sequinned, tell-tale hearts. They look ready for showtime; their shorts cut so high on the leg I can see beyond the tops of their thighs. The folds beneath their buttocks are perfectly visible, and the rounding swells above peek out from under the soft white fabric. This is intentional, designed to make people look where they shouldn't. They can't do moving work in their gleaming costumes and ridiculous painted faces. Which is why, I suppose, they're wearing them. They are lazy girls.

Each girl has a packet of cigarettes tucked neatly into the

waistband of her shorts. They smoke. Making a big show of it. Three shiny red mouths try to blow curls of smoke from pouting lips. The smoke immediately disappears into the morning air, cruelly spoiling their carefully practised film-star effect. Idiots.

These three also work with the horses, doing riding tricks and such, using whips and sticks to make the animals dance, tormenting them for the crowds. They don't care about the horses; they love the authority it gives them, controlling powerful beasts with the lash. And they love Manu. They follow him into the animal enclosure whenever they get the chance, try to tease him with giggles and insinuations. He's too skilled for them. He brushes them off, swipes them away like common moths — always with a smile, of course, Manu would never be rude to a pretty girl — until the harlots retreat, pouting in coy disappointment, determined to return again some other time, to buzz and flutter around his flame. Look at them. They think so much of themselves. They think that one day they will have Manu. Each one dreams she will be the one. They really are stupid if they think they're any match for Marina, even with youth and sobriety on their side.

One of them is called Stella. She's a real Jezebel. Fausto loves Stella — only because he wants to stick it in her, that's what Serendipity Wilson says. She probably lets him. I've watched him paw and slaver over her; a fat man dribbling over a succulent beefsteak. Meat for the master, that's all she is. Serendipity Wilson says that some girls will do anything to get themselves noticed, and that I must never let myself be like that. I never shall. Just thinking about it makes me feel sick.

Stella is not as stupid as she looks. She has a malevolence about her. You can tell the sort she is. She would reveal your deepest secrets to the highest bidder. The other two follow her around as if attached by a magnetic charge. If I were them, I'd leave her to rot in her own pit of nastiness. They seem to crave her attention, her indulgence, and abuse. They're shallow creatures. They get what they deserve. I should pity them. I don't.

Stella is the one to watch, all right. She's always waiting for the right moment, or so she thinks, to get Manu alone, show him what she can really do. Even now, as she's consumed in peacocking and smoking, I can see her eyes swivel in her head, dart glances over to Manu working with the animals. Those other two are oblivious. Tarting themselves up for the sake of it. But I can see her, that Stella, putting on her show, pulling out all the stops for Manu. He doesn't even know she's there.

Here, under the big wagon, I have a perfect view. It's always the first wagon to be loaded. The precious big top already rests on its back, strapped in, ready to go. They'll leave it be now while everything else gets packed up. I'm safe here, invisible in my cocoon (not yet a butterfly, more than a worm). Of course, this is not what I would normally be writing. I would normally write: *Here I am, lying under the big wagon as usual.* I cannot write that today, because it's not true.

Today nothing is *usual*, and never will be again. Not because we're hauling out. That's as normal as hens' eggs. It's because of The Big Change. Although, if you did not know, if you were watching right now (as I am), you wouldn't suspect things were any different from yesterday, or the day before. Everyone is acting as though nothing has happened. Even I'm doing my usual thing: lying on my belly, watching, scribbling in my lined notebook with my sharpened pencil. I sharpened it especially this morning with Manu's knife. Not that he has any idea I used his knife – he never allows me to touch his things. I did it anyway. I did it because I am different now and I can dare to do things, and if I want to use his pathetic little knife, then I will. I did it because of The Big Change.

I am fizzing. A million tiny bubbles are dancing under my skin. I want to run and run and run and never stop. I would like to open my mouth and release my bubbles onto the whole encampment, onto the whole world. My tiny bubbles would engulf the liars, crush and grind them into a sticky paste, carry their remains far away and make their stupid ghosts suffer seasickness in my never-ending sea of bubbles, until every one of them agrees to celebrate my Big Change. But I'm lying in the dirt, hidden. I calm the fizz and don't stir. Still and silent, as always. I'm as bad as the others. I pity myself. Idiot.

I must write everything down about The Big Change, exactly as it happened, only I'm not sure I can. What if I get it wrong, forget something, or put things in the wrong order? What if, in recording things inaccurately, I leave behind a pale imitation of events, an invention, even? I need to be careful, otherwise the truth – the enormity of it – will be lost. Writing is a risky business. There's so much at stake. Maybe I should not write about it at all? Maybe it's too precious for words? And I should let the memory remain intact, in my head, where no one can ever see it. What if I forget? I have an excellent memory, but you never know. One day I'll be old. I might get senile and cretinous, like Big Gen's poor old mam who lives in a home for incurables and no one ever visits, because of the disgrace. Then where will I be? I must write it down. That's why I'm scribbling like this in the first place. Why I used the precious knife to sharpen the stupid pencil.

I will start with this very moment and work backwards. For example, right now my right cheek is lying in the dirt. My breath causes a pool of wet earth to coagulate under that side of my mouth. I'm looking over to the animal enclosure. I can see Manu. He is bedding the animals into their trailers ready for the move. He does it carefully. They do not like being moved. It upsets him to see their distress. He's walking from the big cat enclosure now, carrying a leopard around his neck, wearing it like a scarf. It looks funny and I bury my face in the ground to hide my giggles. My lips brush the patch of wet earth. It smells of spit and muck. Manu is smiling and whistling. He always whistles the same tune. It is called '*J'ai Deux Amours*'. It's the song he sings to Marina when they play together, when they are happy. The leopard looks happy, his sleepy head on Manu's shoulder.

Manu opens the cage door. He bends (he is the strongest man on the encampment, no one can beat him) and the leopard pours gently into the cage, calm, ready for the long journey to the next site. The journeys are always long, especially for the animals. It's not natural for them to be moved around in cages and boxes. I know how they feel. I am more animal than person.

Manu laughs. I hear him quite clearly. The leopard licks Manu's hand. He laughs again. I've never seen him look so happy. Maybe Manu is not laughing because of the leopard? Maybe he cannot contain his joy, but (like me) has to keep it locked inside, or else find an excuse for it?

This whole situation is stupid. I should run up there now. I should throw my arms around Manu, do a little curtsy or a twirl, or simply bow, like I did at the end of the act last night, when, for my first ever appearance in the ring, the applause from the audience exploded, and the noise from their excited, stamping feet was like a mighty storm, making The Big Change final and complete. Oh, how can I ever forget it? The way the big top shook with love for its forgotten child, its bright new star. There, I've written it down. It will not be altered or erased. As I write, I bear witness to the above. Even if these idiots refuse to acknowledge it, what do I care? My star has risen. I am what I was born to be. I am my mother's child.

Imagine how Manu must be feeling. He must want to

shout: *Did you see her? She is my daughter.* He must want to scream it to the whole encampment, so that everyone, even the stupid dancing girls, would go to shake his glad hand, and Fausto would offer him one of his long cigarettes and say, *How proud you must be to have such an artist for a daughter,* and Manu – modest, as always – would say, *She gets it from her mother,* which could certainly be true, but in fact, is not.

Marina has nothing to do with it. It comes from the burns and blisters on my feet, the twisted muscles and cracked bones, from years of fearlessly facing death, practising, falling off ropes and wires, refusing the safety harness, and working, working, working in preparation for my big moment in the ring; for last night. So that at long last Marina would be the one standing in the shadow of her daughter, watching her own flesh and blood – her abomination – become what she can no longer be. Even so, I would smile and be gracious, because Manu is not to blame for saying such things. He is a man and lives in a masculine world. They don't understand things as we do because they are all muscle and mouth. After all, it's what fathers are supposed to say.

But this is not how it is.

Last night, when at last I stood behind the red curtain (blessed be that gateway to another world) hand in hand with Serendipity Wilson as we quietly waited our turn, the circus people saw me in my costume for the first time. They did not bother to conceal their derision. I heard the whispers, saw the way they spluttered and sniggered behind hands and feathers. Some tried to be kind, nodded with weak smiles, sighed and shook their heads, but most made ugly faces. Until they saw me in the ring.

When I climbed the rope, I felt like an angel ascending the heavens. I'd only had a few hours to practise in the big top, up so high. I felt light, so light. When I reached the top, I looked down. Being on the high wire is like being in a different world. It's quieter than the down-below place, the air somehow softer, as if it wants to wrap me up. I'd felt it before, on the practice wire. But up so high, my head almost touching the canvas roof of the big top, and with the hordes sitting in place, eating spun-sugar, their faces looking up – the glimmer of a pair of spectacles here, a gloved hand there – and all of them holding their breath, it seemed more pronounced. I felt protected. If I were to exhale, up there on my perch, I could blow them away like dust.

Then, the music began. It shattered the silence, sending shards of magic ripping through the big top. Serendipity Wilson sat in the rigging, legs dangling into the void, holding the old euphonium to her lips. She played her rough recital, each beat referencing some change of step, some special movement or glissade, as I danced on my wire. She let each note linger softly in the air: 'J'ai Deux Amours'.

I fanned the atmosphere with my feather parasol as I stood on the wooden plate at the top of the rigging, so people could imagine a wondrous bird of beauty and grace. All the while, the circus folk gathered in the ring below. At first it was just the Joey clowns, then I saw them run to the red curtain and gesture to the others. And out came acrobats, the trapeze family, the dancing girls, until the whole company seemed to be there, desperately craning their necks to see, whispering in breathless tones.

As the music played, I listened with a throbbing in my belly for the introduction to end. It seemed to take forever for the first note of the main section to arrive and send me into my routine. When at last my cue came, I felt the cold wire, the grooves of its weave, its hard roundness, pressing into my feet. Flesh fused with metal like an electric charge, giving me energy and strength as the steel cable started to bend with me.

The heat from the lights made me sticky under my costume, and it surprised me to feel a line of wetness in the ridge between my nose and mouth. I stuck out my tongue, licked my salty lips, and laughed out loud. I didn't need to think about my routine, it was there, imprinted in my body, making me move to the music just as I'd practised, only better, more elegant and free. Nor was I bothered that the electric lights were suddenly so bright I couldn't see the audience or the rigging around me. I was engulfed in a pool of darkness, highlighted by spots of bright colours that moved in kaleidoscope swirls as I turned this way and that. If it wasn't for the deep sound of the breathing hordes, and the shuffling of the circus folk in the ring below, I might've believed I was alone.

Up there, performing for the first time in the big top, and for a real audience, without nets or ropes, I was a thing born of air, no longer bound to the filth of the earth like the rest.

I slipped my right foot along the wire, brought my left up behind, and leapt into a full twist, landing with arms outstretched and bent knees, parasol held aloft, keeping my balance. The audience gasped. I went straight into a run, a quick turn, a run back, into a half pirouette, and then the slow walk to the centre of the wire, a gentle slide of both feet, arms raised above my head, using the parasol, again for extra balance, letting the feathers move with the air as I eased, slowly, deliberately, into the splits.

At last I had become what I was meant to be: no more flesh and bone than clouds or mist. Bubbles came up from somewhere down below and began to flood into me. They filled me with joy. Even in the darkness, I was light, in every sense, and shining (without the aid of magical hair). My weightlessness was such, I thought I might be carried away, to drift forever. I imagined I might burst through the patched canvas of the big top, and rise yet further up, make my way through the black sky, pass stars and planets, forego the moon, and burn my feathers on the sun. All too soon the music stopped, and once again the world fell quiet and still. It was done.

Silence rushed into me, fell blanket-heavy over the ring; over the audience; over the wide-eyed circus folk who, I could now see, were standing there, looking up. Serendipity Wilson and I descended in a vacuum of silence so intense it made my ears throb. I wondered what I'd done wrong. I was sure I'd felt the majestic spectacle of my routine. Had I got it wrong? I planted myself on the tarpaulin floor. The throb began to buzz, then to scream. I thought my ears would split and I'd have to leave the ring, running through the silence, with hot blood trickling down my jaw and neck.

Then it came.

The audience got to their feet. I watched as every soul in the big top seemed to rise together, as one. And what a noise, what a glorious noise they made. They applauded, they cheered, they stamped, they shouted and whistled. I thought they'd never stop. The big top trembled with appreciation. I turned towards the red curtain just in time to see several artistes scrambling to get back behind it. The three cowgirls were there, all white shorts and red fringes. Stella was one of the last through the curtain, as cool and calm as ever. She stopped for a moment before making her exit. She looked back over her shoulder, frowned, curled her juicy lips, and although I couldn't hear it over the audience's cheers, I'm sure she growled, like a dog.

Serendipity Wilson held my hand. We smiled as we bowed, waved and blew kisses to our adoring audience. They'd had their money's worth, witnessed the birth of the next truly big star of the circus. For surely that's what I would become. In a few years, when I am a woman, when I've practised so hard no one can come close to my talent, Serendipity Wilson says I will be the greatest. And I will, I'll make sure of it.

Fausto and Big Gen were clapping and cheering along with the audience. Fausto dabbed at his fat red cheeks with his handkerchief. Gen wiped her eyes with the corner of her ridiculous dress. They're not stupid, those two. Not like the rest. They had the scent of pound notes in their noses, the jangle of dirty brass in their ears.

I scanned the audience. Manu and Marina could not have missed the act. Someone must have told them to *come quickly, come and see what your daughter can do*, and surely, they must have run to the big top to see. Marina may have hidden her face in Manu's shoulder, because she's a proud woman and wouldn't want people to see her showing this new emotion for her only child. But I did not see them.

Maybe they left during the applause, needing some time together, alone and quiet, to gather themselves? When I went back to the caravan after the show, all was darkness. Marina was asleep behind the curtain, and Manu sat quietly at the table. He said nothing. He was playing with his knife, shaving strips of wood from sticks to pass the time, as if waiting for me needed some occupation other than just waiting. (How did he know I'd go to the caravan? Imagine how arrogant he must be! It was Serendipity Wilson who suggested I spend the night with my parents. She thought it would be a nice surprise.)

Manu put a finger to his lips as I entered, and gestured towards the bedroom. Then he put his knife away in the drawer, leaving the sticks to scatter over the table as he stood up. He looked at me for what seemed like a long time, and I am sure his eyes glistened, even smiled. But it was dark. He said nothing. He stroked my head with one swipe of his hand before quickly joining Marina in the bedroom and closing the curtain behind him.

Alone in the darkness of the caravan, I listened to the outside sounds; to the audience dawdling as they left the encampment, their voices still giddy with the excitement of the show. Such happy voices. *I gave them that happy*, I thought. And with nothing else to do, with my excitement and pride suppressed, I lay down by the stove, dizzy, fizzing with bubbles. I pulled my second-best blanket to my chin and lay as still as I could, listening to the joy outside. I did not close my eyes. I stared through the gloom at the thin curtain behind which my mother and father were now soundly sleeping. At some point I must've fallen asleep, because the next thing I knew it was today, the caravan was empty, and I could hear people working, striking the big top and rigging, getting ready for the off. I got up, took Manu's knife from the drawer, sharpened my pencil, and with my blanket still wrapped around me like an old woman's shawl, came here, to my *usual* place.

Here I am. Still full of bubbles. The only way to keep last night forever unspoiled by time and spite is to write it down in my notebook. So, I scratch these letters, bold and clear, on this paper. I am unable to move from under the wagon because I'm scared people will look at me, or maybe I'm scared they will not. Whichever, it doesn't matter. The fact is they will see me, and I will see them, and we will all pretend not to see each other. And all my riotous feelings are to be bound up and kept in a quiet place, to be forever locked

in false silence, like I have always been. If someone somewhere is reading this notebook, if it is many years into the
future and I am long since dead, all I ask, dear reader, is that
you pity my ghost.

It's strange to copy out my thoughts from so long ago.
I remember writing them, but they seem false somehow,
the foolish scribbles of an unformed mind. The only thing
that strikes true is my feeling for the wire.

Funambulism is not so difficult. Anyone can walk the
high wire, supposing they have the correct equipment, a
minimum of training, and a stomach for heights. Daredev-
ils do it all the time. They stretch their wires across high
buildings. I've seen these types, watched the dumbfounded
hordes gasp at their audaciousness. At worst they're exhibi-
tionists, at best, athletes. A true funambulist needs to be an
artist, acrobat, prima ballerina, expert equilibrist, poet and
dramatist.

You questioned me about fear. As your little tape recorder
sat between us, turning and listening. I may not have been
completely honest. It's always tempting to play to the audience (in this case, you). It's a performer's dirty habit, their
duty even. I hope you forgive me. Audiences expect deception. That's why they come to the show. I will be honest
now. It's easier to tell the truth when writing it down. Lies
look ugly on the page.

The truth is, I have no fear because I take no risks. It's
bewitching to believe that wearing a lock of hair around

my neck protects me from the void. Every nursery tale confirms it; magic does not require effort, only imagination. I even believe it myself. I would certainly never go onto the wire without my pendant. The fact is, when I'm on the wire, I am in full control. Skill through practice protects me, not superstition. I hope you don't think me an egotist. My limitations and boundaries are well known to me. When not performing, I feel as ungainly and ugly as when I was an eleven-year-old scribbling in notebooks, and my thoughts, for the most part, are dark and unpleasant. My salvation has been my wire.

This is not what I want to say. I should really be writing about the child, about how I lost her and why I must find her, even now, after all these years. It's why I am writing all this down. In truth, there's a morbid pleasure in ploughing through the past, even the unpleasant bits. But this is self-indulgent. I need to take a walk, flee these horrible thoughts. Solitude, although a blessing, can sometimes send me into the darkness.

I will stop now.

# 6

# Tales Told by Serendipity Wilson #1
## *The Termagant Wife*

Afternoons could be long on the encampment, especially in winter when there was nothing to do but hunker down and wait for showtime. Sometimes, like most of the others on the encampment, we'd nap, doze the hours away. Serendipity Wilson disliked laziness for its own sake, so she'd create games for us to play, or teach me how to knit a blanket, sew a seam. There were other lessons too, though I didn't know it at the time.

Over steaming cups of cinnamon tea, wrapped from head to toe in covers and blankets, Serendipity Wilson would tell me stories from her island home. Only later did I come to understand their true meaning and purpose. She wanted me to grow up a wise woman. Perhaps also, to learn from her own mistakes – who knows? Those stories have served me well. I wish I could thank her. At least I can write them down for you, exactly as they were told to me, so you can see what a careful teacher she was.

*You should not be afraid to speak, Mouse. You're a clever girl. It pains me to see how you shrink away, hushed and reduced, when people approach. You have a voice. Find it. Don't let anyone stop you from using it.*

*Do you know women have died for the sake of their voice? Never in vain though, because we carry their voices with us still. Don't be cowed into silence. Men know their voices are listened to. Being heard is an ingrained truth for them. Even so, some men can become loud and brutal, better to ensure the woman in front of them is only the listener, not the speaker, or the thinker. This is a man-lie, Mouse: a lie told for thousands of years. Thankfully, not all men believe it. Sadly, women are sometimes duped. You must never believe it. Never be complicit in it. It exists to mask an ancient fear. When a man speaks to you in such a way, know that they are afraid of you. We must always have an equal voice. That's why you must find yours, Mouse. In the end, good sense is what must be heard, no matter who speaks it. Don't frown and pull at your fingers. Why sweat so? I'm not cross with you. I only want you to know that your voice is as valid as anyone else's, and certainly as valid as any man's.*

*Sit here, closer to me now, and let me tell you about a woman who wouldn't let her voice be ignored, even after the most brutal of punishments.*

*If you find yourself in the valley of St Marks, be sure to cross the brook. For on its banks stands a parsonage. Although it's a small house, it is very fine; built, it is said, from an ancient granite boulder known as Goddard Crovan's Stone.*

*Goddard Crovan, son of Harold the Black, was an ambitious man. He'd already been King of Norway and of Dublin, but that was not enough for such a mighty king. So it was, in the year 1049, he invaded our island and became King of Man. Ten days after the invasion, when the people had vowed to be his faithful servants, he set up house in Manannán mac Lir's own castle, on the summit of Barrule, and took a wife.*

*His wife was known on the island for her charm. She was quick-witted and clever and, although not a classic beauty, she was a beguiling young woman who could hold her own in any tavern among the bands of local men. Before her marriage, many callers came to her door, but she always sent them away with a flea in their ear and a stone in their heart. She'd wanted to be wooed, to be swept off her feet. Sadly, the men who tried to win her favours were never stimulating or interesting enough. Indeed, many were handsome. But she knew that beauty was a fading glory.*

*There were warriors, prize-winning farmers, youths from good families, even boys who fancied themselves poets. But though at first she may have ached for the touch of a certain suitor's fingers upon her hand, she soon grew tired of their chatter, realizing her own wit was far superior to that of the would-be beau. But Goddard Crovan was not a local; he was a king.*

*After spending only one evening with the girl, Goddard Crovan decided she was to be his bride. There was no question of refusal; in any case, she did not want to refuse. Wasn't this exactly the romance she'd been waiting for?*

*The new wife was happy in the old castle. Her husband was attentive enough, to begin with. She would spend her days teaching him games, telling him stories of ancient times, and reading aloud to him from the numerous books she'd sent for, hoping to create a fine library for their draughty castle home.*

*These volumes contain information every king should know, she would tell him. Ignorance can only bring defeat. You must educate yourself in the way of the world, in the ways of the scribes and the thinkers.*

When Goddard Crovan was called away on kingly errands, the wife would coax him to disclose the details of the matter, so she could advise him on the best course of action. *Would it not, she'd say, be better to negotiate than to fight? We cannot afford the loss of even a single man, and our fleet is small.* Or: *Now is the time for action, husband. The time for talk is over. Strike or be struck!*

As the king's wife, she took charge of all financial matters, making sure her husband did not fritter away the wealth of the island. She was a shrewd accountant, and the island prospered under its new king.

Goddard Crovan was not used to being told what to do and how to do it, especially by a woman. No matter that she was more learned than he, more meticulous and intelligent. The situation soon became unbearable to him. He could not move around his own castle without his wife trailing in his shadow, trotting in his footsteps, advising him on this and that.

*Do not wear furs this evening, my lord. The sea is angry and if your ship should fail, the weight would drag you down to the depths.*

*Wife!* he said. *I shall wear furs and do as I please. How many men are followed around by their little woman, nagging in their earhole all the time. Do this! Don't do this! Am I not a king? Am I not a man? Desist, wife! Or I shall be forced to scold you.*

*You ridiculous man. Obviously you're a king! But if you are careless, you will not only lose your kingdom, you will be meat for the*

*fishes, and then where will you be? Listen to my counsel, abandon
your stupid pride and all will be well.*

*Goddard Crovan grew angry. And from that day forwards the
king stormed around his castle like a great bear, his wife always in
tow behind him, quarrelling as they went.*

*How have I become the master of such a termagant wife? he
roared. Leave me be, woman! I shall have none of your harridan
screeching.*

*And so it continued. Weeks and months passed. The wife would
not let her husband be, for she knew she could beat him in the world
of words. She would not let him have the last say in anything, especially when he always said such stupid things. She saw it as a game,
a great amusement to pass the time. Only the king was not amused.*

*Your bawling will get you nowhere, shrew! he would say. Still she
followed, still she spoke. Until finally he ordered her to be locked in
her room.*

*This did not stop the wife. Furious at her husband's use of brutal-
ity, she shouted her counsel from behind the door, telling him she
would not be silenced by the brawn of a man. Her voice rang around
the castle. No nook, no cranny was free from her continuing counsel.
The king could not abide the noise; he raged up and down the chambers of his great home, unable to think, to speak, but roaring like a
wild animal, frothing at the mouth with impotence and frustration.
Days, weeks went by, until he could no longer bear the sound of his
wife's voice and banished her from the castle.*

*I release you from your vows, termagant wife! he cried, and bolted
the castle gates behind her.*

*The woman descended the mountain of Barrule. She listened to* the birds, saw the puffins nesting in the rocks, and as she took in the bright, fresh island air, the woody odour of the heather, the salty taste of the sea, she thought how wonderful a thing it was to have been born on Man. She did not need to be the wife of a king to enjoy the landscape of her island home, to read books, or to eat good food. She would rather a poor husband, a man of wit, who could understand philosophy and science, or even no husband at all, than some idiot king who only knew how to fight and burble on in simple words.

There was no romance in riches, she told herself. No, she thought, she was not at all unhappy to be away from the castle and the king. And as she reached the bottom of the mountain, far beneath the castle gates, well out of earshot of the king, those were the very words she spoke. She spoke them freely, out loud, to the mountain and the air.

Unbeknownst to her, as she began to speak, a wind began to blow. The wind picked up her words and carried them all the way back up the mountain and into the heart of the castle. Her voice once again rang through the chambers and the halls. The king was beside himself.

How dare she rebuke me, and screeching for the whole island to hear? I'll shut her up once and for all! He ran full pelt through the castle gates. In his fury he fell upon a large boulder. The king grabbed the boulder and flung it down the mountain of Barrule in the direction of his former wife's voice. His aim was good, his ears keen. The boulder hit its mark, and killed the woman where she stood, stone dead.

The granite boulder rested where it landed for many hundreds of years. It was a famous landmark and was given the name of Goddard Crovan's Stone. Many writers, artists and poets of renown *have mentioned the boulder in their works. It was seen as a reminder to all young girls of the folly of termagancy. After all, what better warning could there be than the promise of death?*

*Time passed, as time does, and weathered the stone, making it an ugly sight for locals and tourists alike. It was not a fit thing to bear the name of a King of Man. After a while the boulder was all but forgotten. So, in order to preserve its fine history, the stone was smashed into chunks by men with mallets, and the pieces used to build the parsonage on the banks of the brook. Only, that was not the end of Goddard Crovan's handiwork.*

*To this day, the men who live in the shadow of Barrule send their young daughters to spend a night in the parsonage at St Marks, believing the house to be a reliable remedy for a termagant tongue. But young girls can be resourceful things, and many have slept soundly in the parsonage bed, knowing the walls around them are imbued with the soul of a woman who was murdered for her voice. Putting their hands to the walls, they call up the memory of the woman. And soon they feel her spirit come to give them strength, courage to speak, and protection from the brutality of foolish men.*

*Be like the young women of St Marks, Mouse, take heart from this tale. Your voice has the power to change lives, at the very least your own. Use it.*

# 7

# Coffee: The Gentle Sway of a Memory

I awoke this morning not knowing where, or who I was. The world seemed an unfamiliar place. It took several seconds before I could register the facts: I was lying on my bed, the smell of coffee gently filling the room, almost tangibly so.

There was movement downstairs; the rattling of pans; the ching of spoons in cups. The familiar smell of coffee sent me into a quandary, conflating past, present, and future. I breathed in the heavy aroma, closed my eyes, and let myself float away, back to the Formica fittings of my parents' caravan, to the gas-bottle stove, and my small square of shelter between the grocery shelf and the hotplate.

I awake not knowing where, or who I am. The world seems an unfamiliar place. It takes several seconds before I can register the facts: I am lying under my second-best blanket, warm but uncomfortable on the floor, by the stove, in the caravan of my birth. The smell of roasted coffee hangs in the air. Slowly, I open my eyes. Manu is hovering over me. He puts a hand on my shoulder.

I am growing up, one of the star attractions of our circus. I'm expected to forget my childhood. Fausto says I'm to look to the future. I want to forget. What use is childhood to me now? Only, it's not easy. I feel closer to the past than to the future, and the present is unreal: a baffling, seemingly never-ending field of boredom, peppered with moments of joy, when I'm performing on my wire or practising my routines. This is what I am thinking as I shake off the world of dreams and look into my father's eyes.

It's been almost a week since I slept in the wigwam. Serendipity Wilson has started going off on her own. I wish I knew where to. But she won't say, and her nightly absences have become unbearable to me. I cannot stay there without her – not that she would mind; in fact, she'd encourage me to, if she wasn't too preoccupied with her nocturnal wanderings to notice my bed hasn't been slept in. She goes off so much lately. There's an ache in my guts when she's gone. I can't eat or sleep. Better that you cut off both my legs than take Serendipity Wilson away from me. She knows, but still she goes. The wigwam is the nearest thing I have to a home, yet when alone there, I feel like a trespasser.

Manu hands me a mug of steaming black liquid. The first sip makes my eyes water, it tastes as bitter as it smells. But I'm grateful for his attention, and drink without wincing. He sits on the floor next to me. My heart jumps. The effect of his closeness, and the coffee, is like a magic potion (my insides suddenly alive and alert). It also makes me feel sick. Nevertheless, I drink it down in gulps and want more.

When Serendipity Wilson finds I have taken to drinking coffee, she'll soon realize something is wrong. Then she'll stop her gallivanting, come back to the wigwam, everything will go back to normal and I will no longer have to stay at the caravan.

We sit on the floor. It's nice, having Manu close. I hide a smile behind my steaming cup. Even so, there's something sitting between us, something far from cosy. I cannot look at him in case the bad thing shows itself. I stare at the floor.

*I'd like your help, ma puce.*

The unexpected softness in his voice makes me flush. Hot blood rushes around my face. The more aware of it I am, the hotter it becomes. Manu smiles, shakes his head and lets out a silent laugh.

*You're a big hit. Non?*

He pauses, sips his coffee. Am I supposed to answer? Silence. My smile is gone. I continue to stare at the floor.

*I've heard the talk around the encampment. You must take no notice.*

I am terrified. What talk? What do those people say when I cannot hear them? My heart is on the floor. People are so cruel, to speak of me, to my own father!

*You're wonderful on your wire, that's what matters, and you're a clever girl. You know very well that all you need in life is this.*

Manu taps the side of his head with the tip of his middle finger. I can't stop myself from smiling. He doesn't care about silly gossip.

*You've seen my act?*

*Yes, I'm not blind.*

My smile grows so big it hurts my cheeks, and I'm scared it will fill my entire face, like a stupid Joey clown.

*I want to be the best.*

*Like your mother.*

*No. Not like Marina. Never like her.*

*But you are. Look at your eyes, your jaw, here, and your long neck, like a goose.*

Manu brushes his middle finger around my eyes, along my jaw and down my neck. His touch is a magnet. The downy hairs on my skin stand up to meet the tip of his finger. I feel, profoundly, that his meat and bones are the same as mine. I have been cut from his flesh, fashioned like clay by his hands. I shiver, even though I am not cold. When I look down at my arms, I think of plucked chickens; hideous. I want Manu to continue brushing his finger down the length of my bare arm. I want him to stroke to the tips of my raggedy fingers, to not notice, or care, about my hideousness. He stops. He sighs.

*Marina needs us.*

There's ringing in my ears. I have to remember to breathe out because I'm holding my breath. My insides are throbbing and moving, my skin is sweating, and I don't want Manu to see how muddled up I am, so I try to speak.

*She doesn't know I exist.*

My voice is small, high-pitched, like a trembling bell.

*You're wrong. She is only too aware of you, ma puce.*

I shake my head, grip my coffee cup, feel the heat seep

through the chipped porcelain into the palms of my hands. Trying hard to block the tears that are pooling behind my eyes and in my throat, I look at the square of grubby, colourless carpet between my feet.

*She knows what you're growing up to be. Your mother thinks you can fly on your wire, like a raven. That's what she calls you. A big black bird.*

I sniff, wipe my nose on my shoulder, and let out a painful sob.

*My costume is white, not black. She's never even seen me.*

*Be calm. It's simply her way. She sees things differently to other people. You know? Maybe she sees things other people can't — another one of her gifts. And she has given you her artistic gift.*

*She's given me nothing.*

*She gave you life. Isn't that enough?*

I do not answer. Manu smiles and my heart flaps in the hollow of my chest, like the wings of a canary trapped inside a cloth bag, utterly captured. My father is a beautiful man, his hair still black, his skin dark, his body slim and muscular. Despite everything, I am proud to be his daughter. I do not want to argue with him or have him think me an ungrateful child (although I have nothing to thank him for). My attention is so easily interrupted. I find it hard to follow words spoken to me by anyone other than Serendipity Wilson. But I am sure I'm capable of keeping myself here, with Manu, of listening and responding, of appearing normal.

*Marina wants to be a star again. It's her dream.*

*I'm sure she can do it. She's a legend, Papa.*

*A lot of time has passed, she needs to work hard. Marina needs our encouragement. She needs our help.*

*She barely speaks to me. You should ask Big Gen.*

*You're wrong. You and I are the only people who can help Marina. Gen is no good, she coddles her, treats her like a baby, pours drink down her throat! I can't trust her; I can't even trust myself. I give in to her, I'm weak. It's not the way to get her back into the ring.*

*I can't swim.*

Manu laughs.

*But you can fly.*

My father tells me stories now, of how great Marina was in her day. His endless chatter makes me uncomfortable. It's as if he's talking to himself. He doesn't look at me but goes on and on. I feel sick and wish I could leave. The stories continue. Wet patches spread under my arms. Sweat trickles down my sides, under my clothes. My hands are soaked and so slippery that I almost drop my coffee cup. I wipe them on my second-best blanket. Manu is still talking. The wool of my blanket feels rough, as if it has turned against me, as if it wants to cut me. I grip my cup again and let out a low, heavy groan in order to interrupt his string of meaningless words. My voice is louder than anticipated, and because I am ashamed and confused, I scream out that I will do everything possible to help Marina. My voice is too loud and strange for the confines of the caravan. Manu falls silent. My relief is palpable. I look over to the curtain and imagine Marina lying in her bed; her eyes wide and smiling. The most important thing in the world is Marina's smile. If I can put my thoughts in order, stop my mind from racing, do everything in the right way, my mother might smile at me. She would be grateful if I helped her. She'd see my talent. She would be amazed and impressed by my generosity, and she might want us to do an act together; mother and daughter, like other circus families.

The coffee cup, like the day, grows cold. Manu maintains his silence. The effect is calming. Even now, if people talk to me, I lose focus, get flustered, stop listening. It's not only Manu who makes me feel this way, and it's not because I'm stupid, which is what many people still believe. I know this sickness and confusion is due to my years of isolation as a child. I'm learning to fight it, to be brave, hold my ground. Still, noise and talk can make me unwell. Like now. Or perhaps it's the coffee that's to blame.

Manu notices my eyes, flicking up and down, trying to focus on something behind him. He turns, checks the curtain drawn around his bed, and looks back at me, frowning. I stay as still and cold as a pebble. I would like to up sticks, get out of there, but I dare not move. Without warning, Manu stands, says he doesn't know why he even bothers talking to me since I don't want to listen or pay proper attention to anything he is saying. Slamming the door behind him, he leaves. I get up to watch his retreat through the caravan's only window.

Now that I am alone, the caravan is like a cave. I lie on the floor, curl my knees to my chest, and am sick over my second-best blanket.

# 8

# The Disappearance of Old Man Frazer

*Yorkshire Evening Post*, 17 October 1960

A circus performer disappeared last week on the night before his troupe was due to leave town. 'Old Man Frazer' is 49 years of age and said to be in excellent health. Frazer vanished from a circus encampment on Woodhouse Moor, Leeds 6, sometime before 7 p.m. last Tuesday evening.

The former sergeant-major and Desert Rat turned trapeze artiste is said to be a level-headed man and much respected by his associates. Genevieve Callaghan, the circus secretary, better known to audiences as Big Gen, told this reporter that the circus community can't help but suspect foul play.

'He's not the sort [of person] to go off without a word,' she said. 'His family are beside themselves. Their livelihood is at stake.'

Miss Callaghan, herself a local lass, hailing originally from Burley, refutes the accusation of a torrid love affair turned sour, calling him 'a family man', and asks the public to contact this

paper if they have any information as to his whereabouts.

The police, although interested to hear from anyone
who would like to come
forward with information,
say they are not regarding
Mr Frazer's (né John Erskine
Frazer) disappearance as
suspicious.

*Ernest P. Edwards*

Old Man Frazer (who changed his first name from John to
Janus – a homage to the god of new beginnings – in the mistaken belief this would make him more exotic, transform
him into a circus artiste) had a war wound, causing him
to limp around the encampment like a tragic Victorian, all
shiny boots and tight breeches.

His act, the Flying Frazer Family, consisted of mother:
Lady [Muck] Annabel Frazer (Annabel, predictably, not her
real name). Father: Old Man Janus. And the two sons.

She, Lady Muck, had been some kind of showgirl and
had danced at the Folies-Bergère in Paris, which she always
maintained is where she met her husband. Although, what a
man like Janus John Frazer was doing hanging around fancy
clubs in Paris, when he was supposed to be out in the desert
fighting a war, I will never know. I've always presumed the
story of their Parisian love affair to be a fabrication, a mar-
keting ploy to make them look special. But what do I know?

Annabel (real name Annie Dawson), was younger than
him, and didn't mix well with circus people. She'd swan
around the encampment, nose in the air, sour look on her

face. She insisted on having the most up-to-date caravan, and thought herself extremely stylish and talented, far above any normal circus artiste. So did he for that matter, or at least it came across that way. In fact, she was a one-time stripper with delusions of grandeur, and he, a failed gymnast with a gammy leg.

The Flying Frazer Family were (probably) the most dreadful act Fausto had ever put on. He hired them in a moment of folly, being desperate for flyers — *you can't have a circus without flyers* — and impressed at their meagre expectations (they must've been as desperate as he was, if not for the money — they seemed to have plenty of that — then at least for glory, a chance to perform and show themselves off). He took them on without reputation or reference.

Old Man Frazer was a man of few words. Although he would *Hup! Hey!* and grunt his way around the ring during performances, and make all manner of strange noises to enhance his swinging on the trapeze, he was the picture of solemnity around the encampment. So much so, rumours spread of a dark secret. It was believed he'd had a *bad war*.

John Frazer was a Scotsman, who despite not having the tiniest trace of an accent, often favoured a kilt and sporran in place of a pair of ordinary slacks. He was rich, or so the rumours said; his ancestral home, some sort of Scottish castle. It was clear that John was not in need of a regular income, such was his status as a man of means. Other than Annabel and the boys (who were not his, but the product of a failed early marriage to a French contortionist), he had little family to speak of. There was a sister, long since gone to a better place, having met her fate during the war – she was among the first wave of GI brides. He didn't speak of her often, but when he did, you'd think she was the veritable queen of America. Many believed he must have run off to start a better life over the pond, escaping the foolishness of an unsuitable marriage. There was so much gossip it was hard to know what to believe. One thing was certain: wherever he was, John Frazer would never want for much.

The Old Man was tall; short of torso but lengthy of leg. His long arms gave the impression of considerable strength. He was heavy-jawed, thin-lipped and large-nosed. It was a manly face, yet singularly unattractive. His head of short, bristly, chocolate-brown hair resembled the end of a scrubbing brush and gave him the look of a man constantly surprised by life. His eyes were dark and, had they belonged to a different face, they might even have been thought handsome. As it was, they reinforced a sense of deep distrust with the world, and an ugliness of thought to match his outward appearance. And this was the man Serendipity Wilson had taken to be her first, and only, beau.

Old Man Frazer's disappearance took everyone by surprise. Fausto and Gen thought he was terribly ungrateful to run off like that, leaving them in limbo, especially as Lady Muck refused to continue the act – due to the emotional trauma of it all – but nevertheless insisted on being paid in full for each unperformed show. They soon sent her packing. Flyers, it seemed, weren't that important after all.

When I say his disappearance took everyone by surprise, I do not include myself in that number. There are some things we keep hidden, through shame I suppose, even when those concerned are long gone. I don't imagine it matters if I tell you now. Integrity is all well and good, but it doesn't get a story told. If you're to help me in my search for the missing child, it's only right you know all the grimy details. I'll let you in on the secret, then. It's all here in this old notebook. I need to keep my courage while I transcribe this. I hope you can forgive me my sins. I'll type it quickly. I'll do it now.

People are debauched and squalid. Their appetites so great they do not care who sees their lusts. It makes me sick. If it wasn't for my wire, I would've escaped this den of lechery long ago. I wish I could live my entire life upon my wire. If I could, I'd never come down.

Serendipity Wilson is as bad as the others. No! She's worse. She pretends to be made of higher stuff, as if that freakish hair makes her flame brighter than the dirt of her flesh. I know the truth. I've seen her, running about, hiding in dark corners (she should know better than to think there are corners too dark for my eyes) with that decrepit fool. His ugliness offends me. How could she let his big hands touch her? Let that slit-for-a-mouth press against her body, and his slug-of-a-tongue lick her skin? She is everything, and he is nothing. The thought makes me retch.

At first I thought she'd taken up with one of the gruesome

twins. They're young, granted, but the Nathan boy has a look in his eyes that could (mistakenly) be perceived as depth. I've seen him flirt with the girls around the encampment. The thought of her with one of those two made me feel sick enough. Then I saw her and the old man, wriggling out from under the big wagon, fixing themselves.

I was in the animal enclosure, Solomon's head on my lap. I was stroking his ears to help him sleep. Llamas are like people (only better), they suffer from the night. I wasn't there to watch the goings-on of others, not expecting to see anything. In any case, it was late. Everyone had taken to their beds soon after the evening show, which had been a dull affair. Other than the sound of the animals, all was quiet on the encampment.

As I sat in the straw with the llamas, I sensed something pure and still resting on the warm night air. Although the show had been lacklustre, I'd been on my wire. The audience were unafraid to show their appreciation, and how I loved them for it. I was happy.

Then I saw them.

Serendipity Wilson was the first to squeeze herself out from under the wagon. She brushed herself down, did not linger or even turn to see if her collaborator was close behind. She scanned the encampment, no doubt to make sure no one was around (she didn't make sure enough) and skipped off. I was perplexed, thought maybe I should go after her, maybe she'd been searching for me, but she looked content, unconcerned. Then it was his turn.

He pulled himself slowly out, stretched, and leaned against
the wagon as calm and natural as you like. He lit a cigarette.
I watched the red pinprick of light flare and wane as he
inhaled. He stayed long after his smoke was finished, hands
on the wagon behind him. I wondered if there was something wrong. Eventually, he pushed away and walked, not
with a swagger – not likely with that limp – but with his
head down, like a man defeated, across the encampment.

I spent the night with the llamas. It was impossible to go
back to the wigwam and Serendipity Wilson after bearing
witness to her crime. It was repulsive. And I certainly didn't
want to be anywhere near my disgusting parents – they're
even worse. My generosity in agreeing to help Marina has
done nothing to make them speak kindly to me. So I lay
next to Solomon, buried my crying eyes into the top of his
woolly head, kissed him goodnight and let the world of
dreams take me away from the hideousness of the day.

It is morning now.

Although I slept well and feel relatively bright, my hand
trembles as I write. The events of last night continue to stab
at me. I am heavy with heartbreak. How can I face the day?
Serendipity Wilson has betrayed our friendship, our bond
of trust. Not only has she been indulging in unspeakable
acts with that ugly, talentless old man, she has not, at any
time, thought fit to include me in her secret. She could've
asked me to keep it under my hat. I keep secrets better than
anyone in the world. I am the most trustworthy companion. Now she has another, it seems. One devoid of artistry,

one whose face is an affront. And to make it worse, one who is old enough to be her own father. Probably.

What have I done to be thrown into the shadows of her life? I'd do anything, everything, to make up for the injury. There must be something very bad in me. I wish I could find the badness and cut it out. I'd take Manu's knife and gouge it from my flesh. I'm not scared of pain. If it were that simple, I'd happily do it. Serendipity Wilson is not Marina, she would not betray me without good cause. Still, I am cast out, completely alone and unable to leave the llama pen. I'll stay here forever, until I die of exposure, or fever, or something. At least until tonight's performance. Then I must face the world, face Serendipity Wilson, and her lumbering, ugly lover. Does she know what she's done?

There are several blank pages after this. It's odd that I should have left the pages blank. Maybe it was a statement, something about life being empty; the sort of thing young people do. This isn't how I remember things. The events happened exactly as they're written, yet I cannot find myself in the words. My grief spills onto the page as if it were another performance, in the same way Marina would parade around the circus encampment, sobbing and drunk, in nothing but her slip. I hope you don't think of me like that.

All I can do is write the memories as they come to me, transcribe the words I once scribbled, and hope you will see the essence of the young girl who wrote them. My memories may have lost detail over time, they could even be misremembered. Still, they seem more real to me than the hand that wrote those pitiful words. As I tap at the keys, I am bound to stumble upon the truth. How sad that it's only with hindsight we truly see how things once were.

Serendipity Wilson's eyes sparkle. She beams from under her turbaned head. The wigwam sways slightly; the movement of the fabric and the whistle of air passing over it calms me. I haven't spoken to her for three days. I look at her from under heavy brows. She is mocking me. Knitting small stitches with skinny needles. Humming.

*I saw you.*

*What? Don't you see me now?*

*With him.*

*I see.*

*How could you?*

*There's no need to be angry, Mouse. Nothing in this world is more natural than physical desire. You will see.*

I do not respond. Neither do I move. Instead, I continue to glower at her.

*In any case the whole silly thing is over now. I shan't be running around barefoot through the night again. It's a sure way to catch a cold.*

*What? Why?*

*Because.*

*You don't love Old Man Frazer anymore?*

*What are you talking about? Love indeed!*

She laughs, which makes me feel stupid, so I bury my head in my hands and sob.

*You're not so unworldly, Mouse, to think that love is reserved for the givers and receivers of pleasure. Don't be silly. This is something entirely different. Well, maybe not entirely, but different.*

*He looks sad these days.*

*That's no concern of mine. I'm not his wife.*

*That's just it. He has a wife! Why did you do it with him? He's so old and ugly and married to that awful woman. And you . . .*

*Yes?*

*You're the most wonderful person in the world.*

*Thank you. That's very sweet.*

*I don't understand.*

*You're such a child sometimes.*

*You're supposed to look after me, explain things to me.*

*All right, Mouse! It's quite simple. No matter what you may think, in terms of womanly things, I'm nothing special.*

Serendipity Wilson puts down her knitting and wrinkles her forehead, a deliberate attempt at looking thoughtful, which irritates me.

*Let me see if I can give you a better answer.*

*Please.*

*He has nice eyes.*

*What?*

*And very manly hands. You know he doesn't have relations with Annabel anymore? They haven't done it for years. It's all an act with them.*

*But, why you? Why did you do it?*

*I don't exactly have a lot of choice when it comes to these things, do I, Mouse? Who else could I have chosen, really? Who would* consider me a desirable partner, rather than a grotesque conquest? He was, in fact, the perfect choice.

*Why did you have to do it at all?*

*Oh, don't be naive. It makes me cross with you.*

*Then, tell me.*

*There are certain things a woman of my age must experience. Imagine if I carried on in life without ever understanding the pleasures of the body. Because, my dear Mouse, there are such pleasures to be had. I couldn't bear the idea of being an eternal virgin. As romantic as that may sound to a young mind such as yours, believe me, it makes for a thoroughly dull life. Some things are just necessary, that's all, and it was time – my goodness, it was time. But now it's done. I'm satisfied, and it's done.*

She pauses, looks at her fingers, and smiles. She is thinking about him, about the things they did together, about the pleasures that I cannot understand.

*What did it feel like, the pleasures?*

*I'm sure you can imagine. You've felt certain urges. It's normal. Everyone does. There's no shame in it. Anyway, I'm not sure it's possible to describe.*

*Try.*

*Oh, Mouse, it's not easy. All right. Promise not to interrupt and I'll try.*

*Promise.*

*Sometimes it would make me want to scream. Really scream. I mean, there was no control, I couldn't stop myself from screaming. Sometimes it would make me sigh. Not a normal sigh, but something deep that came from the very centre of me, something I didn't even know was there. It was like I had this thing, which was resting, sleeping inside me all my life, and suddenly it was opened up, released. When he pushed his fingers inside me – do not grimace so, Mouse – he woke the thing up. The more he pushed, the more the thing began to pulse and breathe, until finally something broke, like the banks of a river in a flood, and I was completely undone, unleashed and free. These were the times when I never wanted it to stop. I'd be lost, and I'd beg him to keep on, to never stop. Other times the whole thing was funny, ridiculous even. And I had to concentrate, hard, to get any pleasure at all.*

*Marina screams. I hate her stupid screams.*

*Well, maybe they aren't always real. There are times when one must scream, or whatever, to get on with things.*

*I would never scream. I hate screaming.*

*Janus has certain little . . . how should I put it? Problems. Screaming can sometimes help. You see, his old cocker can have difficulty becoming ripe enough for active service. Don't pretend you don't know what I mean, Mouse. Oh, he gets his pleasure all right, he comes as if he was as hard as a cannon, eventually. But, honestly, sometimes it's like trying to squash a marshmallow into a slot machine. It's exhausting.*

Serendipity Wilson looks at me with wide eyes, as innocent as a lambkin. We are still for a second, staring at each other as if suspended on an intake of breath, and then, we plunge. Peals of laughter tumble out of us. We roll on the floor like small children, holding our bellies as tears run down our cheeks. We are unable to speak or even breathe without snorting, until eventually, we fall silent. Our mirth drifts away and we are simply lying together on the floor of the colourful wigwam, each in our own place, but completely, unequivocally together.

Serendipity Wilson turns on her side. We are face to face, nose to nose. She puts her hand over mine, takes it, and places it on her stomach.

*He managed to give me something though, Mouse. Flaccid cocker or not. I didn't know I wanted it, but now it's here, it is the most wonderful thing in the world. I want it more than anything.*

I half-laugh, as if there's been another joke, something else to start giggling about, but Serendipity Wilson has stopped. She's looking directly into my eyes, but she is far away. Her face is serene and although she's not exactly smiling now, there is a trace of something around her mouth, a not-quite-smile, an almost-smirk; whatever it is, she looks like an angel and I love her more than ever. My heart cannot hold my feelings, so it explodes. I feel it; the shards of love rushing through my veins, carving me up from the inside, like slivers of sharpened metal, razor-blades cutting through muscle. My blood tingles and I'm sure that no one will ever be able to put my heart together again. But it doesn't matter. I place my head on Serendipity Wilson's shoulder, breathe in her familiar smell, and without realizing it, I forgive her.

At first, nobody noticed the absence of John Frazer, which, considering all the running around and hiding in dark places he'd been doing, was no surprise. It was business as usual on the encampment, with all the excitement that goes with the last day of a show. Extra streamers waved from flagpoles. Even the animals seemed to feel the thrill of the final show.

Marina was preparing to perform again, or rather, she was thinking about it. No longer a circus star, her new act would simply see her swim around her tank, waving and smiling, tumbling and somersaulting through the water. There were to be no crocodiles, no distractions, just Marina, swimming, and smiling. The act was to be short. A filler to enable the ring to be cleared and rigging made safe for the next big act. My mother worried about her audience; how to make them love her again. Her nerves bordered on panic. I spent the early morning watching her pace up and down outside the caravan, smoking and throwing gin down her throat. It was unbearable; it seemed unfitting to see her so devastated by nerves for such an inconsequential perform-ance. Of course, all this posturing was merely another performance, of sorts. Nevertheless, it made me sad to see how much she needed the attention of others. I decided not to watch.

Strolling around the encampment, boredom feeding off blank thoughts and deep sighs, I didn't notice him at first, trailing after me. Eventually I spotted him, limping in my shadow, and the shock was like a blow to the head. My first instinct was to run. But Old Man Frazer strode beside me, his long legs making short shrift of thoughts of escape. Before I knew what was happening, he grabbed my arm, forced me to stop, to face him. I was little used to people speaking to me directly, looking into my face. In my whole life I'd only ever had direct conversations with four people, and although I knew this man, he was still a stranger.

*I need your help, young lady.*

*Please, let go. I don't like people touching me. Leave me alone.*

*So sensitive! Don't worry, I don't want to hurt you. I need your help, that's all.*

*Why does everyone need my help, these days? Go away!*

My impulse was to spit in his face, free my arm from his grip, and run away. Yet all I could do was stare with terrified eyes into the face of Serendipity Wilson's lover. I didn't want to be close to this man, didn't want to feel his words gently blow across my mouth in warm, coffee-soured clouds.

*There's nothing I can do. She doesn't want you. She told me so.*

*Take this. We can't talk here. Meet me this afternoon. Understand? You'll thank me for this. If you do what I say, you'll be greatly rewarded. Do you understand?*

John Frazer pressed a piece of paper into my hand. I nodded. This seemed to be the correct response. He nodded back and marched away; he didn't turn to look at me; he didn't try to persuade me with more words, more squeezing and bruising of my arm. When I was sure he was gone, I dropped to my knees. As much as it horrified me, I somehow regretted his abrupt exit.

With my knees embedded in the damp ground, I wondered what it would be like to be wrapped in John Frazer's vinegary odour. I fanned my face for air. When I came to my senses and looked at the piece of paper I was using for a fan, I realized it was the note he'd shoved into my hand. It was daubed in hastily scribbled lines and instructions; a map, drawn especially for me. I scrunched the thing into a ball and held it to my face. It smelled of him, so I quickly pulled it away and, lacking a pocket, folded the strange gift into the waistband of my skirt – the way Serendipity Wilson always did, when she wanted to keep things safe.

It was still early afternoon when I left the encampment. We were camped on an open piece of land on the outskirts of a city centre. The dirty common was cut in two by a busy road. The section we were parked on was usually used for children's football games, or dog walking, or dumping unwanted household goods. The greener section, on the other side of the road, had a playground and statues of bears and lions and other animals. Someone had painted them, in mischief, rainbow colours. They were mucky-looking things; chipped and broken.

I sat for a moment on a colourful lion, stroked its chipped nose. From there I could see over the encampment. The big top – a round, blue-and-white-striped leviathan with a pointed tip, topped off with a jolly yellow flag that called to passers-by as it flapped in the breeze – dominated every-thing. Compared to the rest of the structure, from here, the flag looked small. Really, it was an enormous triangle of patched canvas that took two men to fold. I looked over to the trucks parked in a circle behind the big top, designed to house the pens and cages of the animals. And over to the left of the big top, I could see Marina's old tank, covered with its green tarpaulin.

There were plenty of people milling around; artistes practising in the open air, setting up makeshift tables for meals. Someone ran across the field from the artistes' abodes. It was Manu. He disappeared behind the trucks, into the animal enclosure. The caravans and tents making up the dwellings were on the far right of the land, away from the big top. From where I sat, they seemed meagre things. Even the colourful wigwam, standing defiantly alone – as always – looked inconsequential from my vantage point. Still, its familiarity made me smile.

I started to walk towards the city centre. Large university buildings dominated the upper part of the town, and rows of red-brick terraces were nestled together behind the encampment, as if terrified the surrounding trees and roads might encroach on their small streets and swallow them up. They looked sad, dirty, and poor.

As I set off, I looked at the map, crumpled and smudged in my hands, and wound my way down what seemed to be the main street. The white university hall, with its oblong tower, gave extra clarity and light to the day. All the buildings of the university were beautiful and grand, made of white stone. There were people buzzing about, sitting on wide steps, chatting, smoking. They were not the sort of people who made up the hordes that came to the circus. The girls dressed in black, and the boys in ill-fitting suits that looked self-consciously creased. Students.

I imagined my wire stretched between those great white buildings, wondered how it would feel to glide over the heads of the dark girls and shabby boys. They'd stop their chatter then, only breaking their silence with applause. Perhaps the applause wouldn't resonate. Stone and brick buildings are not gentle like the fabric confines of a big top, they might soak up the sound. I decided I never wanted to be confined by walls, no matter how grand they might be. I'd stay forever under the gentle protection of the colourful wigwam (no matter how inconsequential it looked), and Serendipity Wilson.

There was building work going on, the noise and commotion adding to my disorientation. Not knowing where I was or where I was going, I followed my crudely drawn guide. The road dipped through courtyards, past a fire station, a theatre, until I came to a crossroads, at the centre of which, floating like an island between roads and buildings, was my destination; a small public garden.

Another large white building stood at the apex of the garden. It was fussy. Two towers adorned its roof, ornate in contrast to the flat frontage of the university buildings, making it look like a voracious country church. On either side of this stone wedding cake was mounted a large clock made up of what looked to be huge squares of cast gold. They resembled two enormous golden ears. There were further wide steps leading up to three solid doors – shut tight to the citizens of the town. No one was milling around here. Directly in front of the building was a series of plinths.

Atop each plinth stood a proud golden owl, casting yellow light onto white stone. A narrow road snaked around the owls, and a large red-brick building loomed on the other side, massive and splendidly Victorian. Although magnificent, the red-brick behemoth paled into industrial insignificance next to the gold and glitz of owls and clocks. It was a hospital, obviously occupied and in use, but as silent as the grave.

The public garden standing between the hospital and the wedding-cake building, dwarfed by its surroundings, was as neat and colourful as a picture postcard. Perhaps the incurably infirm were staring down from dormitory windows, gazing at the happy flowerbeds, the garden there to allow them one last look at the radiance of life. *How cruel,* I thought.

I found Old Man Frazer standing in the garden, a lone, uncomfortable figure. I was so taken with the architecture of my surroundings that, under different circumstances, I probably wouldn't have noticed him. As it was, he stuck out like a lion in a field of newborn lambs. My throat contracted. I wiped my hands on the now almost sodden paper ball clinging to my fingers. He looked up. It took all my courage not to turn on my heel and run. Serendipity Wilson's lover wasn't surprised to see me, even though I'd not said when, or even if, I'd be there.

*Good girl. You didn't keep me waiting.*

*I'm not a good girl. I'm not anything to you.*

*And yet, here we are. Don't worry, I'll be quick.*

*What do you want?*

*I need your help.*

*There's nothing I can do for you.*

*Ah now, I'm sure there is.*

I laughed because I didn't understand his answer, but immediately felt stupid and ashamed.

*Look, this isn't an easy thing to discuss. Would you like me to buy you a milkshake, or something?*

*I am not a child.*

*True.*

*I know not to accept gifts from strange men.*

He half-smiled, which left me feeling adrift. I didn't mean to sound like a joker, I didn't mean to sound any way at all. Then, he moved towards a nearby bench. My awkwardness about to engulf me, I followed and sat next to him.

*I'm presuming you know?*

There was a pause. He expected some sort of reply or reaction. I didn't move.

*I'd prefer that my wife and her children stay ignorant of my part in this. There's no need for extra upset. I suppose it's inevitable, though. It's a shameful thing, making a child out of wedlock. Your friend, that sweet girl, stands to lose a lot. I'm sorry for her. It should never have happened. No, that's not true. It's the most real thing that's ever happened to me. I don't regret it for a second.*

*What are you talking about?*

He looked at me. I'd never noticed how dark his eyes were. Two hard, black pebbles glaring at me.

*She hasn't told you? I was under the impression you two were closer than sisters. I suppose some things are too private to share, even with our nearest and dearest. Still, won't be long before it shows. She can't hide it forever.*

*Hide what?*

*Do I have to spell it out? Serendipity Wilson is with child. With my child, to be precise.*

My hands rested in my lap. I stared at them. After a while, I realized I wasn't breathing. I opened my mouth. Nothing went in. I must've been a ridiculous sight, sat beside the mountainous John Frazer, opening and closing my mouth like a netted fish. I had the urge to fall to my knees again, but I was sitting on the bench and couldn't find the impulse to move anything other than my useless, guppy mouth.

At last, I drew breath, and with it came a deep moan. John Frazer went to touch my shoulder. I shifted on the bench, escaping his touch.

*Why should I believe you?*

*Because it's true. Why else do you think I brought you here?*

*Leave me alone. You haven't brought me here, I came out for a walk, that's all. I don't understand any of this.*

*You'd better start understanding, young lady, because your friend needs your help.*

*She doesn't want a baby. She would've told me. She must be suffering.*

*She's not unhappy, you foolish girl! But she doesn't realize what she's doing. It will ruin her life, having a child, alone. And in that place.*

*Why didn't she tell me? I mean, tell me properly? She knows I'm no good at puzzles. She should've said, told me straight out.*

*Maybe she's too preoccupied right now to be thinking of you?*

*How could you have done this to her? How could she let you?*

*Don't be a crybaby. As difficult as it is, she's not the first girl in the world to be caught out. Believe me, I want to make everything right. I can take care of her, and our baby. We can be a proper family.*

*She has a family.*

*They're far away. It would kill them to know she'd . . . fallen. They're not her real parents, anyway. They don't have blood-ties.*

*That's not what . . . I am her family.*

*Indeed.*

*She doesn't belong with you. She doesn't want you.*

*I want to make her happy. She deserves it, doesn't she? And our child. You're right. You're her family, in that place. She's deeply attached to you, and that's the problem.*

*I don't . . . I don't need to hear this. I'm leaving.*

*Listen to me. I've offered to take her away. I can't promise a life of roses and romance, but I'll do what's right. I've found us a place to live, a place she'll love. She says she can't leave because of you. Do you understand now?*

*I don't know what you're talking about.*

*You're standing in the way of her happiness! And the happiness of our child. I can provide for my baby in a way she'll never be able to on her own, or in a circus. A circus, for God's sake! I can't bear to think of my own child having to endure that fleapit. It was a mistake ever going there.*

*What about your wife?*

*She'll feel a great deal of shame, but she's tough, she'll get over it. Never mind that now. Do you understand me? Are you listening to what I'm saying? You're the obstacle. If it wasn't for you, I'd be halfway across the world by now, and your friend would be happy, cared for, and getting ready to live a good, clean life, instead of living like a gipsy. You're the only one who can help her. Do you see?*

No.

*Tell her you want her to leave. That she's not to worry because you'll be perfectly fine without her. You need to let her go. You're a big girl now.*

*Serendipity Wilson will need me more than ever. In any case, this is all lies, a plot, because you know she's finished with your little games, and she wants to go back to a life without you. Like it was before. Just her and me. The two of us. Like it should be.*

I can pay.

*What?*

*Money, girl. I won't see you unrewarded. I know you haven't had much of a life, but that's no reason to hinder my child's, or your friend's happiness. I can give you money, enough for you to set up on your own, to go somewhere, be whoever, whatever you want.*

Please stop talking. You're confusing me.

*I want my child!*

We sat in silence for a while. I heard the distant rumble of traffic. There was a bird, I couldn't see it. I wondered if it was a blackbird.

*There are many lives within a life. You'll understand, one day. You're young. I've seen things that would make you sick, things that would haunt you forever. This is my last chance, can you get that through your stupid head? My chance to do something good, some-thing right. I can't miss it, I can't. I understand you don't want to lose your friend.*

*You have no idea about who I am, or what I know.*

*Look, even if she refuses to come away with me, there's no place in that girl's life for a baby. The circus isn't a decent home. I could give the child so much. We could have a real life, a great life. Can you see that, at least? That child is mine. I can provide everything, more than everything. What can she give it? The filthy life of a tramp, living in a tent? I mean, look at her! She's not normal. What good would it do for a child to grow up with such a strange, skinny, horse-faced thing for a mother? Think about it, please. You know I'm right. That baby could grow up with everything, I would give him everything.*

*Stop talking!*

*For goodness' sake, girl. Listen to what I'm saying.*

Carved and defined by the two golden clocks, the min-utes passed slowly, in audible thuds. Although I couldn't look at him, John Frazer was a burning presence at my side. I looked at the lawn; the grass was an implausible green, as if it had been painted. The thought occurred to me that I might be dreaming, and for a moment I felt light, almost free. John Frazer coughed. I flinched and pressed the finger-nails of one hand into the flesh of the other. It was not a dream. I was sat next to the man who'd touched Serendipity Wilson in her most private places, had licked and sucked and pushed into her with his pathetic worm. I moved position, readying myself for escape. Yet, a small part of me wanted to be near him, wanted to put my hand on his, just to know I could. Such a dreadful fascination. Still, it sliced into every half-formed thought.

*She doesn't want you. I know what she wants.*

*You're deluded. What about the baby?*

*I know nothing of it.*

*You're not as stupid as you like people to think, are you? I understand.*

*I never said I was stupid.*

*All right. Enough. I know when to stop. I can arrange things differently, if I must. I have one more thing to ask. Will you give her this, please?*

Old Man Frazer handed me an envelope. It was brown and sealed, with *Dearest* jotted on the front in large letters. Without thinking, I took it.

*You want me to give this to Annabel?* I said with a half-smile, waving the letter.

*Don't trifle with me, girl.*

He tried to pull the envelope back. I was too quick. I'd already folded it up and tucked it into the waistband of my skirt.

*I know who you mean. I'll give it to her, if you promise never to come back.*

*I can't do that. I'm not giving up. She can't keep me from my own flesh and blood. I'll fight if I must.*

*No. You need to leave us alone. Forever. She doesn't care for you. She laughs behind your back. I know all about your . . . thing. I know about the screaming. She tells me everything.*

*Not quite everything, it seems.*

I said nothing and left.

I walked as fast as I could towards the encampment, sweat dripping down my face and under my clothes. I threw my map, now a sodden pulpy mess, to the ground and kept to the path I'd come by. I was afraid to stop or turn to look at the road behind, in case he was coming after me. I pictured him, beating me to death with his big hands, prising the envelope from my poor, dead fists. As I reached the main road, looking up again at the university tower, I found the courage to stop and turn.

There was the street, its buildings and wide road. The students were gone. Two grubby men staggered some distance behind me, drinking from bottles. The daylight was starting to fade. John Frazer was nowhere to be seen.

I didn't deliver the letter. It served no purpose. She'd already told me she didn't love John Frazer. What good would a letter do? I kept it. I considered burning it but couldn't. It's strange, how objects can be loaded with significance. Nor did I feel the need to read the nasty thing. It wasn't addressed to me. The thought of opening it somehow seemed like the ultimate act of treachery. I slipped the folded envelope into the back of my notebook and put it in my glory-box, where it could sit, safely locked away.

I'm tired of this room, tired of recounting the details of my life. So, you see, John Frazer is the child's father. This could be information that might help you to help me?

Or am I grasping at straws? I won't copy out the letter, not yet. Tomorrow may bring a new wave of energy, and excitement (those fluttering wings) for the task ahead. For now, I need to rest. John Frazer's letter has succeeded in preventing sleep for me tonight.

I am thinking about you, my reader, my helper (my friend?). This room is worn with age, all but vacated. The smell of life (someone else's) sticks to the fittings and fixtures. This is what I've become. I wonder where you are now? Not at your moment of reading this, but right now, as I type. You're probably sleeping, resting from your busy working day full of bustle, noise and deadlines. Maybe you're not alone in your bed. It's highly likely your body rests beside another each night. You're attractive, and clever. I'm not trying to flatter you, it just strikes me how different our lives are, even down to our appearance. You are long and lithe; although I am tall and my muscles well shaped, my hips are full, and I'm a mess of curves. You're younger, with beautifully natural hair, while I'm a chemically induced redhead; like everything else about me, it's a lie.

And you? Do you always write the truth, publish with integrity? Are you moral, ethical, principled and righteous? What do these things mean? They're just words (words, words, words), not even my own. I copied them from the thesaurus (the only book, other than my notebooks, I own) which sits, spine unbroken, cover hard and shiny, on my desk. I bought the thesaurus for the specific purpose of writing down my memories. You see? I cannot even trust my own words. The thesaurus is a net I can fall into, in case of calamity. How different writing is from funambulism.

I've never used a safety net. I'm not afraid to fall. Writing scares me, though. Words disseminate. Yet, we are the holders of the pens, the masters of the words. We load them like a gun, and fire them into the world for people to read and to believe. Under the word *Honest* in my thesaurus it says: *adjective*: *moral, ethical, principled, righteous* etc. Tomorrow I'll buy the newspaper, I'll read your column and I'll spend more time wondering about your life. I suppose you're used to such things. You have many readers. They are faceless, shapeless things. I have only one. You've become very precious to me.

In a few hours the sun will rise on a new day and I'll sit again at my desk, continue my stories. Until then, I'll not sleep or write. I will sit on my window ledge and look out at Manhattan, letting the breeze of the night refresh my mind. I will listen to the city. I won't think of words, of memories, or of you. I will, for this small pocket of time, simply be.

# 9

# Assorted Scribbles from a Notebook

I haven't seen Serendipity Wilson since this morning. We met to go through the routine for tonight's show, but her mind was elsewhere. She vanished soon after. I do the work these days. I don't mind, I enjoy being the creator of beautiful worlds. The new routine will have the hordes falling over themselves to buy tickets, and Fausto *creaming* himself (as Stella would say). I've designed the act to be performed without electric lights. Serendipity Wilson's hair is enough.

The routine is based on the story of Titania before she married Oberon, before she was made to look foolish and fornicate with a donkey – because these are the lengths men will go to, to disarm a woman (this should always be remembered). At the pinnacle of the act when the moment is right, I will release the fireflies. No one will have seen such an effect. How beautiful I will be; the queen of the fairies, surrounded by her flitting servants of light. Of course, they won't be real fireflies. I've never actually seen any. But I can make some. I'll collect scraps from Serendipity Wilson's hairbrush, bind them into small balls and attach them to pieces of wire (ingenuity thou art my dearest gift!). From now on the act will be more than a show of extraordinary skill, it will be theatre, magic and spectacle. The hordes will weep for my Titania. Until the Joey clowns come on, throw buckets of muck around the place, fart and kick each other up the arse.

Life is a grotesque and cruel comedy. Why do I bother?

Fausto gave me extra wages this week, said I'm the star and if I continue like this, I'll be bigger than Marina was. I've performed in every show for the past six months, which means three different encampments, and sometimes two or three shows a day. Most of the time I've been alone on the wire, or the main attraction with Serendipity Wilson as my helper. The others are jealous and spiteful. I get more time to practise in the big top than anyone else and can demand to go in there whenever I wish. Fausto arranges it, he kicks whoever's in there out on their arses. Oh, they pretend not to care, but they do. Why else would they ignore me? The hordes love Serendipity Wilson, but it's more for her hair than anything else. Recently, I noticed how she shakes before each performance. The hordes want to gawp at her, as if she's an animal in a cage, or a freak-show exhibit, like those in Big Gen's book. And Serendipity Wilson doesn't mind a bit. It makes me sick, watching her submit to their stares. *It's good to stand back, Mouse. I'm not inviting them to look. Who cares? I'm not ashamed. Let them stare*, she says.

★

She tires easily these days, says she's *getting old*, that soon her hair will turn white and her bones will be nothing but dust, then her day in the ring really will be over. I suspect she looks forward to it. Yet, she is still young and, in truth, looks more wonderful than ever. Her hair has an extra sheen to it. She has a lightness of foot, as if she's made from feathers and unspun wool. Even so, she's looking quite plump and doesn't stop eating. She refuses to hide her condition. It's like she doesn't care who knows about her dirty secret. We never speak of it. I'm not involved in her new adventure. She's never once asked me to help, to be a part of things. Maybe it's better like that, now I'm helping Marina. She'd only worry if she knew. It's a blessing, really. When the time comes, I'll surprise her with Marina's new act, choreographed entirely by myself. Because she'd never want to hurt my feelings, she'll pretend to be delighted and tell me how clever I am. But I know it will irk her, to see how independent I've become. Then she'll be sorry, and never abandon me again.

Manu, Marina and I may yet become known as a great circus family. After we die, people will name stars after us. We will truly shine, the three of us, brighter than fireflies, brighter than Serendipity Wilson's hair. Three bright specks, way up high. One day I'll hang my wire from the stars. The people below will crick-crack their poor little necks to see the girl who walks between the stars. Then we'll see whose head shines brightest.

★

Tomorrow we start work with Marina. My hands shake as I write, it's hard to keep a grip on my pencil. I find it difficult to speak to Manu, to look him in the eye. It's worse with Marina. Still, I am their daughter. Serendipity Wilson always said that blood is of no concern, but I know better (maybe she's changed her mind now; she'll soon see, I suppose). If my veins were opened, my blood spilled, it would be Marina's blood I'd see. Yes, I'm the daughter of The Great Marina. Dare I hope she might love me, yet? Tomorrow we'll work on ballet and movement skills. There's no need to bother with water or swimming. We need to work on poise, on suppleness. We need to keep her sober.

I saw Marina in a film once. A thing shown in picture houses after the war, a ploy to cheer people up in the grey days of rationing. *Roll Up, Roll Up, Come to the Circus and Forget Your Dead Sons.* They called her the Circus Siren. Anyone who saw it would certainly believe Marina to be more fish than human. I've always supposed it myself. I used to have a dream. Or rather, I have the memory of something I believe to be a dream, like a distant echo. In it I see my own hands in front of me. They're tiny. There are snot smudges where my face presses, hard, against the glass of a water tank, behind which I see hair, and tail, and bubbles. The dream seems so real. That's the power of dreams, the power of films, of books, of words. They deceive us, make us believe their lies, until the lights come up, we close the book, we open our eyes, and once again, we're confined to our drudgery. When

I finally see Marina swimming in her tank, it won't be like the dream. It will be a disappointment, because most things are disappointing. Hollywood stars don't look so glamorous in real life. That's what people say who meet them: they're shorter, fatter, their skin is oily, or cracked with lines. It's all illusion. Audiences are willingly stupid; goggle-eyed and dumbfounded by the trick of a dark auditorium and the bright lights of a show. Everything is a lie. Marina is not a mermaid or a siren. She is a drunk. I will remember this. Everything is a lie.

Marina is a pig. I had to push her out of her vile pit again today. The way she lounges in bed, hidden behind that stinking curtain. She is a large pink sow, wallowing in her own filthy self-regard. I never realized how heavy she was until it was upon my shoulders to heave her out of bed, to push-start her into life. She kicked me this morning, hard in the stomach. Then fell back into her pit, laughing and snorting. I could smell it on her, even after a night snoring and spluttering next to Manu. She's a filthy, drunken pig.

We almost got her to the tank today. Manu and I managed to drag her halfway there, although she complained all the time: it was too hot, she was tired, didn't we realize how ill she was? All the same old shit. I just laugh now. Manu tried to stroke her and coo at her, while I held her up and pushed her along. He told her not to worry, if she couldn't face it we could try again tomorrow. Of course, she hates me, bites me and hits out almost constantly. That's fine by me. It shows her up for what she is. I'd think calling your daughter a *bitch* and an *ugly whore* a bit of a joke. *Like mother, like daughter,* I said, as she spat in my face.

Tonight, I told Manu if he continues to mollycoddle Marina, there's no point in carrying on. If he cannot be bothered to help, then neither can I. He's worse than Big Gen — that overbearing, blubbery freak. I will not continue to give up my time if Marina isn't prepared to work. Manu sneaks her beakers of gin. I'm not stupid. Why else would she suddenly put on her best stage smile, meek as a kitten, stroke my hair and call me *darling child*? I can smell it. Serendipity Wilson told me gin is called Mother's Ruin, because women — mothers — have gone out, got drunk, and *ruined themselves* on the stuff, leaving their children neglected and wretched. And because the drink has no odour, no one knows the mother's filthy secret. Serendipity Wilson says *it's a curse and these poor mothers need help.* In fact, Serendipity Wilson hates Marina. Anyway, it's not true. I can smell it on Marina, the stench leaks through every pore. Gin is no excuse for her bad behaviour. Marina is a pig. Drunk or sober. Not that I've seen her sober. I've given up trying to understand why she hates me.

Manu is sneaky and not to be trusted. I am going to write it down again, so I will never forget. Manu is not to be trusted.

★

I don't want to sleep in the caravan tonight. I cannot bear another minute in the company of Marina and Manu. They don't want me there. That's fine with me. I've had enough of their cooing and grunting. They're like rampant dogs with silly children's voices and pouting faces. I will go to the wigwam, even if Serendipity Wilson isn't there (all she does is eat and sleep, or chatter with Gen these days). I'd rather be alone in the wigwam than anywhere else. I only went to the caravan in the first place to teach Serendipity Wilson a lesson. But she never noticed or was too occupied to catch on. Manu and Marina are tiresome, they talk only of Marina: how great she is, how wonderful she's been. Then Marina weeps her gin-soaked tears and Manu caresses her and I'm the bystander, the wallflower. I don't exist, I'm more invisible than ever. So I will go to the only place I've ever belonged, back to the warmth of my bed at the wigwam. I will go home.

Success! We went to the tank today. Marina stopped in her tracks when she saw it, she had no idea we'd cleaned and filled it. Manu and I spent a week working on that filthy old tank, scrubbing off layers of slime and dirt. The water looked fresh and lovely. I was worried it might already be stagnant, but as we approached, it sparkled under the sun like liquid diamonds. I knew Marina was ready. When she moves, it's easy to forget what state she's in. She has a gift. Serendipity Wilson says the body has a memory. Even if the mind is completely gone.

After the inevitable teary outburst, Marina walked calmly over to the water tank. She touched the tips of her fingers against the cold glass, as if it were an old friend. She smiled, first at Manu, then at me, and I had to steady myself for fear my stupid heart might stop. Then she slipped out of her housecoat, revealing a plain blue swimsuit. She looked freshly made. She climbed the ladder to the top of the tank, and as easily as her nylon housecoat had slipped from her shoulders, she slid, soundlessly, into the water. There was no splash as she broke the surface and torpedoed down to the bottom in a perfect line of fizzing Marina. Little bubbles played around her body, covered her in a blanket of translucent pearls. I watched my mother shake herself free from the thousands of bubbles. They whirled around the tank before fizzing to the top, each one giving a short plop as it tore itself free from the surface of the water. The bubbles did not stop there, they continued to float upwards. Foaming, blistering the air as they rose into the sky, until their strange cavorting began to take shape. And there, hovering above the water tank, was an imprint of the woman they'd left behind. This watery replica Marina seemed to move now, seemed to bend and grope in the empty air. I raised my hand to salute her, but it was too late. She swam towards the sun, rainbows twisting around her like colourful ballgowns, covering the encampment in a play of multicoloured light and rain.

Even as I stood, dumbfounded by the miracle, I wanted to scream with delight, to dance and to sing, but Manu touched my hand and directed my attention back to the water tank. There was Marina in the flesh, suspended in the water, hair floating above and around her. *She looks like an angel*, I whispered. We stared, unable to take our eyes from this woman, this giver of life. So still was she, so doll-like, that we couldn't help but flinch a little when she eventually moved. Putting her hands flat on the glass in front of her, Marina smiled. Manu touched the outside of the tank where her hands rested on the inside. Then, still smiling, Marina turned to me. Following my father's lead, I lifted my hand to the tank and placed it on the cold surface. We stayed there, the three of us, connected, until Marina swam quickly away in another gaggle of bubbles, and my father and I watched her magnificent siren show.

# 10

# The Sea-Creature and the Paper Doll

Manhattan bustles outside my window. It's not quite evening. I'm dreamy and restless. There's a confusion between my waking-life and dreaming-life. I cannot always decipher the world of actuality from the world of imagination. If I try to sleep, I cannot. When I wake, it's from the shallowest sleep. But within these snatches of almost-sleep, I dream.

My room looks unreal today, like someone replaced it with a facsimile while I was dozing (was it you?). I daren't touch the walls, lest they topple over like pieces from a film set. I was so tired this afternoon. The sun made patches of light around the room, reminding me of warm afternoons in the colourful wigwam. I must've drifted off as I lay on the bed, legs and arms rigid and sticking out like a paper cut-out doll. Just a doll, waiting to be dressed in paper cut-out clothes by a giant child. And without my realizing it, the fingers of that giant child lifted me from the bed, and I was asleep.

I wake in a cool place. Although there's no sound, the air around me echoes, pulsates. As my eyes become accustomed to the strange light, I realize I'm underwater, encased in a glass holding tank. The water ebbs around the outside of the tank, creating luminescent waves and soft shadows. The glow from my pendant helps this gentle movement of light, and the shadows hover across my skin. I look down, now at my arms, now at my legs. I am naked. I wonder where my jumper could be, why I don't feel cold, only a soft and pleasant warmth.

Slowly, I become aware of sound. The mysterious echo I'd mistaken for silence is the sound of my own breathing. It has a metallic quality, and is somehow insubstantial, as if not coming from me at all. Yet I feel air entering and leaving my body, feel my lungs contract and push. My workings are all too apparent and I throb with every pump of blood.

It's hard to move. My limbs are heavy. There's a weight pressing down on me. I panic a little and tell myself to remain calm. Slowly, I push my feet down, hard against the glass wall of my surroundings, attempt a standing position. The glass is slightly sticky where I touch it. There are no flat surfaces. My tank is a sphere, a bubble. I manage to stand. Struggling at first, I put one foot in front of the other and place my hands on the glass in front of me. The tank begins to shift.

There's a tremendous noise from outside as I push forwards. The water seems to solidify around me, to trap me. I start rocking forwards then backwards, start to push my bubble through the angry sea. I stop. For no reason other than wanting to be still again. The silent echo returns and I'm back inside myself.

Something strikes my craft from behind. I'm startled, knocked off balance. I right myself, turn quickly, and see the large shadow of a figure with what looks like an enormous fishtail, swimming into the darkness. Another, louder strike now from the other side of my bubble. I snap around and see it.

The creature, somehow familiar but terrible, stares at me with the hooded eyes of my mother. Its nose, barely there at all, is two holes in the middle of its face. The lips are red and ghastly, like the flesh of an open fruit, like a version of Marina's smiling mouth on my old circus posters. Dark tendrils of hair sway around the creature's head, reminding me of a squid or octopus.

Its face is up against the glass now, and its hands, like my own only transparent and with a slight webbing between the fingers, are pressing against the wall of my bubble-tank. I'm so afraid I cannot move. The creature blinks. I'm sure it feels my fear, wants to tease me, hurt me. It will crack open my bubble as easy as an egg, pour me into the sea. I'll drown, be spat out onto some distant shore, nothing but a mass of gelatinous muck.

When it opens its mouth, it's an unimaginable horror. Three rows of yellow, razor-like teeth gnash at me. Suddenly the water around the creature explodes into a thousand angry bubbles, and my monster screams an unearthly siren scream.

I turn quickly, try to move as before: one foot in front of the other, pushing my hands on the glass, rocking, trying to move away from the creature. But it swims around and appears in front of me again, still screaming. My every cell is filled with its noise. I'm in a state of complete terror. For some reason, at that moment of ultimate fear, and without warning, I become aware of my nakedness. I begin to shiver. My body is weak. I fall, limp and trembling, to the bottom of my bubble. The screaming continues.

Helpless now, I let the creature rock me. The rocking is violent and cruel. I try to find some solace in it, hum a lullaby, let my body fall and bruise as I'm rolled through the sea at speed. Something hot spills between my thighs, it runs down my legs, and although I'm mortified by my own body, there's something strangely comforting in it. I know I've lost control, that I'm about to be murdered by the sea and her monsters.

The rocking finally stops. I flick open my eyes.

I'm lying on the bed in my room in Manhattan, as rigid as a paper doll. I've been sweating under my jumper; my skin is sticky and itchy. I roll onto my side and realize I've wet myself. I lie still for a moment, unable to think or move. Then press my face into the velvet pillow, and cry.

# 11

# Tales Told by Serendipity Wilson #2
## The Lost Wife of Ballaleece

*A man might find it difficult to understand why a woman might prefer liberty to the constraints of living under his roof, and therefore, as he might see it, under his rule. Especially when he's prepared to give her (what he considers to be) everything. Perhaps he simply can't believe that autonomy is the greatest gift. So, if she should tell him their union is over, thank him for his time, but explain that now she must be away, he might say that she's away all right, away with the fairies. Or maybe he'd prefer to live as a widower, rather than be seen to give her the agency she so desires. In times past, women have had to be cunning in order to have what they need, what they want.*

*There was once a farmer in Ballaleece. A well-known bachelor. As a young man, he was known to countless women. For many years he kept himself free, preferring the taste of ale and whisky in the evenings to that of a woman. But as time went on and his hair began to grey, the farmer started to feel the need to leave his bachelor years behind. So it was he found a beautiful young woman, who was soon to become his beautiful young wife.*

*Everyone around Ballaleece saw the devotion the farmer had for his new wife, and she for him. They were the moon and the stars, the*

sun and the earth to each other. Even when the crops went to rot in
the fields and the cows went without a milking, no one complained to
the farmer whose bedroom curtains were nearly always drawn at this
time, and who was often seen without his shirt collar.

One fine morning the farmer's young wife went up into the top
meadow. She told her husband she wanted to cut some meadow
flowers to adorn the table for his breakfast, which she had prepared
and left warming on the stove. A half hour passed but she did not
return. The farmer began to be agitated. He felt angry that his wife
would leave for such a long time, when he hadn't yet had his breakfast. As punishment he decided to take his eggs, lamb chops, and
warm buttermilk from the stove and go ahead and eat them without
the lady's presence. Next time she would think twice before going off
to frolic in the meadow when she should be home seeing to her duties.

Having finished his meal, the farmer sat for a while, but his young
wife did not return. He smoked a pipe, made coffee from the last few
grounds in the pot, adding cardamom and brandy to the mix, but still
his young wife did not appear at the door. Again, he sat and waited,
thinking up punishments he could inflict upon his disrespectful wife
on her eventual return. But she did not return, and the next morning
the farmer ran outside, frantic with worry.

He gathered a search party to sweep the meadows, top and bottom.
He checked the wells, the rivers and ditches, in case there had been an
accident. Neither he, nor any of the search party, found any trace
of the farmer's beautiful young wife. Many said the poor thing had
died, that she had fallen into a river with a heavy flow and been
dragged to the sea. Or maybe she'd tripped and gone down a very
deep well (one too deep to search), her lovely broken body never to be

recovered. Many others, including the farmer himself, believed it was the work of the little people. So jealous, they must've been, of the farmer in his marital bliss, that they took her away against her will, and forced her to stay with them somewhere in the fairy world.

Ballaleece grieved for the young wife. The farmer searched for her all the way to the Calf of Man, but no one had seen his lovely bride. After some time, the farmer became weary of looking and decided to accept his fate, treat himself as a widower and mourn the loss of such a lovely prize.

Not long after, the farmer married again. This time the wife was not so young, and certainly not beautiful, but her family had money and she was as healthy as a heifer, and a fine cook. What more could the farmer want from a union? But soon after the marriage, after failing to excite either himself or his hearty new wife enough for the newly-weds to share a bed, the farmer's beautiful first bride came to visit him in a dream.

Husband, oh husband, she said. The little people took me. You can free me, if only you do exactly as I say.

I'll do anything you say, said the farmer.

On Friday, at midnight, she said, the little people will ride with me through the Ballaleece cowshed. We'll enter by the north door and gallop straight out through the south door. I'll be on a horse, riding with one of the fellas in front. All you have to do is sweep the place clean, make sure there's not even a single straw left on the cowshed floor. When you have done this, then you can catch hold of my horse's bridle as we ride through, hold it tight, and this will free me.

When Friday evening came, the farmer went to the cowshed.

*He swept the floor so clean, not even one bit of dust was left in the air, or on the ground. Then he sat alone in the darkness and waited.*

*At midnight, as his lovely lady had said, the doors flew open. There was music, like the playing of pipes, and in came a throng of little people wearing smart jackets, riding on sleek horses. On the final horse, exactly as she had described, naked, and sitting astride the mare and behind a little fella, was his beautiful first wife. She was as pretty as the flowers in the meadow, with an odour as sweet. Without further thinking on the matter, the farmer grabbed hold of her bridle. He was thrown side to side like a boat on a wild sea. So violent was the movement that he could not hold her, and he fell back onto the cowshed floor. As she galloped through the south door, the lovely girl pointed to a clay pot in the corner of the cowshed, calling out in her melodious voice:*

*Husband, oh husband. You were not thorough enough. A straw has been placed under that clay pot. This is why you were thrown from my horse and could not hold on to the bridle, now I will be gone from you forever!*

*The farmer sat in misery, when suddenly he heard a noise behind him. Hoping that maybe the beautiful young girl had been wrong, that the little people had been moved to mercy by her pleas, he stood quickly, ready for any action he might need to take. But standing at the cowshed door, dressed in her calico nightgown, was his second wife, smiling and pointing to the clay pot.*

*Husband, she said, I put the straw under the clay pot. You've been talking in your sleep lately and your voice is stupid and loud. What did you think you would do with me, if your dream was indeed a fairy visitation and your true love was restored to your bed? Perhaps you thought I would stay to serve you both? Or maybe I would be the next to disappear, for I know how handy you are with an axe and a spade. No, husband. You will honour our union, and if in your sleep you speak of ridding yourself of me, I will not pay your debts and you'll have more to worry about than fairy stories then.*

*The farmer told his tale to the people around Ballaleece. Some people felt sorry for the farmer. Many of them said they knew all along that the beautiful young wife had not died or gone away of her own accord, but that she was taken from them by some fairy spell. At least, said the people, you have married into money now, with such a fine strong woman. And as things are, the cows will never go without a milking again. And they never did.*

*Do not be defined by a lover, or by anyone else for that matter. You are not an appendage, an add-on to the masculine world. And so, you must have your independence — not only of thought and spirit, but physical and financial. Independence will be your strength. Find it. Hold on to it. It is freedom, Mouse, and it will serve you well.*

# 12

# A Storm. And the Queen of Light

Serendipity Wilson waddles across the circus encampment. This is a big field. She's quite a long way from the caravans and tents. The wind eddies around her, blows her dress tight against her round belly. She struggles on, hands hovering around her head, grasping at the heavy yellow turban whose weight threatens to topple her backwards like an oversized cartoon bowling pin.

A small crowd of adoring fans watch from the edge of the encampment. They hold fast, breath drawn, awaiting their heroine's approach. They're willing to risk being blown to pieces for their efforts to be rewarded.

The wind begins to worry the turban, pulling at frayed ends until the loosened fabric relents, unravelling spectacularly. Serendipity Wilson grapples with yards of billowing cloth but fails to keep any part of the precious headdress in place. She gives up, performs a laboured curtsy of faux-defeat for the crowd as, with a theatrical flourish, she pulls the final wrappings clear. The long yellow sheet undulates behind the still advancing Serendipity Wilson, now gloriously illuminated under her halo of shining, orange hair. Waves of orange light are cast into the darkness of the day, and a communal squeal of delight is emitted from the handful of onlookers. It could be a scene from a romantic painting; *Madonna in the Wind* or *The Queen of Light Approaching Her Minions*.

I sigh and watch from the wigwam.

The faint sound of giddy laughter blows towards me. I've seen enough, there's work to be done. I turn away, fumble with ropes and pegs, trying to keep our home and its contents from flying off. The colourful fabric of the wigwam balloons and flaps in the wind, wrapping itself around me, slapping my legs and arms and face. I look over again. Serendipity Wilson is trying to move away from the road and to step over the muddy ditch dividing the encampment from the street. The hordes, too afraid to cross that sacred barrier, continue to grab at her, to pull her to them. She is dodging faceless hands. They've come here to stroke her hair, pat her belly. Even between shows, even when she's no longer part of an act, she's a star turn. The wind turns their cries of joy into a ghoulish wail. I sigh again. They'd pull her to bits if they could.

Serendipity Wilson steps across the ditch. She places both hands on the small of her back and rocks slightly on her heels. She looks tired. Those leeches would never notice. I secure the wigwam as best I can (it pulls at the pegs and rattles on its central pole) and start to make my way over to her. I'm stopped in my tracks as Stella and that other girl

(they all look the same) run across the encampment, cour-
ageously battling to get to their new friend. Ever since the
baby became common knowledge, those girls have not
left off cooing and fussing over Serendipity Wilson. You'd
think she was suddenly a different person, the way they go
on. They're the ones who wave the crowd off, who put their
arms around her, guide her over to the wigwam.

I look for somewhere to hide, but it's too late. Stella gestures to me like a mistress to her maidservant. Devoured by
anger, I nonetheless comply; opening the flap of the newly
secured wigwam; allowing the three of them to push past
me. Serendipity Wilson gives me a look as she enters. I don't
understand her the way I used to, can't tell if the look is one
of compassion, or pity. I swallow hard, try to think what
Serendipity Wilson would do if the sock were on the other
foot. I decide to stand my ground. Be present, strong, let
my voice be heard. I cough. The other two do not register
my existence.

The wigwam jolts and thrusts, and there's a noise like
thunder as the wind continues to assault the fabric.

*She shouldn't be living in a tent in her condition, the situation's*
*barbaric,* Stella says to no one in particular.

Serendipity Wilson assures the girl she is fine, that she
wants to be here, that this is a wigwam not a tent, and it's
her home. The presence of these two harlots is horrible. They
don't belong here. Now they're putting themselves all over
everything; contaminating; defiling. Serendipity Wilson
is smiling at them. My hands are moist, my arms feel lank,

boneless. The girls are settling down now, purring like cats as their painted claws tug at cushions and blankets. Afraid I might cry, I leave. No one notices.

The wind has not abated. The circus encampment looks desolate. It's unlikely there will be a show tonight. The animals are moaning but there's no sign of Manu. I make my way over to their enclosure, walk past cages of sleeping leopards unworried by the weather. The tiger paces and rattles his cage, yells at the wind and swipes at the bars of his cell. I ignore him, there's nothing I can do to comfort him. The horses are skittish, frightened by the clattering wind. Everything scares horses. They're stupid animals, slaves to their human masters. I unbolt the horse box, take a handful of apples from the bag by the door and approach them with outstretched hands, the way Manu showed me. They let me get close, pat their flanks, feed each one an apple and speak to them in a low, soft voice. I don't stay long, though. I can hear the llamas bleating their poor hearts out. They're out in the elements, straw blowing angrily around them. Llamas are not allowed the comfort of shelter.

I go to Solomon. Putting my arms around his neck and burying my face in his side, I tell him everything is going to be all right, that he's a good boy, a special friend. I feed the other llamas fresh hay, brush their woolly backs, get them to lie on the ground, to relax and let the wind sweep over them. Then I return to my Solomon. We sit on the ground together, he rests his head in my lap and I stroke it. His long-lashed eyes blink up at me, his nose twitches as he sniffs at my pocket, instantly locating the apple I saved especially for him. Solomon knows I wouldn't come empty-handed. His tongue tickles my hand and I laugh, hold out the apple and kiss his head.

*I'm not a bad person*, I say.

I take the snip of luminous orange hair from its knitted pouch around my neck – like a secret pendant. The orange glow lights up my face, but its promise of heat is a lie and I shiver. I try to fight the urge to cry, but the sadness is too big.

*I didn't mean to hurt her. I never would. I just want things to go back to the way they were. Before she started going off, before the stupid baby started growing in her stupid belly.*

Watery snot and tears pool onto llama wool, I rub it away. Solomon stirs before closing his eyes again.

*I shouldn't have persuaded her onto the wire. I knew she wouldn't balance well with that belly. I only wanted to see . . . if I said I needed her to . . . if she would. I only asked her to go on the low wire. I didn't want to hurt her.*

Solomon sighs. He is asleep. I shift onto my side, snuggle into him. His smell is musky; the smell of childhood, of comfort, and love.

*The wind was already up. I told her it was the perfect time to practise, what with no one around to bother us. She looked pathetic, tottering along the wire with that big belly. I don't know what came over me. I was angry and sad at the same time and didn't know what I was doing. I only shook the wire a little bit. The wind could have done worse. It was the tiniest tremor, honestly it was. I wish I could go back in time, I'd stop myself from doing it, from even thinking of doing it. Anyway, she wasn't hurt, was she? The baby wasn't hurt. She banged her arse and twisted her ankle, that's all. She said herself, she should've known better, a woman in her condition. It wasn't my fault. She should've known better.*

A noise close by shocks me into silence. It sounds like laughter or singing. I sit up, call out into the wind. Someone is giggling, they seem to stumble or trip. Standing, I see Marina, Medusa-like, hair blowing free and wild. My mother is naked but for her open nylon housecoat, which swirls around her like a diaphanous red flag. She sees me, shouts something, but it's not a language I understand.

*Marina. Go home. You're drunk*, I call.

She stands in the wind, like a savage thing. The moon is full and bright behind her. How has she managed to choreograph this scene so perfectly; standing there, ghost-like, her stillness utterly at odds with the violence of the storm? I call out again, worried now she may have heard my confession. She does not move. She stares past me. Perhaps she does not see me. But my mother is sneaky, I know not to trust her. Solomon grunts in his sleep, shakes his head and flicks his ears. I look down to check on him and when I turn back, Marina is gone.

More noise now. A commotion across the encampment. People are assembling around the wigwam. Beams of white light criss-cross through the dark. Big Gen shouts at the gathering mob from the door of her trailer. I cannot hear what she says. There's a throbbing in my throat and I am dizzy with fear, and still the words *should've known better* echo through my mind. Gen wraps herself in a blanket and hurries out. Bare-footing it, she trots across the encampment, piggy-like, leaving the door of her trailer to clank manically as it blows open and shut, open and shut. Finally, she pushes through a huddle of girls and disappears into the wigwam.

My ears sting with cold. I want to lie down with the llamas, go to sleep. But there's screaming now, deep, terrible screaming, and I know it to be Serendipity Wilson. I put my hands over my ears, but the screaming continues, as if inside my head. I want to disappear, go away and never come back. Not knowing what to do, I make my way out of the enclosure.

Some strange light ripples across my face, across the moonlit landscape. Turning towards the source I find the tarpaulin cover gone from Marina's water tank. It must have blown off. I'm not strong enough to lift it back by myself so resolve to leave it until morning. Manu can fix it.

Securing the gates with numb fingers and trembling hands, it's only now I realize that the night, although full of tumultuous wind, is clear and bright. The moon is as sharp as a candle. There are no mists, no fogs in which the heavily pregnant descendant of an ancient Celtic sea god could hide, in fear of losing her unborn child. No, I can see all the way across the encampment. I take in great gulps of air, feel light-headed with relief. Serendipity Wilson is safe. I am saved.

I lean against the gates of the llama pen, think about the rabbit in Serendipity Wilson's belly. I've already seen her. Sometimes I look at the sky and there she is, smiling with her big white head. I've heard her too, many times. She calls out to me when I'm asleep in the wigwam. It's a funny voice, muted because she's still inside. We have such fun, nattering like old friends, like sisters even. Being older, I know when enough is enough, and eventually tell her to simmer down and rest. There'll be plenty of time for chatting and playing, I say. But she ignores me and doesn't shut up. There are times I'm afraid she'll wake Serendipity Wilson with her din. I've told her to stay where she is, if she's going to be bad and not attend me when I know best. I cannot promise to protect her once she's out. But as Serendipity Wilson's belly gets bigger, the bunny's voice gets louder. *Don't say I didn't warn you*, I say.

Still not sure where I'm heading, I turn to go. Something blows across my path, brushes my leg like a whisper. I grab it and find I'm holding Marina's housecoat. I decide to go to the caravan, fetch Manu, tell him to come and get her before she catches pneumonia. My mother's housecoat is rough to the touch, crumpled, worn and thoroughly inert in my hand. As I'm thinking how strange this is, how I'd always imagined it to be smooth and soft, the wind stops.

Everything is still. Silent.

I look up. An explosion of cheering voices breaks the peace. And another sound, a shrill, newborn cry. She is here, screaming at me from across the encampment. It is a harsh, piercing sound, like sharpened metal. My limbs feel soft, my body weak with exhaustion, so I fall. First to my knees, then flat, face down on the ground. I have never felt so heavy, so close to the ground, or so far away from my wire. The damp grass is cool, but there's no solace in it, only a gnawing, aching cold that seeps into me.

The wind starts up again.

I turn onto my back, run my mother's housecoat through my hands, feel it catch on my skin, and with nowhere to go, I close my eyes and hope for sleep.

I wake up shivering. The top of Marina's housecoat is twisted like a child's comfort blanket around my right hand; the rest of it covers my torso, a flimsy protection against the morning air. The encampment is deathly quiet. The remnants of last night's storm linger, but the wind, although cold, blows gently and without anger. I blink into the light, try to get my bearings: I am flat on the ground. My back hurts, as does my head. There's a deep sense of sadness in me, but I'm unable to focus on why.

I pull myself into a sitting position. The encampment looks peaceful. The dwellings behind me, at rest. The big top is a shadowy giant, happy as it sleeps. Nothing stirs. I think I hear the many bodies sleeping behind trailer doors and tent flaps. They breathe deeply and in unison, like a midnight choir unable to wake. I envy them.

My legs are stiff from the cold and damp. What a stupid thing it was to fall asleep outside, unprotected. It's true what they say: the light of day makes the evening's stresses and strains seem trivial. I stretch, Marina's housecoat still wrapped around my fist. It flutters into my face as I yawn. The scratchy texture against my lips all too quickly reminds me of the previous night's chaos, and my sadness returns.

I want to stave off the day, make time slow down so I can walk, alone, around the encampment, without thinking about the future, at least for a few hours.

*Just a few hours*, I whisper, as I inhale the synthetic odour of man-made fabric mixed with sickly sweet scent and night dirt.

The caravan is only yards away. I walk slowly, steadily over to it, scared that any sudden movement might wake the whole encampment. I open the door, step inside, hang Marina's housecoat on the hook by the window and look over to my parents' bed. The curtain is open. Manu is lying diagonally across the mattress; he is fully clothed and alone. My first urge is to wake him, to ask where Marina is, maybe she was up early to see the new baby. No, Marina doesn't care for babies. The thought that my mother would get out of her trough to visit a newborn child is ludicrous, to the point where I cover my mouth to stop myself snorting.

I depart without a word, leaving Manu to his dreams.

Standing by the caravan, still unsure what to do with myself, my attention is caught by the sound of bleating from the animal enclosure. The llamas are awake. I take a step forwards, and freeze. Memory grabs me. Images flash through my mind: a shadow play of ripples through moonlight; Marina stock still, almost naked; the wind; the red housecoat. I remember the wind whipping at my skin, making my eyes water, my flesh raw. How beautiful the moonlight was, bouncing off the uncovered water tank. I am pinned to the spot now, momentarily unable to move. I look over to the animal enclosure, and although I cannot see it, over to where the water tank stands, uncovered. Realization hits. And at last, I take off, running and screaming into the morning.

Marina stands on the bottom of her tank, naked. She stares through the water, hair swaying like pond-weed. As serene as an angel. I am screaming and crying. Shouting for help. Banging on the glass. She must have been there for hours, all night. While I slept on the damp earth, clutching her nylon housecoat. Her skin is translucent, opalescent. Maybe it's a trick of the light, but watery colours seem to pulse from her body and sparkle around the tank. I scream so hard, until there's no more sound, only an open, screaming mouth and a rasping silence.

Resting my hands and face against the glass, I close my eyes and feel a movement from inside the tank. Startled, I push myself away from the glass and watch as my dead mother points her toes, lifts her feet from the bottom of the tank, and blinks at me. She may even be smiling. A single bubble spirals up from her left nostril. There's blood coming from somewhere. It rises in a thin cloud, blossoms, then vanishes back into the water.

Marina floats up, and rests face down on the surface of

the water. Finding my voice, I call out again. My screams full of atrocity. This time Gen appears, trotting around the corner in high-heeled mules and a cloud of black chiffon. Falling, missing rungs, I scramble up the ladder to the top of the tank. I thrust my arms into the ice-cold water, and with every bit of strength I can muster, I drag my mother's body free of the tank. Big Gen is shouting, but I do not know what she is saying. It is a frantic yelling of disconnected words. I struggle down the ladder, the weight of Marina's naked body leaning against me, until we flop to the ground. Gen falls silent. Her fingers are stuffed into her mouth.

Marina lies in the dirt. I kneel over her. Her eyes are open and staring. I am frozen to the spot, and violently shaking. Someone throws an old blanket over the corpse's head and shoulders. All that's left of Marina is her nakedness. And the thick tails of dark, wet hair, poking out from under her improvised shroud. Big Gen taps my shoulder. I turn, but see nothing. The world is black.

# 13

# Unwanted Gifts: A Siren Song

Here is a letter.

This envelope, with its contents still resting within, left as if to sleep these many years, was my mother's gift to me. A legacy of sorts. Once pink, now yellowed with time, it is ragged and dirty. I have carried it with me every day since it was handed to me by my father. It is the only tangible thing my mother ever gave me, and even then, she was dead by the time I received it.

I have read it only once.

The letter has been calling to me over the years, begging me to once again spill its secrets. Until now, I have refused. I'm not so deranged to think it has a will of its own. It's a thing devoid of life; an object, an artefact. Still, I wonder if somewhere within the structure of this paper hides the spirit of my mother. Perhaps she is captured in the ink, locked into each letter. I wonder if her spirit suffers, if she wants to be released? Are the words her prison (as they are mine)? Maybe this is why I've kept it: to keep her spirit close. I will release her, soon.

The envelope is thick with folded pages. On the front, written in violet ink and in fine hand, is the word *Daughter*. I shall not read the letter before I copy it out for you, before I tap each of my mother's words onto my clean, white paper.

I picture my mother's pen now, looping each letter together. I imagine her hand, moving as my own does when I trace the beautifully formed letters with my finger; a synchronicity which seems to bring her into the room. I can smell her. The sweet odour reaches into my nostrils, like the tendrils of smoke from my cigarette.

Copying this letter for you might, in some way, help to show you that my life has been nothing but the broken shards of a mirror. I have tried to patch things together, but in the process my fingers have been cut to shreds and there are so many missing pieces. I must do this now. I fear if I do not begin this very instant, courage will fail me and the letter will be left forever sheathed in its envelope. My cigarette is out. It is time.

*Daughter,*

*I don't insult you by calling you* Dear *or* Darling Child, *or anything we know you aren't. I call you* Daughter, *not from affection, but because it's fact. You were born from my womb, from my screaming wound. You're my daughter.*

*Don't think this a romantic gesture, a calling to the heart. My heart was hardened long before your unfortunate birth. I'm not trying to ease my guilt. I've none. The world is full of murderous evil. It's the reason behind your neglect. I'm not sorry I never loved you, never wanted you. It was beyond my control. However, it's only right you know your true identity. It doesn't matter to me if you believe what I say or not. You're at liberty to carry on the fantasies of a childish mind. There's only one truth: humanity is a disgrace. We are worse than any monster imaginable, the little good to be found outweighed by mountains of badness.*

*This is my story.*

*My name was Marta. I grew up with my sister Agnieszka, our mother Róża and our father Jerzy. My parents were educated people, teachers. Although we weren't rich, we weren't poor.*

*Our house was filled with books, with conversations about art, literature, philosophy and sport. Mother and Father grew vegetables in our garden. Our food tasted of goodness and earth. Like you, I was a fiercely intelligent child.*

*My parents came from wealthy families. They met studying languages at university. Mother and Father had a passion for language, for words. By the time I was six years old I understood some French, English and German, even if I wasn't able to speak it. You'll want to know where we had our house and garden, what language was our own. We were Polish.*

*Agnieszka and I didn't know our grandparents. My parents' families didn't approve of the match and both sides refused to acknowledge their marriage, or their children. This wasn't a problem for us. We were happy.*

*I was a strong girl and soon proved to be a good swimmer. Whether in the lakes where we spent our summers, or later in*

the pool, I'd cut through water like a blade. Mother said
I should've been born with a soft fishtail instead of bony legs,
and a shield strapped to my back. She called me her Syrenka,
because you were born to swim and to fight, *she said.*

When I was fourteen my father took me to Krakow, the
nearest city to our town. I became part of a swimming club.
I'd stay the whole weekend in Krakow in my swimming
teacher's apartment above his baker's shop. We trained hard
and won competitions, to which we travelled huddled together
in the back of a baker's van, the smell of freshly baked dough
in our noses and fine flour dusting our skin and clothes.
We'd arrive at competitions white as ghosts.

They called us The Angels.

After winning many races, myself and two other girls from
Krakow qualified to swim at the Olympic Games in Berlin.
Father travelled with me to the Games, leaving my sister
(who'd fallen in love) and my mother to spend the summer
tuning the wireless. I'd never been so far away from home.

The train journey to Berlin was as exciting as the events
or all the pomp and ceremony of the Games themselves.
We three girls were like small children again; running after
each other through train carriages, sticking our heads out of
windows to fill our lungs with the thick black smoke of the
engine, laughing when ash got in our eyes and wiping our
dirt-streaked faces with spit-covered fingers, only to recoil
in false horror at the thought of such indecent acts.

It was August. Berlin was hot. The adventure seemed
unreal. I almost won the bronze medal, missed it by a finger.

*On my return home, I was greeted with great affection by everyone we knew in the town. Even people we didn't know came up to shake my hand, or smiled at me in the street. Coming back from the fishmonger one day with my sister, an old man rushed up to me. He clasped my face between his bone-white hands, declared to the whole street that I was* the true angel of the town, *and after kissing me on both cheeks he rushed away, leaving myself and my sister standing in the middle of the street with our brown paper parcels of dripping wet fish.*

*There was a party in my honour. I wore a white dress. Our neighbours made delicious food, put out tables and little flags in front of their houses. I wandered around, telling the story of my great adventure. I was shy, and a bit embarrassed because I hadn't actually won the medal.* But everyone knows how close you came, *the neighbours said,* it was just luck that other girl got there first.

*The excitement soon died down. Life went back to normal. At least for me. Not for my sister. She got married.*

*My sister's new husband was a barber. He owned his own shop. He was a good man with smiling eyes and a gift for laughter. Within the year Agnieszka was pregnant. The little one came early. We were filled with joy. She was small, beautiful like my sister. And like her father, had the gift of giving happiness.*

*And then the war.*

*I won't tell you what you already know. Poland was invaded. Bombs fell. People died. Fear and chaos were everywhere.*

*My parents' fear was solid. Like another person, an uninvited stranger in our house. It walked with us, ate from our dinner plates and tied itself around our hearts. Our house became a dark place, the curtains always drawn. No neighbours came to call. No visitors. Until the day the soldiers came. Then we hid under chairs and tables listening for muffled voices. They did not knock. Papers were pushed under the door, then the soldiers left as they came; in silence, other than the sound of their boots.*

*The next day my parents called us together. We sat in the back room, around the table with the white cloth. The baby gurgled, everyone else sat quietly as Father spoke. I don't remember his words, simply the sense of what he said.*

*Mother was a Jew.*

*Father held Mother's hand as he told us. I saw tears in his eyes. This great big man had tears in his eyes, and Mother kept repeating the same word:* sorry. *Once again life felt unreal, like I was on the outside looking in. I pinched myself in order to feel my own existence and went to kneel beside my mother:* sorry. *I put my arms around her:* sorry. *I rested my head on her stomach as I'd done as a child, felt the rise and fall of her breathing, her warmth:* sorry. *She stroked my hair with shaking hands, tucked loose strands behind my ears and brushed my cheeks with the soft, white pads of her fingers:* sorry. *I looked up at her beautiful face, my mother's beautiful face, and placed my own hand softly over her mouth, so she couldn't say that word again.*

*My parents lost their jobs. My family were outlaws. Our friends disappeared. A neighbour who'd made cakes for my return from Berlin, the one whose twin boys died when still children because one caught a spark from the open fire on his shirt-tail, and as he went up in flames his brother jumped on him, rolled him on the floor, but was himself engulfed in the blaze. They'd burned to death on their own hearth, and this woman, their mother, our neighbour, watched it happen. This same neighbour, who'd smiled and kissed my forehead when we took her long beans and potatoes from our garden, the one who'd poured us glasses of cold milk for our kindness and asked us how we were getting on with our lessons. This woman, this receiver of long beans and kind thoughts, the one who'd baked the cakes, she spat at me in the street. My mother told me not to cry, not to let it upset me.* Be strong, Syrenka, *she said.* She is afraid.

*The first thing that struck us when we arrived in the ghetto was the stink. No amount of soap, soaking, scrubbing myself raw, dousing myself in the sweetest perfumes, has ever rid me of it. There were many new things. Hunger. Lice. Mother made us promise not to scratch because wounds could become infected and maggots were known to feed off the bad bits. I was afraid of maggots. And death. I saw the body of a boy lying on a street corner, just lying there in the daylight, alone. People walked around it. Some glanced but didn't linger. It was a child. Curled up as if asleep. I stopped beside him, wondered about his family. I wanted to touch him, brush his cheek with my hand, tell him he was safe now.* You can

only die once, *I whispered. Mother pulled me away.*
*The next time I passed by, his clothes were gone.*

*Bodies were piled up beside the heavily guarded fence.*
*There was no land for graves. When the stench got too much*
*and the good people from the town complained, the soldiers*
*came with trucks and took the dead away. Then the trucks*
*came again. This time they came for the living.*

*We were driven to a railway siding. Soldiers herded us out,*
*but there was no time to take in the air or relieve ourselves.*
*One man tried. The soldiers shouted at him. He ignored*
*them. They shot him.*

*Again, we were hauled into trucks; railway trucks meant*
*for cattle, not people. They still held the stench of the farm.*
*It was enough to make you sick. Some were. There were no*
*windows, no smell of the roaring engine, no ash in our eyes*
*or smudged on our faces.*

*Treblinka was cold.*

*Father and my sister's husband were taken away. Let me*
*tell you, Daughter, although you think yourself badly abused*
*by life, you have no idea what cruelty really is.*

*We were sent to work in a forest behind the camp. We*
*chopped large logs into smaller logs. I was still strong. My*
*sister suffered the most. The little one was unwell. My poor*
*darling Agnieszka, who couldn't live with her husband or*
*watch their child grow and play happily in a garden filled with*
*flowers, as she'd dreamed on her wedding day, became weak*
*in body and spirit. She couldn't understand why her child*
*was forced to live in such misery. Because a man decreed it?*

*No, it wasn't just one man. It was the people. They shouted
their approval, cheered and roared it. It was the people who
spat at us in the streets, starved us, let us wallow in our own
shit and vomit and then let us be killed. The people killed us.
For what? Hate? Give it any name you please, hang
whatever flag you like to the flagpole, people will do the same
again, when decreed by the person they choose to decree it.
Humanity is a lie, Daughter, you are a fool if you trust it.
I hope by showing you no love you've come to understand this.
It'll serve you well. Maybe I wasn't such a bad mother after
all. But I didn't do it out of goodness. I did it out of hate.*

*The inevitable happened. We buried my niece in the forest,
alongside the other dead babies.*

*Then, I was taken.*

*There were maybe a hundred of us taken that day. We
were silent as we walked away from the others, away from my
screaming mother, my stunned sister. It was almost peaceful
among our crowd of chosen ones. There was nothing to be done.*

*We were taken to a building inside which we entered a long
white corridor, with benches on either side. We were told to sit
on the benches, to wait. Those who had shoes were told to
remove them. Then we queued up. My hair was cut off and
thrown onto a pile. We shuffled on. Eventually I walked
through a door at the end of the long white room.*

*You're wondering, Daughter, how it is that I've lived
all these years, when I'd been condemned to the ovens?
Remember, life has no meaning. Anything can happen at
any time.*

*Once through the door, I took all my clothes off as ordered.
It wasn't cold, in fact, a pleasant warmth echoed around the
walls. I felt calm. When all the women had come through
and we were all naked, the discarded clothes were removed,
and the door closed. Some people were speaking softly,
praying perhaps, but most were silent. We waited. After
a time, I heard only my own breathing, the beating of my
heart. My body was deafening. I told myself to concentrate
on those sounds, my last ever sounds of me. I waited,
listened, and closed my eyes because there was nothing
more to see.*

*Soon enough, there was a terrible banging. I braced myself,
felt the body of every woman in the room tense. But then,
silence. Nothing. I opened my eyes. Now I was afraid.
I began to shake.*

*A woman standing behind me saw my distress. She took
my hand. There wasn't much light, but I could see her. She
was old. Her breasts lay flat and shrivelled against her body,
her belly protruded but was loose, floppy. Her hand was thin
and cold.*

*At last, the door opened. White light flooded the chamber.
Nobody moved. We, with our chalky bones and naked flesh.
We lived our forevers in that second of light because the
certainty of existence was in it. For the briefest of moments we
bathed in clarity and essence. Can you understand? We were
joined together by this fierce white light, therefore we existed.
Even as I lived that moment I knew it would soon be finished,
like everything else. And so it was. A scream. It was gone.*

*The guards began shouting. Though my German wasn't bad, fear prevented my understanding. They barked. They shouted. They pushed us around with batons and guns. Gradually we understood. Strangers threw themselves, naked, into each other's arms. There was laughter, excited chatter. I couldn't share their grotesque euphoria. This wasn't how it was supposed to be. What about the guns? I'd seen a man shot for wanting to relieve himself. I'd been ready for the gas chamber, I wasn't ready for a bullet.*

*But they let us live.*

*You see how anything can happen? One man decides not to check some pipes, to play cards with his friends instead, write home to his sweetheart, lie in his bunk and dream of sausages, and through this simple decision, I live. Which means you live. The contingent perversity of life means you owe your existence to the laziness of a Nazi guard.*

*We were ordered back through the doors, back into the corridor with the benches. The pile of cut hair was gone, but there was a heap of rags on the floor. It was impossible to find our own clothes. We had to cover ourselves, quickly, with whatever soiled clothing came to hand. It was no relief to be clothed in someone else's filth. But we were alive.*

*How are you enjoying my story, Daughter? It's not a very nice story to be told to you by your dead mother. You're disappointed. You thought me a mermaid. You want so much to believe in the myth, so you'll ask again; if this is true, how was I washed up on a beach in England at the end of the war? The magic of the Syrenka? Yes, hold on to that last bastion of*

the great mythology. *I survived the gas chamber, after all. Ah,
but forgive me, there was no magic in it, just broken motors.*

*Don't believe in fate, child. That's the idiot's way. It
wasn't fate that killed my family, it was contingency; people
chose it to happen. It was through choice that I was sent to
the gas chamber. The guards chose me, I didn't resist. The
accident was that I was sent back. But no, even that was
down to choice and error. Manu says I'm special because
I was given back the gift of life, but that's not true. That it
was me was pure fluke.*

*There was a young man, an interpreter, allowed into the
women's section to translate orders. In fact, there were several.
My mother, sister and I didn't let our captors know we
understood German. We thought it safer. This particular
young man became my friend. He was a prisoner, Polish, a
Jew, but his family was German, and he spoke as fluently as
any guard. He had blue eyes and the face of a cherub, like a
religious painting on a stained-glass window. He liked sport.
He liked me. He'd followed the Olympics, called me the*
angel of the water, *spoke softly to me, said soothing things.*
The good people of our country won't let us suffer
for nothing, *he said.* I'll see you swim in clear waters
one day, when all this is over. *I told him it would never
be over, that he was blind to think there'd ever be an end
to it. We'd die there, even him, with his perfect face and
German voice.*

*The young man often laughed at me. He smiled a lot.
Too much. Then, he found my sister's husband, brought*

*us messages, comfort, maybe even hope. Father wasn't to be found.*

The war will end soon, we'll be free again. We're closer than you think, *said the young man. I told him we were already free, no matter where we were. I could lie on the concrete floor of our block-house, I said, and never move again, let myself slowly die, be rid of this place once and for all if I wished. I didn't have to go to the forest with the others, I said. I could easily get myself shot, I could make that choice. Freedom is choice, I said. We are all responsible for our own actions, we have that power. He didn't understand. He put two fingers under my chin and lifted my face up to his. I stood in ruins, death and stink everywhere, looking into the blue eyes of a cherub-in-tatters, thoughts of first love completely abandoned, obliterated by the absurdity of it all.* I promise you freedom, *said the cherub, and I wanted to laugh in his dirty face.* There are things you don't know about this war, *he said,* hidden things. *He thought me stupid, I told him he was the stupid one, that his smiling mouth wasn't going to cure the disease of life.* No, but it will change the world, *he said. And although I gave him the smile he desired, I walked away, back to the coughing and the vomit and the shit, with a sneer distorting my pathetic, grinning mouth.*

*As time went on the young man told me he was a fighter.* A revolutionary, *he said. He told me about a Polish resistance.* An underground army. *That they were* small in number, but effective through solidarity. *They hid in forests, helped Jews. It was* a network, *he said, an* international network. *His passionate speeches cheered me, not because of their content, but because it'd been a long time since I'd seen such animated conversation. It brought back some sense of normality. But I thought him naive and foolish.*

*Mother was taken.*

*We chopped wood. The chimneys puked out their smoke. We waited. Mother didn't come back.*

*The young man started spending time with my sister. I was jealous. They'd decided to save me. My sister wouldn't be saved, wouldn't leave without her husband, needed to stay close to the buried bones of her child. But I must, they said, at least try to be saved. The young man knew how to do it. We'd escape.*

*I refused.*

*You think it strange, perhaps, that I'd refuse? It wasn't through courage, through loyalty or love for my sister; my heart was already turning to rock. No. I thought it ridiculous. I'd survived the gas chamber, I didn't want to be shot in a stupid escape plot. No. I wouldn't let them do what the Nazis couldn't. But here I am, writing this letter, and you are in the world reading my words. I suppose something akin to hope got to me in the end. If human existence is a project, I thought, if the past and present are nothing, then there's only the future. I couldn't bring my mother back, but I could control what came next. Staying in the camp wasn't a real choice, because I hadn't chosen to be there in the first place. But if I was shot attempting to escape, that would ultimately be my decision. The person behind the gun would only be reacting to my* actions. I would be the trigger to my own death. On the other hand, if it worked, if I escaped, then the future was a crisp, white, blank page. Whether I escaped or was killed trying didn't really matter. What mattered was not letting my future be determined for me.

Oh, but let me be honest now that I'm dead.

For all my existential high-mindedness, even if it meant leaving my sister to die in that place, I wanted to live. Eventually, I agreed.

The young man stole an SS uniform, used engine oil from an old tank to grease down his hair, and marched into the forest where we were chopping logs. I didn't expect it. The day of our escape hadn't been set. My shock was genuine. I wasn't prepared. He grabbed my arm, told the guards he needed to take me away, that I was to be punished for something.

I was winded, couldn't get my breath as he marched me through the forest, away from the others, away from the camp, holding on tightly to my arm, pushing me forwards. He didn't look at me, not once. I kept falling and tripping but he wouldn't stop. He marched me all the way through the forest behind Treblinka. He shouted to some guards who were smoking and lazing around on the edges of the forest. They stood up, shouted back, questioned him. But the young man had a stern, cold voice. He said I'd get what I deserved, and the guards relaxed, went back to their smoking; one of them laughed. They let us pass without looking at our faces.

It was impossible to think we'd survive this ridiculous display. The young man didn't react. He marched on, still

*holding on to my arm, still pushing forwards, until we were
away from trees and walking along a dirt road. After some
time I looked back; the forest, the camp, was out of sight. But
we didn't stop. Images of my sister in her wedding gown, of
my father's hands as he held a book to read aloud before our
evening meal, of my mother's face, of barber's shops and
gardens, of lakes and swimming pools, parcels of dripping wet
fish and photographs of dead boys now flashed quickly through
my mind. I was blinded by my past now, a past that didn't
exist, which was already dead, but it prevented me from seeing
the road ahead. I believed at any second my life would be
extinguished, that death was only moments away.*

*We skirted the edges of a town, passed through its boundaries
and out again. Into countryside, away from roads and into
another forest. Still the young man didn't stop, didn't speak.
I was tired and felt sick with nerves and then, at last, without
word or warning we stopped in the middle of the forest.*

*It was quiet.*

*The only sound was the wind in the trees and bird song.
The smell of the place was unbelievably real, sharp and vital.
I fell to all fours but couldn't sob. Tears wouldn't fall. I sank
my fingers into the earth, it smelled fresh and good. I began
to shovel handfuls of earth, grass and moss into my mouth.
The young man jumped on me, held my hands down.
It's all right, he said, but it wasn't all right. Then he
held me to him, as if that's what I needed, to be held to
the body of a young man. It's all right, he said. It wasn't
all right.*

*The young man pulled us both to the ground, he pushed his hands up my legs, moved them over my buttocks and under, between my filthy, lousy legs. He plunged his fingers inside me, pushing them in as far as they'd go, pulling them out and pushing them in again. I let out a short, surprised gasp. It's all right, he said. It wasn't all right.*

*He pulled at his stolen uniform, grappled with buttons and fastenings. He pushed my legs as wide open as he could, put his hands, all his weight onto my hips, and wriggled until I felt his hardness inside me. There was a sharp white pain. I didn't make a noise. He was heavy. I didn't move. I looked up at branches, at trees, at leaves in all their different colours, at patches of white sky. The smell of engine oil from the young man's hair, mixed with the fresh mossy odours of the forest, made me gag. Then I felt the thick roots of a tree under me, hard and solid against my back, and more clearly than anything I'd ever seen or would ever see again, I imagined their black knotty mass. At last, I screamed. I understood that existence was real, this moment was real. And the horror of it shook my body into resisting. I tried to pull away, to scream again. The young man covered my mouth with his hand as his body tensed. He was strong, wanted to finish his business. He began to thrust harder into me, to hold me tighter. I couldn't move.*

*And then, something inexplicable happened.*

*There was a mighty crack as something split. Something at once deep inside yet all around me, like the breaking of a shell. My body, my famished corpse, crab-like, with its hunger and*

bones, with its dead eyes and grey fish-flesh, cracked open.
A hard layer, a carapace of thick flesh, peeled away, and like
the giant decapods I'd seen at the lakes as a child, I slithered
out, pink and raw. I shed my skin on the forest floor. As the
breeze rustled the leaves and the birds sang. As the young man
went ahead, regardless. My tired skin melted into the earth,
into the moss, into all the rot that had ever been and down to
the centre of everything. There was nothing beautiful left, no
shiny new shell or bright silver-scaled skin hiding under the
old, just slime and maggots, eating away at my badness.
It's all right, *he said.*

*When he finished we sat in silence. It grew dark. We didn't
sleep. The next morning we continued through the forest. After
some time, the young man stopped, told me to get down, to keep
still. Then we saw them. Two boys, dressed in poor farmers'
clothes, carrying guns. The young man whistled. The boys
whistled back. These were the resistance the young man had
spoken of. Two fresh-faced farmers' boys not old enough to
shave were to be our saviours. I wanted to laugh out loud.*

*They took us to a grotto by a stream. There were others
there. They said they'd get me papers, help me, get me to
a safe place. I said thank you. The young man went away.
I never saw him again.*

*My helpers (there were many, I was passed from person
to person like an old shoe) helped. It's not important to say
how. We made our way through various countries and across
borders. Eventually I reached the French coast, where I was
left to continue my journey alone.*

*Cap Gris Nez was swarming with soldiers. But it was my chosen route and where I wanted to be. Before the war I'd followed the brave swimmers, who swam from England to France across the English Channel. As a girl I'd dreamed of being among them. But not like this.*

*Batteries and concrete huts filled with guns and bombs were everywhere. Although tired, I was well fed and strong again, my muscles tight with energy from walking long distances through fields, forests and mountains. I waited for a night filled with rain, that it might somehow cover me. When eventually it came, I was ready.*

*The rain soaked into me as I crawled, crept and ran over wet rock. I heard shouting, laughter, shots, explosions in the near distance. I took off my shoes, felt for landmines with my toes, took off all my clothes and moved towards the sea. The water engulfed me, surrounded and swallowed me. The cold and strength of the water as it pulled me into its ebbs and tides, rocked me with the violence of a murderer. But I soon took control, started to swim and fight, like the Syrenka.*

*My mother came to me in the white water. Her hair was made of seaweed, but her face was that of my Róża. She sang as she swam with me. Sometimes it was a hard fight, to keep on swimming. There were moments I thought I'd have to let myself drown, let the sea take me. But my seaweed mother took my hand. She swam before me, to guide the way. She swam under me, to hold me up. Her legs were nothing but a thick fishtail, all muscle and strength. I held on to her. We curved our bodies as one, entangled hair and limbs as we rolled through the water. I could breathe easily with her by my side, the water was as air to me, and I wasn't tired with Róża as my companion. We laughed together as we swam, played games with the fishes and crabs. Sea-snakes tried to wind themselves around my wrists and ankles, tried to drag me under and tie me to the sandy depths. But my mother wouldn't let them. She flung them away, dashed their brains against rocks and stones. Every watery monster cowered when they saw her, they dared not kill me, not under my Róża's protection. There were times I thought myself alone, but even then I could hear my mother's sweet voice, urging me forwards. I swam until all was blackness and awoke freezing on the sand.*

*I don't remember being found. I remember Gen, all soft and kind with her skin smelling of stewed apples.*

*The sea had given me new life, birthed me onto her shore, allowed me to live as someone newborn. But things are never that simple, are they?*

*It was Gen who first mentioned it, what she called my condition. She'd seen it many times, she said, knew immediately what it was. My belly, my sickness. I was carrying something inside me and it was eating away at any bits of goodness left.*

*We tried to flush it out. Used gin and hot water. But you clung to me. Gen said maybe it was a gift. I couldn't bear the thought of this thing, the young man's gift growing inside me, like a worm, a maggot. I told Gen about the forest and the shedding of my skin. She said she'd sort it out.*

*The worm refused to be destroyed.*

*Yes, you killed any hope of my salvation. You were not conceived as a child should be; you were thrust into me, a constant reminder of the price I had to pay for being saved. So, now you know. Obviously, this means you're older than you've always thought. I shouldn't think that matters. As for Manu, you didn't really believe kind, generous Manu could be your father? He will love you now, if you let him. You're all he has. I give him to you, as a gift.*

*Lastly, Daughter, I ask you not to keep this letter. What right have I to ask you anything? I ask only to save you, or anyone else, the pain of seeing these words again. Once words are on paper the events they describe are given forever to history. Don't let them be. The past is dead. These words are already dead.*

*Take the letter, read it and burn it. Don't pore over it night after night, looking for some sign of love, some crack in the veneer of my story which might let you in; you won't find it.*

*I don't apologize for your life. I couldn't prevent it and I couldn't love you. Despite what you may think, I'm not purposefully cruel. Let's not torture ourselves any longer than we need. Forget everything you've read here if you must, and believe that I was the Syrenka, born of men's desires and fantasies. Burn this letter, and throw the ashes into the sea, that we might all, eventually, rest in peace.*

*Marina. Marta. Mother.*

★

I will now go downstairs to the communal kitchen. I will take a heavy-bottomed copper pan from the top shelf of the large dresser and bring it back up to my room. I will hold each page, in turn, over the pan, and set it alight with my silver-cased lighter. When I am done, I will take the pan over to my window, open the window as wide as it will go, and throw the ashes out. Let the city breeze take them, let them float around this glorious metropolis until they melt into the concrete and dust of Manhattan, and are gone forever.

It is done.

# 14

# An Apparition. And Other Monsters

I went out today. It wasn't planned. I found a clean sweat-shirt in my suitcase under the bed, pulled on some jeans (I've lost weight, they are slack around my middle where once I'd struggle to join metal button to frayed hole) and made my way out of the building.

You might think this perfectly ordinary, but I don't go out much these days. I don't have an appetite for strolling, or for any kind of interaction with the city and her inhabit-ants. Obviously, I must gather the essentials for living, but I can usually rely on the old lady downstairs for that. She'd do anything for a peep around my door. She likes having me here, it gives her something to talk about. It's amazing what you can learn about yourself through an open win-dow. People are so easily pleased with their own chatter, especially on the Lower East Side.

The morning was bright when I left the building. Every-thing sang of early summer and reminded me of my first days in New York, how I believed anything could happen (and of course, it did). These days, even on bright mornings, the city seems dull, muted and washed out. This morning was different, though. The spectrum had shifted back into full colour, and sound was once again restored to glorious stereo.

As I stepped out onto the warm asphalt of Delancey Street, my thoughts inevitably turned to my wire. I don't miss the hordes or the adulation, nor do I yearn for the thrill of performing. I miss the feel of it; cold metal contrasting with warm flesh, hard and tight under my feet; the sound of my own breathing, louder than anything else around me. I never stop longing for the quiet and calm of that upper world. That's what I miss: the separateness. Being on the wire feels like you've passed through, into a different realm. It's a place of quiet, but never of silence. The air touches you in a different way, like feathers stroking your skin. After a while, you don't notice the sweat, even though you smell it more acutely than when you're on the ground. Neither do you feel the tickle in your gut when your weight shifts and your foot slips into the void, before landing safely back on the wire. No, that's not true; you feel it. It's thrilling.

Walking made me hungry. My taste buds tingled with every mouthful of air that touched my tongue, so I made my way to Ratner's. It was busy, which was no surprise, but there was a single empty seat at a table by the window. I took my place, lit a cigarette, and ordered potato pancakes, hot onion rolls, and coffee. The waitress was small and skinny. She made pleasantries, but I couldn't focus. I stared out the window while she chattered on, and smiled when she took her leave.

As the food arrived, the smell was so keen it almost

knocked me off my chair. My stomach growled, I lurched forwards, then I paused. It's good to hold off, to feel the hunger for as long as possible. When at long last I ate, I ate quickly. As expected, it was delicious.

Then, I noticed her.

She was sitting at a table on the far side of the room, almost directly opposite mine. Her back was against the wall, her eyes fixed and staring. It's been some years since our last encounter. I froze.

The room was all movement, all sound and clatter. Yet everything – the people, the walls, the tables and cutlery – started to blur and fade out of focus. I thought myself a construct then, something not quite real. Around me was nothing but a watercolour wash. And through the blurring, surrounded by diluted sound and colour, sat Serendipity Wilson, clear, honed, smiling.

My stomach growled again. This time I felt sick. There was a song playing in the background. I couldn't be sure where it was coming from. A radio? Did it drift in from the street, through the open window? Maybe there was no music, and it was a song of the mind? In any case, it was an old song. I'd been fond of it, once. It had been the inspiration for my last Coney Island routine, a lifetime ago. I couldn't help but think of my costume: a cluster of stars, covering my breasts and groin, making my body shimmer, while the singer told his tale of a Starman. Whether real or imagined, the same song was playing again as I sat in Ratner's. Now it was the soundtrack to her stare.

The hair was gone, of course. They took it. It was far too precious a resource to be lost. They did a good job, shaved the head good and proper; sheared it so her pate shone, not in any magic sense, but with a clean, squeaky shine. It was no surprise to see her looking like this. I've seen her many times since my arrival in New York. In the early days she was an almost constant companion. That was years ago. Her stare was hard now, cold. Maybe she was an imagined apparition, the result of being locked up with my memories for so long without a break. Even so, she was there.

Her mouth moved, silently.

*Hello, Mouse*, it said.

I began to sweat. My hands were shaking. The risk of embarrassment was high, and as you may have gathered, I cannot bear public shame. I pushed my chair away from the table, fumbled manically, toppled the chair to the tiled floor as I searched my pockets for change. The coins fell to the floor, making a sound like metal hitting glass, or breaking windows. The music stopped. Every head turned to look in my direction. I must've looked quite the madwoman — *a complete nutjob*, mouthed lips from across the busy restaurant.

I'm not sure how I made my way back here. I remember that I tripped as I ran, that cold sweat dripped down my back, but I didn't notice the passing landscape or traffic. The front door of the building must've been open because I didn't stop. I rushed in. There was someone on the stairs. They said something, maybe even yelled as I pushed past. Finally, I was forced to a halt at the locked door of my room.

I fumbled for the keys, thrust them into the lock, and slammed the door, bolting and chaining it behind me. Only then did I rest my cheek against the cool wood of the door frame and begin to calm down.

So, here I am. Back in my yellow jumper and tartan pyjama pants, sitting at my desk. The blind is closed. I closed it without looking out the window, in case she's out there, on the street, looking up. It's dark, save the orange glow that shines from my pendant. We get the seraph we deserve, I suppose.

Now you know: the lost child is without its mother. A ghost can't search. I'm the only one able to do it. I'm starting to believe this laying down of words is not only a plea for help to find a missing person, it might also be my act of contrition. Which begs the question: are you my deliverer?

# 15

# Tales Told by Serendipity Wilson #3
## The Sad and Tragic Story of Nora Cain

*A foundling can never know their own story. Sometimes we over-hear things, then we dream, create our own mythologies. This is a tale I keep close, to remind myself that I too was born into the world through love, pain and blood.*

*Nora Cain was a pretty child. She lived with her grandmother, mother and aunt by the craggy shores of Port Soderick. Nora was a happy little girl. Each time she went to Douglas, shopping for meat with her mother and aunt, the people of that town would remark on her gay face and sweet smile.*

*She was good and kind at heart. Many a winter's evening saw Nora Cain crouched by the turf fire in the kitchen of their cottage overlooking the bay, unwinding wool for her grandmother, who would be spinning at her wheel. Nora listened as the wheel clicked and the yarn scraped rhythmically through the rotating grooves. Most of all, she listened to her grandmother's tales. Nora's favourite story, the one she asked for most, was about the lost enchanted island of their ancestors. And by the time she was grown, Nora knew the story of the Great Fin MacCooil so well, she could recite it in her sleep.*

*Fin MacCooil was over fifty foot tall, a powerful magician, and no friend to the people of the beautiful isle off the coast of Port Soderick. Claiming some ancient insult as his motive, Fin MacCooil had cast a spell over the island, sending it and its inhabitants to the bottom of the sea. Those lucky few who swam to the surface, thinking themselves saved, were immediately transformed into pillars of granite. Even today, if you walk along the sands of Soderick bay, you can see them standing proud among the waves.*

*The spell was strong, but as with all magic, there was a crack, a weakness that even Fin MacCooil could not overcome. Every seven years, the submerged island would come to the surface for thirty minutes. During this time, it was said, the enchantment might be broken. If someone were to place a Bible on the island, during the thirty minutes when it was wholly and fully visible out of the water, then the isle would be saved from its sad enchantment, and all the inhabitants would come back to life to live out their days in happy serenity. However, if this person failed, there was said to be a terrible curse. For anyone trying to break a giant's spell must be punished. The curse, like most bad magic, was widely thought to be nothing a good God-loving soul should fear. In fact, no one had claimed to see the island in many years, and those who had, had been far from any place where a Bible might be to hand, and rather closer to flagons of ale and wine, so they hadn't bothered.*

*Nora grew to be a strong and beautiful young woman. When she was barely sixteen years old she fell in love with a fisherman's boy. Although mighty handsome, with thick curls and olive skin, the boy was a dreamer. He could not be trusted to go out on the boat with his father. For whenever he did, his eyes filled with the beauty of the sea* and his mind would wander into a world of dreams, leaving nets to be lost, bellies to go hungry, and pockets to be empty.

Nora Cain's mother thought the boy silly and reckless. How could he take care of her only daughter, especially once the mother was in her grave? The match would see Nora breaking her back to put food on the table and, judging by the boy's charming face and finely sculpted hips, with many a bairn to feed. Lovely Nora would end up old before her time, and then where would she be? No other man would pay any mind to a sagging old hag, abandoned by her good-for-nothing handsome husband, and her dripping with nippers. But Nora Cain burned for the boy, and in turn he loved her back, with all his body and all his soul.

They met in secret, in the caves and rocks by the shore. Here, they learned the beauty of skin touching skin. One fine moonlit night at the end of September, Nora and her lover were playing their usual sweet games in a cave along the bay when, quite by accident, she spotted something in the distance. She told the boy to stop. She pointed, and as they looked out through the dusk, they saw a block of land, slowly rising from the sea. The land appeared bit by bit, increasing in size as it went, revealing trees so green, and mountains so pretty, that the two could do nothing at first but hold their breath and stare.

Realizing at last what she was seeing, Nora sprang into action. Untangling herself from the boy, she raced away, pulling down her skirts as she ran. Her lover shouted after her not to believe in old women's superstitions. Nora could only think of her grandmother's voice, and hastened home with all the speed she could muster.

The Bible! The Bible! cried Nora Cain as she burst in through the side door.

*It's where it always is, child, came the astonished reply.*

*And so, wrenching the old book from its place behind the larder door, Nora made off as quickly as she had come, running all the way, leaving her grandmother shouting behind her.*

*What shall we do for a doorstop now, young lady? And where to goodness are your shoes?*

*Nora was already beyond earshot, jumping over hillocks in stockinged feet, breathlessly shouting out to her lover and tripping over pebbles in her haste to reach the edge of the sea. But already, she could see it was too late.*

*Nora Cain and the fisherman's beautiful son stood hand in hand on the shore. Together they watched as the last visible part of the island subsided once more to its watery destiny. The lovers stood as still as statues for a long time, looking out, saying nothing. Until finally, Nora tossed the tattered old Bible into the sea. Remembering their Sunday-school lessons, a sudden dread clutched their hearts.*

*What have we done? said Nora.*

*What have you done? replied the fisherman's beautiful son.*

*We've been brazen and shameful with our bodies, she moaned.*

*You tricked me into it.*

*You said you loved me.*

*We're bound to be punished. How could I have been so foolish?*

*And with that, the boy slipped his hand from Nora's, told her to fix herself, and took one step away.*

*We must never meet again, he said. That way we might make amends for our terrible acts, we might seek forgiveness. Eventually, we will each marry a good person from a good family, and our shame shall be forgotten.*

*Nora Cain felt her heart break, but she could do nothing but agree. They parted, and as she slowly made her way back along the sands and up to her house, the girl was filled with great misery. Before she even reached her own front door, a terrible sickness struck her.*

*Weeks and months went by, but Nora would not eat nor rise from her bed. She had a fever, and with it came such nightmares that her body shook, and she cried out.*

*The sickness soon filled out her stomach. Her slim, young girl's figure was lost. Bloated of belly and gaunt of face, Nora shuffled from her bed to the window, looking more like her wizened old grandmother than the lovely young girl she had been.*

*On a quiet, still night when everyone slept soundly in their beds, Nora summoned up all her strength, and slipped silently out of the house. Once down by the shore, she stepped into the water. Feeling the waves lap around her ankles, she began to cry, and between her tears she begged old Fin MacCooil to end her misery.*

*As if in answer to a prayer, the sea rose up, formed itself into a giant hand and took Nora into its watery grasp. Her poor broken body was thrown onto the rocks, and as her blood mixed with the sea, some say they thought they heard the sobs of Fin MacCooil himself, echoing around the island as they slept warm and safe in their beds.*

*It happened that, unbeknownst to Nora, the fisherman's beautiful son was wont to wander down to the sea late at night. He pined for Nora, regretted bitterly the way he had discarded her. Each night as he patrolled the shoreline, he'd imagine how he might find her there and they would run away together, leaving Port Soderick forever.*

*On the night Nora Cain gave herself up to the sea, the beautiful boy was watching from a rocky ridge. He called her name, but she did not seem to hear. He began to run as fast as he could to the shore, just as the sea grabbed his dearest love and flung her to her death. Unable to contain his grief, the boy swam to the rock where Nora's body had landed. He lay down next to her amid the foaming water, now pink with blood, and closed his eyes to the world forever.*

*The lovers were found the next day. And beside them, alive as you and I, lying upon the rocks between the two bodies, was a tiny new-born baby, washed clean by the sea.*

*The islanders took the child away, believing it to have been left by the fairies to ease the sadness of the grieving families. As a thank you to the little people for such thoughtfulness, they buried Nora and the fisherman's beautiful son together, not in a churchyard, but deep inside one of the fairy caves by the bay. There, their souls could stay forever cleaved as one, looking out towards the sea and the magical place, where it is said that, every seven years, if you happen to be there at the right time, you might see the enchanted island rise from the water. And if you are bold enough, and pious enough, you might even be the one to break the ancient spell.*

# 16

# A Mute Man's Voice, Fever,
# and Stella Gets Her Man

Serendipity Wilson was not performing. She spent her evenings in the wigwam, with Bunny. Sometimes someone would pay her a visit, hoping to have a moment to coddle the baby, but Serendipity Wilson wouldn't let them in. Even Big Gen was refused admittance. When, finally, she barked at Gen, accusing her of trying to undermine her, saying that Gen had told the whole encampment she was incapable of looking after her own child, I had to intervene. I was in the big top, awaiting my turn in the ring, but there was such a commotion that I had to run back to the wigwam. Apart from the big cats, all the animals were out of their cages, and boards had been put on the ground, to guide them into the back of the big top. Manu watched, holding on to Solomon's reins, as I ran over the boards and past the enclosure, still in full costume, over to the source of the noise. After much shouting, finger-pointing and back-biting, Gen eventually agreed to leave the wigwam. Serendipity Wilson fell to the floor then, as heavy as a bag of stones, and wailed. Bunny was busy playing with balls of wool, and didn't seem to notice her mother's distress, or the loud disturbance that had ensued. I sat by my friend, put my hand on her burning brow, and whispered in a low voice. She did not want my comfort.

*Leave me alone, Mouse,* she bawled. *You belong with your father. Why don't you go and live in the caravan once and for all, leave me and Bunny in peace?*

At the mention of her name, Bunny seemed to catch the thread of her mother's unhappiness and joined in with her own chorus of yowling. I ran to her, scooped her up and kissed her head. She immediately stopped her noise and started playing with my face. Feeling and prodding and giggling.

*Oh, Mouse,* said Serendipity Wilson, her voice quieter now, her eyes glassy with tears. *I didn't mean it. I'm horrible. Look at me, not fit to walk outdoors. I haven't washed for days, and everything's a mess. But look, Bunny's fine, isn't she? She's clean and happy . . . and . . . clean. I'm a good mother.*

*Of course you are. Why would you think otherwise?*

*I dare not think about it, Mouse. I'm not right.*

*You're just tired. I can help.*

*If only you could. It's not that simple. Sometimes it's all too much . . . and I think I . . . I think I hate her. Oh, Mouse! How can that be? How can a mother feel such things? It's wrong. I'm wrong. Inside. I worry people might see it. They'll think I hate my little girl, but I don't! I don't! It's not that sort of hate. I'm not even sure what to call it, it's different. It's because I love her so much! Do you see? I need to keep her close to me, make sure she never knows*

*I have those terrible thoughts. She must only feel how loved she is. I have to protect her. You mustn't tell anyone, do you hear? Not ever. I'm not like Marina! I'm not! I'm a good mother!*

*You're so hot. You might be proper poorly. Shall I ask for a doctor?*

*No, you mustn't do that, Mouse. You mustn't. The ancestors wouldn't like it.*

Serendipity Wilson lay on her side, sobbing, mewling. I crept out of the wigwam, found someone quickly and gave the message that my friend had a fever, so I couldn't do my act as I needed to sit with Bunny.

When I returned, Bunny was on her mother's bed, as before, balls of wool unfurled and scattered around her. She was quiet and still, but staring wide-eyed at Serendipity Wilson, who was convulsed with silent sobs, and writhing on the floor. I took my blanket from my own bed and laid it over her. She didn't seem to notice. Then I climbed into Serendipity Wilson's bed, still dressed in my costume, and with Bunny by my side, we snuggled up. Soon the baby was snuffling, gently snoring, her warm body nestled into my own. I kissed her soft head and slept. In the morning I left early. Mother and child still soundly asleep. One on the floor, one in her mother's bed. Once again there was peace in the wigwam.

The encampment was still and quiet as I left. I dressed myself in clean clothes, out in the open air, regretting a night spent sweating under the blanket in my tulle and satin. I could smell my own skin, sour and milky, as I scurried over to the caravan, and to the task of ensuring Manu ate some breakfast before his busy day with the animals.

Sometime after Marina's death, Manu stopped speaking. He wasn't an instant mute. It was more like a gradual eroding of his will to communicate. For a while, we'd walk around arm in arm, and when he saw someone he wished to speak to, Manu would bend down, whisper what he wanted to say in my ear, and I'd say it for him. Manu needed looking after, and I'd become quite domesticated in my role as his daughter. I cooked for him, cleaned the caravan, washed his clothes and turned his sheets. His initial attempts to curb his grief through hard work and doing his duty by the animals seemed relatively successful, but without Marina he was a lost soul. After a year, Manu's whispered words were few, his skin had grown pale, his gaze vacant. When the words came, they were French, sparse, and slow. And then the silence.

It was the day Manu spoke his last words (the last words I ever heard him speak) that I scampered across the encampment, having left Bunny and Serendipity Wilson snoring in the wigwam. Unusually, I let my father sleep late into the morning. I saw to the animals myself, and when Manu finally came out from behind the curtain, full of sleep and scratching his head, I was all set to start cooking omelettes. But Manu was waving a thick, pink envelope at me, and smiling, as if teasing a child with the promise of butterscotch.

Manu sat down at the table, lit a cigarette, and gestured for me to sit opposite. He slid the letter across the polished tabletop with his middle finger and nodded. I picked the envelope up. On the front, written in violet ink with lovely handwriting, was one word: *Daughter.* Searching his eyes for a clue as to what to do next, I stared at Manu. He half-smiled. Then, he watched as I read my mother's letter.

I felt his stare, heard the pull of his cigarettes in short intervals as I read. When I finished, I put the pages back in their envelope, tucked it into the band of my skirt and, without looking up or saying anything, left the caravan. I went straight to the wigwam, where my two bunkmates were still soundly asleep, placed the letter in my glory-box, and locked it away. Then, I went back to the caravan and without giving any indication that anything unusual had happened, got to the task of cooking omelettes.

Manu stood behind me as I stirred the eggs, put his mouth close to my ear, took a breath and stopped. I listened, waited, expected to hear a word, but nothing came. I thought maybe I'd missed it, but the flow of air from his lips was slow and steady on my neck. I stopped stirring the eggs, took them off the hot-plate and readied myself by standing as still as I could. Staring at the yellowy phlegm cooling in the pan, I tried to concentrate my mind on hearing a whispered word, or even the trace of a breath in the shape of a word. Manu was close, his breath warm on my skin, but instead of speaking, he placed his hands gently on my hips. I did not move. I continued to watch the eggs. They shivered at the touch of air from a crack in the small window above. Manu began to move his hands over the soft mound of my stomach, started to stroke and pet as he pulled me into him. I held my breath, bit hard into my lip, closed my eyes, but still, I did not move.

*I am not Marina*, I said at last, blurting out the words.

Manu stopped. I felt him turn and walk away from me, heard him sit again at the table, and then another sound. The groan was coming from somewhere so embedded in Manu's flesh, it was hardly recognizable as human. I turned. Manu, the heel of each hand pushing into his eye sockets, was swaying slightly where he sat. Saying nothing, I went over and sat opposite the man I'd always thought of as my father. After some time, I put my hand on his elbow. He released his own hands and looked at me with red eyes.

*I want to be near her, again. I'm half mad with it.*

His voice was clear, loud, without the hint of a whisper. Manu wiped his nose on his hand and pushed a packet of cigarettes towards me. Without reflection, I took one. My head swam as I sucked in the smoke. Still, I smoked harder, taking deeper, heavier pulls. When I began to feel sick I held the cigarette away from my face. Manu took it and crushed it into the bottom of an empty coffee cup.

*You're all that's left of her . . . I wasn't thinking.*

He was staring at me, now. His eyes dark, boring into me. I felt my face get hot and redden. I couldn't hold his stare. He was beautiful. We sat like this for a long time, me not daring to look up, until eventually I had to break the silence.

*The letter. You should've given it me sooner. Why have you waited so long?*

*It's something of her. A thing she made. I thought while I could hold it, touch the paper, she was still here, with me. I hear her, speaking the words as she wrote it. See her, biting her lip, trying to get it right. I smell her scent on the envelope. I wanted to keep it close to me.*

*It wasn't yours to keep.*

Manu raised his hand, shook his head, and gestured to me to keep quiet.

*C'est fini. J'ai plus rien a dire.*

I made him omelettes, sat opposite him, watched as he spooned each mouthful, carefully, into his glorious mouth, without once looking at me. He ate in silence, a silence which lasted forever, at least the forever in which I knew him.

On my way back to the wigwam I scribbled on the last page of my notebook, tore it from its bindings, folded it, and carefully wrote the name *Stella* in my best writing on the folded side. I pushed the note under her trailer door. The mealy-mouthed cowgirl was about to be delivered everything she ever wanted, and I was giving it to her, like an omelette, on a plate.

For the first few months of their union, Stella flounced around the encampment wearing Marina's clothes and looking down her nose at the other girls. The nylon and other cheap fabrics suited her. Although heavier than Marina, she still had a fine-looking figure. I watched at my usual distance, recorded their comings and goings. Manu spent most of his time with the animals, returning to the caravan and its new hostess late each evening after the show. She always had his dinner, and herself, ready for him.

After a while her steps were no longer as light and bouncy

as before. When she wandered around the encampment now, it was with a slow, heavy tread. Manu's influence could be seen peeking out of the pockets of her hand-me-down house-coats. She stopped hanging around with the other girls (they had little time for their old friend now), preferring to sit with Big Gen on the steps of her trailer, drinking gin from the bottle, chain-smoking, cackling and sobbing in equal measure, mourning the cards life and love had dealt her.

Stella soon became chubby, her face bloated and sad. Fausto gave her less to do in the show, she no longer had the pull of the other girls, and frankly, the cowgirl costumes looked ridiculous on a girl of her size. Neither would Manu let her help with the animals: that was his job. And I was always there to help if any were needed. Stella became surplus to requirements. She knew her place was merely to feed Manu's appetites, that she was not his special dove; any girl would do. She just had to make sure she was the one who was always there.

She was still there the day I left, some years later. I went to the caravan to say goodbye to Manu. We hugged (as step-father and daughter should) as she watched from the bed, half hidden behind the curtain, wretched, bereft at the tender-ness her lover was able to show another, even if, as she must have believed, it was his own flesh and blood. You might think my heart would ache for the girl. It didn't. As Manu held me in his arms, perceptibly moved by the idea of never seeing me again, I looked over to poor Stella, all bloated and undone in her second-hand pit, and gave her my biggest and best smile. Poor Stella. She buried her peroxide-infused head in the faded sheets to stifle her screams, prompting Manu to turn quickly and slap her bare leg, in something that resembled disgust.

*Look after him*, I said, blowing Manu a kiss and, for the very last time, closing the door to the caravan of my birth.

# 17

# The Passion of Bunny

The following are snippets, collected and collated from various documents. Some, where I feel weight should be added, are punctuated with a snatch of memory, or re-written with nuance. These entries are the glue to my tales so far. I am a curator now, sticking things together as I type, shaping them, building them up in order to make sense of the history so you can get a real idea of what is missing, and why it needs to be found. I hope, above all, you will find this a truthful collection of words.

Bunny smiles, her large head tips forwards, propelling her body to follow. Two fat arms reach out, pleading. I go over, pick her up, straining as I do. She's not yet two years old and growing.

*She's put on weight again.*

Serendipity Wilson does not answer. She sits, bedraggled between her bedclothes, knitting. She, unlike her ever-expanding child, looks thinner than ever, her face gaunt and tired. Her hair is dulled almost to the point of looking tarnished. Only the occasional faint throb of orange betrays its former glory. It makes me sad to look at her. I speak, avoiding her gaze.

*What you making?* I ask.

*Hat.*

*She has hats.*

*Don't fit. Nothing fits.*

*They're fine.*

*Look at my fingers. Look at them! It's never-ending. I don't do this for fun, you know. Oh, you have no idea. No idea!*

*I thought you liked making Bunny's outfits.*

Serendipity Wilson stops knitting. She glares at me, leaving me no choice but to give her my complete attention. Her eyes are wide in their sockets, but empty. She looks like a blind woman; the surface of each orb covered in a milky sheen. She sees only her fat child: the big, hairless head, the grasping chubby fingers; hears only her crying, her screaming. Bunny pulls my hair. I let out a sharp *no*, and struggle to hold her wriggling bulk.

*I need to keep her safe.*

Serendipity Wilson's voice dwindles to a whisper as she continues to stare with unblinking accuracy at nothing in particular.

*There's danger. Do you see? And misery. I'm an artery for it. Awful things pass through me.*

*What things?*

*They're like snakes, hissing and moving under my skin, trying to find a way out. But I won't let them out. Do you hear me? I won't let them get to Bunny.*

*Stop saying things like that. It scares me.*

*You should be scared, Mouse. We all should.*

*It's silly. Bad things wouldn't live in you. Not ever. You're too good.*

*You don't know what's happening, here, inside. Maybe misery is a virus. And I've caught it, like a bad cold.*

*No one can be happy all the time. Not you, not even Bunny.*

*What do you know? Your life has been nothing but misery. Your family stink of it.*

*I can't help it if I was born a monster.*

*No, no. I'm sorry, Mouse. What am I saying? My poor Mouse. I've tried my best, goodness knows. It's not your fault, it never was. You're not a monster, please don't say that. But it's true, isn't it? Misery is your shadow, it follows you, sticks to you, like an infection. Perhaps, unknowingly, you gave it to me.*

Bunny giggles, her fingers search my nostrils, pull at my lip. I have an urge to throw the child across the floor, to tell Serendipity Wilson to look after what is her own and not to rely on me to be a plaything for her brat. But I love Bunny. I know my friend is tired and worried. I look at her, shrouded in a faint mist, shrivelled up like an old balloon.

*Sorry,* I say.

She seemed happier today. I offered to take Bunny out for a while, so she could rest. She smiled. Her hair lit up in a momentary flare. Sometimes I think she may be fading away, soon there'll be nothing left but Manannán mist, then even that will be gone, blown away on the gentlest breeze. She's afraid of going on the wire. It's not the vertigo of old, this is a deeper fear. She can no longer afford the risk. Not now she has Bunny. She stays in bed a lot, sometimes complaining of a fever. Today was no exception. I think she's ill. I spoke to Gen about getting a doctor. Gen said I should not be so dramatic. Then she went to the wigwam and gave Serendipity Wilson some of her special poultice, and a beaker of gin *to calm the nerves*. Thankfully, the patient refused to drink, but she accepted the foul-smelling paste with a weak smile and a cough.

Gen's such a quack.

Bunny and I are pals, the very best of friends. If she is happy, I am the one she comes to. We play peek-a-boo, shadow animals, tickle-me-silly, all manner of childish games. When she's tired and grumpy, she goes to her mother, looks at me through crossed brows, as if I am the cause of all her woes. She slaps me too, when she's angry, spits at me, shouts *no*, calls me *ugly bouse*, and crawls to her mother, pointing at me in villainous accusation. There are times when I do not want her near me. I try to be nice, tell her to leave me alone, but she insists until I cannot hold my tongue any longer. Then I call her names, like *brat* and *fat-faced monster, bald-headed freak* and *bastard child*.

★

Bunny has been as sweet as strawberry jam. I love her to distraction. I was glad to have time with her today, all by myself. We are very close these days, *as thick as thieves*, her mother says. And I reply, *not as thick as you think*, and I laugh, but Serendipity Wilson doesn't see the joke. Bunny laughs along with me. She doesn't understand. Hers is a ritualistic laugh. Our life is a ritual now, with Bunny as the icon at the centre of our observances. Much depends on her bodily functions. Does the little rabbit need to feed; to drink; to sleep; to shit? And on we go in our liturgy of love, of cleaning and feeding, accompanied by a benedictus of cooing and witty quips – *not as thick as you think, ha ha*. I can walk away whenever I wish. I am not bound to the child as she is. It's a never-ending Mass for her: the Passion of Bunny.

Bunny sucks the life from Serendipity Wilson. Everyone sees it, yet they avert their eyes. The circus folk do not add insult to her injury by asking if they could mind the child a while, so the mother might get some rest. In truth, they dare not. She'd bite their heads off. They are such cowards. The only one who bothers is Fausto. He is so fond of the baby. *Let me take her a bits*, he says. *She likes old Fausto. See? Bunny rabbit like his silly face.* And although, at first, she protests, in the end Serendipity Wilson hands the child over with a coy smile and gentle *thank you*, then goes to bed.

Serendipity Wilson slept for a whole day and a whole night. I was scared she might sleep forever. When she finally woke up, she was not refreshed, or hungry. She said she was still tired and wished she could sleep more. I had to mind Bunny all by myself while she was out of it. Fausto allowed it, but he won't stand me being away from the ring for too long. I can't say I'm fond of it either. I am not the child's mother. I wonder if there's really such a thing as sleeping sickness?

I took Bunny to a café in the town today. We had milkshakes. The rabbit is a glutton, though. She wanted another, then another, and I never want to disappoint her. I like it when she's happy, when we laugh and I coddle her. There's nothing like it on earth. We are two peas in a pod, *as thick as thieves.*

I dressed Bunny in haste this morning, in her red dress and matching cardigan. The buttons don't quite reach at the front and the wool stretches tight around her bulging arms, but it's enough to keep the chill out. Her mother was in an agitated state, so I wanted to make a quick exit, before she changed her mind and decided the child could not go because she wasn't *properly dressed.* She's obsessed with the rabbit's clothing. I threw my yellow jumper over my head, pulled on my rubber boots, set Bunny down in the wooden trolley Fausto made, so we can push her around the encampment (now she's too big to carry, and too slow to walk) and, without thinking how I must've looked, set off.

The rabbit chuckled and babbled, her fat fingers grasping the sides of the trolley as I ran over bumps and stones. I looked for anything that could make the stupid contraption jump up and down. Bunny loves to go fast, to be jolted around in her trolley. We laughed so much as we hurried along. Although autumn is upon us, the day was bright and warm, and we were happy. The trolley is painted pillar box red. She was a sight in her matching red outfit, like a fat red imp. *Bumpy, bump, bump,* I said as the rabbit screamed with glee. I don't care how we look to people outside the encampment. They give us sly glances, call us dirty names because they think we are gypsies. I would rather have gypsy blood than be one of the hordes, with their boredom and their ugly lives. I'm proud to be thought a gypsy.

As we trundled out of the encampment, down the long street towards the town, I began to recognize our environment: the seam of a road between two patches of common land, the large white buildings, the groups of young people. We regularly return to the same places, but I rarely take notice. The landscape of this place, however, remains emblazoned on my memory. How strange it was to find myself there, pushing the rabbit around in her funny trolley.

Sometimes I think I am a witch. That I have the power to conjure people up. It's happened many times. I will dream about someone, no one important, usually someone who worked in our show but went off (there are many, Fausto's wages don't motivate people into fidelity). It's always someone I haven't thought of for a long time, if ever. On waking, I pay it no mind, until days later, when they fetch up. Some might call it coincidence. But if the descendant of a sea god, with a head like a beacon and the power to create fog can join a travelling circus, then why should I not have the power to conjure people up? Anyway, what harm could it do? First, I tried to picture his face: skinny lips, large nose, brown thatch. Then the long arms. It was more difficult than I thought. I never paid much attention to the man, not until I had to. I thought back to our meeting in the municipal garden between the large buildings, thought about his sullen eyes, his big hands, imagined his flaccid worm. It was too much. Bunny and I were having fun, I didn't want to ruin things by making myself dizzy and unhappy. I abandoned the exercise. Why would I want to conjure him up, anyway, of all people? No, I did not. The thought made me shiver. I concentrated on pushing the trolley and producing squeals of delight from the rabbit within.

We found a café on a busy road, the other side of which was another large building, blackened with street-filth. I thought it must be an old palace with its great dome rising from the centre, seemingly endless Grecian columns, and stone lions lolling on plinths as if lazily bathing in the light drizzle, which now brought a sombre aspect to the afternoon. The milkshakes kept Bunny quiet, thankfully. The dreariness of the town centre (other than the glorious building opposite) and the darkening day, began to affect my mood. The café was almost empty. The girl behind the counter stared through the window at the dull street. *Dull, dull, dull*, I said under my breath, as Bunny slurped pinkish milk through a white straw. *Dull!* she screamed.

I felt sorry for the behind-the-counter girl. I'd rather be dead than stand behind that counter every day. Perhaps she is dead, her skin embalmed in chip-fat and grease. She looked sad. I wondered whether I should tell her about the circus, ask her to come, tell her she could be my guest. I imagined her, sucking on a toffee apple, smiling as she watched me on the wire. We might become friends. It would be nice to have a friend from the outside world, someone just for me. Who was I kidding? I have enough trouble talking to people as it is. Ordering the milkshakes was an ordeal. I couldn't even look at the girl, and speaking to her made me stutter and sweat. Sometimes I'm glad I wasn't born to live in the mundane world of the hordes, and sometimes I wish I wasn't such a freak.

I browsed a crumpled newspaper, something to do as the rabbit slurped and gurgled. Local news for local people. *Dull as dishwater.* I wasn't really reading it, not until the centre spread hit me like a slap in the chops. There was a picture, depicting two feet (mine), standing on a wire, with ankles, calves and thighs showing. Joey clowns and acrobats could be seen cavorting below. The page was ringed with coffee stains, smudged by fingers sticky from buns. It made me want to scream. You would never know who the star of the show was. I am half a woman. Cut off from the backside up. Marina would never have stood for it. She would've grabbed the page, run all the way back to the encampment, stuck the nasty thing under Fausto's nose and demanded answers. But I am not Marina. So, I fumed as I snapped and turned the pages. One day Fausto will understand the value of who he has heading his troupe.

How false and silly those words look, even as I write them. Fausto will never see me as anything other than Marina's messy problem. It doesn't matter how wonderful I make myself, or how much money I make him. I am not Marina, as Bunny is not Serendipity Wilson.

I looked again at the dull girl. She was still staring out the window, biting her nails. How I envied her now. To have never put a foot upon a wire; perhaps that's what it is to be free and independent. The girl turned quickly, snatched a look at me, and grimaced. I looked away, flushed and humiliated.

Bunny started to moan (inevitably). Her paper straw, now a soggy mush, the source of her torment. I tore the top off, stuck the straw back in her drink, and she spat at me. *Ungrateful brat*. In my attempt to ignore the bastard child, I continued to turn the pages of the newspaper. There were two pages filled with short, personal messages. One read: *My darling Wasp, forgive me. Your Bumble Bee.* Another: *Mr H. If you're not at the statue by 6 p.m., I will know. Miss D.* I was amused, so I read on. *SW. I will wait for you every night. Life is a circus. Midnight. Town Hall steps. JF.* My heart almost stopped.

At first, I was giddy with excitement. Had I really done it? I live it again as I write. *Oh yes*, I thought, *that's the way to conjure up the devil, all right.* Then, an overwhelming wave of dread hit me, and I couldn't breathe.

Stuffing Bunny into the trolley, I could hear myself panting, like a dog. There was a beading of sweat on my top lip. The café girl turned to look at us again, scrunched her nose up and frowned, as if confronted with a bucket of piss. I no longer cared. I tore the page from the newspaper and the girl tutted, clicking her tongue hard against the roof of her mouth. I had to get back, show the message to Serendipity Wilson. It might lift her spirits to see how much he was pining for her, and we might laugh at him as we'd done before. How clever I was with my conjuring trick, but how my heart pounded.

As we rushed into the street, Bunny latched on to the excitement of it all. Forgetting the milkshakes curdling in her belly, she clapped and laughed as we ploughed headlong through the town. By the time we reached the encampment it was dark, Bunny had been sick, and I was shaking and breathless.

The encampment was busy. People sat at makeshift tables, draped in blankets, finishing off meals, or stood around in groups, smoking, chatting, readying themselves for the night's work. I stared at them, frozen by confusion. *Bouse!* shouted Bunny, jumping like a flea in her trolley, bringing me to my senses. I couldn't let Serendipity Wilson see Bunny in such an excited state, it would send her into all kinds of furies. I looked at the newspaper page in my hand, its white edges now smudged with my own inky fingerprints. What idiocies had been going through my head? I couldn't show her Old Man Frazer's message, that was a sure way to bring on her sickness. Neither could I ignore it. I'd conjured him up, after all. The message was a gift. Like the tales Serendipity Wilson told me as a child said: if you're the receiver of a bestowal, there must be some good reason for it. Such things should not be disregarded. My thoughts were spinning.

If Old Man Frazer is here, I thought, closing my eyes to concentrate my mind, he could help us. His presence does not have to mean calamity. I wouldn't have been party to bringing him back if it were to make mischief. Yes, of course – when the penny dropped it fell hard, and I could barely contain myself – he could take Bunny for a while! That's it! He is the daddy, after all. It would be good for everyone. If Bunny was to go on a short holiday, Serendipity Wilson would have time to recover. She could sleep as much as she liked, then. No one would bother her. And she couldn't complain or worry about the baby because she'd be with her daddy, and that is a natural and right thing. It went without saying that I would miss Bunny, and Serendipity Wilson would miss her dreadfully. But surely, that's not a bad thing. By the time Bunny came home, everyone would be so happy to see each other, and all worries and sickness would most likely be forgotten.

I parked the trolley next to a group of dancing girls, asked them to mind Bunny, and ran around the encampment like a chicken with its head off, looking for Gen and Fausto. When I couldn't find either of them, I started to panic. There was nothing else for it. Even though it was something that had always greatly disturbed me, and as a child had given me nightmares, I went to Big Gen's trailer. I found her there, dusting herself in talcum with a large, pink puff. She listened quietly as I spat out my ideas, waving the scrap of newspaper at her. When I finished, she set down her puff and gestured me to sit. I tried to regulate my breathing as Gen read the page I'd thrust at her. *Don't move. Wait here,* she said, turning to go, but stopped and turned back, as if struck by an afterthought. Moving towards me, Gen put a large, paw-like hand lightly on my cheek. Instinctively (and only for a moment), my face snuggled into her podgy palm. It was soft, dry and warm, and smelled a little of bleach, but not unpleasantly so. *You're a good girl*, she whispered and smiled at me before rushing away, slamming the metal door behind her.

I sat on my hands and crossed my ankles, trying hard to keep still. I'd never been inside Gen's trailer before, and it was the source of many circus stories. As I'd always imagined, it was dark. Lit only by one thick candle. I watched as wax spilled down, creating landscapes as it rolled onto a cracked dinner plate, forming solid pools. The empty bird cages, silver and gold pendants and broken bits of porcelain doll that hung by lengths of string from the ceiling of her trailer, looked sinister and strange in the flickering darkness. The feathers and bows of her enormous clothes, strewn about the place, moved slightly in a faint breeze. I wondered if it was my breathing creating the draught, so I gulped and held my breath for as long as I could, until it came bursting out in a loud gasp, just as the trailer door clattered open.

Gen and Fausto were speaking in loud voices, but being so shocked by their sudden appearance, and by my own exclamation, I didn't catch what they were saying. They stopped, looked at me, and in unison as if perfectly rehearsed, they smiled. Fausto put his small hands on his wide hips.

*Not a bad plan. Might work. You're not stupid as you look-like. No, not stupid. Gen and me, we been at a loss, see, not knowing what to do about the situation. S'not sustainable, having the girl out of things like these past times. I can't keep her for nothing. Good timing, this newspaper thingamajig. Yes, we try this. A rest from the child is good idea, what Doctor Foster orders, as they say. And good to protect little one from Mama's madness. It's good. All round good. We do it.*

I felt so proud and could not stop a smile from creeping up my own face as Fausto left, throwing the trailer door open with a satisfied grunt and nod of his head. Gen said she would take over the proceedings, get in touch with the newspaper, give Old Man Frazer a message so that everything could be arranged properly. For now, all I had to do was keep it under my hat. I am very good at keeping secrets, and I told her so. I liked the way Gen looked at me then; her eyes, small and wrinkled, went into slits, the way a cat's might do, when they're fast asleep. I'll show her how good I am, I thought. I'll make the plan work, and soon Serendipity Wilson will be back to her old self, Bunny will have had a nice holiday, and we will all be back together, facing the future, hand in hand and best feet forwards, as Fausto likes to say.

# 18

# Doctor's Orders

Serendipity Wilson's sickness worsened. I kept my counsel about Old Man Frazer, waited for a word from Gen, and hoped it would come soon.

When at last Gen and Fausto came to the wigwam to tell of the arrangements they'd made, Serendipity Wilson's face turned scarlet. The mere mention of John Frazer made her lose her temper, shouting that Gen and Fausto had no right to interfere in things that did not concern them. The duo insisted it was *all for the best,* but Serendipity Wilson screamed, threw herself about the place and tore her hair out in clumps. Gen was firm, though I could tell she was moved. Still, she folded her great mottled arms across her enormous bosom and said it was too late for all that, everything had been organized and there was no need for dramatics. Serendipity Wilson knew she was powerless against the iron will of Gen and Fausto. I sat silent on my bed, and other than the occasional blinking of my eyes, as motionless as a rock. My friend lashed about the place, only falling still when every bit of strength had been forced from her.

The fits of anger made things worse. Over the next few days, stricken by fever and visions, Serendipity Wilson became a shivering wreck, entirely bound to her bed. Sometimes there were ravings, and I wished I'd listened when she'd tried to teach me Manx. Big Gen was worried, too. For two days she patrolled outside the wigwam, sticking her head in at intervals, asking *Has owt changed?* and offering to lend a hand with Bunny. Scared for my friend's life, not knowing what else to do, I knelt by her bed and prayed. I begged her island ancestors to intervene. I pleaded with Manannán mac Lir himself to lift the fever that now consumed her waking moments and called upon any kindly deity who might be passing over the wigwam to hear my supplications, give us relief (I've never been fussy about gods, they're all the same to me, dishing out rewards and punishments, desperate to be worshipped), but none was forthcoming.

When Gen persuaded Fausto to summon a doctor, and he, with his big leather bag and heavy tweed suit that smelled like soil and fire, proclaimed Serendipity Wilson to be suffering from nervous exhaustion and womb-fever, and gave her medicine in a heavy glass bottle to be taken with a spoon, Serendipity Wilson's sickness seemed to recede a little. How the doctor scolded Gen for not letting the girl see a proper midwife when she'd needed one, and how Gen went quiet and red and looked at the floor and mumbled that she'd wanted to, but Fausto had been against it. There was even a tear in her eye. It was enough to make me feel sorry for her.

As the fever broke, Serendipity Wilson saw that the holiday might not be a bad thing after all. The doctor thought it an excellent idea, indeed he was emphatic, saying the father ought not to be shirking his duty, and complained about how some men are nothing but dogs and should be kept on a lead. *You know what they do to dogs who can't control themselves*, he said.

When the day came for Bunny to leave, Serendipity Wilson was still in her bed. The fevers had gone, but she was as thin as cotton and just as frail. With eyes barely open, breathing slowly, she spoke in a low voice, the trace of a smile brushing her lips.

*I want to get well*, she said. *For Bunny. I don't like her seeing me like this. But I'm afraid, Mouse. I'm so afraid.*

*There's nothing to be frightened of. You need some proper rest, that's all. That's what the doctor-man said.*

*No, it's not that. I know what my sickness is and where it comes from. I shouldn't have had a child so far from the island. The ancestors are trying to make me take her to them by giving me fevers. They don't like to give their children up entirely to the mortal world. I don't think the ancestors mean to punish me, they're not cruel. But it's a strange way to go about things. Anyway, I'm not afraid of them, or of the sickness.*

*Then, what?*

*Can't you see? I'm afraid of me. I'm scared that one day . . . I have no patience. I'm terrified to touch Bunny in case I do her harm. I don't trust myself. And the fogs have gone. I can't muster the energy anymore, so I can't hide. I can't protect myself, or her. What if they never come back. What if, after all this . . . what if I hurt her?*

*When Bunny comes home, you'll be well again, and she'll be happy because of spending time with her daddy. She has his blood too, remember. The ancestors know that. Don't fret. All will be well.*

Serendipity Wilson sat up and held my hand. Her grip was stronger now, and her hair flared and waned in gentle throbs.

*See? I'm feeling better already. Thank you, Mouse.*

*I'm happy to help you.*

*Listen carefully, Mouse. If you need me, wherever or whenever, I will come to you, and I'll hold your hand, as you've held mine. That's a promise.*

*Don't go on, you'll tire yourself out. Bunny will be here in a minute. You need your energy, so you can spend the afternoon playing, and packing her bag for the journey. You're sure you're strong enough? I can do it, if you'd prefer.*

*Oh yes, I'm strong now. Look.*

Serendipity Wilson gave my hand a squeeze. I laughed, and rubbed my hand as I pulled it away, feigning a twinge of pain from her new-found strength.

*Good. Fausto and Gen will wait outside the wigwam, in case you need anything. They've got a table and chairs out there, I think they're planning to have a feast.*

*They never stop eating, those two.*

*Gen needs the fuel, for the dragon that lives up her arse.*

We started to laugh. I snorted, and Serendipity Wilson called me a pigwig. When I snorted again, I thought we might split ourselves in half, laughing so much, until Fausto came in with Bunny and we had to contain our giggles, which burst out each time we caught each other's eye. I didn't want to leave my friend. She was looking better already; simply the idea of the oncoming rest and respite was doing a marvellous job. I wished I could stay, but mother and daughter needed to say their farewells.

*You'll come back this afternoon? You know I can't trust anyone but you. You must be the one to take Bunny to John. I won't allow anyone else to do it. You'll find it hard though, seeing him, and leaving Bunny. You won't let me down now, Mouse? Remember, it's only for a few weeks. You'll be strong, won't you?*

*You can trust me*, I said.

Outside the wigwam, Gen was sitting on her throne: an over-large, heavy wooden chair that took at least three people to move. It was a monstrous, gothic-looking thing, all spirals and carved tendrils. The high back stopped behind her neck, and two great mahogany twists jutted up at each side of her head, topped off with fat cupids in crowns that seemed to hover over their greedy faces. The throne had been made especially for her. *Have you ever seen such fine work?* she'd say, then she'd sigh and rub her great doughy paws over the wood. It had been painted gold, back in the day, before she was married (and a sad tale that turned out to be), before the world lost interest in her art. But the paint was mostly gone now, worn away and faded. If you looked closely enough, stuck your nose right up to the thing, you could still see the odd fleck, dulled, deeply ingrained into the old wood. The last bastion of her former greatness.

Oh yes, she was the queen back then, no one could touch her. And she'd had lovers galore, men from all walks of life, *all wanting a bit of Gen for themselves*. Naturally, she'd oblige them, for a price. *If they wanted it (and they wanted it), they could bloody pay for it. You get nowt for nowt, not in this life, not from Big Queen Gen*. And don't imagine she hadn't had real royalty between her thighs. Gen's talents were well known, word got to high places back then, or so she said. There was something sad about seeing her sat there now. Gen wanted to be regal, to hold court. What a pathetic queendom to reign over, nothing but mud and dirt and old, torn clothes.

Fausto sat opposite her at the tottering, makeshift table, balanced on a low three-legged stool. He looked like a pig on a thimble, grunting as he made his way through thick slabs of cooked meat, bread and lard. I stood and waited a moment by Gen's throne, watched as she finished stuffing the end of a cream horn into her mouth, licked her fingers, dabbed the corners of her mouth with a grubby lace hanky, and nodded. I took that to mean I could stand down from my duties. Then Gen took a breath as she swallowed, as if she might say something. But, having nothing to say myself, and mortified by the sight of them both in their glorious gluttony, I turned quickly away.

Nervous and out of sorts, I made my way into the town, something to do in the hours before handing over Bunny. I came across a jeweller's shop, and without thinking, went inside. The man behind the counter asked how he could help. I took the lock of bright hair from its knitted pouch around my neck and showed it him.

*What's this, then?* he said.

*Hair.*

*I've not seen hair like this before.*

*It's special.*

*You can say that again.*

*I want to keep it.*

*Aye, I can see why.*

*Not for me, for someone who's going away for a while.*

*What you want is a brooch, or pendant, to keep it in.*

*Yes. Something special.*

*I think I've the very thing.*

The man turned his back, opened tiny drawer after tiny drawer in a large wooden cabinet until he found what he was looking for, and presented it with a theatrical flourish. There on the counter, lying on a velvet mat, were two glass lockets hanging from long silver chains.

*One for you, and one for him*, he said.

I sat on a simple chair by the door, waited while the man crouched over the countertop, bound the hair into two little bundles and placed them in the lockets. There were no other customers. I could hear the rumble of traffic outside, wheels crunching on wet roads. It was warm inside the jeweller's shop, protected by the dark wood and glass shelves. It was a relief to sit, and not think about Bunny, John Frazer, Serendipity Wilson, or anything.

The man rose to his full height, dangled two bright pendulums, glinting, orange, between his fingers, and smiled. He held them up to the light and their brilliance shone, like fire captured in ice.

*Looks like amber, see?* said the man. *Brighter than any I've ever seen, mind. The world is full of wonders.*

Something sharp stabbed at my heart. Beauty can be a painful thing to look at. A million reveries ran through my head, tangled up like strands of unravelled wool. Mind pictures that could not quite form into thoughts: Serendipity Wilson clicking her needles – click, click, click – cinnamon tea – *J'ai Deux Amours* – Marina, hair like tentacles – red nylon housecoat – a kick in the guts – strong soap and cold water – the warm touch of Serendipity Wilson's fingers on my arm.

I didn't realize I was crying.

*Now then, don't take on so. You're young, there'll be many people pass through your life yet, no need to break your heart over the first one.*

His voice was soft. I smiled. The man put the pendants into two velvet boxes, and I paid the money. When I got back to the wigwam, Fausto had vacated his stool, leaving Gen still sitting at her table by the entrance, keeping an eye on things and picking at the carcass of a roast chicken. She sucked at her fingers, raised her eyebrows and smiled as I approached. Then, as if I needed her permission to enter, she waved me through.

Bunny was ready, her things packed in a knitted bag.

Serendipity Wilson handed me the knitted toy rabbit the baby liked so much. *Babbit*, said Bunny, as I stuffed it in the bag. Serendipity Wilson kissed her daughter's head, said something in her own language that I couldn't understand, and with great effort, smiled weakly up at me from her bed.

*Time to go*, I said, lifting Bunny into her trolley. Serendipity Wilson lay back and closed her eyes. *Remember what I told you*, she said. *Be a good girl for Mouse.*

*Bouse!* screamed Bunny.

The Town Hall was the large blackened building with Grecian columns and sleeping lions. By the time I got there, Bunny was fast asleep.

John Frazer was waiting for us, standing tall in a long raincoat, at the top of the steps. He looked like a character from a film, his collar turned up, one hand in a pocket, the other holding a cigarette; poised to perfection, as still as the stone lions beside him. I couldn't hump the trolley with Bunny in it up those steep steps; in any case I didn't want to get close to him.

I bent over the sleeping child, took one of the velvet boxes from my coat pocket and tucked it under her arm. I told her I'd come back for her very soon, and if she got lonely for us, she was to look at the pendant and know we were waiting for her to come home. *We'll miss you every day*, I said.

Gen had pinned a note to the baby's woollen jacket with instructions for Bunny's diet, and for her return. I kissed Bunny's soft head. Then looked up to where her father stood, as if frozen in time, and with a deep breath, I waved my hand to beckon him.

*Make sure you follow Gen's instructions. Don't let her eat too much!* I shouted in a half-whisper, so as not to wake the child. *I'll pick her up myself, so don't get any ideas about Serendipity Wilson, you won't be seeing her.*

John Frazer flicked his cigarette to the ground and started to descend. I turned and ran. He shouted after me, but I didn't stop to answer. The noise of the shouting must've woken Bunny in her trolley. Her familiar high-pitched yowl took me by surprise. My pace slowed, I hesitated. A force stronger than my own will was urging me back. I stopped, turned to go to the child, but as I did, saw John Frazer bend over the trolley, pick her up, and hold her to him, as natural as a cat with its kittens. The crying stopped. He was swaying now, kissing the baby's head. He looked over, took one of Bunny's chubby hands and brought it up to his lips. I watched her fingers search his face. Then he straightened up and saluted me, like a soldier. I turned again and ran all the way to the encampment.

The wigwam was dark and quiet when I got back. Serendipity Wilson was breathing heavily under her blankets. I climbed into my own bed, pulled the covers to my chin, and slept soundly until the morning. When I awoke, Serendipity Wilson was sat up in bed, the wigwam was flooded with orange light, and I blinked into the clear aspect of a new day.

# 19

# Endings, Returns and Invocations

This is not the end.

A pile of pages, typed and neatly stacked, sits at the back left-hand corner of the writing table. The stack is tidy. It looks like a solid block, as if all the individual pieces of paper have defiantly merged together, creating something strong and concrete. It gives me an extreme sense of satisfaction. I'm efficient in my work; there's no room for a slattern, not when such a messy life can look so neat. It's easy to forget about the stories held within the stack. For the moment, those stories seem unimportant. After all, they're only words. What can they do, locked as they are in their tidy pile? They cannot bring back the dead.

The old documents, from which I transcribe, remain strewn over the table. Ugly reminders of work yet to be done. The disintegrating paper giving off a musty smell as the faded words escape. At the end of my task, these old documents will go the way of Marina's letter. Ashes and dust. If I look at them now, I think I hear voices from long ago calling out. Their whispers creep around the walls.

*Can you see the light at the end of the tunnel yet, Mouse?* I want to answer, to shout out, but I'm not too far gone to have forgotten there are other people in the building. *Can you see the light?* insists the creeping voice. *Shhhhh*, I snap. *Be still.* But the voice will not stop.

As always, her lamp hangs about my neck. My tunnel is as dark as pitch. Maybe she doesn't want to light my way, maybe she wants to watch as I thrash about in the dark. If I keep typing, each letter will push me forwards, until at last I will see my tiny spot of light in the distance. Eventually the pinprick will become an orb, a gaping mouth, and finally I'll be standing outside, bathed in cool light, looking back into the shadowland of my tunnel. Then I'll probably regret the calming terror of darkness. I might even hate the light. We can be such morbid creatures.

It's the darkest day of the year. New York City knows how to set a scene, helping to paint the picture of my life. The sky through my window is grey velvet, swirled with black, like the dramatic icing on a Halloween cake. People stay indoors on days like this. A city squall clears the streets, gives us something to hide from, something to talk about, other than ourselves.

I've always loved storms. They're a primordial reminder that we're not in control. Every big event in my life has been accompanied by the elemental swish of wind and darkening of skies. At least, that's how I remember them. My thumbs itch for thunder now, for the vault to break and the rains to fall. Come quickly, storm, help me get the most difficult words onto the page. Without it, I might lose my nerve. But listen, I don't need invocations. The thunder is coming.

Serendipity Wilson gained strength quickly. Every day we made plans for things to do on Bunny's return. We talked about the picnics we'd have, how it might be time for the child to take to the wire (it's never too early). We made lists and drew pictures. Serendipity Wilson began to knit new blankets, clothes and toys for the homecoming. I was still performing alone, but my friend had started practising again. Just a little, enough to regain her confidence. There were moments of sadness too, when we missed Bunny, and we wept together. But we learned to look to the future. Serendipity Wilson, her head of fire a beacon again, shone through the days and nights, so that Bunny might know how her mother waited and longed for her return.

At last, the day came. Serendipity Wilson was bouncing like a gnat around the wigwam. Our home was ablaze with colour and light, and the smell of cinnamon and cedar wood drenched the air. We put Bunny's new clothes and toys in a neat pile, by her bed things. Everything was in place. When I left at the appointed time, Gen came by to wait with Serendipity Wilson, who could not keep still. She made Big Gen roar with laughter with all her dancing and nattering. *Quickly now. Bring Bunny home, Mouse*, said Serendipity Wilson, pushing me out of the wigwam, into the day.

I ran practically all the way.

As I arrived, the Town Hall clock struck twelve. I turned

the corner, arms open, expectant, ready to receive the child, but stopped in my tracks when I saw the empty expanse of stone steps, sleeping lions and Greek colonnade. Realizing then I was breathless, I put my hand flat to the plinth beside me and rested my weight against it. Three smartly dressed young women clicked by, in a gaggle of conversation. Probably secretaries, I thought. The cold stone started to bleed through my clothes. I shivered, looked up, and searched the steps again for the shape of a figure in a trench coat, pulling a trolley. Nothing.

Having imagined John Frazer would be the one waiting when I arrived, I was at a loss. Treading carefully at first, graduating to a run, I climbed the stone steps. At the top, I could easily see the length of the road before me, going out of the town one way, and in, the other. There was plenty of traffic. People in their work clothes marched about, and a tramp sat between two tea-chests in a mass of rags and string. But there was no sign of John Frazer and his daughter. I sat down on the top step and looked over the town.

When the Town Hall clock struck one, I was in a panic. I didn't want to leave my place on the steps in case I missed the rendezvous. It was possible that John Frazer was late because Bunny was acting up. I knew how difficult she could be. Then I noticed the boy, sat on a lower step. He'd arrived not long after me. I'd paid him no mind, then. Now, I stared at him. The boy seemed restless, he kept snatching glances at me. I stood and started to descend. He also stood up, as if in greeting.

*Are you waiting for someone?* I asked, panic now surging through me, making me tremble and twist my ankle, as I reached his step.

*Aye, a lass. Might be you.*

*Did someone send you?*

*Might 'ave.*

*Don't be daft with me, little boy. Who sent you?*

*A man. Said I was to deliver this. Is it you then? No one else 'as been waiting.*

The boy held out an envelope. I took it. It was sealed, but I recognized the writing on the front. I'd seen it before, in this very city, it had been my map then. Now it said *My Flame-Haired Funambulist*, in thick, red letters. My chest felt tight, and I thought I might faint.

*Who gave you this? Who?*

*A man. Paid me. Said I was to give this to a lass on't steps. Is it you?*

*Yes.*

The boy ran off.

I wasn't sure what to do. I felt sea-sick, even though I was in the middle of a city. I sat down because I thought I might fall. When I looked around and saw that everything was as before, other than the boy's absence, I took a breath, wiped my shaking hands on my skirt, ripped open the letter, and read.

*Dearest one,*

*It's time for me to be heard. What correspondence I've had from the encampment (Gen's attempt at literacy leaves a lot to be desired) is poor, to say the least. The moment has come to show my hand, so to speak. I know it will hurt you, but there's no other way. Once the initial shock passes, you'll see my actions are taken through love, not spite or anger. If you'd thought fit to answer my first letter, it might not have come to this, but here we are. Now I will explain how things are going to be.*

*For just over two years I have been forced to live in purgatory. I haven't been able to leave this country or set up a real home, following your every move like a stray dog pining for its mistress. Though it was not for you I pined, your silence spoke volumes and I know when to retreat, it was for my child.*

*Do you remember telling me how my seed had taken in your belly? They were your words. I recall every intonation of your voice that evening, as we lay under the wagon in that disgusting place. When I told you it was impossible because the war had finished any hope of fatherhood I might once have had, you said everything was possible. You believed your ancestors were blessing us. I was chosen, that's what you said, many years before we met, perhaps even at my own birth, to sire your child. I loved you for your imagination and stories, no matter how ludicrous they were. You didn't know the strength of your words that night. I'd accepted my fate years ago. My astonishment at your condition was beyond words. Do you remember? My complete allegiance to you and our child was never in question, even when you said you didn't want me, that our love affair was over. I told you I'd do the right thing. You didn't once take my feelings into consideration. I was redundant in the matter.*

*I had to get away from that place. It was stupid of me to think I could persuade you, but I was desperate (what men will do for love!). I wish you'd had the decency to reply to my letter. So you see, I was left, hanging between one life and another. What would you have me do? I found ways to watch our child grow. I couldn't abandon her. She is my miracle as much as yours, no matter what you think, and I claim her now.*

*What a bonny girl our child is. She has a look of my family, we were all big babies. She's a healthy specimen. It would break my heart not to have her in my arms. When I received Gen's communication, I thought it the second miracle of my life, and I can't let that go, especially in the circumstances. I will not allow my child to be returned to a life of precarity and dirt. It's for this reason alone I write.*

*My love, it is time to end all this. I accept your silence as a refusal of the life I offered. After deliberating hard on the matter, I see you're right. You belong in the circus. Any fool can see that. I've no wish to take you from it, or to destroy your spirit (which I've so admired). But how diminished you are. When I see you (as I have done many times, sometimes from closer than you might think), I barely recognize the darling girl who once ran to me with such bloom and enthusiasm. Believe me, it's as difficult for me to write this as it is for you to read it. Motherhood is not your friend. What a pathetic creature you look, trying to hold on to our*

*little one, struggling like an old woman. You're in a bad way,
my girl, and I fear you're unfit to be a mother to our child.
A mother needs strength, and you're so depleted. Even if this
break from the baby has served you well, as your colleagues
hoped, after a while things will go back to how they were.
I won't let that happen. I won't risk the safety of my child.
But I will help you.*

*I will give our baby more than the scrapings of a circus
life and a mother at her wits' end. Obviously, you can see
her. I don't suggest stealing her from you (as you did from
me). She'll want for nothing and have a good life with
decent prospects. Think also of yourself. You're not made for
motherhood, that much is evident. See this as an opportunity.
I'm letting you have everything: your life in the circus, the
possibility to know our child, and for her to know and love
you, at my behest. This means you can come and visit,
but you will only have access to the child when I am present.
I don't want any trouble.*

*Don't dismiss this letter. If you think you can ignore me,
you're mistaken. I won't be pushed away. I have friends in
the law. I shan't hesitate to call on them if my hand is forced.
I've taken advice and am assured that every judge in the land
would grant me sole guardianship of our child considering the
circumstances — a mother in poor health, with delusions of a
magic lineage, existing in poverty, living on the fringes of
society, in a travelling show! It needn't come to that. Do as
I ask. Meet me. If you're not yet strong enough, then don't
concern yourself with the matter until your health returns.*

*I'll wait. The details of the arrangement are not urgent.*
*What's important is that our daughter is happy and safe.*
*You needn't worry, she has everything she needs, including*
*a father's devotion. But do come, as soon as you're able, so*
*we can sort this out and get on with our lives. If you have*
*ideas of going to the police station, I must tell you I've already*
*informed the necessary authorities and they know about the*
*entire, sorry mess. It would do your case more harm than good*
*to show them how you've been living with our child, in a state*
*of hysteria. I'm sorry to insist, but you understand, dearest*
*girl, I must protect my daughter.*

> *Yours always,*
> *John Frazer*

The Town Hall clock struck two. I was unable to move. The letter was still open in my hand, but my mind was gone. I was a shell. It was only panic that shook me awake. I had to think. This was my fault. I'd conjured him up. I closed my eyes, pictured him as I last saw him, kissing Bunny's head, and let the sobs flow. Tears splashed down my cheeks and onto the stone steps. It never occurred to me he might not bring Bunny back. I thought he would try everything possible to see Serendipity Wilson, but not this. Why had Gen and Fausto agreed to such a stupid, childish scheme? Did they know this would happen? I wiped my nose on my sleeve.

The more I thought about it, the more it seemed that Gen

and Fausto might be in cahoots with the Old Man. This was happening, it was happening now, and I had to make it better. My entire life people had underestimated me, and yet was I not the best wire walker anyone had ever seen? I could do anything, if only I focused, put my mind to it. The letter had a post office box number written at the top. It was all going to be fine. I needed time to think, but I would make it right. Somehow, I would bring Bunny home.

It took two days for Serendipity Wilson to rise from her bed. She had not moved a muscle since I came back without Bunny; no stretch of an arm or leg, no turn of the head on her pillow. Once ensconced under the covers, she lay immobile, as if imbued with some paralysing poison. There was the gentle rising of the bedclothes as her slow, steady breathing betrayed the fact of life beneath. Other than that, not a twitch. I wanted to shake her but kept my distance.

I had explained everything as best I could. Bunny had been taken unwell with a bad head cold. Old Man Frazer, not wanting to risk moving her around while still poorly, suggested I go back next week, same time, same place, to collect her. Gen and Fausto both looked at me through squinted eyes as I went through the story. I was glad I knew not to trust them. Serendipity Wilson shouted at first, clenched her fists and pummelled the air. Then she disappeared for a while. There was a fog. When she emerged, after pottering around the place, mumbling to herself for an hour or two, she took herself to bed.

In the meantime, money had to be made and there was a show to put on. And put it on we did. In came the audience, up went the lights. The dancers danced. The horses looked pretty trotting around the ring, leaving steaming parcels for the Joey clowns to collect, who in turn chased around the slippery tarpaulin in colourful clothes and painted faces, carrying their bags of shit. Yes, ladies and gentlemen, we had buckets of magic. Why would the audience not be delighted? Why would we not stand in the ring with smiles on our faces and stars in our eyes when all the time the rustle of money could be heard rising above the din? By the time the hordes traipsed into the big top that first evening, although I refused to perform, claiming a head cold of my own coming on, everything seemed normal enough.

When things were quiet, in a couple of days, I would slip out of the encampment, contact John Frazer, and by whatever means possible (I'd get Manu to help, he was the strongest man alive), I would bring Bunny home. There was no need to panic. That's life, after all; you must balance things out, steady the wire. If there's too much weight on one side, then down you go, flapping your useless arms in dead air. Funambulism is all about balance. Sometimes you get it wrong, it's unavoidable; when you fall, bones break. But I was an expert, the star of the show, a conjuring witch, and the daughter of The Great Marina. I may have fallen in rehearsals, but never in a performance. I wasn't about to start now.

The next night I was back in the ring. I took my applause

and went to bed exhausted. Serendipity Wilson continued to sleep like the almost dead. I pulled my blanket over my arms, looked across the wigwam, and stared at the pile of knitted clothes, neatly folded, awaiting their baby owner. My heart lurched and creaked like an abandoned ship, broken in a becalmed ocean. I couldn't swallow. A pool of saliva collected in my mouth, throat, and lungs. I thought I might drown in a bodily sea of sorrow and worry. Closing my eyes, I pictured Bunny. She was smiling. Rasping with each word, my oesophagus contracting like the belly of a snake after a good meal, I whispered to my little rabbit. I hoped her fairy ancestors might hear me, that they might some- how carry my words on their wings, or if they be wingless creatures, on their backs, and deliver my message to her soft baby ears. Then she need not feel alone, or cry for want of us.

*I will come for you*, I sobbed. *Do not despair. I'm on my way. I will not rest until I bring you home. I promise. Just a few more days. I won't let you down, my Bunny. Good night, don't fret, all will be well.* Eventually my sobs broke into smooth, regular breathing, and at last I was asleep.

When I awoke, Serendipity Wilson was standing over me, smiling, as bright and shiny as a new sixpence. *Time to get up, lazybones*, she said, and danced out of the wigwam, spreading her light on the dark morning. I thought joy had come back to me. As I rose, the sadness and worry of previ- ous days was blown away by the wonder of all that might now come to pass. I decided, as I dressed, that it would be a good day. From now on, all days would be good days, and

I would become a kind and gentle person, full of goodness and grace. I would make up for past errors by being the best I could be. Things were going to change. Bunny would soon be home, I would see to it. I was going to make everything better.

Before leaving the wigwam, I fumbled under the bedclothes for my notebook. A stab of panic hit when I couldn't locate John Frazer's latest letter. I was sure I'd placed it between the pages of my notebook. No need to worry. I was always so careful with my things. The letter was not lost. There had been so much confusion recently, and my mind was a muddle. Serendipity Wilson's voice floated through the fluttering walls, calling to me. It was silly to waste time on childish thoughts. There was a bright new day waiting for me. From now on I would take control, I would be strong. The letter was in my glory-box. Of course it was. Didn't I put it there last night, before I cried myself to sleep?

I left the wigwam without looking for the letter, leaving my notebook hidden under the bedclothes, and vowing that, from now on, I would only write down happy thoughts. In fact, I would burn all my notebooks. Everything they contained was dark and sad. How childish it was to keep diaries, reminders of a past better forgotten. I decided there and then that all childish things must end. After the show, I would take all my papers from my glory-box, make a fire, and burn them. I left the wigwam congratulating myself on my wonderful, grown-up insight.

The day was dark and blustery as I hurried across the encampment, but I could easily see Serendipity Wilson's light in the near distance. That great orange sun that had the power to turn even the darkest pocket of England into a paradise. Her head was brighter than ever. She was moving slowly some paces ahead of me, but with soft, dancing steps, as if silent music surrounded her. Sensing my presence, she turned, beckoned, and I ran to her. I slid my hand into hers and we walked in silence, side by side, until we reached the big top. I could not take my eyes off her. Her face was serene, the way it had been years ago when we sat in the wigwam telling stories and eating cakes. How I longed for those days. How I felt, deep in the very substance of my being, that we would have such times again. *I'm happy to see you so well*, I said. Serendipity Wilson did not answer or look at me. I squeezed her hand. And smiled.

The day passed by in a sort of bliss. We rehearsed, rigging our wire up outside in the open air, letting the grey day leak into our bones, as we danced and shed light on the encampment. Many came out to watch us practise. There was a silent admiration from below, the palpable esteem of others.

I caught sight of Stella, leaning on a guy rope. She was alone, smoking, staring up. I didn't care that she watched with spiteful eyes. I couldn't think badly of her now. We all try to make our way in the world, as best we can. There are so many roads and it's easy to take a wrong turn, find yourself at a dead end, as she had. I was lucky, I had Serendipity Wilson and my shining pendant. I could always see the road ahead. All Stella could see was a brick wall, plastered with posters of Marina. A part of me wanted to wish her well, to tell her not to worry about Manu, to think of herself. But I was busy on my wire. In any case, Stella would never listen to me. I had to concentrate on myself.

Serendipity Wilson and I danced in unison, as we'd done many times before. Two women of equal stature, of equal grace and gifts. There were no set pieces, no steps to learn or follow. We improvised, followed each other's motions, patterns, and breathing. The wire became a third dancer, providing rhythm to our silent movement. It was a complete feeling of togetherness. I don't know how long we were up there. I don't remember breaking for lunch, or ablutions, or any other reason. I only remember the feeling of air rushing over my skin as we moved; the smell of Serendipity Wilson's hair as it blew across my face. I remember her touch, strong, but gentle, and the great ball of love filling the gaps that life had opened in me, packing the deep chasms, sealing off the loneliness.

As evening approached, we took down the wire, reassembling it in the big top for the evening performance. We did not speak. There was no need for words. Serendipity Wilson sang to herself as she worked, her cheeks flushed and pink. My heart was wide open. The audience started to arrive as we finished rigging up. I lost sight of Serendipity Wilson but was happy to dress alone. I've always liked the solitary moments before a performance. The ritual of putting on my costume; the smell of it, synthetic, and faintly musky with traces of my own sweat. The making up of my face to become that other person – the one who's always there but can only be seen under layers of paint, and by strangers – I felt no alarm, not seeing Serendipity Wilson before the performance, there was nothing unusual in it. Even as I stood behind the red curtain, alone, and when Fausto began to introduce our act, I wasn't concerned. I knew she'd be by my side when needed.

We had no music to accompany us as we flew up the ropes to the wire. There was the heavy but electric sound of stillness; of people breathing, watching. Serendipity Wilson ran across the wire, as swift as the wind itself. When she reached the other side, she turned to look at me. We were mirror images. She, standing with one foot on the wire and the other resting on the step of the rigging behind. And I, facing her at the opposite end of our thread. We waited like this for a moment. Then something passed between us.

Without signal or sound, relying only on our shared feelings, we began to move towards each other. Bare foot by bare foot, I slid along the wire towards my friend. We met in the middle. I heard her breathing, felt her heat, looked deep into her eyes as she looked into mine, and we began our improvised dance.

We each had a large feather fan, to beat the air for balance, and for show. Our movements were slow at first, there was no leader, no follower. If she moved, it was as if my own thoughts had been behind the movement. The dance progressed seamlessly, becoming quicker, quicker still. Nothing could stop us.

We were flying; two beautiful seabirds swooping and diving. I forgot everything; Bunny, Marina, Manu – they were all gone. No, they'd never existed. This was all there ever was. Exhilaration, movement, balance, grace and love. There was no big top. No Fausto. No audience.

Then I became aware of the hordes in the blackness below. It was a full house. Where there was no place to sit, people were standing. Every available space was taken, making the big top seem smaller than usual, but more alive. I started to enjoy the fact that so many people were watching us. My performance became more pronounced and theatrical. I gave an extra flourish here and there to my movements, reacting to the gasps of the audience as much as to my partner. The wire bounced without jolting as our legs slid, our arms swayed, and our bodies bent to create, not a bird now, but a two-headed, four-limbed winged serpent. The light from Serendipity Wilson's hair made magic of the big top, waving around the ring as her head flicked this way and that. And then, without warning, she was still.

The shock of her sudden stillness made my foot slip. I tried to steady myself with my fan, took a step back as the wire jumped. My feet gripped the metal, my knees bent. I had to crouch, wrap my fingers around the wire, secure myself, anxious, for the first time during any performance, at the lack of a net. With thoughts of falling rushing at me, I was nevertheless highly conscious of how ugly I must look; crouched there like a cowering schoolgirl, sweating and gormless. I slid backwards into the safety of the rigging, while Serendipity Wilson stood, strong on the wire. I sat for a moment, scowling, heart bashing in my chest, anger and confusion flushing my face, wondering why my friend would want to make me look so stupid in front of the hordes. Was she jealous? Did she want to be the star? Was this her way of showing me, after everything we'd been through, by shaming me? I watched as Serendipity Wilson raised her arms above her head, dropped her feather fan – which seemed to glide, swan-like, to the ground – and stared into the distance, as if entranced by some fabulous thing. There was an intake of breath from the crowd. My anger faded into reverence.

It was not long until the fear and panic came again. She was so still. I felt sure something was wrong. I didn't have a clear view from the rigging, so made my way down the ropes, as quickly as I could, and planted my feet on the ground, gratefully pushing them into the cold tarpaulin.

Serendipity Wilson was alone on the wire, arms stretched upwards. She, the foundling with Manannán blood feeding her earthly flesh, was at last holding ceremony. A hundred ancestral ghosts flooded the big top. I could not see them, but I heard them. Like the ebbing of a sea, or the murmuring of wings. She was summoning them. They were to come to her now.

The hordes hummed in uncomfortable confusion, then fell silent. They were looking up, breath held, frozen in time, awaiting some magic thing, some spectacle of light. There was a palpable spark of anticipation. Something wonderful was about to happen, and they were the chosen ones, the soon-to-be-witnesses to this great happening. And from behind the red curtain, how many pairs of eyes were peeping out, looking up to Serendipity Wilson convening with her ghosts? Yet, there was no human sound to be heard, and in the silence, a shiver of infinite possibility passed among us. I had never known such beauty, such magic, or such horror.

In the end, it happened quickly.

Serendipity Wilson stepped off the wire. When I think of that moment, I often imagine she does not fall. Rather, she hovers for an instant, the big top disappears, and she is standing in a black sky peppered with stars. Under the halo of her hair I can see she is smiling. She looks down to me, waves a slender hand, then floats away. But that's the dream version, an invention to make the incident bearable. In truth, she did not look at me, she did not wave or hover. She fell.

Serendipity Wilson's hair streamered behind her, comet-like, in a trail of orange fire. The light was blindingly bright as she fell, brighter than I'd ever known it, although it dulled on impact. There was no soundtrack to her falling, no shuffling of feet, no whispers. It was utterly quiet, as if for that moment, in respect to the act, the audible world had been shut off. There was barely a sound as she hit, only a soft thud.

At first, she stirred; her legs trembled and she twitched like a sleeping cat. Then she lay unmoving. Her stillness infected us. There was a deep hush, the blinking of a thousand eyes, and silence. Nobody moved. Until the horror struck home and I broke the peace with a scream. The sound seemed to rip through the solid air. It had no echo or depth, just a tearing and fraying as if the very elements of the universe were breaking down around us. The effect of the scream seemed to free my body. At last, I ran to her.

Her hair lay bright, splayed like coffin silk across the tarpaulin. She was on her back, one arm and shoulder twisted under her, the visible hand resting on her hip. I went to touch it, to caress it, to give some comfort to the corpse. She was clutching something under the waistband of her costume. I lifted her hand away, and there, nestled in the soft fabric of her tutu, was a crumpled envelope addressed to *My Flame-Haired Funambulist*, the handwriting smudged but clearly visible under the folds of her fingers.

With panic thrumming through every part of me, I took the missing letter as deftly as I could, bending over the body in heavy sobs to conceal my actions, and stuffed it into my own costume. When all was safe, I began to shout and scream for help.

There was some movement from the audience, now. And sound. Just whispers at first – the hordes never sure when the spectacle ends, and the awfulness of reality begins – then sobbing, and finally, screams. The ring flooded with circus performers, some shouting to *move away*, others professing to be trained medics; a dancing girl (whose name and face I no longer remember, or never knew) put her arm around me. I let her lead me out of the ring. Fausto, as if only now aware the show was over, rushed onto the tarpaulin, waving his chubby arms, begging the audience to leave as quickly and quietly as possible, reassuring them that refunds would be available.

Leaving the chaos behind, the dancing girl found a quiet spot, sat me down among costumes and silks, and gave me a beaker of strong liquor, which I refused to drink. She spoke softly, saying something about shock, stroked my shoulder, then my knee. Although my legs were weak, I pushed the girl away and made my way to the wigwam. I thought that if I could just go to bed, if I could close my eyes and go to sleep, then morning would soon come and this night would be finished, gone forever. All I had to do was sleep and everything would be fine. That's what she always said: *Sleep on it. You'll see, things will look better in the morning, Mouse.*

Undressing, I put the letter in my glory-box, all thoughts of burning my precious notebooks gone. Words were all I had now. The only witness left. *Things will look better in the morning, Mouse.* Without my notebooks, I would be erased. *You'll see.* The idea of putting a flame to them appalled me. *Sleep on it.* I would not be aborted from history, not for Serendipity Wilson, or Marina, not for anyone.

I pulled on my yellow jumper, climbed into Serendipity Wilson's bed, pulled the covers up tight and closed my eyes. I could smell her, she was close, she wouldn't leave me, the thought was ridiculous.

*Shall I bind your hair?* I whispered.

*Not tonight. There's no need anymore. Go to sleep now, Mouse. Things will look better in the morning.*

I wriggled down into the covers, let her scent soothe me, curled my legs to my chest and imagined myself small – so small – and floating, protected by a filigree of blood vessels and trembling flesh. *Go to sleep now, Mouse. Go to sleep.*

Before the funeral, they cut off her hair. It was discussed among the circus folk and thought to be for the best. The idea that something of such beauty, something worth so much to so many, might be left cankerous and decaying in the ground, or burned to ashes, was out of the question. So Serendipity Wilson was shorn of her light. Big Gen did the deed herself, told me how gentle she was, how respectful, how she even *spoke to the child.*

Once off, the tresses had to be cared for properly and pre-served. The hordes needed something of their darling star to worship. The hair was placed in a mirrored case – *imagine how it will shine*, said Fausto – and locked shut to protect it from sticky fingers that might fancy a bit of the light for themselves. A special tent was erected, made from old flags and pieces of silk, to neatly house the tragedy. It was a fit-ting shrine. A fluttering chapel for the grieving people.

A banner was put up and, as Fausto had predicted, the hordes came weeping and wailing to pay their respects. They didn't mind the expense, it was only a small fee. They left flowers and other offerings at her altar, some threw pennies or silver coins, for luck. This soon became a custom. Fausto erected a second banner pronouncing: A PENNY A WISH. How people wept at the death of such an extraordinary young woman. In death, as in life, Serendipity Wilson could certainly put on a show. She was a sensation.

Due to all the ceremony and wish granting, the hair became known as a magical thing, which, if ever touched by human hand, would make the toucher fearless, as fearless as Serendipity Wilson had been in life. (Fausto omitted any mention of vertigo; why spoil things for the mourners?) Security had to be stepped up. Two Joey clowns patrolled the tent by day. They carried sticks, resting them against their shoulders as if they were guns. Another two sat by the shining case, their painted faces illuminated orange by the never-ceasing glow, showing the cracks in their make-up, revealing the deception in their smiles. At night, Big Gen took the relic to her trailer, tucked it under a heavy blanket to extinguish its light, and wrapped her girth around it.

As for Bunny, it was generally considered a good thing she'd been too poorly to come home, what with a mother who'd go and do a thing like that. Serendipity Wilson was obviously a complete fruitcake. The child might even have been in danger. Thank goodness Old Man Frazer had been found. *Let the sleepy dogs lie*, said Fausto, insisting that Bunny and her daddy be left in peace.

I was given the wigwam and all its contents. A sort of compensation. Mr and Mrs Wilson came to the encampment after the funeral. Fausto made sure they didn't see the shrine, find out their daughter was going to her final resting place *chauve*. They sat with me in the wigwam for a while.

I made cinnamon tea, which they politely sipped but did not drink. Mrs Wilson wept a little, but she was happy to meet me and was grateful her daughter had found such a good friend. I asked if there was anything they wanted. Mrs Wilson took the long yellow piece of fabric their adopted daughter had used to bind her hair, but said I was to keep everything else. Their child had been an *unexpected blessing*, they said. They knew, even before she joined the circus, she was not really theirs to keep. There was no mention of Bunny. Serendipity Wilson, everyone supposed, had kept her pregnancy from them, and Big Gen made sure everyone kept mum. There was no need to kick up a fuss. Bunny wasn't blood-related. What did it matter?

That was that.

I stayed with the circus, performing, doing my duty, for what seemed like an eternity. In truth, it was no more than three years. For the most part, I kept myself to myself, apart from the odd occasion when I'd sit with Gen outside her trailer. To begin with, she would ask me to join her so she could *keep an eye on* me, because she was *worried* for me, but later it became as natural as waking in the morning and sleeping at night. We'd sit there, saying nothing much, Gen gently humming an old song under her breath, sighing, and smiling at me every now and then, head to one side in a kindly way. Days ran into nights ran into days. Life was fluid and dull. I spent most of my time alone, or with Solomon and the llamas. Sometimes I'd spend an hour or two with Manu. We'd sit in the animal enclosure, silent but comfortable in each other's company. He was looking thinner; not unhealthy, but not the fine man he'd once been.

For a while, I couldn't imagine life being any different. I thought I'd eventually moulder away alongside Fausto and Gen and the crumbling big top. Maybe one day, when my mind was finally gone, I'd be sent to a home for the confused and deluded, and that would be the end of me. Still, I was young, and dreamt of a different world. And I did not forget my promise.

I tried to find Bunny. Soon after Serendipity Wilson's fall, I sent a message to the post office box mentioned in John Frazer's letter. There was no reply. I sent another, and another. Finally, I wrote to the postmaster who informed me the person I was trying to contact had closed their account. There were no forwarding details.

I saved my money. My earnings were hardly a fortune, but other than on my wire and ropes, I didn't spend much. There were little bags of notes and coins in my glory-box, and I found bundles of pound notes, tied together with colourful strands of wool, at the bottom of Serendipity Wilson's box. Not knowing what else to do with it, I took the money. As I put the bundles with the rest of my things, I noticed, on top of my notebooks and papers, as if someone had that minute placed it there, the letter John Frazer had handed me in the garden, still unopened. I hurriedly put the money away, closed the lid, and locked it. But I couldn't take my eyes from my glory-box.

The unopened letter was calling to me. Really calling.

I could hear it; a muffled voice coming from inside the box. I stared harder, eyes wide, ears straining to hear. There it was again. The voice, although small and smothered, was unmistakably that of Serendipity Wilson. I thought I might be losing my marbles. I wouldn't have to wait to be old to be put in a home, because lunacy was obviously looming. I turned away. The voice came again. Louder this time.

*Read the letter, Mouse*, it said. *Please.*

This time I was sure it was Serendipity Wilson's voice. I stepped backwards in fright, tripped, and fell onto my mattress. I lay where I fell for some time. I wanted to hear the voice again. Now all I heard was the distant sound of the animals in their enclosure on the other side of the encampment, and the wind, winding its way around the wigwam. After a while, when my heart had stopped its thumping and my breathing was steady, I approached my glory-box. Key held out before me – pointing it like a weapon – and moving slowly, I unlocked and lifted the lid, took out the envelope, and with trembling hands, opened it.

*My darling,*
*I know there's no chance for you to love me. Those days are*
*behind us, and I accept, with a heavy heart, your rejection.*
*It was a wonder you ever came to me in the first place, but*
*how glad I am you did. Although heavy with grieving for the*
*love we've lost, my heart sings when I think of the miracle*
*we've made. I'm leaving Fausto's rat hole. I can't bear to be*
*with Annabel and the boys, and at the same time watch you*

*grow heavy with our child. But never fear, my love, I have
made provision for us.*

*Some time ago, imagining how one day I would take you
away from that pit of hell, I charged my sister to find us a
home in your dreamland (you see, I never forget, you're
always in my thoughts). She's done just that. The house is
big enough to accommodate three separate families. My sister
and her husband are occupying the top residence, you and our
child can live together in peace, in your own part of the house.
It will be a lovely home (my sister has furnished all three
residences — she has impeccable taste), and I will never be far
away, my own rooms being in the basement of the building.
I won't ask for your love. Your life can be your own. But we
will bring our child up together, in a good home. If — and
I must stress this is a last resort — the only way you'll consent
to leave that foul place is to bring your funny little friend with
you, then do so. It's not what I envisaged, but then, none of
this is. It's so much more than I ever imagined. A child! In
losing your love I have gained the most precious gift. I'm
eternally grateful to you. Don't spend too much time thinking
about things. Just send word soon. I'll get money to you for
the journey. You'll be well looked after. Everything's in hand.
Have no fear. The future is happening.*

*J. Frazer*

There was another, smaller piece of paper in the envelope,
folded in two. It was a picture, torn from a book, depicting

a young woman in Victorian dress. Her skirts had been short-ened, and beneath them, instead of the usual two legs, there were four. Two little ones (in the middle, as if coming out of her heavenly slot) and two normal ones, all done up in stock-ings and neatly laced boots. Across the page, scrawled over the picture, and in a (now) recognizable hand, were the words:

*Cpl and Mrs James Macveigh,*
*2863 West 20th Street, Coney Island,*
*Brooklyn, New York,*
*USA*

Time passed slowly. Every day I'd take out John Frazer's unde-livered invitation, and read it, over and over, as if trying to make up for the fact Serendipity Wilson never did. I looked at the picture on the torn-out page, read the address, then put it all back in my glory-box. These, along with my shin-ing pendant – that I never took from around my neck – were now my most precious things. I spent a lot of time in the wig-wam, sitting in front of my closed box, listening for Serendipity Wilson's voice. I wanted so much for her to visit me. I prayed for it. But she wasn't the type to respond to invocations.

Fausto's circus was all I'd ever known. Things were so miserably stagnant in that small world. It always had been so, I suppose. But I was different now. My protracted child-hood vanished when Serendipity Wilson fell, as if with that single action I suddenly caught up with myself. Quite simply, I became more measured, less childlike. Gradually, the feral girl disappeared, leaving behind only her shadow, which followed me.

My talent was going to waste, not to mention my life. I'd waited too long already, caught in the snare of laziness, fear of action. What might I be beyond the confines of the circus, without Gen or Fausto or any of it? And as the days, months and years fell away, even though I tried not to hear, one thing kept chipping away at me, like a hammer on stone: I had made a promise.

I wrote a short letter to Fausto, one to Gen and a longer, carefully thought-out one to Manu. I didn't tell Fausto where I was planning to go, merely stating that my time at the circus had come to an end. Fausto Flavio showed no reaction to his letter. He paid me my dues, eventually, but would give me nothing in advance. Gen was kind, though. When I got up the courage to ask, she gave me papers she'd been keeping, the ones that registered my birth, and without telling her darling Fausto, agreed to help me. Really, she arranged everything.

Gen took me into the town. I had all my hair cut off, as short as the cutting lady would dare. I thought there was something subversive about being a woman with cropped hair, ridding myself of some of the trappings of so-called feminine beauty. And that, I decided, was what I wanted to be. Or it was what I wanted the world to believe me to be. In any case, it felt liberating to be shot of the stuff. Then we went to a post office. I gave Gen the money, and she paid my passport fee to a ratty-faced man behind the counter, speaking sternly to him, making sure everything was in order. She stuck me in a booth, closed a small grey cloth behind me, and told me to look at a square of light. The whole booth flashed, and I screamed and thought I might be blinded. Afterwards we had to wait for a strip of photographs to be spat out of a slit in the side of the booth. I looked shocked in the photographs. They made me think of the pictures of freaks in Gen's book.

Later, Gen took me back to the post office. We picked up my new passport. This time the man behind the counter wore spectacles which hung on a golden chain around his neck. He handed me the passport and smiled, showing tiny sharp teeth, pointed at the ends. I wondered if he might also have claws. The slim book felt warm in my hand. It was mine; an object made just for me. I turned away from the counter and sniffed back sobs. Gen hugged me and mumbled something about it being for the best and wiped a tear from her own cheek. Then we went to a travel agent's shop. The lights were too bright and made me squint. Gen did all the talking as I watched a television set. It showed a film of an aeroplane. All the passengers wore smart, colourful clothes and they smiled all the time. They looked like dolls.

Manu was sitting next to me in the llama pen when I handed him his letter. He gestured for me to read it to him as he sighed, took hold of my hand, stroked my head. It wasn't a long letter. In it I addressed him as Father – after all, I had no other. I'd tried to suppress my feelings since discovering I was the result of the worst form of violation and violence, tried to pretend it was of no consequence to me now, only to the person upon whom it was rendered. But when I read the word *father*, heard my own voice say it aloud, the dam burst. I sobbed. My body shook with misery, shame and every possible sadness. Manu held me to him, rocked me back and forth. He took my face in both his hands, his dark, beautiful eyes staring into mine, kissed me on the forehead. Then, he dug in his pocket for the pencil and pad kept there, scratched something quickly, tore the leaf from its bindings and handed it to me. I read the words in silence and have kept them with me every day since.

*Ma pauvre fille, c'était pas de ta faute.*

The rest of the letter simply explained I'd made mistakes and was sorry, that leaving would give me a chance to make things right. It said I should've left sooner but grieving for Marina and for Serendipity Wilson had prevented me doing so. I thanked Manu for taking care of my mother. His love, I said, in the end, was all she'd lived for, and one day I hoped myself to find such a person as he had been to her. *See, I wrote, what a powerful and positive influence you've had on me, when all is said and done.* I thanked him, then, for playing the part of my father, an impossible role under the circumstances. I saw that now, I said. Still, I was grateful.

We spent the afternoon cleaning the animals together, and then I watched as he slowly shuffled back to the caravan. A few weeks later I said my last goodbye to Manu, and with my passport, aeroplane ticket, maps and instructions, left the encampment, the circus, and England, forever.

# 20

# Tales Told by Serendipity Wilson #4
## *Fairy Cakes*

*Trust is a precious thing, Mouse. We earn it through our actions, through showing we are stable in friendship, reliable, honourable and true. Of course, we should never trust the fairies — that would be folly, no matter what they promise. The problem, really, is with people. They can be difficult to fathom.*

*Sometimes we might see someone and feel them an instant friend. This might be the case. And if the feeling is strong — goodness knows I wear my heart pinned to my chest for all to see — who would resist the pull of human affection? Maybe I'm not a good example. Perhaps you should heed the story of the scatter-headed servant girl.*

*Did you notice the tree by the railway tracks, Mouse, with its bushy leaves and blossoms like tiny white stars? Beware, for that is a Tramman Tree.*

*It has long been known, by all Manxmen and Manxwomen, that fairies inhabit the Tramman Tree. And tree-dwelling fairies are a very particular bunch. For these are the little people from the Otherworld, a place still ruled to this very day by the spirit of Manannán mac Lir. Each tree-dweller holds the soul of a long-dead ancestor within its form. In modern times people know to take heed,* to keep away from the Tramman Tree and the supernatural things hiding in its branches. But back in the old days, people were not so cautious of fairy ways.

Newly married couples would often plant a Tramman Tree in their garden and when the fairy ancestors came to make their home there, as a reward for such a lovely place to live, they would offer fairy protection to the planters of the tree. It was a tricksy business all the same, as it has never been advisable to put your trust in fairy magic, especially in a form so imbued with the spirits of the dead. Take heed, for this is as true today as it was then.

There once was a house in Glen Rushen, and although only a simple house, it was larger than most in the area, and with a fine garden out back. Against the far wall of the garden stood a Tramman Tree. The family who lived in the house planted it when their children were small and the tree was nothing but a twig. They fed the sapling with scrapings of black tea, tended its leaves and branches, and watched it grow into a fine, healthy specimen. The family believed the fairy ancestors would surely come to such a beauteous tree to live happily and protect them from any evil that might pass their way. And so they did. For many years the family lived in watchful harmony with the fairies. No harm came to the family and the little people had a fine home in their tree.

One day, when the Tramman Tree was fully grown, a beggarman was passing by. He saw the large house, the spacious garden with its stony path, and thought it a fine place to accommodate a stranger for the night, for the sun was nearly to bed and he must find lodgings, and maybe a bite to eat, before darkness covered the island.

The beggarman knocked politely on the door. The family were all *away and would not be back until morning, so it was a servant girl who answered. She was a kindly soul, although known in the area to be a scatter-headed thing. She took pity on the stranger, said there was plenty of room to sleep on the kitchen floor, and that indeed she would be most pleased of the company, and invited the beggarman in.*

*Earlier that morning, before leaving, the family had given the servant girl her orders. There was not much to be done, just the usual chores. But she must not forget to fill the large jug to the brim with water and leave it out on the table before going to bed. They impressed upon her how important this was, and that it would be at her own peril if she were to forget. The servant girl did not understand the family's insistence, but promised that, no matter what, she would not forget.*

*Unbeknown to the servant girl, who after all was only the hired help and had no need to know the affairs of the family, the fairies had, a few days before, requested the use of the kitchen that evening. This was not a strange thing. The little people often spoke to the family and took favours in return for their continuing protection. This time the fairies had asked for a jug of water, the biggest the family owned, to be placed on the table ready for their use. The family, knowing better than to ask questions and having no real cause to do so, readily agreed.*

*As the evening grew late, in the kitchen the scatter-headed servant girl and the beggarman spent a happy time together. They told each other tales of adventure and woe, ate soup and salty bread, drank water freshly pulled from the well that afternoon, and having such a thirst after their meal, drank the large jug dry. After a while, when the sun finally disappeared, and the kitchen was in darkness, the* servant girl showed the stranger to a quilt laid out on the floor behind the kitchen door, where he could take his rest. When she had seen him safely settled in she went off to sleep in her usual place, by the fire-hearth.

Sometime after midnight, when the kitchen was still, and the only sound was the ticking of the clock, the fairies came. They went straight to the kitchen to start their baking, for it was that purpose alone which brought the little people to the house that night. But when they looked on the table, they found no jug, and no water.

What will we use to bind the flour to make our cakes? they asked each other.

How can we bake cakes without water?

If there was a cow to milk, then that would do.

But the family has no cow.

It's surely the fault of that scatter-headed servant girl.

We'll teach her a lesson.

Yes. Let's show her the error of her scatter-headed ways.

They all agreed. So, taking off their fairy shoes, the little people crept across the floor to the hearth, and silently gathered around the sleeping servant girl. Then without a single word, as if reading each other's minds, one of the little fellas took a long, sharp fairy-pin from his fairy-hat, stuck it into the servant girl's big toe, and, through the puncture, after whispering some magic fairy words, drew a fountain of thick, red blood. Following on, each little fella took his own hat pin, stuck it into her toes or feet, said their magic and watched the blood flow. The girl was a virgin, so the blood was extra pure and good.

This is better than we thought, said the fairies, without using words — for fairies are able to communicate in ways humans are unable to fathom — and they greedily watched the blood flow in smooth, unctuous torrents.

Taking the largest jug from the kitchen, some of the little people began to fill it up with blood, while the others watched, licking their lips and rubbing their bellies.

Fill it right up to the brim! they said.

When it was finally full, the fairies stopped the stream of blood with their magic, left the sleeping servant girl alone, and with titters and whispers of, Can you believe it, not yet been had by a man! they got on with the business of baking.

Meanwhile, the beggarman, who we must not forget, for he is more than just a passing stranger in our story, was lying on his quilt behind the door. He often had trouble sleeping due to rheumatics and this night was no exception. In his sleeplessness the beggarman watched — with one eye open — as the fairies filled their jug. He now began witnessing such an event, as the fairies went about baking their terrible cakes. And what a thing he saw.

The cakes were a deep, deep red. They smelled sickly sweet and were plentiful indeed. Although the beggarman knew he would never be tempted by such a horror as blood-cakes, he could not help but lick his lips and savour the smell of such sweet confectioneries. It had been many years since he'd had the chance to taste such virgin sweetness.

After the cakes had been left to cool for a while on the kitchen table, the fairies began carousing. They drank their special fairy-wine, ate their blood-cakes and had a fine old time. Much laughter was heard by the beggarman as he lay unnoticed, as still as death and quieter than the grave, under his borrowed quilt.

*The fairies had their fill. There was belching and farting, every sort of odious noise and smell made by their full fairy bellies. The little people sprawled around the kitchen, moaning and holding their fat, full stomachs, so stuffed they could barely move. But all was not well in the kitchen. There was still a chunk of fairy cake left. The fairies looked at it, uneaten on the table. They rubbed their rounded tummies and thought of sleep. Not one could eat a morsel more.*

*It would not do for fairy blood-cake to be left unattended, and in a place where anyone could stumble across it. The fairies knew that, if not eaten, this chunk of cake must be hidden away. For fairy cake, as you may well know, cannot be destroyed. They broke the chunk into three pieces, stashed each piece high in the rafters of the roof, then, with shuffling feet and satisfied smiles, the fairies left the house.*

*The next morning when the family returned they found a beggarman lying next to the still sleeping servant girl. On being asked what on earth was going on, the beggarman explained that he had heard the girl cry out, and wanting to assist, he had just that minute come to her, but try as he might he could not rouse the girl. She was completely insensible, he told them, and had been making the most terrible noises.*

*How she moans, he said. And lets out such groans of deep, torturous pain.*

*Then, the beggarman touched the girl's face and she cried out, and indeed they were dreadful cries. The beggarman, sitting up and adjusting himself, recounted what he had seen the night before, and the family shook their heads.*

*That scatter-headed girl, they said.*

*The beggarman pointed to where the pieces of blood-cake had* been hidden, and climbing the rafters, the family found the last three ghastly pieces of the bright-red cake.

The morsels, still smelling sickly sweet, were brought to the sleeping girl. The mother of the family, being the only woman, forced the servant girl's dry mouth open. She pushed the pieces of hideous blood-cake in, closed the lips tight shut, then smothered the girl's face with her hands so the poor thing could not spit out the horrible mess. After much thrashing about, the girl swallowed, hard. Within moments, the scatter-headed servant girl was revived. Her eyes were bright, and she remembered nothing of her ordeal.

The beggarman went away and was never seen in Glen Rushen again. The family, having been so touched by the awful incident of the blood-cakes, moved to another place, leaving the Tramman Tree and the fairies behind.

And the scatter-headed servant girl? She became a wise woman. After the family moved away she gave birth to a child. Of course, this was a great surprise to her as she had never known a man. She took the child to be a gift from the fairies, payment for the use of her blood, and brought the little girl up within sight of the Tramman Tree, so the child would know where to go if ever she was in need of fairy help.

The scattered-headed servant girl was a scatter-head no more. She became known throughout Glen Rushen for her wonderful memory and never forgot anything anyone ever told her. Like all of us, she had her troubles and she had her fortunes, but for the rest of her days she always kept a full pitcher of water on her table after dark, and even though she was a kindly soul, she never opened her door to a stranger again.

*Why should I tell you such a tale as this, Mouse? Do I think a kind word from a stranger may do you more harm than good? Of course not! You are already far too reticent and mouse-like when it comes to people. I want you to be bold, comfortable with yourself around others. Dare I say, I even advocate a certain amount of reck-lessness on your part? Oh yes, Mouse. Be reckless, do. But there's room for caution, that's all. Be hospitable, be kind, be impulsive, but don't be a scatter-head. Never be off your guard!*

# 21

# New Worlds and the Power of Wings

There are crowds of people around me.

Alone, or in small cloistered groups, the people walk with purpose. They remind me of clockwork toys, wound up and set on their way; eyes fixed, seeing nothing. I am one of them. Isolated; invisible; unthinking; moving forwards.

Lost, I continue pushing my bags, up and down shiny airport concourses and concrete walkways in a rattling metal trolley. Up and down I go, round and on, not knowing where I am or where I'm going. An eternity passes, and I wonder if I'll ever leave this place. Maybe this will be my life from now on: looking through windows at aeroplanes taking off and landing; taking moving electric staircases to different levels, even though I'm scared I'll be toppled over and eaten up by the crunching apparatus. I take them anyway, because I can. Because everyone does. There's a rhythm to my plodding and trudging. *Ever onwards*, it says. *Ever onwards* in this strange new world that has no llamas and no leopards, no hand-dug privies, no wigwams, and no big tops.

I follow signs this way and that, and even pluck up courage to ask passers-by if they think I might be going the right
way. Eventually I find myself in a queue, talking to a blonde
woman in a striped silk scarf and fancy little hat that manages to balance, just so, on her perfect head. She looks like a
dancing girl, only neater. Nicer.

When the blonde woman smiles, I think I hear applause.
It's her turn in the ring now. As I hand her my tickets and
papers there's a sparkle in her eye: the performance begins.
She takes a pen, makes long sweeping marks on the papers,
flicks over pages, does it again. She pulls strips of paper from
a roll, ties them around my bags with lengths of string from
a box by her hand, always smiling. She is perfectly rehearsed;
her timing is impeccable. She pushes my ticket and travel
documents – in a pouch now, marked with golden letters –
back over to me.

*I'm never coming back*, I say.

The performance is coming to its end. She laughs, showing pearls for teeth. Putting my bags on a moving platform
beside her, watching them roll into an opening behind, she
sighs, then turns back to me.

*Everything but the kitchen sink*, smiles the girl. Then, raising
a neatly gloved finger, she looks over my shoulder, and calls
*next* to the person behind me.

My time is done. Her performance was a triumph. I shuffle away, leaving a line of eagerly waiting faces, panting,
searching for eye contact, for some form of recognition from
the blonde artiste who will, for a few minutes only, give

them her full attention. I am one of the hordes now. She is the star of the show, and how we beg for her regard.

When it's time to board the plane, I am surprised. It doesn't look like the one on the colour television set in the travel agent's shop, with its spiral staircase inside, and a lounge, and ladies in silk scarves and hats and high heels. This one seems very modest in comparison. At least from the outside. And mucky. It's big. A monster.

Following a winding line, mechanically we make our way down some tiled steps and out onto the concrete, to stand, lost, beneath the enormous wings of the aeroplane. Before long, it's my turn to put my feet on the movable staircase (it has wheels), and to walk through the door into the plane. The door looks small for such a beast. Still, it's a gaping mouth waiting to swallow us up. I stop for a moment and think that this will be the last time I'll ever touch English ground. I look around. Bright modern buildings painted white, with all their glass and windows sparkling in the dying sun, twinkle at me. I could be in a film or one of Big Gen's magazines. There are aeroplanes waiting, and baggage trains darting this way and that. The concrete ground stretches out forever, until it shimmers on the horizon. There's no poignant feeling of leaving my life behind. The things around me are unrecognizable. They have nothing to do with me, with anything that has gone before. And without even realizing it, I see I've already left.

A man in a suit is standing behind me with his son, who is complaining and whining. The child tries to push past me, but the man grabs the boy's arm and pulls him back. The boy squeals. I look over my shoulder and the child sticks out his tongue. I smile and move on.

My seat is in the middle of the aeroplane. I'm between two older men. When the plane takes off, it rattles and shudders. I sit as still as possible, enjoying the feel of it; the tilt of the machine as it takes us up into the sky. Girls in knee-high boots, sheer nylons, and short, starched blue dresses with high collars, dole out food and drinks. I refuse both and keep my eyes on the seat in front, letting myself feel each shake and judder of my flying pod. Eventually a sea of cigarette smoke fills the cabin. My eyes sting, so I close them. I think something is happening to my body. I can hear the gentle beat of my heart and feel the warm blood pumping into every part of me. My skin tingles and I think of myself as sand, moving and reforming into something more solid than before, more real. I listen to the sound of the engine, and soon it lulls me into a deep, dreamless sleep.

I wake up as the plane lands. I've never felt so rested, so well. I step onto the concrete, feel the hot ground through the soles of my Dunlops, and smile into the day. Modern buildings glint, and tow-tractors spin around the waiting aeroplanes. For a moment, I wonder if we haven't moved at all, and this whole thing has been a joke. In truth, I could be anywhere. Nevertheless, I feel different now. A girl in knee-high boots and a short, starched blue dress hands me a bag with a wet facecloth in it.

*Welcome to New York*, she says.

# 22

# New York: A Palace of Concrete and Light

Walking through Manhattan on my first full day in New York City, I decide it's neither bigger, nor dirtier than I expected. Everything is both utterly familiar and completely alien. I have come through the mirror, and Alice-like, find myself shrunken. Taxis are yellow, hairy-armed policemen direct traffic in rolled-up shirtsleeves and stiff hexagonal caps. Buildings are impossibly high; they look like fairy-tale towers, crystal behemoths, staring down at me. If I look up to find their summits, the world spins under my feet, and I feel giddy. I've seen large, old buildings before, but nothing as tall and elegant as these. I think of the big top, how I believed being up on my wire, the top of my head brushing its canvas roof, was the nearest thing to touching the stars. These buildings reach so far into the clouds, I can't even see their tops.

This is my rebirth. The city is my new mother.

I'm on the edge of everything. I put my hands on the low wall in front of me and lean over. It's a hot day and the bricks are warm and welcoming. I look out over the water stretching before me. It's calm. Golden shafts of light seem to glint and shoot off its surface, and I wonder if the water might be liquid gold. There are boats gliding across the glinting water, ferrying passengers over to the island in the distance, where I can see the Statue of Liberty holding up her torch. She looks tiny from where I stand, and she's green, which surprises me.

I turn and look across the wide, tree-lined avenue at the forest of buildings clustering together, forming this part of Manhattan. The buildings in front of me are all different, made from glass and metal, or brick and stone, and differing heights. They look like a crowd of giants, peeping around and over each other, curiously looking at me. They're red, or grey, or silver, or brown. Some have points and spikes, some are flat at the top. I walk across the avenue, over one crossing, then another, and like a child in a nursery rhyme, I enter the enchanted streets.

There's the constant sound of traffic. Even at this time of the morning, sirens and car horns keen in the near distance. Every face I see looks the same: their features vague, incomplete; blanked out by the city's wails and cries. They seem to stride through the streets like they know where they are and what they're doing (I wish I was in on the secret). I wonder what it's like to be one of them, understanding this city, knowing my place in it.

The smell of the place is vaguely familiar, a mix of smoked meat, onions, and warm sugar emanating from the many street hot-dog sellers. Even when you cannot see them, you can smell their trade, wrapping the city in a delicate film of filthy delight. I see them, the food hawkers, setting up shop as I walk through the Manhattan streets, on this, the first morning of forever. They turn knobs, press buttons on the sides of metal boxes. One has erected a miniature tent-top of yellow and red stripes over his box.

*Look! All the fun of a big top, in the shape of cheap comestibles.*

I stop, clamp my hands tight to my ears. Serendipity Wilson's voice is at my shoulder. I turn quickly, but she's nowhere to be seen. I search the faces of passers-by, reminding myself to look hard at each in turn, hoping to see a trace of the one I've come to find. If I close my eyes, even for a minute, the bald pate and green eyes of Serendipity Wilson will glare at me, accusing me of forgetting why I'm here. So I keep them wide, try not to blink, and scrutinize the hordes. Still, I can't stop her voice from nattering at me.

*What's wrong, Mouse? Cat got your tongue?*

I stand and watch as the man sets up his stall. A board leans against his metal box, showing the stars of today's show; bread buns filled with long brown sausages, smothered in greasy onions and bright, gloopy mustard. A smaller picture shows something called a Pretzel. It's also brown. The seller puts on a paper hat in the style of an American soldier, and a long white apron, only slightly stained.

*Sergeant Sausage! The standard bearer for processed meat.*

Even though I don't want to give her the satisfaction of knowing I can hear her, I can't help giggling. I turn to the vendor and have a deep desire to salute. But I resist and leave my hands in place over my ears.

*Shush, be still*, I whisper, as I suppress another giggle.

Steam rises from metal as the food slowly warms. The smell induces an initial, rather violent urge to retch, but this is soon followed by hunger, which I know can never be sated. I'm a gaping hole. The place inside me where a frightened little girl cowered, or where she'd preen because she was the star, has been voided by my journey here. It's empty now, bottomless. I could eat a million of this man's nauseating hot dogs and still need more.

The thought occurs that I'm not in New York at all, and that I might be dreaming. But cells and molecules tingle. My nerve endings feel exposed. My body is as light as air. I wish I was on my wire. How perfect it would be. Instead, I start to run. Steam rises through iron grids in the street as my feet spring off concrete and macadam. The elastic ground seems to bend to meet each footfall, and again I recall the sensation of galvanized steel rope beneath my feet.

Trying to focus, I attempt to picture the inside of my head as I bolt across roads. It's chock-full of cobwebs that tremble like strings on a violin. The notes ring with Serendipity Wilson's voice, which, because I'm running, is being blown away by the moving, gushing air. Although it somehow makes me feel guilty, I run faster. Daring myself, at last, to take my hands from my ears, I rush through the city din until I'm out of breath. Laughing now, thinking the voice gone, and myself alone, I come to a halt.

I buy some postcards. They're gaudy things depicting sights I haven't seen yet. I choose a bright picture of the

Empire State Building, and write across the back: I AM HERE. I AM FREE. I place it with the others in my knitted shoulder bag. The postcard will not be addressed. There's no one to send it to, no one to read it with envy, to wish they were here. It's a keepsake.

Marina and Manu do not exist in this place. Maybe they never did. They feel made up, like characters in a book; once read, easily forgotten. All the circus people are gone forever. I never have to think about them again.

*Not all, Mouse.*

I flinch.

On the other side of a road, busy with traffic, I finally catch a glimpse of her. She's leaning against a tall building, staring at me, smiling. I look away, close my eyes, then turn back and look again. There's no one there. A trick of the light? My imagination running riot? I could swear I saw her eyes, as green as they ever were, looking at me from across the street. And her voice is still here, not blown away like spiders' webs, but lurking around corners, waiting for me to fulfil my promise. My chest tightens. But there's a strange comfort in the pain, in knowing she's never far away.

*No. Not all*, I say, speaking in a loud, clear voice, so she might hear me over the city noise. A young couple stare at me as they pass.

I plod on.

My body is transforming. Muscle tone has started to twitch through lack of use. I rub my thighs, my shoulders, my arms. Soon I'll be changed into something else: a grounded thing. I think of Marina, grasping for the bottle, screaming and desperate. And for a second, I close my eyes, and sigh.

It's daylight as I copy down these words from the back of this crumpled map, this handful of old postcards. They leave me hazy and breathless. Was I still so unformed? I feel the excitement of that first day again. I'm smiling as I write. My heartbeat quickens with the exhilaration of it all, so does my typing. Sunlight hits my face, and I stop.

The sun has fingers today. Streaks of sunlight reach in through my window, stroke my neck with their warmth. If I stop writing, lose focus, they will lull me into waking dreams. *Regard, ma puce, les doigts du dieu.* I wonder, just for a moment, where Manu might be now. I've no idea what happened to him, or any of them, after I left. Surely Fausto and Gen are long gone? And the circus? Is Manu still feeding the animals? Or is he here, sending rays of sunlight into my room? Whatever might've befallen him, somehow I know he thinks of me as I think of him, with a melancholy only true fondness can inspire. At least, that's what I tell myself. It helps.

Specks of dust float through the light, taking me back to another dusty place. I remove my fingers from the keys, sit back and enjoy a moment of stillness. It's tempting to let myself fall under the spell of warmth and light. But my thoughts linger in the place of memory. My machine calls me back. I rest my hands on its cold casing, and before I know it, I am typing again.

★

The lady behind the hotel reception desk hands me a map. Her eyes are colourless and grey, a couple of joyless, glassy orbs with no depth. She is middle-aged, wide around the middle, and wearing a woollen suit far too heavy for a warm July morning. Drops of sweat cling to the downy whiskers on her over-powdered upper lip. Her hair, chemically hewn to resemble straw, is piled high and held with brassy pins in a solid, lacquered mass. She swats at a bluebottle with her right hand and fans herself with the map before handing it to me with her left. The bluebottle circles the mountain of her hair, lands on its surface, crawls around its rocky out-crops, and rubs its legs together.

There's a mirror on the wall behind the reception desk. It's held in place by a short chain (tarnished) and attached by a nail that casts a brown stain on the wall around it. I stare blankly at the woman. She continues to talk at me, to look at me with her dead eyes. I blink several times to avoid looking at my own reflection behind her. There I am. Marina's heavy-lidded eyes, my newly cropped hair, dyed firebrand red. I look fresh, young – but not a youth – and interesting. And I'm here, in this place, far away. I touch my face; my reflection moves with me. It's real. The back of the woman's over-large head also reflects back at me. It draws my attention again to the bluebottle, which is now quickly crawling its way up her solidified hair. I take the map, smile – *be nice, Mouse* – and ask how to get to Coney Island.

*You don't wanna go down there, honey,* says the woman. *You wanna see the Empire State Building, the Chrysler Building. Don't* go outside of Manhattan, understand. *Brooklyn's a cesspit. And don't take the subway. A young woman alone could get into a lot of trouble. Coney Island's no place for tourists, not these days. It's full of Blacks and Jews.*

I stare at the woman for longer than is comfortable, until eventually I say, *There's a fly in your hair*, and flick the folded map at the woman's head, narrowly missing her ski-slope nose. She gives a surprised yelp as I turn quickly and leave.

I walk for hours, but time seems to be standing still. From the Upper East Side I find my way to Central Park, linger in the sunshine, listen to conversations, scribble on the back of my map and on postcards. For a while I watch a group of young girls (identical in denim shorts) practise a dance, but they make me think of Stella, so I walk away. There are children in the park, holding hands with mothers, playing together in groups while the adults chatter on. I think of Bunny, her big moon head, her high-pitched squeak, but shake the images from my thoughts. I know better than to think I can conjure her up with mind-pictures. I tried it hundreds of times back at the encampment, believing in my silly, childish daydreams. I will no longer let myself fall into such traps. In any case, Bunny will be older now, she might look quite different.

Graffiti scars benches and walls in great bursts of colour, giving life to dead things. There are people on roller-skates. I cannot decide whether I'm comfortable in Central Park. There's a mixture of serenity and danger. So I make my way out and curse the stupid receptionist for planting her seeds of suspicion and fear. *Bitch*.

With the day passing I find myself on Park Avenue and, finally, I look at my map. I walk a long time to get to where I need to be. Unsure of my map-reading skills, I find my voice at Union Square, stopping to ask several people the same question to be sure that I'm boarding the correct train, travelling in the right direction. I'm more nervous than I care to admit. I am a tourist – *Coney Island's no place for tourists* – and horribly earthbound. I wish again that I was on my wire, walking slowly above Manhattan, my bare toes feeling for the grooves in the metal. I'd dance over the East River if I could, stop short at the ocean (which I'll never cross again), and at my destination, like one of Jacob's angels, I'd descend. That's the way to enter a new place, not on some rattling, graffiti-covered subway train that radiates a perfume of urine.

Coney Island has been in my consciousness ever since I can remember. Big Gen's picture book, *Coney Folk*, dazzled me as a child with its stories of human curios. How Gen would sigh as she looked dreamily at its pages; at images of Jolly Irene, Coney Island's Favourite Fat Lady. A proclamation our Gen never tired of reminding us was entirely unsubstantiated.

Gen couldn't help but admire Irene's silhouette – indeed her vast forty-nine stones was most impressive. But frankly, the girl got lucky. Jolly Irene, the book informed us, had been a perfectly normal-sized, slim young lady before falling pregnant. Then, what with all those hormones whizzing around her body, the lucky thing couldn't stop piling on the fat.

The book told us that when she died, Jolly Irene's coffin was so big, and so heavy, it couldn't be carried into the church. That wasn't a problem for the Coney Folk. The ceremony was performed outside, the churchyard full to bursting with all her Coney Island pals, standing around the hearse, applauding and cheering one last time for their friend's final triumph. Although impressed by this, Gen believed Jolly Irene to be *a bit of a fake*, having come by her voluptuousness through good fortune rather than hard work.

Gen preferred the other fat lady in her book: Baby Doll, the Pulchritude Queen of the Avoirdupois (something she'd called herself, *back in the day*). Baby Doll was of similar size and shape to our Gen. *She's so much more natural*, Gen would say. And Serendipity Wilson would wink at me from across the wigwam and try to suppress her giggles.

The book was our favourite thing to read. It had every kind of freak you could hope to imagine. Like Lady Olga, who was something of a film star. She wore a full evening gown, a spray of summer flowers in her hair, and had a silky beard on her chin. There was Monkey Girl, Spider Boy, the Armless Wonder, and Serendipity Wilson's favourite, Mrs Myrtle Corbin, otherwise known as the Four-Legged Girl Prodigy.

Myrtle Corbin was a dipygus, which, the book told us, meant her bottom half was completely duplicated. She had two pelvises, two vaginas, two wombs and four legs. Two of her legs, the outside ones, looked normal enough, other than one was finished off with a club foot. Then there were the smaller, inside legs. Serendipity Wilson liked her because she was said to be an intelligent and cultured young woman who could hold her own at the dinner table, and use her wit and intellect to charm audiences, as much as her overburdened lower quarters.

Myrtle married when she was nineteen. Her husband was a doctor, and well off. It was obviously a match of true love. Soon after her marriage, Myrtle started experiencing strange pains in her left side. She went to her family doctor and was surprised to discover she was pregnant. Myrtle was amazed, not by the fact of her condition but more that it should be in her left side. Her doctor later wrote that, judging by her shock, the girl's preferred vagina for intercourse was obviously her right. She went on to have five children, using both her wombs, left and right.

The freaks I liked were the self-mades. These were people born without deformity, or anomalies. They'd chosen freakdom, rather than work for peanuts in some dead-end café or other job. I liked the artistry of the contortionists, the snake charmers and escapologists. It takes hard work to become that sort of freak. I've always admired people who work hard. I was particularly impressed with a curious character called Mortado, the human fountain.

Mortado was from Germany. Having no artistic skills and being of two legs, two arms and average build, there wasn't much he could offer the Coney Island sideshows. Until he hit upon a bright idea. He asked a local surgeon to insert thin rubber pipes into his skin. These pipes could be pumped full of water which would spurt out, gloriously (he hoped), through incisions in his fingertips, turning him into a living fountain. The cuts where the pipes came out never healed (due to being blasted with water three or four times a day). He must've lived in ceaseless agony.

My personal favourite Coney Island freak was Princess Maria, otherwise known as the Girl of a Thousand Eyes. Maria was quite the young beauty when she came to Coney Island in her adolescence. Whether she was bewitched by the pull of the show, by the promise of stardom, or simply by the idea of making herself into something different from all the other pretty girls – so abundant on the streets of New York – into becoming something beguilingly monstrous, we cannot know. The book only presented us with a muddy photograph and a few lines describing her extraordinary beauty. It also informed us that by the time Princess Maria was twenty, she'd covered her entire body – including face, buttocks, palms of her hands, eyelids, and the bottoms of her feet – with tattooed pictures of eyes, complete with lashes.

Serendipity Wilson liked to be in control of the book, as if she was the only one in the world with the right to look at Gen's special book, the only one with the right to be a freak. She would often slam it shut as I gazed on Maria's photograph. And I'd be left angry, with Gen blubbering and sighing next to me, assuring the air around her that she'd had her day in the sun too, when things weren't so frowned upon, and didn't she and her late hubby – poor man – cause a storm in their day? Oh, she would say, how she missed those heady days when Little Len and Big Gen were legends of the English sideshow circuit. Sadly, it didn't last long. *Can I help it if I was born too late?* And when hard times hit, Little Len ran off with a lady of his own stature and Gen was left alone, broken-hearted and unaccepted, until Fausto came along. Big Gen also liked to tell us how, soon after he left her, Little Len was crushed to death when an elephant sat on him. But I've never believed the story. Revenge is a funny thing.

We'd pore over that book. Then, at night, I'd slide under the covers, lie close to Serendipity Wilson in her bed, and listen to her stories about how, one day, she would go to Coney Island and become the star of Dreamland. I wanted to belong to that faraway place, too. To cover myself in eyes and put fountains in my hands, to walk the wire for the self-mades, the authentics, the outcasts. Now, here I am, closer than I ever believed possible. But here, on this dirty train rattling through Brooklyn, I miss the gentle movement of the wigwam, the warmth of wool, and the smell of spiced wood, of cinnamon and cedar. I'm an alien, and completely lost. People look at me with dirty thoughts plastered on their faces. I don't need to be covered in tattoos. I'm a stranger, and the biggest freak of all.

# 23

# Dreamland, or the Final Act
# of an Ageing Showgirl

Stillwell Avenue is an elevated mass of iron, steel and concrete. I step onto a seemingly deserted island platform, accompanied by a smattering of sleepy passengers. The heat is dense, almost solid. I stand for a moment, watch as my fellow end-of-the-liners trudge towards the exit, disappearing down concrete stairs to their lives beyond subways and trains.

I like the station. I like its decay. From my elevated position I can see across Coney Island. She's an ageing, monstrous showgirl with all her delights on show. I imagine I see this spirit of degeneracy, dancing on the once pristine, now broken station platforms. She was a trickster, lying in wait for day trippers and holidaymakers, picking their pockets, promising wondrous things in return for a few shiny coins. She was probably fat, like Gen.

I make my way through the empty station. Weeds grow through cracked concrete. I want to applaud their struggle. As my eyes begin to focus, I see this is a desolate place. What was I expecting? A big top at the end of the line, the welcoming smiles of jugglers, fire-eaters, bearded ladies and stilt-walkers, or men with stumps for legs doing tricks for loose change?

My footsteps are a dull smack as I head to the exit. The gates of hell would seem more inviting at this moment. Confined to the station, I am safe. No one would ever know if I snuck away. I think of my Manhattan hotel – that palace of floors covered with carpets; of hard bedsprings and soft furnishings; of heavy-curtained windows, polished surfaces and soft-pile rugs; of large silver spoons for eating eggs at breakfast; of staircases and elevators; of tiled bathrooms and stained porcelain bowls to shit in – and I wonder how people manage, with all these trappings, to ever go outside.

Graffiti and dirt decorate every surface in the station. The heat doesn't help. I stop for a moment, listen. There's a clappity-clap in the distance, delighted screams muffled under the heat of the day. There are voices below, a high-pitched buzzing which I cannot place – traffic? Perhaps a boat? – and footsteps. There are plenty of people, I hear them, feel the throb of their lives, but the station has become a labyrinth, a Brobdingnagian land, and although I know that beyond my concrete shell the streets are bustling with hordes, I see no one. I glance around, hardly daring to lift my head. The station looks deserted. But I'm not alone as I plod towards the exit sign.

She is here.

I turn quickly and see her bald head reflecting white light where once a fire burned. In truth, I'm terrified of this spectre. I thought I'd lost it on the streets of Manhattan, and again in Central Park, but it's cunning and hid in the cracks of walls and pavements. I don't trust it. I turn away, shut my eyes. *Keep going, Mouse, you've come this far*, it says. Having no one else to rely on, I nod, take in a lungful of air and make my way down the final set of steps and out onto the street.

The high-pitched buzzing gets louder. A long-haired boy is sat on the ground, his back grazing the wall of the station. He is shirtless. His legs, browned by the sun, stick out from cut-off jeans. He is leaning forwards. His hair covers his face as he draws on his leg with a vibrating metal pen. Next to him is a box of Kleenex. Every now and then he stops, takes one, and dabs it at his leg, wiping away blood, dirty with ink. He looks up.

*Not much to see.*

My face reddens. I look at the ground, shuffle my feet in an attempt to move away, but they're heavy and slow. He's older than I thought, a man rather than a boy.

*I call it doodling. Can show you some good ones, though. If you like.*

I nod. The man stands up, pats the dust off his cut-off jeans, turns, raises his arms above his head, and leans against the wall.

Across his back is a mish-mash of pictures and colour. There's a green dragon across his shoulders, with its tail wrapped around a long-haired girl; it's breathing red fire that mixes with her red hair. The girl is naked and unafraid, far prettier and more womanly than any real person. Above the dragon are a series of blue clouds with a yellow sun bursting through, and a rainbow that falls all the way to the bottom of his back, past the girl and her dragon and down under the waistband of his jeans. Playing amongst the rainbow's colours are some other figures. They look like angels. Their wings are full and feathery, as one would expect, but there is something lustful about these naked angels who proudly display their swollen, ripe breasts, and large, shining cocks that sprout from between their legs.

*Designed it myself. Like it?*

*It's very beautiful. Yes, I like it. A lot.*

*Nice accent. Where you from?*

*England.*

Blood rushes to my face. I don't raise my head but flick my eyes up to catch a glimpse of the man. He has pale blue eyes, his hair is thick with blond curls, and his smile is slight and pretty. He laughs. I ask him if the needle hurts, he laughs again. The palms of my hands are moist and slippery. I'd like to speak, but my heart is beating too quickly, and I don't know what to say. Without thinking, I wonder out loud what it might be like to have a tattoo. I am gabbling on now, about eyes. I hear my own voice, but it's like another person is speaking, and I have no control over what they're saying. I ask if he knows about the tattooed ladies of Coney Island. Do they still exist? Has he seen any? Then I ask again what it's like, not the needle this time, I can imagine what that feels like, but to be eternally marked with ink and pin, and then, without even taking a breath, I say that perhaps I could have a tattoo. And I wonder if he wouldn't mind, awfully, because I'm in no rush, so he can take his time about it.

*To be perfectly honest,* I say, *I don't know where I'm going or how I'll get there. So, if you can spare the time, I'd be grateful . . . I mean, is that all right?*

The man laughs. It makes his eyes sparkle. Other than his two sharp-looking doggy teeth that stick out when he smiles, he has small, perfectly straight and very white teeth hiding behind his lovely mouth.

*Sure, I can make you a tattoo. It's what I do. What do you want? A butterfly, a bird?*

*Oh, really, no, I . . . eyes.*

*Eyes?*

*Or, perhaps just one eye.*

*Like the evil eye? Don't you want something less obvious, more artistic?*

*Yes. I mean, yes, I do.*

*Surprise me.*

*A mermaid. I mean, a mermaid swimming in a tank with a crocodile.*

*Well,* he laughs, *that's very precise.*

*Yes.*

*Okay. A mermaid swimming with a crocodile. Sure, I guess it's appropriate, considering where we are. Where do you want it?*

I am completely confused. Minutes ago, I was in the station, avoiding the ghost of Serendipity Wilson, getting ready for the task of winding my way around more new streets, in order to find Bunny (and rid myself of the ghoul).

And now I'm sat on the street next to a blond man with a cupid smile holding a vibrating needle. I've been talking, and now the man's about to tattoo me.

I point to my thigh.

*That's a small thigh.*

I nod. The man gets very close to me. He strokes my thigh, over and over, and looks at my face.

*You sure about this?*

I nod again. He takes a bottle from a canvas bag, drenches a Kleenex with the clear liquid and rubs it on my leg. Then the high-pitched buzz; the scratching pain of the needle and the smile of the man with pale blue eyes.

When it's done, I stare at my leg. The image is speckled with blood. The skin around it, raging and pink. The man shuts off his pen, leans back and beams. I take my hands from his shoulder. There are little white half-moons on the blue clouds where I've dug in. He takes a pot of Vaseline from his bag, pops the lid and, taking a big blob, smooths it over my reddening leg. I flinch.

*Some kind of calling card?*

*Sorry?*

*You know, the mermaid?*

*Sorry?*

*Well, I just thought . . . don't you know? That's Mermaid Avenue, right there.*

I say nothing and concentrate on the burn in my leg as the ink works its way into my skin. Of course it is, I think.

*It'll smart for a few days. Don't pick at it, okay?*

*How much?*

*On the house. You can pay double next time.*

*Next time.*

*Let's say, I like to give gifts to pretty girls.*

I have no idea what to say or how to react, I stare at my leg, feel the pain, see the blood, listen to myself breathing. My face is hot, and I wonder if I'm being a scatter-head. If I am, at this precise moment, I don't care. There are no fairies here, only a tattooed picture of a mermaid and a man with sparkling eyes.

*You can buy me a drink, if you like?*

*I don't drink. Alcohol, I mean. But, I'm happy to buy you a drink.*

*You have some place to go?*

I struggle to get up. My thigh is hot and sore. The man holds out his hand, I hesitate but take it. He helps me to my feet.

*I don't much like the idea of a girl from England being alone around here. Especially one who doesn't drink. Alcohol, I mean.* He smiles.

*I'm not alone. I have her.*

I point to the tattoo, still raging on my thigh. The man laughs, holds out his hand again. This time I take it without hesitation.

*I'm Cubby.*

*Nice to meet you.*

*I definitely need a drink. Let's find some decent refreshment.*

*Yes. Of course. But . . . would you happen to know where this is?*

I dig deep into my knitted bag, pull out the folded piece of paper with the picture of Myrtle Corbin on it, and an address written in thick red letters.

*Sure. It's not far. That where you're heading?*

*I'm looking for someone. It's why I'm here. I mean, I think she might live there. I haven't seen her in a long time and she probably doesn't even know who I am, but . . . I have this address.*

*Sounds mysterious. Let me drop my stuff off first, won't take long. Plus, if you don't mind me saying, you might need to rest up before you start knocking on doors. You don't look great. Not bad, in fact you look really nice, just pale.*

*I'm tired. It's so hot here. I suppose I'm not used to it. And . . . I don't normally talk. I mean, I never talk very much. Not if I don't have to. I'm a bit of a mouse . . . I feel quite light-headed.*

Smiling, Cubby stuffs his things into the canvas bag, flings it over his shoulder and winks at me. I try to ignore the discomfort in my thigh as we walk. I can smell his sweat (sweet), mixed with ink and methylated spirit. We talk about England and about my wire. Naturally, I mention the circus, and how strange everything is to me since I left, especially the beds and the toilets, and the hot running water. I like it when he talks about his artwork, his friends, and especially his family. He makes his life sound like a storybook adventure, and I think he must have a golden tongue to match his golden hair.

I'd seen the Wonder Wheel, and all manner of cage-like contraptions, from the train coming into Stillwell Avenue. Walking at ground level now, the excitement of the fairground is tempered by piles of discarded food cartons, tin cans, bottles, odd items of clothing and even household goods. A whole sofa, its torn leather upholstery spilling springs and frothing with bright yellow sponge, sits proudly abandoned on a pavement. We do as the other passers-by do, and walk around it, as if street furniture was as normal as hot-dog vendors, or traffic lights. I think again about my childhood vision of Coney Island, with its rabbits and palm trees, and snort.

*I don't know why people need sofas anyway*, I say.

*Evidently, they don't.* Cubby smiles, and we continue on our way.

Here, in Coney Island, land of dreams, home of freaks, as I walk and chat with Cubby, I'm transformed into something normal, someone quite run-of-the-mill. Yet now I'm the tattooed lady, a real self-made. I feel completely happy and find I can't stop smiling. Cubby tells me his stories, runs through details of his life. Although I want to hear everything he says, I feel my eyes widen in their sockets as I crane my head, this way and that, trying to take in the Coney Island landscape as he speaks. Then, as if suddenly waking from a dream and remembering who I am, I turn quickly, search the shadows. She's not here. Other than Cubby, and the various pedestrians, I am, at last, completely alone.

# 24

# Our Strangest Curiosities

Cubby Couney was the last of the Coney Island freakshow exhibits. Born two months early, he arrived at Doc Martin's baby incubator show wrapped in an old felt hat, the fleshy cord from his young mother still dangling from his tiny belly. Like the many other babies before him, Cubby was so small he could nestle in the palm of the hand of the nurse who delivered him.

By the time Cubby was born, the freak shows of Coney Island had lost their appeal. It was the dog-end of the dog-end of an era. Nevertheless, the *All the World Loves a Baby* sign still hung above the door of the preemies show, which opened every day without fail, and the cash register bell rang often enough to ensure the show continued for as long as possible. Giving hope to those who had nothing but.

Dr Martin Couney had come to the show circuit back in the glory days, on an inspired whim. After his life-saving machines were turned down by every city hospital in the country, the Doc hit on the idea of showing premature babies off, for the cost of a cup of coffee, to anyone willing to pay.

The ticket price would fund the running of the incubators and the general care of the babies. Families wouldn't have to worry about finding enough money to save their little ones. The Doc would save them, taking in any child offered to him, regardless of background, or ability to pay. Who wouldn't want to see miniature human newborns, in all their diminutive perfection? The incubator show was an instant hit. Years later, Cubby was to be the show's finale, when a frightened girl, in the last months of the show, turned up and tapped on the glass of the viewing window, behind which a few impish creatures slept in transparent boxes. It was nothing Betty, the nurse, hadn't seen before. Begging her to take the minuscule baby who lay quietly folded in a soft hat cradled in the crook of her elbow, the girl kept her eyes to the floor, avoiding the sweep of the nurse's gaze. Worried for the health of the young mother, Nurse Betty tried to persuade the girl to see the Doc. But he was an old man, and the girl was terrified. So, after carefully handing over the hat, in which the wide-eyed baby wriggled like a desert lizard, off she went, promising to return once her baby was healthy and big.

And she did return.

Every day, for three weeks, the girl would quietly appear at the viewing window. Betty, not wishing to cause the girl any alarm, would pretend not to notice her. Discreetly going to Cubby's incubator, Betty would lift the lid and take the child out, so the mother could see him. He was strong for one so small, had a good appetite (which never left him), and grew quickly.

Betty couldn't help but be drawn to the blue-eyed child. The first time she saw him, squirming in the hat, she thought she felt his heartbeat deep within her own body. Later, as he grew up, she would tell him how beautiful he was, full of joy and always smiling. Even when he cried for his bottle, as soon as it arrived, he'd stop his noise, stare right into the nurse's eyes, and smile. When the young mother stopped her daily visits, Betty did everything she could to find out who and where she was, but to no avail.

*She was only a child herself. A frightened angel*, she told him, if he ever asked.

It was no surprise when the Doc announced the preemies show was to close. There'd been so much talk, especially since the hospitals had finally opened their doors (and their minds) to the incubator machines. The Doc was old. It was time he retired. There were only a few babies left in the show, and for the most part, they were doing well. Their parents came to take them home, or to one of the hospitals equipped with nice, shiny new machines.

On the last day of the show, there was one baby left. Little Cubby Couney, named after the doctor who'd saved him (and so many others), lay on his back, kicking his legs and blowing spit bubbles as he blinked his shining violet-blue eyes. He was beguiling, like the child of an angel. Betty had already made arrangements to take the baby home.

Some years earlier, Betty had married her sweetheart and things were going well for them. They had a conjuring act on the boardwalk. Bill, her husband, was good with his hands. Wearing a top hat and tails, looking every bit the Hollywood icon, he could charm the poison from a snake. He'd wanted to join the air force, but a childhood bout of polio put paid to those ideas, so he did card tricks instead. Betty, when not playing nurse at the preemies show, dressed in a long aquamarine silk gown, cut on the bias. She was quite the spectacle when, seemingly out of nowhere, she'd produce doves, bunnies and kittens from all kinds of receptacles. If you had a pocket, Betty could find some creature hiding in there. She was an expert at pulling rabbits from hats.

For the denouement of their act, Betty, with her glittering smile and soft, bouncing hair, would put the 'found' animals safely in their baskets, then lay herself down in a pine box. She'd wave to the crowd as she closed the lid behind her. The box, which rested on trestles at either end – so it looked like a long thin table – had a hole at one extremity, where Betty's smiling head would stick out, and another, smaller hole at the other, for her feet, which she'd flex and point, beautifully adorned in high-heeled pumps. When she was settled, Bill would appear with his saw, and set to work. It was a classic act, and the crowd must've loved it, as they were always willing to pay.

The conjuring act, along with Betty's work at the preemies and Bill's casual labour on the rides at the fun fairs, made the couple a decent living. Enough to put a bit away each month, enough to build their dream: a roller coaster, with an integrated house for them to live in (why build two structures when you only need one?), designed and constructed by Bill the conjurer himself.

Aunt Betty and Uncle Bill brought Cubby up in the roller-coaster house. Betty, being home with the child now, and with the preemies show gone, became known around Coney Island for her cooking. She still did the odd trick; pulling kittens from the pockets and hoods of unsuspecting children's raincoats, just for fun. The roller coaster did well, bringing the family a fine income, and on top of that, the house was so big, and Aunt Betty so prolific in her baking and cooking, that for a time, they opened it up as a hotel.

As a young boy, even though he knew every inch of the house, Cubby swore he'd sometimes find empty rooms that definitely hadn't been there before. He'd tell Aunt Betty and Uncle Bill that he'd played in a strange room with a puppy, or with another child, a stranger come for a ride on the coaster who'd lost their way, and once, even with a snake. Then, the next day, when he looked for the room again, all he'd find was a perfectly papered wall, and the steel bones of the coaster, crisscrossing above him, just as Uncle Bill had made it.

Aunt Betty didn't mind the stories, she told him that all great artists had big imaginations, and Cubby was such a creative child. She'd sit him on her knee, push the curls away from his eyes and tell him, as best she could, why he was their only child.

*Before you came along, the girls at the preemies said I wasn't normal, not wanting one of my own. But I never wanted to have a baby grow inside me — even the thought of it makes me queasy. You're the most precious boy. An angel brought you to me, see. I'm sorry if you get lonely sometimes.*

Then the boy would throw his arms around her neck and cover her in kisses until they were both giggling. As Cubby got older, the mysterious rooms stopped appearing, until he all but forgot about them, except as the product of a fertile imagination nurtured by a caring adoptive mother.

Eventually, they closed the hotel. It was hard work and the family didn't need the money. Besides, Uncle Bill wasn't as energetic as he once was, and it was all he could do to work the roller coaster. A few days after Cubby moved out, proudly setting himself up in his first two-roomed apartment, Uncle Bill had a heart attack. It was a grey and windy afternoon, so they'd kept the coaster locked up. Bill had felt fine that day, it was a rare chance for him to put his feet up. And that's exactly what he did. On the sofa, in the second-best parlour. He died a few days later.

Aunt Betty refused to let Cubby move back home, telling him that every bird must fledge, and it was his time. He was an artist, and he must spread his wings. She carried on as she always had, taking on a man to run the coaster, never once showing any sign of weakness, only the odd glimmer of sadness for the loss of her dear Bill. She was well known in the community, and well loved; the matriarch of the roller coaster, cooking for the acts on the boardwalk, looking after any strays that might come her way, human or animal. Obviously, Aunt Betty always kept an eye on her darling boy. He was the greatest prize she'd ever pulled from a hat.

# 25

# A Missing Moment of Destiny

These memories derail me.

It's still early. There's time to push on. It's easy enough to mechanically copy out words. No need to read them first – *your mind is an empty box, Mouse.* If only I could block out sound. Although I don't listen, I hear things: traffic; birdsong; aeroplanes above; voices below; the ticking of the clock on the landing. I've started to hate that particular sound; the audible plod of time moving ever forwards. To where? To what?

I no longer walk my wire, but you already know that. Let's not be coy about it. Serendipity Wilson knew what she was doing when she stepped off that wire: she wanted to teach me to suffer for my crimes, and I was always a good student.

My left hand holds a notebook – another sticky thread into our web of tales. There are more stories here yet. More creatures awaiting their release. Let's slay the monsters together. This notebook is larger than the others, and better quality. I bought it in London's Paddington Station, on my

final day in England. The cover retains the soft, smooth texture synonymous with its brand. The first time I picked it
up I had a deep desire to own it and spoil its pages with
words. I wasn't used to being out in the world of the hordes,
crowded into shops and railway stations. Still, I didn't rush
to the counter to pay. I took my time, knowing that once
I'd paid the ticket price, some of its magic would be lost.

This was my final notebook.

Cubby lives at 1520 Neptune Avenue, under a fish restaurant. The stairwell down to his basement apartment is
slippery and smells of rotting fish. His apartment has two
rooms, they are quite big, but dark. The walls of the first
room are covered in his paintings. They are colourful depic-
tions of people, all of whom are half man, half woman;
their breasts large with swirling colourful nipples, their cocks
shiny, long and stiff. Like the three figures etched into Cubby's back, they all have wings. I stare at the pictures as we
enter, feeling my eyes widen, my heart thrash. Excitement
sparks in every part of me, as if soft, fiery fingers were running over my body, lingering in sensitive places. The hairs
on my arms bristle. I rub my hands over my neck and shoulders, give myself a squeeze, and am thrilled by my own
touch. For all my interior exhilaration and clatter, I'm
strangely calm and feel a hitherto unknown sense of empow-
erment. I can do whatever I wish here, in this place, with
this man. And I like it.

The door to his apartment opens directly on to the first

room. There's a large couch made up of two single mattresses, one on top of the other, and covered in printed sheets and blankets made of knitted squares (which I find strangely comforting), and a scatter of threadbare cushions. I wonder if this is where he sleeps, imagine him pulling off his T-shirt and laying down his head.

There's a low table in front of the couch, covered in candles. They're stuck to the surface with melted wax. There are overflowing ashtrays, paints and paintbrushes, half-drunk cups of coffee, empty cigarette packets. There's no other furniture.

Piles of books are stacked around the room. Wooden crates act as shelves or cupboards, holding all manner of treasures and everyday utensils. A series of glass jars are stacked against the walls. The soles of my Dunlops make a tacky sound as I walk on the bare floor.

The door to the second room is propped open. I look in. It too has a mattress on the floor, bigger than the one in the other room, covered in a mess of patterned sheets, blankets and thin cushions, and obviously serving as a bed. I step lightly over the threshold without being shown, Cubby follows. I try not to blink, I don't want to miss a single detail of this wondrous place. The walls are just as colourful as the first room, but the pictures more diverse. As before, some are Cubby's own, others are prints of famous paintings. One is called *Isabella and the Pot of Basil*. It depicts the heroine of a famous poem. She's wearing a long white dress. It reaches down to her naked feet which are large and masculine.

*Look, Mouse. Perfect wire-walker feet.*

Serendipity Wilson's voice is loud and seems to come from behind the painting. I look wildly at Cubby, and around the room; there's no sign of her. I wonder if Cubby heard it too, but dare not ask, in case he thinks me deranged, or in case he did hear her and she is right here, crouching behind the large fridge in the corner. I look back at the painting, conscious that I've broken out in a sweat. A blue cloth drapes around the girl's middle. *Big feet*, I blurt out. Cubby laughs, he is staring at me with shining eyes.

Isabella caresses a large ornate pot adorned with Arabian-looking patterns and macabre skulls. There are tall stems and leaves growing from the pot. I touch the picture.

*She looks very dreamy.*

Cubby laughs again.

*She looks like you, you mean.*

Then Cubby explains that the severed head of her murdered lover is planted in the pot, which is why the plant looks so healthy, because the head is rotting and nourishing the soil.

*Imagine, tending the basil every day. Willing it to grow so you could have something of your dead lover to nurture and love. That's why I like it, see? Because Isabella's love isn't rational. Love should be crazy like that, don't you think?*

Cubby's not sure who murdered Isabella's sweetheart, either her father or her brothers. I mention that as far as I'm concerned fathers are not always to be trusted. Cubby laughs again, louder this time. He takes the picture from the wall, rolls it up and hands it to me.

*Take it, I want you to have it.*

Then he sits on the mattress-bed and gestures for me to sit next to him. I do. He takes my hand. I don't pull away. I shuffle closer, press myself to him, feel the length of his leg touching mine.

Cubby's apartment doesn't smell entirely of fish. There's something sweet and heady too. Apparently, a mix of incense and weed. There's no kitchen, but a basin sits in one corner of the bedroom next to a slim table. A hotplate, adequate for heating water and canned produce, along with coffee maker, various cups and cutlery, are crowded onto the table. Everything looks dulled in the darkness. On the opposite side of the room is the enormous fridge, on top of which sits an old felt hat, faded and dusty. I've never seen a fridge like it, all curved corners and shiny edges. It reminds me of Manu and Marina's caravan. I point to it, giving voice to my thoughts.

*That thing's the size of a caravan.*

The fridge is not used as a fridge, it doesn't work (there's no plug). It's used to hold Cubby's clothes and belongings. He runs a hand through his hair, then touches the nape of my neck with the tip of his index finger.

*You're lovely*, he says.

His voice is full of kindness. Almost unbelievably, I feel the loveliness he sees in me. It's Cubby himself, this man who as a baby was taken home in a hat, who paints pictures of hermaphrodite angels, who tattooed my leg and who, by looking at me here on his bed in Coney Island, makes me

into this new, lovely being. He's an alchemist and I'm transformed. Although I say nothing, I'm euphoric.

I shiver, even though my skin is sticky from the heat. We
lie together on the mattress for a while, we do not speak.
The sound of the street rumbles outside; even so, the rest of
the world feels far away, like a distant memory. My thigh
starts to throb and itch, but I resist the urge to scratch. Looking up, I see the ceiling is painted dark blue, like a midnight
sky, and is littered with hundreds of stars cut from silver
paper. The corners of the stars lift off slightly, and tremble
in a draught of air. They make a soft fluttering sound. I want
to touch and be touched under this synthetic night, so turn
to Cubby, but find he's already looking at me, his thick curls
spread on the pillow, his face slightly rough with stubble
and his breath close, warm, filled with the musty smell of
life. He is smiling.

We kiss for a long time, and touch. After which he takes
a half-smoked cigarette from an ashtray on the floor, lights it
and inhales. He offers me the cigarette, assuring me it's only
a normal one, and I'm glad of it, even though it makes my
head swoon. He seems surprised at my extravagance, staying in such a *swanky hotel*. I admit I've only enough money
to last a week, then I'll have to think about rigging up my
wire. We kiss again, and again, and in between he asks how
long I plan to stay. *Forever*, I say.

I'm writing this from the hotel. It's late, dark outside, and
I've only come back to collect my things. Cubby asked me
to stay with him, because he doesn't like me spending my

money on hotels. I reacted badly, and he looked embarrassed, stared at his hands. I didn't think he was serious about wanting to know me, getting close to me. So, I panicked and became agitated. When I started to pace the room, Cubby looked genuinely concerned. He touched me gently on the shoulders, guided me to the mattress and sat down next to me, stroking my hand and looking into my eyes until I was calm. He said he was sorry he'd come on so strong, he was only trying to help. After a while, he told me he does know a nice, safe place where I can stay, and that I'm not to worry, he won't bother me if I don't want it. But I do want it.

When I got back, I told the bluebottle lady I'd be leaving in the morning because I've met a man in Coney Island. She looked like someone had slapped her in the chops, and I laughed loudly in her face, but immediately felt bad about it.

I need to sleep. In the morning I'll make my way to Union Square and find the train back down to Brooklyn. It's been a long day. I'm deathly tired. I wish I had a tap on the side of my head, so I could turn off the thoughts. As it is, they gush. Tomorrow might be the day I see Bunny again. I wonder what she'll say to me? How strange, to think of her speaking in sentences. Is that how it will be? I hadn't thought of it, until now. I've been so preoccupied with the events of the day. I'll have to be calm, and ready for any questions she might have. I'll tell her about her ancestors, of course, and that her mother was the best and brightest person I've ever known. I'll tell her that her mother loved her deeply, and never wanted to leave her or send her away. I'll tell her it was my fault. I'll tell her I'm sorry.

If it's not tomorrow, then some other day will do. No matter. I'm in no hurry. Not now. To think, this torn-out page from Big Gen's book is the thing guiding me to Bunny. It seems incredible now. How out of place it looks, here in this hotel, in this country. Like me. Yet how many times have I run my fingers over the scrawl and imagined myself there – here – with her? I'll put it under the thick hotel pillow now and lie as still as I can under the starched cotton bedclothes. The throbbing in my leg, which has been bothering me all day, is fading. I'll fall asleep tracing the lines of my tattoo with my finger. The picture is in relief, raised and scabby, and with the sound of Manhattan rumbling through the open hotel window, I'll dream, as I always do, of a big top, of cold tarpaulin, and of a water tank.

*Marina [one], Marina [two], Marina [three].*

I'm surprised to find Cubby waiting for me at Stillwell Avenue when I arrive. It's early, I don't know how long he's been here, but he's smiling. His eyes are wide, blue and staring. He's been up all night, *but it would've been more fun being with you.* Cubby holds my hand as we wander down Mermaid Avenue. He wants to make sure my leg is okay, I say it's beautiful, but that's not what he meant. He asks if it hurts. I reply no, even though it does.

We take a right turn up West 15th Street – I've started to make a mental note of all the street names – and walk past pretty brick houses on both sides of the street, with flowers in window boxes and wooden steps up to the front door. Past low buildings with painted fronts in light, pastel colours, that might be someone's home, or perhaps a workplace, an office? Past an auto-repair shop with a large, hand-painted sign of swirly red, white and blue letters. Past parked cars, all along the street, packed along the kerb, making the road look thinner than it is. And past the wood-and-steel skeleton of a roller coaster which, other than the skyscrapers of Manhattan, is the biggest thing I have ever seen. Cubby points at the beast, as proud as if it were his own.

*That's Aunt Betty's place. Do you see? The house under the roller coaster? That's where you'll be staying. There's plenty of space. Aunt Betty's great. I told you I grew up there, right? She's expecting us later.*

I nod.

When we get to the fish restaurant, Cubby opens the door to his apartment and tells me to throw my stuff anywhere for now. While he waits outside and smokes, I drop my bags on the floor. A minute later, I rejoin Cubby on the street, he hands me a cigarette and we smoke as we walk. Cubby leads us back down Neptune Avenue, past West 15th Street with its thundering roller coaster and Aunt Betty's house shivering beneath, and along to West 20th.

The streets are busy. It's another hot day, and I am grateful for the Atlantic breeze which seems to envelop Coney Island on days like this. It's not far to our destination. We chatter as we walk. Cubby asks me about the picture of the four-legged girl torn from the book. I try as best I can to explain, but it seems I'm not in the mood to talk today. I feel stupid; everything I say sounds babyish – Big Gen, Fausto, Marina. Even Serendipity Wilson, when talked about now, sounds like a silly fairy-tale goblin – I'm ashamed. Cubby doesn't seem to mind or notice my embarrassment. He smiles and nods along, tells me how he loved playing on the rides in the theme parks when he was a kid. Even as I walk through the Coney Island streets, I imagine the mysterious island of my childhood, that dreamland filled with bearded ladies and rabbits. There's only one rabbit I want to find now. Still, I wonder if I should wait a few days, get used to my surroundings before barging in on Bunny's life. I mean, I have the address, there's no rush. Perhaps I should get my own bearings first. Nothing feels real at the moment, every-thing's moving so fast and I wonder again, what harm would it do, to wait for a while?

Then, we are here: 2863 West 20th Street.

Seeing a real building, on a real street, made of bricks and glass and concrete, makes my throat contract and I must stop myself from sobbing and spluttering. It's a large house at the end of a row of similar houses. The windows on one side are built into a rotunda, making it look like the turret of a castle, very grand. I stare at the piece of paper in my hand – a relic now – then stare at the house across the street and find it hard to make a connection between these two things.

*This is it*, says Cubby.

*Yes.*

*Who lives here?*

I look at the paper again, show it to Cubby, point at the names and shake my head.

*I suppose these people do.*

He takes my arm as we cross the road, holds lightly on to my elbow as we climb the steps to the main door, and I knock. At first, there's nothing. Then the sound of movement from below, a door unlocking, and a voice calling from beneath the steps.

*Can I help you?*

I look down to see a middle-aged woman standing in a doorway under the stoop. Cubby goes towards the woman. I follow him down the steps.

*My friend is looking for someone at this address. Is this you? Or, do you know these people?*

Cubby takes the piece of paper from my hand, shows it to the woman. I feel uncomfortable with him holding it, as if his touch is sullying it. I want to grab it back and am relieved when he hands it to me. The middle-aged woman smiles and nods her head.

*You missed 'em.*

*They live here?* I ask, pointing at the paper.

*Yes. Well, no. They moved last week.*

The three of us stand there, looking at each other, saying nothing. I am so hot. Sweat is pouring out of me. It trickles from my hairline, down my forehead and into my eyes. I wipe the back of my hand across my brow. Water splashes from my face. I want to run away, to hide from this woman, this stranger, this house. I sway, put my hand to the metal rail beside me, steady myself. The metal is warm; for some reason this surprises me and brings me to my senses, at least enough to break the silence.

*Thank you. I'm sorry to have bothered you*, I say, and not knowing what to do next, or how to react, I turn to walk away.

*Are you a relative? You're English, right? The accent.*

The woman moves closer. She is staring at my chest. Then I realize, it's not my chest that interests her, but my pendant. She goes to touch it and I take a step back, avoiding the sweep of her fingers.

*Where'd you get that? That belongs to the little girl. Why've you got it?*

*Little girl? Is there a little girl here? With a pendant like this?*

*Not* like *that, that's the very same one. She's always playing with that thing.*

*There are two. Pendants, I mean.*

*If you say so. It's not my business, anyway. I keep myself to myself. I'm not one to pry into other people's—*

*Where is she? The child?*

*Like I said, you missed 'em.*

*Yes, but I have to find her. Do you understand? To give her the pendant! They both belong to her really, see? I've just been looking after this one for a while. So, if you'd tell me where I can find her? I'd be very grateful.*

*Upstate, that's all I know. They didn't leave an address. Sad to*

*see them go. Such nice people. It's a pity you didn't come by yester-
day, she was here. Spent a few hours clearing things up, her and the
little girl. They won't be back again, that's what she said. This place
has gone downhill. All the good people are leaving. Who can blame
a nice family for wanting to move upstate?*

*You said the lady is English? And the man, I mean, the child's
father?*

*Look, I don't know what you want, but . . . I guess it's common
knowledge that she's not their kid. The kid was her brother's little
girl. He died, not long after they arrived. Fell from the top of the
parachute jump. Climbed all the way up there one night by himself,
blind drunk. Personally, I think he jumped. The man had mental
problems. Seen things in the war. That's what they said. But what
do I know?*

*Oh. I see.*

*They adopted the kid.*

*Is she big? I mean fat? I mean the little girl? The last time I saw
her she was putting on weight so quickly and I thought . . .*

*Fat? Heavens to Betsy, no. She's a skinny thing.*

*And her hair. Does she have hair?*

*Well, you ask the strangest questions. Yes, she has hair! Why
wouldn't she have hair? She's a real carrot top! I guess that's the
British thing . . .*

Her voice fades as I turn quickly away, my only thought
being that I need to get away from this woman. I scurry
back down West 20th Street, Cubby at my heels, panting
like a puppy.

*What was that?*

*Sorry. I can't breathe properly, I have to get away from here.*

*All that stuff about the guy who jumped off the 'chute, and your necklace?*

*Please. I can't think. I need to move, to walk, anything.*

*I'm sorry you missed your friends, but slow down. Where are you going, rushing around like a crazy person?*

I stop dead in my tracks, taking Cubby by surprise so that he almost trips as he forces himself to come to a stop. He looks like a clown.

*I could've been here, yesterday. In fact, I could've been here years ago.*

*But you weren't. I don't mean to sound cruel, but that's just the way it is.*

*That woman said they were here yesterday. So that was destiny. I mean, I was actually here, in this place — it makes sense: that was the day I was supposed to find her. I missed my own destiny. It's so ludicrous, it's almost funny. I mean, if it wasn't so miserable.*

Cubby squeezes my hand, but I pull away. I start walking again, so quickly that he has to trot to keep up, reminding me again of the Joey clowns at the circus and causing a wave of anger to engulf me. Finally, he comes to a halt. I continue a few steps, then stop, and turn.

*How am I supposed to find Bunny now?*

*I'm sorry,* he says. *I didn't force you to spend time with me, so don't look at me like that, as if I'm to blame. You captain your own ship, like the rest of us.*

*I don't blame you. I'm just . . .*

*It's okay. I get it. Disappointment is a terrible thing.*

301

*It's my own fault. I've spent so much time dreaming about finding Bunny but doing nothing about it. Even when I dream of her, I don't speak to her or even imagine what she looks like. She's like a cloud, a big white cloud in the sky. There's no face, no voice. She's fading, do you see? Blowing away, like the clouds. I don't know what I'm doing here. I don't know if any of this is real. All I know is, I must find her. I must.*

Cubby walks slowly over to me, takes my head in his hands and kisses me on the lips. It is intimate; private; his tongue softly pressing into my mouth. It makes me light-headed. I find that I'm balancing on my toes, teetering on the edge of a precipice. But I don't want to feel like this, not right now. I ease myself away, and although I'm fighting against it, I cry.

*It's so stupid and useless*, I say.

*No, it's not. There's still hope. We don't have to give up. We were close this time. If we can get this far now, there's no reason we won't find her next time. We could do it, you know? Nothing's lost. There's always hope, right?*

Cubby smiles. Not knowing what else to do, but feeling sure, somehow, that we are collaborators now, I take a breath, reach for his hand, and slowly walk on.

Coney Island, although shabby, is full of colour. Along its main streets, every sign, every boarded-up window seems to be painted in bright blues, reds and yellows, albeit chipped, scrawled upon and filthy.

Cubby and I don't speak as we walk together, back towards

the fish restaurant. My body is heavy with disappointment; my companion steadies his pace, as if instinctively understanding the need to be slow, to tread softly. I feel the extra heat coming from Cubby's body, the tension in his muscles as he moves; his wrists; his arms. I take a step closer to him, so that our hips and legs touch as we walk. It comforts and excites me. The confusion makes my head spin.

When Cubby looks at me, I am already staring up at him. He's tall. I hadn't noticed his height before. Now I do, and I want to scale him, like a building. I want to get to the top and conquer him. If I never find Bunny, at least I'll have that, I think. I'd like to tell him how beautiful he is, but there are no words. It's not the time for words. Emboldened by our new-found complicity, I continue to look at him. Even when he looks away, I can tell he's aware of my face, staring up at his own. He smiles, lets out a short, breathy laugh and shakes his head, almost imperceptibly. But I see it. The energy that winded me back at the Macveigh house, and pooled in my belly, is spreading through me again now, fizzing.

A little along the way, there's a group of people. They stand on the pavement, some sit on the kerb between parked cars, most are drinking alcohol from bottles. They're all dressed the same; in blue jeans and T-shirts. They are boisterous and self-conscious. Cubby waves to them as they call to him, but I tighten my grip on his hand. My message understood, he doesn't approach the blue jeans. We walk on.

The roller-coaster ride looms above us, like the delicate

bones of some primordial beast; the giant protector of Aunt Betty's wooden house. I've never seen anything so huge look so fragile. It could be made of French lace. If not for the heavy noise of the cars as they barrel along, I'd swear you could blow it away with a single breath. I feel its gentle vibration resonate through me as we pass, as if I'm connected in some way to its inner workings. I imagine myself growing until I'm as big as the coaster. My skin tingles.

Once at the fish restaurant, we go straight to the second room with the mattress on the floor, and the fridge that's not a fridge. Without saying a word, we undress and lie under the thin sheets, pushing cushions away with restless legs. I feel Cubby's weight, the softness of his skin, his heat. I push into him, move under him, push faster, so that we're both gasping, pulling at the air as if it were made of liquorice ribbons. Afterwards, we stay in bed until the late afternoon. When the light begins to dim, and we need to get up, I rise from the mattress and walk to the basin, naked. Cubby is still in bed, watching me. I feel his gaze, like a physical thing, as if his eyes are touching me. Then he calls me over, presses down on my breast bone with his middle finger and tells me that there is an invisible silver line between us, a thread that cannot be broken by distance. I knock his hand away. He looks hurt, so I kiss the ends of his fingers, and smile.

I may not be used to this new world of the hordes, or to this city, with her hot dogs, blue-jeaned youth and painted hermaphrodite angels, but I seem to know how to play its games, and I'm starting to enjoy them. I wiggle as I pull on my shorts, reach out for my new lover's hand, pull him to his feet and kiss his wet mouth.

*Will you help me find Bunny?*

*Of course. Anything. You only have to ask.*

*Promise?*

*Promise.*

## 26

# Tales Told by Serendipity Wilson #5

## *The Fisherman and Themselves*

*To dream is to live with your face brightened by moonlight. Yet dreams are only a shadow, my Mouse, a pale and rippled reflection of the way things could be. I know what a dreamer you are; we are cut from the same fabric where that's concerned. But, if our dreams come true, we risk tainting them with the hard edge of reality. Sometimes it's a risk worth taking, like working hard to become the greatest funambulist who ever lived. And, sometimes, it's best to leave well alone and let daydreams stay in the world of our imagination. The trick is, finding which to leave and which to follow.*

*Being true Manx, from childhood Fintan the fisherman's son knew the little people were everywhere on the island. Even if he couldn't see them, his belief was strong. He lived with his family, surrounded by thick gorse bushes, the Mourne Mountains looming beyond the sea in the mists, and Bay Mooar, with its soft sand and sloshing waves, down below. At night, he'd sneak out, run down to the bay, scritch-scratching his legs on the sharp gorse as he went, and hide behind a rock to wait, hoping to catch Themselves reeling a jig or playing their little fiddles out on the sands.*

*Fintan's dearest dream was to see the little people, or perhaps just* one he could befriend and who'd like him so much, he'd be taken to fairyland and granted wishes. But that was wishful thinking. For Themselves won't stand to be spied upon, even by a child.

The more you believe in something, the more likely you are to hear a voice in the wind or catch sight of a shadow in the corner of your eye. So it was with Fintan, who could hear fairy music on the furthest breeze — if any were there to be heard or not — and would follow it, like a dog sniffing for a bone. But Themselves are not ones to suffer the whimsy of a little boy and would play games, sending out the sounds of fiddles and laughter, weaving it like a thread to be followed, and as soon as Fintan came near, they'd say some fairy words, and vanish.

Fintan would lie behind rocks and gorse, sighing with disappointment. Just one glimpse of the fairy world would make him happy. He'd never bother the little people again, he'd simply smile if anyone protested that fairies were long gone from the island (as often they did) and nod a gentle salute to the little hidden eyes he knew were all around, blinking invisibly under their caps.

Sometimes, Fintan saw lights, shining like stars on a frosty night, skipping in the bay. He knew they were fairy boats, setting out their nets to catch herring. The next morning, he'd beg his father to cast out their own nets, even the broken ones. And, no matter what the weather or the state of the sea, on those days, they'd bring in great hauls of fish. Fintan's father, like many islanders, had a fear of fairy magic. But, if the fish were good, he didn't ask questions. He was grateful for an easy day's work.

During the day, Fintan rubbed his eyes and napped in his lessons. But at night, he refused to sleep. He lay under the blankets, listening *for the wind to stop and the waves to calm, in hope of hearing a tap-tap-tapping on wood or metal, or any sound that might be Themselves going about their business in the caves around the bay. One night, the tapping was particularly loud. It was surely down in the caves on the other side of the bay, but how loud and clear the sound rang, like a sign, a calling to a small boy from Themselves.*

*In a moment, Fintan was out of bed and through the window, nightshirt flapping in the breeze, the fabric curling around his skinny legs, catching on the gorse. Flying towards the sound that grew ever louder, ever closer, and taking no notice of his surroundings, before he knew it, Fintan was in the water, weighed down by his bed things and swimming towards the caves. Eventually he was there, kneeling exhausted on the rocks. The tapping didn't stop, and at the mouth of the first cave, to Fintan's delight and surprise, was a little fella, chipping away with chisel and hammer at a large wooden box. Unable to contain his joy, Fintan let out a cry.*

*It's young Fintan, is it? said the little fella, without turning to look or stopping his work.*

*Aye, said Fintan, I've come to be your friend, so you can grant me wishes. As it's me what found you, you're surely duty-bound to do so.*

*Fintan's voice was shrill with the excitement of what was to come, but still the little fella did not give up on his work or turn to look at him.*

*Is that so, said the little fella. Well, now, to grant a wish, first you must tell me what it is I'm making here.*

*That's easy, replied Fintan. A box so big, too big for a fairy box, must be to hold all your treasure. I say you're making a treasure chest.*

*Ah, you see, that's wrong. This might be a chest, of sorts, but not* one for holding any fairy treasure. And there's no second guess, Fintan. That's your lot. Now away with you, boy.

Fintan, although disappointed, knew he must accept the fairy way and didn't try to press for a second guess. Instead, he begged the little fella to tell him what it was he was busy making.

Until then, the little fella had kept his back to Fintan, and all the while had not once stopped tapping at the wood. Now, he stopped and turned. What a fright Fintan got. The little man's face was all jumbled up so that you couldn't tell an eye from a nose, and there was a blackness, a hollow that the fella seemed to see through, and talk through. The boy was so terrified he froze.

Young Fintan, said the fella, I'm making you a coffin. And if I or any other fairy folk catch you looking at us ever again, you'll be seeing the inside of this box and nothing else ever more. And with that Fintan jumped into the sea, swam as fast as he could across the bay, and ran without stopping all the way to his bed.

In time, Fintan grew to be a man and all but forgot his childish ways and dreams. Like his father, he worked to bring in the catch. Fintan the fisherman lived in the same cottage he was born in. One misty morning, when the fog got thick, Fintan abandoned his boat, tied it up in the bay by the caves and waded to the shore. In the evening, when the moon was up and the night quite clear, Fintan went back to collect his boat. As he undid the rope, he thought he heard singing. He looked about him. There was no one. Then again, he thought he heard a fiddle, and played so well that he couldn't think who might be holding the bow. The sound seemed to be coming from one of the caves. So, leaving his boat tied up, Fintan went to see who was there at such an hour.

*As the fisherman approached the cave, the music seemed to grow. There was laughing and shouting and tankards clattering together. The sound was so merry that Fintan started to relish the idea of joining the feast. Whoever was in there would surely not mind another reveller.*

*The mouth of the cave was dark, as if the light from the moon could not reach it. The merrymakers must've forgotten their candles, as there wasn't a flicker of light to be seen. Thinking this strange, but not so strange to stop him looking in, Fintan put a foot inside the mouth of the cave. Immediately, all the sound stopped dead.*

*Everything around him was dark, dank and cold. Fintan couldn't see his hand in front of his face. Not put off, he took further steps into the cave. Now the cave was a blanket of darkness. In fact, the mouth of the cave seemed to disappear altogether. As if it had closed behind him. He couldn't see the moon outside, or hear the waves moving around the rocks.*

*At last he found his voice, and let out a gentle but firm: Hello, who's here?*

*There was the sound of shuffling feet, of movement and whispering. Who indeed? said a voice, and other voices giggled and snorted in muffled laughter around him. Fintan felt something brush past his leg, and then other things, like the ends of tiny coat-tails and feathered caps, all brushing against him, and more giggles and whispers.*

*Do you not know us, Fisherman? said one small voice. Perhaps we should light a candle, so you can see? With that, Fintan remembered his boyhood. His heart began to beat so loud that Themselves commented on the clatter he was making. Fintan understood. He* spun on his heel, and although it was darker than any place he'd ever known, he ran back in the direction he'd come.

At last he was outside. His boat was before him, bobbing on the waves in the clear light of the moon. Fintan, breathless, leaned against the rocks for a minute. He was sweating and shaking. The music and laughter started up again, making him jump into his boat, and row, as fast as he could, back across the bay.

The next morning, Fintan refused to go down to the bay, claiming that Themselves were trying to trick him. Later that day, one of the older fishermen came knocking at the door. He told Fintan there was the most curious sight down by the caves: hundreds of tiny footprints, going hither and thither all around the sand. And in the cave, they found a fine oak box, the size and shape of a grown man's coffin.

Fintan lived to be an old man himself. But he never forgot what happened that night. Often, on cold evenings, when the people of the bay would gather together, Fintan told his tale, just as I'm telling you now, as a warning.

Be careful what you wish for, lest your wishes come true.

## 27

# Aunt Betty and the Thunderbolt House

By the time we get to Aunt Betty's house, it's evening. The air, still hot from the day, buzzes with the electricity of thick cables, and fun seekers. No one cares about the mounds of rubble behind broken wire fences from housing projects that ran out of money and never got built. Lights, food and fun are still in abundance. What more could anyone need to believe in the magic of the place?

The Thunderbolt, proudly showing its name across the entrance to the roller coaster in large, electric letters, is a hubbub of excited people. Light bulbs flicker occasionally as the body of the structure shakes and wooden cars roar past. Cubby shouts up to a podgy middle-aged man, obviously running things. The man waves, and gestures for us to go through some large gates. Once through the service gates, we bend under steel poles, climb over beams, cables and ropes to get to the front door of Aunt Betty's house. There's the smell of industry mixed with earth and sugary food; the smells of the circus. My eyes close, and for a second

I'm thrown back into that other world. I even think I hear an accordion playing somewhere in the distance.

Cubby pushes the door (almost too small and slender for the entrance to such a large building) without knocking. With a gentle squeak of the hinges it yawns open on to a narrow staircase. The walls on each side of us are a dark wood, rich and beautifully kept. It reminds me of old photographs of ocean liners. I let my hand run against the wood; as smooth and cold as polished stone. Everything smells of beeswax and rose water. There's no hint of summer dirt in here, no whiff of sticky fried food. It's dark outside now, but on the wooden staircase we're surrounded by a hazy, reflective light. Looking around I see no possible source of illumination, no lamps, no bulbs. Still, everything shines, as if imbued with the finest crystal, creating rainbows of colour in the corners of my eyes. The orange flame around my neck jumps, as if responding to the light. I'm a child again, walking into a land of dreams, my face lit with amber radiance. My eyes widen with anticipation and something that's not quite fear, not quite excitement.

*What is this place?* I whisper.


The Thunderbolt House is a warren of rooms and corridors. Twenty rooms in all, including two parlours (one for best), one large kitchen, a dining room, Aunt Betty's bedroom, and two bathrooms. All the other rooms are guest bedrooms.

One of the guest rooms has been made up for me. It's at the

furthest end of the house, away from the parlours and kitchen. There's pink paper on the walls, printed with faded bluebells. Although the style is old, it's neat and clean and suits me perfectly. I have an oak wardrobe with matching chest of drawers, a dressing table complete with mirror and a pretty dressing set made from heavy pink glass, and a shaded lamp (the lampshade matching the bluebell wallpaper) is set atop a bedside table. The bed, which has a headboard of black wood, is tightly made up and covered in a pink-and-blue candlewick bedspread. In the centre of the room – as throughout the house – two thick metal girders rise up through the floorboards, piercing the room like enormous needles, with their points disappearing into the ceiling. These are the ribs of the great roller-coaster beast. They make the gentility of the pink room, with its bluebells and prettiness, seem a sham.

The room is almost always in semi-darkness. It has one large window, which must let in plenty of light, but because the coaster track passes directly in front of the window, only inches away from the pane, it's hidden behind thickly lined pink damask curtains, drawn tightly shut.

Aunt Betty is waiting for us in the main parlour when we arrive. She stands, hands folded in front, smart in a close-fitting floral dress that wraps tidily over her ample bosom. Her shoes are ivory leather, low-heeled, and garnished with silver buckles. Aunt Betty's hair is a cotton wool cloud of whiteness. She smiles as we enter the room, her pink lips making a perfect moon of her large, soft face.

*So this is your English girl? What short hair, and that colour!*

Aunt Betty pauses for a moment. I feel my hands moisten, my heartbeat throb in my throat. Then her smile broadens and she reaches for my hand.

*I like it*, she says. *So modern.*

Aunt Betty sets an occasional table for us, chock-full of food. There are plates loaded with things I've never eaten before. I find an armchair and sit, ready to pick at the delights. Cubby and Aunt Betty chat quietly in quick, light voices, but I'm not listening to them. I reach out for something to eat. There's a sudden burst of movement and noise. There's screaming; the building shakes; the tea things clatter on the tray, and the many framed photographs on the walls swing violently on their nails. I hold on to the seat of the armchair, every muscle tensed, every neuron readied for catastrophe, wondering what dreadful mistake I could have made, to be punished in such a dramatic way. But as quickly as it comes, the thundering noise stops, and all is still.

Realizing my eyes are clamped shut, I open them to see Aunt Betty and Cubby sat on the sofa, chatting as before, as if nothing has happened. I glance around the room, checking I've not been under some illusion, that my mind isn't playing tricks on me again. The tea things are immobile, the framed pictures remain in place on the wall, every one of them slightly askew (just as before). I seem to let out an exclamation, as Cubby and Aunt Betty stop their conversation, look over to me and smile in unison. *It's only the coaster, dear. You'll get used to it,* Aunt Betty says, waving her hand towards the table of food.

I fill myself with bourekas, kugel, potato latkes, sufgani-yot, and chocolate cake. They're the most delicious things I've ever tasted. Aunt Betty laughs as I shove handfuls of food into my mouth. *Oh yes, I can see we're going to get along fine*, she says. Cubby leaves, kissing me lightly on the lips. To be kissed, so publicly, and in front of that nice old lady, makes my face hot and red. *Aunt Betty will look after you*, he says.

It takes some time for me to find my voice, but by the time Aunt Betty shows me to the pink room, I'm twittering away like a baby chick, telling her all about the animals on the encampment, about Solomon and how he'd let me sleep snuggled up into him, and Aunt Betty laughs saying it prob-ably wasn't the most hygienic of places to sleep, and I say that actually llamas are very clean creatures. I feel like a dif-ferent person, a good person.

*Settle yourself in. Don't feel you need to spend time with old Betty. I know how things are. It must be hard for you, so far from home. You know where I am if you need anything. Breakfast will be waiting for you in the kitchen, so don't wait. Well, you know where I am.*

And with that, the lady with the cotton wool hair sighs, brushes the dresser with the flat of her hand, and turns to go.

*Aunt Betty*, I say.

*Yes, dear?*

*Thank you.*

Aunt Betty waits a moment before speaking. She takes in a deep lungful of air.

*That's perfectly all right,* she says. *We all need a helping hand every now and then. This house is a good place for lost souls. It seems to know what people need.*

After she closes the door behind her, I unroll the picture of Isabella and her pot, and with the tacks Aunt Betty gave me for the purpose, pin the picture to the wall opposite the bed. I'm standing in front of it when the shattering sound of the roller coaster breaks the world in two. I turn quickly to look at the window just as the damask curtains blow apart, revealing a blur of screaming faces.

# 28

# The Boardwalk Spectacular

Are you wondering if there's to be a happy ending? I wish I could tell you. We must find the answer together.

I admit that this period of time in Coney Island was a happy one. You may ask why I didn't fall apart, after crossing an ocean to find Bunny, and failing at my first, sorry attempt? Why I wasn't frantically continuing the hunt? Well, I suppose in the end we must live each day as well as we can. I had Cubby. I had Aunt Betty. I had agency. And, I had my wire.

I was far from Fausto's circus. The badness that had clung to me my entire life was dissolving. This was the really big change in my life: I was no longer invisible. In truth, I could have done much more to find Bunny. But I didn't forget her. She was always there. Bunny was the air, the stuff under the wire holding it – and me – up. Sometimes I'd wonder what would happen if I found her, how I'd live without my one important task? She was, as she continues to be, simply my reason for being.

I must type quickly now, before I'm too tired to think

and can remember nothing. You need to know all about my search for the child. There will be no more breaks, no sleep to calm the mind, just the quickness of my fingers and the blinking of my eyes.

A few days after I move into Aunt Betty's place, with little else to do but chat with Aunt Betty and fret about Bunny, we decide it's time for me to get back onto my wire.

*The way you talk about your act is enchanting. Why waste time talking?* Aunt Betty says. *It's the doing that counts.*

Having walked the length of the beach looking for somewhere suitable to rig up, we settle on a spot at the end of the boardwalk, away from the main hub.

*The crowd must come to us,* I explain. *It's an old performers' trick. We don't go begging for attention.*

*That's right. We whet their appetite, make them curious,* Aunt Betty continues, as if knowing what I'm about to say. She laughs as Cubby frowns and scratches his head.

The boardwalk is a wide wooden thoroughfare running the length of Coney Island beach and Surf Avenue. It's elevated where we are, so the beach, with its soft golden sand, is below us on one side. And on the other side, at ground level, are concessions selling everything from seashells and T-shirts to hot dogs and fortunes (*for a pretty penny,* as Gen would say). This is also where the theme-park rides are, and where, back in the day, the freak shows barked for custom. Further along Surf Avenue, Dreamland once stood. I look for signs of it, but there's nothing left, save a few dreams,

I suppose. The spearing red tower of the old parachute jump, visible all over Coney Island, looking like an enormous flower with its cage-like petals, is just ahead of us. I can't help thinking about Old Man Frazer when I look at it, like he's still up there, clinging to its structure. Wherever I am in Coney Island, it's as if he's there, waiting, ready to fall.

We rig up between two lamp posts. They're high enough, at least twenty-five feet, and metal. I use a short wire, thinner than I'm used to. It was all I could carry from England. It's the perfect length, as if made for this place, and this reinforces my conviction that I'm exactly where I should be. I have all my slings, ropes, and foam blocks for fastening the wire. I bought and paid for them, I took nothing that didn't belong to me or Serendipity Wilson. Cubby is a quick learner, good with his hands and practical, he understands how to work the tension, he couldn't be more exemplary if I'd made him up.

As soon as the wire is ready, I scale the post. I'm so eager to get off the ground, I practically sprint up. Then I'm there, above the ground, leaning on the lamp-head. I take a breath and blow a gentle stream of air from my mouth, put my right foot on the wire and start to walk. There was a worry that once on the wire, I'd be haunted by the streaking comet of Serendipity Wilson's hair as she fell, and freeze. But the familiar feeling of my upper world, with its soft, quiet air, is such a relief and a comfort to me. The squeezing of my stomach muscles and the bending of my knees; the twisting of my bare feet on the steel cable, and the slight bounce as the wire moves with the shifting of my own weight, makes me feel like I'm home; in a place where I belong. The sensation is so strong that for a moment I think my limbs will collapse and I falter. Yet I don't fall. I slide my right foot forwards, bringing both my arms out to the side, and lift my left leg high, in a faultless arabesque. Now I am as free as the fresh sea air. It's such a relief. Tears roll down my cheeks, evaporating quickly in the breeze.

When I finally look down, I see Cubby; handsome and a little dumbfounded, with his mouth gaping open, staring up at me. Aunt Betty is smiling, the picnic she brought spread on blankets around the boardwalk, as she beckons passers-by to join the free feast. I watch her as I move along my wire. She points up to me, tapping people on the shoulder, clapping her hands in exclamation. A small crowd gathers. They shove piles of sandwiches into their mouths before, taking Aunt Betty's lead, they look up and gasp with delight.

Aunt Betty knows how to play the hordes. Her eyes twinkle as they catch mine, and I see her goodness. It's soft, comforting, and solid. I think she's glowing with goodness, as bright and orange as the pendant around my neck. I smile at her. She blinks and nods in reply, then touches Cubby on the arm, and makes her way through the thickening crowd, down the boardwalk and back to the Thunderbolt House.

The first day goes well. There are the usual Coney Island noises: laughter, food hawkers, mechanical contraptions and excited screams mixed in with the rhythmic sliding of the ocean. I balance above the heads of the holiday hordes who, despite what the bluebottle lady said back at the hotel, still flock to Coney Island on warm days like this. At last, I feel dense human energy moving around below me, the freedom of empty space above, as I move and listen to the waves lapping against the shore. And all the while I'm keeping a lookout for the one I'm here to find.

I can clearly see the faces of the people on the ground. It's not like being in the black hole of the big top. Here, they dress in colourful clothes. They're full of life and chatter. The wire is my watchtower, that's what Aunt Betty said when I told her about my search for Bunny, about the address on the paper and the near miss. If Bunny is among the crowds (her family might bring her for a day out at the beach, you never know, especially with their connection to the place), from my wire, she said, I will see her.

I must also watch for Serendipity Wilson, although I haven't mentioned this to Aunt Betty. My bald phantom has been absent since my move to Thunderbolt House. I know she's lying in wait, hiding behind my fellow performers on the boardwalk: the jugglers, the drag queens and fire-eaters who work their acts during the day. I'll not let her take me unawares, not anymore. When she shows herself again, like the perfect hostess (like Aunt Betty), I'll be ready to receive her.

Down on the ground, Cubby continues to stare up at me, loose-jawed. His uplifted face so alive, his skin almost sparkling and his soft blond curls resting against his neck.

Once again, I feel the touch of his gaze. There are plenty of others too, clapping and sighing, their picnics pushed aside now, as I improvise my way through a complete act. Cubby is the only one whose eyes I feel on my skin. I perform for him.

There are no further diary entries to prompt my Coney Island memories. This is the last page I will copy out for you. I'm not sure why I stopped writing in my notebooks. There was no dramatic incident, nothing to firm up my decision to halt, not that I remember. My life had taken such a turn that, I suppose, I didn't want to waste time; like Aunt Betty said, I could be *doing* things. Everything comes to an end, eventually. Even my search.

Days on the boardwalk follow a pattern. Cubby helps to rig up in the morning, and I perform all day. I don't have set pieces at this point. Although I do plan things out, sometimes.

I have an act based on the Joey clowns at the circus. (I still have the notes and sketches, written on the back of a paper napkin.) It's full of jumping allegro movements along the wire. Nothing slow or graceful. Instead of parasol, fan, or balancing pole, I have handfuls of balloons on long strings, which I hold out, and every now and then, as if by accident, I let one go. Then I grab hold of my battered old top hat with one hand and pretend to shake. I tremble the wire with one foot, holding the other leg out to the side, as if I might be losing my balance and about to fall. It's a fun act. I wear shorts and a patchwork jacket that used to belong to Cubby and is too big for me. The Joey clown act doesn't last long. It makes me hot and out of breath, bounding along the wire in demi-plié, sometimes doing simple juggling tricks with batons as I go. It takes a lot of effort. The holiday crowd love the act, though. Especially children. So I dust it off every now and then, just for fun.

Mostly though, I improvise. Soft melodies are blown in from somewhere seemingly far away. I use them. From time to time I take a break, sit on my wire and look at the people below, or out to the endless ocean (it's not endless, I've lived at its end). Or I descend and sit with Cubby for a while. He wraps his legs around me and we kiss until it's time to go back on my wire. Sometimes Cubby sits on a hessian rug, gets out his buzzing pen (he tells me it is called an *iron*). I smile down at him as he engraves butterflies and eagles into the skin of strangers with alcohol on their breaths. My years of hiding under trailers and wagons are over. I'm as vibrant and bright as the sun. I'm a buzzing iron; a wingless angel; a resident of the Thunderbolt House; a boardwalk funambulist.

At the end of each session, Cubby passes a battered straw hat around and collects the money. When the sun goes down, he helps to de-rig the wire, as if he'd done it every day of his life. Sometimes I go straight back to Aunt Betty's house, sit on my bed and stare at the curtained window. Or, if I don't want to be alone, Aunt Betty prepares our meal and I sit in the kitchen with her. We eat and tell each other stories. One evening she tells me not to worry about Bunny. Saying, even if I don't find her, she's sure she'll grow up strong and well.

*I feel her heart*, she says. *It happens sometimes. It's difficult to explain. All I can say is, when you talk about her, I feel her heart alongside mine, small and red and beating inside my own breast. I felt the same thing when I worked at the preemies. The Doc said it's a heart murmur, but I know it's not medical. I felt it with Cubby, when I first saw him. She'll be fine.*

Of course, there are times when I want only to be with Cubby. We stroll back to the fish restaurant together, hand in hand. We're like playful children: grubby and silly. Cubby's enthusiasm for everything we see and do is relentless. When he speaks it's always in long strings of words and accompanied by big gestures. He reads a lot of books, so compares each experience of the day to something he's read recently, or to some author's train of thought that interests him. Everything interests him. Especially me. When he looks at me, I'm the only person in the world, the only one who matters.

As we skip through the crowds of families packing up after a fun day out, yattering about this and that, I automatically search the faces of passing children, hoping to catch a glimpse of the child I once knew so well; the one who'll *be fine*. In case I don't recognize her, I also look for a shining pendant. My own, I keep hidden under a T-shirt, or cotton shift. There might be a time when I want to show it off; for now though, it's enough to know it's there.

I'm often tired at day's end. And as much as I want to be with Cubby and to feel his energy, I crave silence; it's what I'm used to. Cubby isn't one to keep quiet. So, when we get to the apartment, I head straight to the second room and pull him to the mattress. Afterwards, Cubby lights us both a cigarette, and I tug the covers over my head. He's quiet then. There's a heady odour, a sour, human smell in my lover's bed. It makes me think of Solomon, and I long to be comforted by something other than the hum of waxy flesh, by something innocent, far away from the wrappings of everyday life.

The light is fading, and my thoughts begin to wander, my memories falter. Although they remain sharp, pictures of my time in Coney Island come back to me in fragments, like shards of a broken mirror. I wish I could rewind, locate the missing moments and live them again; live them better.

What happens to all the lost memories; the moments of silent thought, the complicity of long-gone lovers, when our minds are so far gone our still breathing bodies may as well be thrown into some dark oubliette? What happens to a life once lived? I'd like to think that, somehow, we leave our mark, like a footprint in the snow. But I don't believe it. Eventually snow melts, the footprint is gone. We leave nothing behind.

Cubby and I lived, for the four years we were together, in a sort of balanced collusion. In the summer months I worked on my wire, and in winter we plotted the next summer. Aunt Betty was our ballast, keeping us upright and on track. It was a cyclical, seemingly uncomplicated life. But I needed more than the constant turning of the seasons, and the heavy tramp towards oblivion. Then, as now, I needed to find Bunny.

# 29

# Sea Angels

I am small again.

With my hands, red and sore with effort, pushing into wet brown slop, I dig. My mother sits on a rock nearby. She is naked. Sunlight bounces from her skin, and she shines, pearl-white. I can't contemplate going over to her, putting my hands on her, so I continue my labour, digging down, my eyes fixed to the rock, to my mother. From where she sits, I cannot see her legs. I imagine them gone, and in their place, a long, slick and glistening fishtail. My own skin – salty, smudged in dirt and crust, pink and scorched by the sun – itches under my thin dress.

My mother sings. The words are strange, unrecognizable. Now, she stands, legs visible. Her voice is a flute, calling out to the sea. I stop digging, letting my dug hole fill with sea water. She turns, looks at me and I freeze. A wave of panic as she makes her way towards me, trying to work out what wrong thing I've done to warrant her attention.

Eyes wide with fear (will there be a punishment?), I don't move when she crouches before me. Soft-voiced, she speaks.

The words are like her song; unidentifiable. Only in dreams has she spoken to me with such tender-sounding utterances. I concentrate on the gentle movement of her mouth. Her words drift over me; into me; through me. There are no other sounds now, only the melody of my mother's voice. Spellbound, I follow her to the water's edge. Her steps are slow, graceful, steady as I trot behind her, avoiding the jellyfish scattered along the way.

At last she turns to me again, bending now, unhooking my dress, pulling it, roughly, over my head. I watch the dress fall onto wet sand; it looks like a dead thing. Head to one side, my mother laughs. Her teeth glint like stars in the universe of her mouth. She looks at me, raises her eyebrows, prods my arm and I catch her laughter. She takes my hand as we move into the waves, laughing.

Waves splosh and break around my ankles. At first, it makes me laugh. I enjoy the cold rush of it on my skin. When I feel the wetness reach past my thighs, into the dirty place, I catch my breath. I try to stop. I've not been this far into the sea before. My mother has hold of my wrist. She doesn't let go. She continues. I pull back, but she's stronger than me. As she pulls me closer to her, my legs rise beneath me. Kicking wildly, I search for the ground. The water is loud, gushing, rushing through my ears, and somewhere beyond that, I can hear laughter. I go under.

My mother releases me.

With all my strength, I strain my neck upwards, sticking my chin out as high as it will go, searching for a gap, a moment to grab at the air. Waves pull me down, then up. I struggle against them. When my head feels the cold air, I cry out. But I'm under again. My body is getting tired, my mind is reeling. The more I fight, the weaker I get. My hands are out in front of me. They are small and pink. When I try to push down, the water won't give. Reaching up for one final breath, I fill my lungs.

At first, I float near the top. Closing my eyes, I let the rolling motion move me along. Feeling myself sink, I am calm. If it wasn't for the burning in my lungs, the terrible need to push the air out and pull something, anything, back in, it would even feel peaceful.

Opening my eyes, I am in a cloudy, milky sea. Then there are tiny pinpricks of light. The lights come closer, slowly growing until they're each about the size of my little finger. They are many, surrounding me, flitting this way and that, examining me. Their substance is jelly, but they're nothing like the rotting, stinking globs that cover the beach. These creatures have eyes, and jelly-like wings that move so quickly they almost seem to be still. They dash around me, nudge at me. I thought my body numb, yet I feel them nipping at my skin. Pleasure calms the rage of my lungs. Now I see that they have faces; mouths that smile at me.

The pain in my chest is becoming unbearable. My insides are burning, yet I am surrounded by these beautiful angelic creatures. I want to let go, so I can stay with them. The little angels seem to be telling me to do it, to stop holding on. They buzz and flicker, egging me on with their eyes and mouths. Finally, I let the air out. It bursts and gushes, making the water around me churn in a frenzy. Pushing my angels away, stirring them into the murky soup. Then, just as I'm about to take in the sea, let the water enter me, my arms are yanked upwards and I am pulled free from the water.

My mother throws me onto the wet sand and tramps up the beach, picking something up along the way. Back on her rock, she pats herself down with the skirt of her dress before dropping it over her head. She calls to me, all the melody gone from her voice now, leaving a flat husky sound.

I try to stand but my body is too heavy, so I pull myself along through the muddy sand, avoiding lumps of jellied muck. When I eventually manage to get to my feet, I'm covered in brown slop.

Reaching my mother's rock, I lean against it, holding myself up. She jumps down and, without looking at me, orders me to follow her. We head back towards the encampment. She stops, and I almost walk into her. My mother throws my wet dress at me. It lands with a stinging slap on my belly, and sticks to me.

*Put it on*, she says. *I should've known you wouldn't swim. Stupid me for trying to find some good in you. Why couldn't you drown?*

She turns, and we walk back to the encampment.

# 30

# The Tidy House of Tarrytown

At the end of each season, when the air cools and the holiday traffic trickles away, Cubby spends his time in the library.

Every morning he stands at the reader's shelf, his back to the lady librarian, and surreptitiously tears pages from telephone directories; numbers from places I've never heard of, towns with strange-sounding names like Syracuse, Yonkers, Ithaca, Poughkeepsie and Tarrytown in Greenburgh, Westchester County. Any page listing the name, or a near enough version of the name scribbled in red pen over Myrtle Corbin's four legs, suffers the fate of Cubby's destruction. It's a slow enterprise. Sometimes he only manages to purloin one page before the eyes of the bookworm glance up from behind her counter. At first, I go with him, but this results in childish snorting and giggling as the threat of being caught in the act of our paper-tearing savagery leaves us holding our bellies in fits of laughter. Cubby is an efficient page thief, if I leave him to it.

I save small change in a large, empty bottle that once held

strong liquor, a curiosity given to me by Aunt Betty, who swears it wasn't her who drank the contents. Once a week I empty the coins into my old knitted bag. It sags under the weight, so I must hold it by the bottom, and Cubby and I make our way to the phone booth on Mermaid Avenue. Cubby does the talking. It was his idea, after all. Taking the torn-out pages, he makes his way down the list of names, calling up each one, in turn.

*Hello, I'm looking for a Mrs Macveigh, formerly of Great Britain. I have a letter for her, from her late brother John Frazer. I'd like to deliver it. Would that be you/your wife?*

And the answer comes that they've never heard of a John Frazer from Great Britain and they're sorry they can't help.

So, the game continues. I stand outside the telephone booth as Cubby makes his calls. If the mood takes me, I make faces at him through the glass and he gives me his mock-angry wide-eyed look and waves his hand at me, as if to scold a naughty child. Otherwise, I stand, and wait, and listen to his voice from behind the glass. We both know it's a game, but it's kind of him, so I play along. Anyway, what else can we do? We've both made promises.

In the autumn before I leave Coney Island, at the end of a cool October day, I sit slumped on the ground outside the Mermaid Avenue phone booth, distractedly knitting my fingers together. I'm restless, glum and out of sorts. When Cubby starts frantically knocking on the glass and waving his arms, I don't make any sudden move. I slide the door slowly open and, feeling slightly put out at being dragged away from my sullen daydreaming, stick my head in.

*That's right, yes. I can deliver the letter personally. You have no idea how long it's taken me to find the lady, so I don't want the letter to get lost in the mail. That's fine, I've got the address here from the directory. I'll make my way over and put it in the mailbox myself.*

When he puts the phone down, Cubby lifts me from the ground, laughing and shrieking *I've found her!* I am instantly happy, as though someone has flicked a switch, but I'm so surprised, and so confused, that I burst into tears. Cubby holds me tightly to his chest and rocks me in his arms, saying nothing, until I stop sobbing.

*Did you speak to her, John Frazer's sister? Did she sound nice?*

*No. I spoke to the landlady, I think. Some lady who lives in the same building. They seem to share a telephone. But she assured me that the 'Mrs' is the lady we're looking for, and with a little girl, just as I described.*

*What do we do? I mean, we don't have a letter, what are we going to say, when we see them?*

*Tell them you've been looking for Bunny all these years, tell them you're delivering their cheese, tell them anything you like. Who cares? We've found Bunny!*

Although I tell her I have enough, Aunt Betty insists on giving me money for the bus fare to Tarrytown, Greenburgh, Westchester County. Cubby and I take the subway into Manhattan and board at Penn Station. My pulse is racing and I'm full up with the excitement of seeing Bunny again, but as soon as we get off the subway my focus

wanders. I'd like to walk around Manhattan, maybe stop
for something to eat, look in through the windows of the
big stores. Cubby says we don't have time to waste, and we
can come back one day soon, maybe even with Bunny, for a
nice day trip. I throw my arms around his neck and he lifts
me from the ground, twirls me around in the bus queue. An
old man in a light jacket with a wooden walking cane steps
away from us. He looks frightened, so I smile at him and say
*sorry*. But the man looks at the ground while shuffling aside,
trying to get as far away from us as he can without losing
his place in line. Seeing how this bothers me, Cubby takes
my hand, kisses the top of my head, and holds me steady.

The journey seems long. But really, the ride's just over
two hours. Though the windows are open and there's a
chill, the air in the bus is stagnant. I'm as jumpy as a flea. It
feels like forever.

Prospect Avenue is lined with tall trees. In fact, the whole
place seems to be surrounded by a forest. Number 31 is a
tall, wooden house with a triangular roof and a little round
window in the attic. I wonder if that's Bunny's room. It's a
tidy, pretty house, painted beige and white.

The day is cold, but bright enough. The trees crisp with
red and yellow leaves, and the air, although chilly, feels soft
on my face. I close my eyes and imagine a wire stretching
from the round window to a large oak on the other side of
the way. There's a girl on the wire, her back is to me, and
cascading down to her waist is a plume of soft, orange hair.
She edges gently along the wire, her white cotton dress

brushing the tops of her bare feet. When she reaches the window, she pushes it gently open and turns. She has green eyes and a wide smile. The child giggles and waves to me, then climbs through the window and into the house. When I open my eyes, I almost expect to see her face, smiling at me through the round glass pane. Without thinking I raise my hand to wave, then realizing my mistake, rest it on Cubby's shoulder and kiss him on the cheek.

*It's easier to breathe here,* I said. *I can see why she'd want the child to grow up here and not in Coney Island. It's so pretty, it feels enchanted. Old Man Frazer's sister must be a good person, to give his child a fairy-tale home like this. I wish I knew her.*

*Maybe you will. It's unlikely she'll let you speak to her daughter alone. I think you need to be ready for her to be suspicious of you. Okay? Anyway, now's your chance. Come on.*

Cubby knocks on the door. I stand beside him, readying myself. When the door opens there's an old lady, ancient and wrinkled, standing in the porch. She looks about a hundred years old. Her hair is beautifully coiffed, and she's wearing a dainty grey day dress, with buttons up the front.

*Are you the landlady?* asks Cubby.

*I'm sorry, what do you want? Can I help you?*

*We're looking for Mrs Macveigh.*

*Well, you've found her.*

There's a pause. Cubby and I look at each other. I cross my brows and take a breath before speaking, because I don't want to say the wrong thing. The day is growing colder now, and darker. I shiver.

*I'm looking for Mrs Macveigh, from Great Britain. I mean, my companion telephoned. It's about her brother, John Frazer, and his daughter . . . I mean, Bunny.*

*Oh no, I'm sorry, I think there's been a mistake. You see, I'm Mrs Macveigh and I never had a brother so . . .*

*But I telephoned. You remember that? I spoke to you . . .*

*No, no. I mean yes. I've got a telephone. Have you come to fix it?*

*What? No, we've come to deliver a letter. I spoke to you about it, on the phone. You said Mrs Macveigh lived here with her daughter. A little girl with orange hair,* insists Cubby.

*Yes, I know. There was a girl with orange hair, but that was before the war. She grew up and moved away, you see. I'm sorry, did you say you came about the telephone? I forget things, sometimes.*

*You don't remember? I called about a letter from her late brother, from England?*

*Oh, yes. I remember now. Yes, a letter. How kind of you to come all this way. I get confused, you see? I'm on my own most of the time.*

*I don't understand,* I say, my eyes pooling with tears.

*So, there's no child living here? No little girl? And you're Mrs Macveigh?* Cubby says, putting his arm around me.

*Well of course I'm Mrs Macveigh, who else would I be?*

*And you live here alone?*

*Just me and Mr Pilkington.*

*Who?*

*My cat.*

Before the old lady has time to close her door, I break free from Cubby and run into the forest. He calls after me. I don't care. I want to find something that will take reality away.

All I find is wet leaves and damp ground. I can smell fungus and rotting vegetation. I close my eyes, hoping to catch another glimpse of my red-headed child in her plain cotton dress. But when I do, it isn't Bunny I see, or even Serendipity Wilson. It's Marina, lying on her back in a Polish forest. I think then of the young man thrusting into her, giving her the gift she would never want. It starts to rain. I open my eyes and don't know which way to turn, so I stay perfectly still. The rain becomes thick and heavy. I long to dissolve into the nature around me. I take off my shoes, my coat, my thick stockings and my dress. Now I am standing in the forest, in my underwear, letting the rain soak into me. Still, I don't know what to do. There's a large tree beside me, it must be two hundred years old; that's what I'm thinking: *How old is it?* I want to be like that tree. I want to be still and rooted, ancient, consumed by the forest, and eternally silent. I put my hands on the nearest branch and, pulling myself up on to my toes, start to climb. Before I can hoist myself up, a heavy weight falls upon me, and I am forced to the ground.

*What the hell are you doing?* shouts Cubby. *Why didn't you answer me?* But I cannot move or speak. It's only then I realize I am screaming. My voice is desperate, shouting over and again.

*Mother! Mother! Mother!*

Cubby, holding me to him like a wet rag, strokes my hair and kisses my face.

*It's okay. Everything is going to be okay. I promise. I won't let*

338

*anything hurt you. I'll make it all right. I'll make whatever it is
better.*

Our journey back to Coney Island is silent. I'm sodden
and spent. I look at Cubby, hoping for some kind of com-
munion, to let him know how sorry I am for putting him
through such a spectacle, how ashamed, but he's staring
straight ahead. He doesn't blink. He doesn't move. At Stillwell Avenue, Cubby takes my hand and says, *I think you have
to stop looking now, you know. It's not doing you any good. Sometimes you need to let things go.*

Pulling my hand slowly away, I tell Cubby I need to be
on my own and make my way back to Aunt Betty's house.
I'm exhausted. Thoughts of telephone directories, phone
calls and trips to possible reunions are hopeless and stupid
dreams, I see that now. I need to find another way, but for
the moment, I want to forget everything.

On the way, I stop off at a store. I buy some bread and a
half-bottle of gin. When I get there, the house is empty. My
relief feels like a physical thing, like I'd been carrying a
large rock through a crowd of shouting, wailing people for
years, and only now was I permitted to lay the rock down
and enjoy some solitude. I dry myself on a faded towel,
wrap it around my shoulders, sit on my bed in the pink
room, and look at the drawn curtains across the window. I
open the half-bottle of gin, enjoying the crack of the metal
screw-top as it gives way. Then, wincing even at the thought
of it, I take a sip. Soon enough the thunder breaks, and the
curtains blow open.

There she is, as I knew she would be, holding on to the sides of her little wooden cart; Serendipity Wilson, looking straight into my eyes as she speeds past my window.

Waiting becomes my pastime. All through the winter, I make cinnamon tea, lace it with a swig of gin and take it to my room to sip. I sit on the bed and wait for the roller coaster cars to thunder past my window. I can sit for hours, watching, waiting, sipping. Sometimes I think I see the faces of dancing girls from Fausto's circus among the screamers as they hurtle by. One time, I think I see the bulk of Big Gen fly in and out of view. I'm convinced if I sit in this place long enough, everyone I've ever known will one day fly past my window. So I watch for Bunny. But it's always the bald-headed phantom of Serendipity Wilson that appears among the few out-of-season funsters. Its face does not smile and scream like the others as it thunders by; it is blank and staring right at me through the gaps in the curtained window.

I stare back. And drink my gin.

# 31

# A Hand in the Darkness

Coney Island is beautiful in her winter weeds, she is a bride deserted at the altar, beautifully sad in her fading gown. Nowhere is desolation more magnificent than Coney Island. There's a general feeling of calm when the season ends and darkness spreads its wings from ocean to high-rise blocks. Apart from a few desperate concessions along the boardwalk — and Nathan's (World Famous Hot Dogs), which never shuts its doors — almost everything is closed, locked and bolted. Thin wooden boards quiver over shopfronts and barren attractions. Padlocks clank against metal bars, guarding against miscreants and junkie mischief-makers. Empty bottles scatter the sidewalks, seemingly abandoned by a lone late-night reveller, now long since departed. The constant movement of the waves, foaming white and crashing to the beach, only enhances the stillness of the joyrides; the machines are turned to stone. The Thunderbolt is still most of the time too, only opening for short periods in the evening, and on weekends for the local youth. Aunt Betty's house feels like a slain beast without the coaster's constant noise and rattle.

At these times I wish more than ever I had a big top. I would pitch it on the beach, I would dance on my wire for the November dregs of this bleak and demented dreamland. Darkness is full of beauty. But I do not have a big top. So, I spend the dim daylight hours walking by the ocean, or looking at my window, or simply sleeping in the pink room. Cubby goes to bars with his friends. Aunt Betty cooks, and feeds me, until I tell her to stop because I am getting fat. I wonder if I will be the first person in the world to die of boredom. *You'll have to get in line*, Cubby says.

For the time we were together, Cubby was the world to me. There was a silver thread between us, connecting us. It's still there. Even though we parted, the thread lingers. It floats from my breastbone like the tail of a kite. It's another ghost, attaching me with umbilical clarity to the past. If I tug at it now, the memories will rain down onto the paper, helping me to get to the end. No matter what the outcome, the words will be written.

When the weather grows warm again, before the start of the season (my last in Coney Island), Cubby and his friends organize a party on the beach. I rarely speak to Cubby's friends, can barely distinguish one from another. Even if we pass on the street – if I recognize them at all – at most I smile, then quickly put my head down and walk away. No one really bothers with me, there's no need. Cubby is loved and cherished, that's enough.

After hovering on the outskirts of the party for a while, I slide unseen under the boardwalk, kicking away hot-dog cartons, spray cans and other manifestations of human consumption to find a comfortable spot. The sand is cold under the boardwalk. Someone else might think it unwelcoming; not me. I let myself sink into it, feel the spread of it under my belly and legs, close my eyes and imagine each grain of sand as a minute sticky bud, holding me to the earth. The darkness, the thick air of the enclosed space and the feeling of isolation, soothe me. My mind settles. Thoughts of childhood are strangely comforting now. I am back where I belong; invisible, unseen.

Further down my burrow, I hear voices. People are having sex. Neither the furtive lusts of others nor the piles of refuse bother me. This is New York City, after all. I am one of her adopted children, a denizen of her trash. I continue to think about the sand, how it has been swished around the world by the might of an ocean, made up of minuscule pieces of rock and fishy remains, and how now, it cushions my cheek. I breathe in its peculiar aroma of dead and crumbled things, sink deeper into it, let myself feel my body resting upon each grain. I am just another grain, battered, annihilated by the water, ready to fade into the vastness of the beach. I let my thoughts float away until I believe I have all but disappeared. My relief is so great, I feel the wet trail of a tear squeeze between my cheek and the sand. I'm hidden again. I'm safe.

I have no recollection of how long I lie there before it

happens. Perhaps I drift into sleep, but soon enough, as if trying to pull me back from my dreams, a hand reaches for mine. Cold fingers move across my knuckles, fold around them. I flinch, and for a moment my body tenses. But the fingers are soft, and utterly recognizable.

*I am not afraid of you*, I whisper.

*Good girl. The first lesson is never be afraid. Well done, Mouse. But you need to move forwards now. Stop wasting your talent. Dreamland is gone. How would Bunny feel, if she found you performing on a beach boardwalk for coins? You should be the greatest funambulist who ever lived. Instead, you're hiding like a scared kitten in a rotten seaside town. Didn't I teach you anything?*

Her voice is close, warm; a stark contrast to the icy fingers clenching my hand. It's a reassuring song from the place of my beginnings, from warm evenings under knitted blankets. I wonder now if she is an angel rather than a ghost. Cubby always says *everyone needs an angel*. I relax further into the sand, begin to focus on her touch. Happiness spreads over me, burns through gristle and flesh, and I lie with my eyes closed, in a sort of ecstasy. But the next thing I know, I'm cold, scared to open my eyes, and have an overwhelming feeling of dread: I am a woman, lying under the boardwalk in Coney Island, holding hands with the dead.

The fingers start to tighten around my hand. It begins gradually, so although it has the effect of easing me back into the waking world, I think nothing of it; until it does not stop. They tighten more. My heartbeat ricochets in my chest, the sound strangely dampened by the sand beneath me. There's a thumping panic in my stomach, a throbbing in my windpipe, and still the fingers tighten. It takes me a moment to register the pain. I try to pull away, but the grip is too strong. *Let go*, I say. She doesn't answer. I think I hear my bones cracking, I think she will not stop until every bone in my hand is shot to a thousand pieces. Is she giving me the opportunity to experience physical pain, perhaps even to mourn the loss of some function or other?

I open my eyes, and scream.

Cubby is at my side, arms around me. I cling to him, kiss his neck as he fishes me out of my hidey-hole. He helps me up and, stumbling, takes me away from the boardwalk, the beach, and the others. Cubby strokes my back, my hair, my face as he carries me, falling through the yellow-lit streets of Coney Island. It's just the two of us. The ghoul is gone. Back at the fish restaurant, Cubby looks at my hand, presses softly on each bone and tendon.

*Nothing broken*, he says.

It's late. I don't want to go back to the pink room, so we go to bed. I can smell the warm intoxication on Cubby's breath and skin as he falls asleep. The room is dark, but I'm wide-eyed, looking up at the silver-paper stars, illumin-ated by the familiar glow of my pendant. I touch its cold casing, roll it between the tips of my fingers, make shapes with the light around the room. I use it as a torch, scan the walls: there are his painted angels – so many of them – with their swirling breasts and shiny cocks. I turn my light on Cubby, but he's facing the other way, breathing heavily. I study the angels etched into his back, watch them rise and fall with the rhythms of his body. *You are plagued with angels*, I whisper, *as I am plagued with ghosts*, and then I fall asleep.

# 32

# Tales Told by Serendipity Wilson #6

## *The Blackbird*

*What are you doing, lying under a dirty old wagon on a lovely,
sunny afternoon?*

*Nothing.*

*Nothing?*

*I'm doing nothing.*

*Well you won't mind if I do nothing with you then. Budge up.*

*There's no room.*

*Nonsense, Mouse. There we go. Now, lie still and listen,* said
Serendipity Wilson.

*What?*

*My friend the blackbird, he's back.*

*Is he your friend?*

*Of course, don't you hear him singing?*

*Yes.*

*But I forgot, you don't speak Manx. Silly me.*

*A blackbird can't speak. That's ridiculous. It's a bird.*

*Oh, really, Mouse, must I explain everything?*

*What does he say, then?*

*Kione jiarg, kione jiarg, Vel oo cheet? Vel oo cheet? Skee fleau, skee fleau. Lhondoo, Lhondoo.*

*Not funny. Tell me in English.*

*Red head, red head, Are you coming? Are you coming? Tired waiting, tired waiting. Blackbird, Blackbird.*

*This is another tall tale. You're making fun of me. Birds cannot speak.*

*That shows how much you know. And I would never make fun of you, Mouse, you are far too precious to me. The truth is, blackbirds are very impatient creatures. Every summer when I was little, one came to see me. I'd hear him in the morning, up on the roof calling to me to come and play, but I wouldn't go out without my breakfast, so on he'd go, singing and calling. Until one day, he didn't come anymore.*

*That is a sad story.*

*Not really.*

*Were you afraid he might be dead?*

*No. What dark thoughts you have, Mouse. Why would I think such a thing?*

*If he stopped coming to visit all of a sudden, I would consider him dead.*

*Nonsense. I knew he'd come to find me again one day, and that our time for playing was over for a while. I was growing up, and playing with blackbirds is such a childish thing to do. But I'm fully grown up now, I like childish things.*

*How did he know where to find you?*

*So many questions. Let's wriggle out from under here and sit in the sun, so I can show you something. That's better. Ready?*

*For what?*

*Now, look.*

*It's beautiful, can I touch it?*

*Yes, but be very careful. It's a tail feather. He gave it to me when we were playing on the beach one day. It is the pitchest black in the world. No light will pass through it. Not all his feathers are like this one. This feather was hidden in his tail and has the power to protect against dark thoughts. See how black it is? You will never find anything blacker or darker. It is a very special thing. It's an honour to be the guardian of his most cherished feather. You see, a blackbird will only ever have one truly black feather; if he gives it away, no other will grow in its place. That's why he will always know where to find me. He follows his instinct, the instinct to find his treasured thing. And now, I want you to have it.*

*Me? But won't he be angry if you give it away?*

*Oh, no. On the contrary. He'll be very happy that I've someone so special in my life that I'm willing to give up his feather, and all the protection it holds, to them. Maybe one day you'll pass it on to someone else. But that will be a long time yet. For now, it's your turn to be the blackbird's friend. Listen out for him, my dear Mouse, for he will come to find you wherever you are and sing just for you. All he wants in return is that you remember to salute him, as a thank you for such a powerful gift.*

*What about his song?*

*What about it?*

*In his song he calls to a girl with red hair. Mine's mousey brown. Would you like red hair, Mouse?*

*I'd like to have hair like yours.*

*I'm not sure anyone can have hair like mine, but we can make you a redhead. That's as easy as eggs. And then, when the blackbird sings his song, you can be sure he is singing to you.*

*What if he dies?*

*There you go again. You have greater need for this feather than I originally thought. Why such dark thoughts? It's more likely you will give the feather away before the blackbird dies. Let's say he is an eternal soul. If you believe it is true, then it will be so. The power to believe in things we do not understand is the greatest power we possess, don't you think? Just make sure you don't misuse that power. Don't put your trust in paternalistic deities and other nonsenses. Now, take the feather, put it in your glory-box and banish the dark thoughts, forever.*

# 33

# Rising Stars and Falling Planets

When summer finally comes, all my energy goes into my wire and my new boardwalk routine. I create a masterpiece: an elaborate act based on astronomy and space flight. It pulls together some of my previous acts. The Stargirl is a space-age Titania. The queen of the universe, flitting and sliding over the wire with her stars and planets. She can be playful too. And I use the balloons idea of the Joey clowns act, so she holds on to strings with planets attached at one end, and all of a sudden, she lets one fly away. And off it goes, a lonely planet floating up to the Coney Island sky as the Stargirl now plays the part of an embarrassed empress, having just clumsily lost one of her empires.

I wear a one-piece costume, on to which I sew hundreds of swirling stars, pale planets and bursts of galactic energy. It clings to my body, as if my naked flesh were covered in all things astronomical. Around my head, stars twinkle from a headpiece sprouting satellites on seemingly invisible stalks, and I move across the wire to the strumming sounds of a guitar, and a singer who tells his extraterrestrial tale in lilting English tones.

People flock to see my Stargirl, invoking aliens, gods, and all manner of interplanetary beasts. Since the moon landings, everyone is so excited about anything to do with space travel. I've read magazines and books, and there are television shows all about *the science behind the fiction.*

Balancing above the crowd in my astronomical costume, I really am the Stargirl. I feel what she feels, with her moons and her satellites. I think I see the dreams of people below float towards me as they lift their heads. I sprinkle them with stardust, which I keep in a pouch around my waist, and they sigh aloud and clap as if I've done some especially tricky move. But it's only glitter powder. When, finally, I back-flip, turning my body through the air as I go, landing with a gentle bounce of the wire, the crowd explodes. Sometimes people even lift their hands up to me as if reaching out, wanting to touch me. Why do they do that? I make them believe the Stargirl is powerful enough to give them whatever they want. It works. I'm the biggest act on the boardwalk. I'm the toast of Coney Island.

During the day, my section of the boardwalk is packed solid. It's hard to get down from my wire, so I take fewer and fewer breaks, until eventually Cubby has to climb up the lamp post to pass me food, so I don't faint from hunger and fall off the wire. *Now, that really would be a show,* he says.

Cubby tells me he met some people from Boston, come to Coney Island just to see the Stargirl. Their friends had seen my act and told them all about it, and apparently, everyone is talking about wire walking these days. I spend my evenings now writing letters to local newspapers, even to some of the nationals. As I write, I drink my gin. Not wanting Aunt Betty or Cubby to know how important my bottles are to me now, I hide them. I'm good at hiding things. The newspapers respond well to my letters, send reporters and photographers. Finally, no one can touch me.

Cubby paints a huge sign, all circus swirls in red and gold, reassuring the passing public that they're witnessing *The Greatest Funambulist Who Ever Lived*. He makes photo-cards proclaiming the same thing, and I sign them. At first, they sell for pennies but by the cartload. When one young man asks Cubby for my image to be tattooed down the length of his arm, the price of tattoos goes up. Cubby starts to call his tattoos Skin Paintings. He gets so busy that, with the money he makes, he rents a shop on Neptune Avenue. The walls are painted silver and are covered with pictures of mermaids swimming with crocodiles, of the Stargirl on her wire, and of hermaphrodite angels.

I stay on the boardwalk, but now I employ blue-jeaned boys to make sure the audience pays for what they're seeing. They sell the photo-cards and little pouches of stardust. I remember what Fausto said about never selling yourself too low, so I put the prices up. The blue jeans also make sure there's enough room around my wire, so my act can be seen at its best. Eventually I make a deal with the owner of Astroland, who I spot, day after day, watching my Stargirl act.

He prints large colour posters of me and hangs them all over his amusement park. He also sends them out to newspapers, who print them on their front pages, inviting everyone in New York State and beyond to visit Coney Island to see the Greatest Funambulist Who Ever Lived.

Finally, my act is too big for the boardwalk, so without signing any contract (Fausto taught me well), I agree to move to Astroland. A small version of a shiny big top is set up, all ribbons and flags and blue-and-white stripes. Tickets are sold at a little wooden booth at the entrance to the tent, and the audience sit on neat benches eating cotton candy as spotlights follow me this way and that.

Cubby thinks my new title a bit tacky, especially the Who Ever Lived bit. *The bigger you make yourself, the more the hordes believe it*, I snap. My patience is running out. I'm often irritable and snappy, especially around Cubby. I'm sick of biding my time in Coney Island. Sometimes it feels like I'm cloistered away, living at the ends of the earth. Bunny is lost to me here. She's the reason for my new act, for the letters to newspapers and the photographs. The more I'm seen, the more likely she'll see me.

The best way to hide my drinking from Cubby is to hide myself, so we see less of each other. I spend hour after hour in my pink room, where I can feel the glorious crack of the bottle-top under my hand, watch the clear liquid dance in the white porcelain cup and feel the burn as it runs down my throat. Sometimes I forget what I'm doing and slip out, make my way to the fish restaurant and to Cubby's bed. He doesn't seem to notice my drunkenness, or he doesn't let on.

*Do you ever see her?* I ask him, lying under colourful sheets, my head gently spinning, eyes trying to focus on the pictures hung around the place.

*What?*

*I mean, really see her?*

*Who?*

*Your Angel. The one you paint.*

*Sure, all the time.*

*Does she follow you?*

*What?*

*On the street. Do you hear her footsteps, like an echo of your own? Do you know she's there? Do you turn around quickly, to see her before she has a chance to disappear, only to find her gone?*

*I don't hear her.*

*But you know she's there? I mean, a tangible thing, really there?*

*What? She's a construct, baby. I'm an artist, it's what I do. Like you, I construct, I create. What do you think, I'm some kind of crazy?*

We are reaching our finale. Of course, I need your help to piece the last few pieces of this puzzle together. We're not quite there, but I have a feeling something is about to happen. Bunny is closer than we dare imagine.

The calling card was hand-delivered. One of the blue jeans brigade brought it to the fish restaurant early one morning.

I was still wrapped in a haze of sleep, my head dulled and sore, when he burst in. He said a woman was looking for me down at Astroland the night before. He guessed I'd be at Cubby's, so brought it round first thing.

### PEACHES AGENCY
#### Melba O'Doherty
#### Artiste Management and Talent Agency
#### 415 Lafayette Street, NY 10003
#### Telephone: ★★★ ★★★ ★★★★

As soon as blue jeans leaves (after lingering much longer than he needed to), I forget my thumping head, jump out of bed, take the card, and go straight to the phone booth on Mermaid Avenue. I run all the way and have to wait to catch my breath before picking up the receiver and dialling the number. I put my hand on the glass. It's cold. The last time I'd been inside this phone booth was when Cubby thought he'd found Bunny. Images of the beige-and-white house flash through my mind. My mouth is dry. I force saliva into my throat, swallow, and ready myself to speak.

The phone is answered by a woman. Her name is Mel. She has a rasping, grating voice. Yes, she'd caught my act, both on the boardwalk and at Astroland. There'd been so much talk about the Coney Island Stargirl that, as busy as things are, she couldn't resist a few journeys down to Brooklyn. She loves the act.

*Honestly, you can't compare talent like yours to most of the acts on my books. They are A M A T E U R S*, she says.

Then she starts talking about a tightrope-walking Frenchman, how he's captured the imagination of the world. I make a positive noise and laugh delicately into the receiver, but also explain that what he does is wire walking and is different from my own work on the wire. *I'm a funambulist*, I say, *I don't do stunts.*

She thinks it a pity that I'm English and not French, but concedes that *you can't have everything, and you, darling, have a lot.* When I tell her my stepfather is French, she squeals and drops the phone.

*Perfect!* she says.

Mel wants to lose the Stargirl act because *the gays don't go for that stuff, they want glamour, the whole Bettie Page deal. I never really got it. But who cares. If it sells, it sells.*

Looking out of the phone booth I see Cubby running towards me. It's another hot day and he's sweating. Dark rings spread under the arms of his T-shirt. I think about the boardwalk and wonder aloud if Mel's seen the drag acts over there, because some of them are really great, and I'm sure they'll be ideal. Mel says queens are ten a penny in New York. Wire walking, though, that's something new, exciting, fresh.

*We could really have something with this*, she says. *I've got the Continental Baths at the Ansonia all lined up and ready to go for you. They're gonna L O V E you.*

Mel's idea for an act is to have me dressed up as a French

357

maid, *à la* The Page, complete with feather duster. She thinks it would be good for me to have my own band, nothing fancy – a brass section, guitar and some drums.

*And it's not just the Baths. We can do the family circuit, there's room for everything. I can get you variety stuff on television, E E Easy.*

Cubby pushes the phone booth door open as I am replacing the receiver. He looks expectant, hopeful and happy. I step out onto the sidewalk with my head down and say nothing. He seems to melt before me. I meet his gaze, he looks like a fallen soldier. Then I smile and nod and watch as Cubby's face lights up. He takes off his T-shirt and swings it around his head, whooping and yelling. Then, lifting me from the ground, he throws me in the air like a paper doll.

I wish I could tell you what I did was fair or kind, but I don't want to lie to you, not since we've come so far together. At this point in our story, I was desperate to leave Coney Island. Not only to find Bunny, although that was always paramount in my mind, but because boredom had set in, and I wanted more. Perhaps I was selfish. Without shame or regret, I did what I had to do. Sometimes, when we think we're high enough, on top of the world, we nevertheless keep on climbing, wanting to see what it's like, to rig up at the furthest point, to balance above and beyond the natural order of things. We get used to being good at what we do, which means we get sloppy. And then, we fall.

★

In the end I pack everything – which other than my wires and ropes is very little – with the exception of the Stargirl costume, which I leave hanging in the wardrobe in the pink room, and the picture of Isabella with her pot, which stays pinned on the wall opposite the bed. I tell Aunt Betty and Cubby that I need to go up to Greenwich Village to sort out the contracts and legal arrangements for my new representation. Aunt Betty hugs me in the second parlour, gives me a whole chocolate cake for the journey, and tells me how proud she is. I leave the Thunderbolt House and walk slowly to the fish restaurant. It's a clear day and the air seems purer than usual. I want to breathe it in, to hold it inside for as long as possible.

As we stand in the dreary light of the front room, familiar sounds trickle down from the fish restaurant above: the clatter of pans, cutlery being washed and stacked. They're getting ready for the lunchtime rush (*not so much of a rush these days*, says Cubby). Soon there'll be the cooking smells, the faint odour of frying which always makes our bellies sing, even if we aren't in the faintest bit hungry.

I will always remember Cubby, standing smiling before me, the sleeve of his old shirt ripped at the seam, his curls tucked behind his ears. He lifts me off my feet, kissing my face, my neck, my hands, telling me he always knew I was a star. We laugh. I say, *See you in two days*. He says, *Miss you*. I say, *Miss you too*.

I never go back.

# 34

# Angels, Demons and the
# Final Deliverance

We are almost at the end.

So, now you know my story. I am the girl who went from fleapit halfwit in an English circus, to glamorous cabaret star of New York City. I am the Greatest Funambulist Who Ever Lived. Above all, I am someone who has spent over half a lifetime searching. Which brings me back to you.

No one lives in isolation. Our words, actions, even thoughts, can send people they touch spinning into orbits they never dreamed of or imagined. A simple song, for example, inspired me to create a routine that would propel me from a Coney Island busker into the wider world of entertainment, national recognition, and eventually to be interviewed by you. The singer never knew what powerful magic awaited me inside his song. He could never know of my existence. Yet he was the pebble to my ripple. Those ripples don't stop. They continue. Even now. There's more to these pages than meets the eye, unless, that is, it's the keen eye of a careful reader.

You know the later part of my story already, it's been

widely documented: the cabaret scene, the wild parties, the drink (how hard I fell into the lap of my mother's demon, once unshackled from my Coney Island angel), the purchase of a strip club. (Did I do it for publicity? Let's say I did, just to clear up the question.) Surely you were brought to one of my family shows, as a youngster? Every child in New York state saw those shows. Then there's that drunken television appearance; you might think burning a hundred-dollar bill in one hand while balancing a Martini in the other, wearing nothing but a postage-stamp-sized bikini and ten-inch heels, in front of the vice president of a cable TV channel, to be a crass, egotistical stunt — and that might, in some way, be true.

Yes, I wanted to be seen. But it wasn't entirely a matter of ego. It was for the ripple effect. If I couldn't find Bunny, then at least she might know me. I did all I could to ensure as many people as possible would see me wearing my shining pendant. If that meant destroying myself in the process, it was the price I'd have to pay. Even Serendipity Wilson knew that. Of course, there was no point killing myself. I was playing a long game. The ripples were slow-moving, going back and forth with the ebb and flow of my life. Eventually though, my impatience took over, something had to give.

I've explained how I'm in complete control when on my wire. It's practice. I remember watching the Joey clowns when I was a child. It was a great lesson. They rehearsed harder than any other artiste. Their act had everything;

acrobatics, even funambulism. But they taught themselves the one big lesson most of us miss: how to fall.

For all my hard work, my attention to artistic detail, for all the carousing and showing myself off with my shining pendant, if anyone remembers me at all (and perhaps that includes you?), it's because they watched as I fell.

A one-off Times Square performance with special effects, light-show, full orchestra and a blonde-haired singer in a ballgown, provided the perfect stage. There'd been gossip about my sobriety, which only served to boost my popularity. Tickets were said to be like gold dust, so the show was to be broadcast live on the Saturday Varieties; family entertainment in the heart of the home. Ideal for reaching as many people as possible.

My wire didn't need to be as high as the buildings around Times Square. I made it clear, as always, this wasn't a stunt, rather a show of artistic endeavour. The stroke of genius was having the wire strung only a few feet above the heads of the standing crowds. People give a softer landing than concrete and asphalt. I wore a plain white costume, no rhinestones or flashy colours, so my pendant might be seen at its shining best. I even made sure I'd had just enough to drink, to allow the reporters to run wild with the story.

But I wasn't drunk.

From the window of my hotel, I watched the crowds gather. They came early. Parts of the square were cordoned off for ticket holders and the wire was rigged up, but people went about their normal business. Traffic screamed, billboards flashed, and hawkers hawked. The wire was between two scaffold podiums on either side of the square. I'd check everything before daylight faded, but aside from that the only thing I could do was watch and wait.

As night fell and the streets pulsed with excitement, I admit being taken aback at the size of the crowd. I'd never seen so many people crammed into one place. They seemed to soak up the light, making Times Square, with all its brightness and continually blinking billboards, appear a darker place than usual.

Wearing coveralls over my costume, I made my way out to do the final checks. Officials were running about, TV cameras stood on stages with directors and goodness knows who waving their arms, shouting commands. The orchestra was in place; tuning up, checking instruments. I'd put a miniature bottle of vodka in my coverall pocket, more for show (in case anyone was looking – and they were) than anything else, but it would provide a decent top-up. When everything was ready, I sat on the podium and took the coveralls off.

The noise was tremendous as I took my place on the edge of the podium, drew a deep breath, and lifted my arms above my head as a sign of readiness. Everything went dark. All at once, the street lights and every flashing billboard were extinguished, plunging us all into deep darkness, and other than the odd yelp of delighted shock, there was a sudden and profound hush. Then, the strains of an orchestra, a slow and plaintive introduction to a well-known jazz classic, and golden lights – appearing one by one at first, then in clusters, creating shapes and patterns over all the billboards – flooding us with light. I saw the uplifted faces of the gasping crowd. It was magnificent. Tears filled my eyes. I sniffed them back and stepped onto the wire.

As soon as my toe touched the taut steel, the crowd burst into spontaneous applause. The lady in the ballgown opened her mouth. It seemed all Manhattan could hear the words as she slowly sang: *J'ai Deux Amours*.

Even I was thrilled by the spectacle. But there was work to be done. I danced holding a large white parasol for balance. I was a swan in flapper garb. My parasol a great wing, helping me fly along the wire. The lighting ensured that my pendant shone at its very best. The orange glow seemed to emanate from my breastbone, as if it was part of me. It gave me the reassurance I needed. She was with me, lighting my way. I remember little of the routine after the first few beats. My heart was heavy in my chest. I listened to the music, danced and was lost.

In the centre of the wire, sliding down into the splits when the song came to its end, I was suddenly and completely alert. My skin sparked; pure electricity. I had to concentrate hard on the tight feelings in my muscles. As the last note sounded, I pushed out my hip, knocked myself off-balance, and fell.

Falling, I pulled my pelvis around and stuck my right arm, slightly bent, underneath, aiming myself sideways on. My left arm was wrapped around my ribs, for protection.

Then, just as the Joey clowns did, to reduce injury, I went limp. My timing was impeccable. It wasn't far to fall. I hit at exactly the right moment, in almost the right place. My bruised hip, twisted knee and sprained ankle had all been accounted for. The only accident was bashing my head against an unforeseen street bench and smashing my cheekbone.

There were screams. At first all the lights went out. Billboards soon came back on though, illuminating the pool of blood that, due to the gash in my face, now seemed to cover me. I hadn't expected blood, and felt a quick rush of shock. When I recovered and saw how well my white costume contrasted with the red streams running down my front, I couldn't help but smile. Although it hurt, it was perfect.

I didn't enjoy the pain. But strangely, Bunny or no Bunny, it wasn't the worst way to go into retirement. My wounds have healed, for the most part. There's no permanent damage and, by looking like I cheated death and coming out of things sober, I've created a small legend for myself. Two years on and a self-confessed recluse, journalists still want to interview me. As you know, until you came along, I've turned them down.

Now, I will tell you what you certainly do not know. During every single moment of my glittering cabaret career, with its limousine rides through SoHo, nights filled with champagne and cocaine, and numerous sexual conquests, I was numb. From the moment I left Coney Island, my life has been a tasteless meal; all the treats I can eat, but with no flavour. Even my faithful tormentor kept her distance. I'm glad to be done with it.

I thought Serendipity Wilson's ghost was gone forever. It's strange, but sometimes I longed for her, and so acutely I thought my mind might break. Even in her absence, she haunted me. Losing her a second time helped my demons do their job that little bit better. How clever of her. I know now she was biding her time.

Through it all, I missed Cubby the most. I didn't allow myself to think about him. So, I stopped feeling. You could've pricked me with a thousand pins and I would've felt nothing. But it doesn't matter, because, dear reader, I wasn't doing it for myself. I was doing it for you.

Something has been playing on my mind since I started this correspondence, this task. Will we meet again? Face to face? I'd like that, very much. I wonder if you've been thinking the same thing? How I wish I knew your feelings, now, after reading this. If we do meet, I may be tempted to put you on the low wire. Are you afraid of heights? I know such things can be family traits. No matter. We'd keep you low to the ground, avoid any accidents. You'll find it easier than you think, your long limbs are perfect for it.

I'm thinking about when we first met for the interview, how your eyes lit upon my pendant. Professional curiosity? Oh, I was sick with nerves. Did you notice my hands shaking? The chain-smoking? Perhaps not. I've become very good at feigning confidence over the years. I must confess something to you now: even before we met, I knew who you were. I did my research. And of course, I recognized your name.

I have in my hand the section of a page torn roughly from a picture book. On one side is a photograph of a young woman in Victorian dress. Her skirts are shorter than one would expect, and beneath them hang four legs. We know her name is Myrtle Corbin and that I found the thing in my glory-box after Serendipity Wilson's fall. It's the reason I came to America and to Coney Island. Written across the image, in bold, red letters, are some names and an address.

I'm sure of one thing, it's not really my life story that interests you; you've been thinking about this note for some time. It's the reason you've continued to read on, right up to this moment and these very words. Had you expected to see the names of your parents written down in these pages? The name John Frazer may already have been a giveaway. I had considered keeping to his circus persona, but it's a common enough name. I wonder, do you remember him? It almost destroyed me to learn how he left this life, and you. He was a selfish man. Did they ever speak to you about your mother? About your origins? Was anything ever said about your birth? About the circus? Or, about me? No, they wouldn't know of my existence. Did you know where your pendant came from, at least? Anything of its significance? So many questions, and I'm not sure I deserve to have them answered, but I cannot help but pour them onto the page.

Oh, Bunny, did you really think I wouldn't know you?

I travelled an ocean to find you. My task, when I crossed the sea with a bald-headed spectre at my heels, was to deliver her to you. Perhaps you've known all along? Was it the pendant? Did you look me up because you'd seen me perform years ago, and saw I wore a strange pendant, identical to your own? Was it the Times Square performance? Did you see the pendant then? And the fall? Did it work? I wonder if it's been eating away at you all this time, until eventually you found a way to meet me. An interview was the perfect thing. You had a good look at the pendant then, didn't you? Asked me all sorts of questions about it. Was it during the interview that the penny dropped? Surely you don't remember me? Unless that is the gift of your ancient ancestors. Do you remember me, Bunny?

This is all conjecture.

You couldn't have been sure. Until now, you were merely curious. You had your suspicions and so you read on. It's a relief to finally cure that curiosity. Please know that I never stopped thinking about you, not for a single day. I knew our story wasn't over. Cubby once told me to never lose hope – do you remember? I wrote that down for you – so I didn't. The pages left in my notebooks are blank. But let me get to the end of my story. I want to be tidy in my tale-telling. In any case, having read this far, you deserve a proper ending.

One month after I left Coney Island for Manhattan, I wrote to Aunt Betty. I explained myself as best I could and sent a cheque, paying back the money for the trip to Tarrytown.

Of course, she wrote back immediately, with the cheque ripped to pieces. And there began our real friendship. She kept me informed on things in Coney Island, even sent parcels of chocolate cake and bread pudding (made from an old English recipe she found, to remind me of home, she said). We've written of our feelings, discussed world events, she's even recommended books for me to read. Aunt Betty never scolded me for my behaviour, she never judged me, no matter what might have been printed in gossip columns. Through her letters, she's shown me love. I suppose you could say, a mother's love; something I never thought I'd know. I've received it with a great deal of gratitude and tried my best to return it. Her letters have been a lifeline, especially since my fall. I told her that since leaving Coney Island I've felt her heart beating in my own breast, right next to mine, guiding me and helping me through difficult times. And until a few months ago, when that gentle pulse stopped, I think I really did feel it. Aunt Betty died peacefully in her sleep. I knew she was gone before anyone informed me. To my surprise, it was Cubby who wrote to tell me the news.

As expected, there was quite a crowd at the funeral parlour on Mermaid Avenue. The place was filled with flowers, the smell heady. I knelt and laid a small spray of bluebells (her favourite) with the rest. As I got to my feet, I felt a tugging at my chest, the pull of an invisible thread. I turned, and there was Cubby.

He was smiling. His hair, now short, looked neat and smart. We talked softly to each other. He showed me a scrapbook Aunt Betty had kept, full of newspaper cuttings outlining my various exploits, not all of them good. She had, he told me, been very proud of her funambulist. After everything I'd done, this caught in the back of my throat. Cubby handed me a white cotton handkerchief, still folded from where he'd taken it from the packet, which made me smile. I dabbed my eyes and handed it back. There were little wet patches on it, smeared with black. He shoved the handkerchief into his breast pocket and followed me into the garden.

*Did you ever find her?* he asked.

*No. I mean, she's found me.*

*You know, I saw you fall, watched it live on TV.*

*Yes. Aunt Betty said.*

*I wanted to pick you up. I wanted to go right over there and pick you up.*

*I'm sorry.*

*It was for Bunny, right? That was the point.*

*Right.*

Cubby took my hands in his, they were big, warm.

*I've missed you*, he said.

Enough. Let me finish and be done. When I get to the end, I'll be free from the ghosts, free from the angels, and most importantly, free from my search for you. This is my task then, to pass these characters on. I'm not convinced they will go willingly, or even at all. They're stubborn and set in their ways. Nevertheless, I give them to you.

Marina and Manu are yours now, as are Big Gen, Fausto, Stella and even my darling Solomon. Look gently over their memories, they deserve your care. Then, there is your mother, my mentor and tormentor. You should treasure Serendipity Wilson most of all. She has spent a lifetime haunting me in your name. Remember to hold her light high. The darkness is always around us, your pendant is a torch, bright enough to keep you from falling from your wire (whatever that may be). Do not put aside Manannán mac Lir as mere myth; there are truths within those tales. It's why she told them. Keep them close so they may work their magic for you.

As for the faceless blue jeans, they're here, I suppose, somewhere in this city. In any case, I commend even them to your care. I will keep hold of Cubby, the memory of our time together is what I need to keep myself upright, balanced, and safe. Our silver thread is as strong as ever, I feel it, pulling me away from this room and into the future.

With all the imagination in the world, I couldn't have stopped your mother from falling. No matter how many words I put on the page, I cannot unwrite it. Róża, my grandmother, too can never be saved, and Marta is forever the victim of a cruelty too terrible to contemplate. None of this can be changed. I cannot get my childhood back or live a life that was never mine. In spite of everything, I wouldn't want to.

All we can do is perform our lives as gloriously as possible. For my part, I'm happy to take my applause where

I can. This is the end because I cannot write the next chapter, it needs to be lived.

As I look out of my window, every person I see has their own wire to walk. I wish them luck in their endeavours, and hope they manage to grip their toes around the metal, feel its power, and somehow hold on. It is what I'm doing now, it's what we will always do.

When I pull this page from the spool of my machine, I will do so quickly. It will make a sharp zipping noise and, like at the end of a performance when I bathe in applause, it will fill me with joy. I'll hold the page up to the window, gripping it lightly between thumb and index finger to avoid spoiling the crisp surface of the paper. The pale light will filter through its whiteness, showing it to be unblemished by anything other than my words. Then, I will go to my bed, climb under my velvet sheets, and close my eyes. I will be aware of my breathing and, like a cat that purrs in spite of itself, I will fall asleep, smiling.

In the morning, I will rise early. The old documents left sitting on my desk will burn in the copper pan, their ashes tossed from my window. They have no power now. I'll package up my typed pages into a brown paper parcel and tie it up with a length of yellow wool, unravelled from my old jumper.

My pendant is my parting gift. I am, at last, taking it from around my throat as I type. It will be the first thing you see when you open the parcel. When I'm done with all this, I will leave my room, break out into the day and deliver everything to you. Responsibility for the parcel and its contents will rest entirely on your shoulders. You are the reader, you own the stories now.

At last I'll be free to walk my wire again. But I'll choose not to. I will not perform for the hordes. I will be one of them: a faceless body in the crowd, perfectly balanced in grace and complicity with all around me. It's also time for me to be moving on from this squalid little room. I'll follow my silver thread, take the subway back to Coney Island, find Cubby, and give him the blackbird feather your mother once entrusted to me. Other than myself, it's all I have to give. I can only hope he will be happy to receive it, and me.

If, on my journey into the future, anyone sees me, if they ask who I am and what I do, I will not shy away. I will tell them that I am the Funambulist, come from across the sea to make my home in a city that requires the full attention of my art. Then, I will put one foot in front of the other, feel my heel strike the solidity of the street, and like the mass of people around me, I will walk.

# Acknowledgements

Writing *A Girl Made of Air* has been a fascinating voyage of discovery. There have been calm waters and tempests, burning seas and cold winds, but through it all I've learned so much about writing and about myself. To everyone who has supported, helped, facilitated and taught me, thank you.

First and foremost, thanks go to Samar Hammam, my wonderful agent. Thank you so much, Samar. Your unbending support and passion for *A Girl Made of Air* has given me a strength I didn't know I had. Thank you for guiding me through difficult times. Thank you for your tenacity and your ferocious belief in this book and in me. I bless the day I met you.

A million thanks to my editor Emma Capron, without whom this book would simply not exist. Thank you, Emma, for your enthusiasm, your wisdom, and your gentleness. Also, to Pip Watkins, whose beautiful cover design has left us all breathless, and thanks to the designers at Quercus for working tirelessly to bring the beauty to life. Special thanks go to Milly Reid and Hannah Winter, you are both amazing and I am so grateful for all your hard work. And to all the team at Quercus, thank you so much.

To Bruce Coker, my very first reader, eternal thanks. Time is precious and you've never hesitated to give yours. Thank you for talking me through the tricky bits, thanks for your friendship, and for the many pints of stout. You're a star.

And to my other first readers: Tracey Rees-Cooke, Anna Tagg and Tim Lewes Gibbon, I am grateful beyond words to each of you. Thank you, thank you.

This novel began life quietly, on a short course at Birkbeck University. Thanks go to the tutor Carol Barker, your early enthusiasm spurred me on. And to my tutors on the Creative Writing BA course at Birkbeck, many thanks all. I am especially grateful to Luke Williams whose teaching and early guidance was crucial. Thank you, Luke, you were a marvellous and inspiring teacher.

I must acknowledge that this novel was produced through a time of grief. It has become a homage to those I lost during its creation. So, to Simon, for your friendship and care, which I will always miss, thank you. To my first hero David Bowie, whose universe and music will always be *the pebble to my ripple*. I'm beyond grateful. To Prem, I still can't quite believe you're gone. Simply, thank you.

Words of acknowledgement go to the writers, books and people that inspired and helped form the background to *A Girl Made of Air*. The works of Sophia Morrison and A. W. Moore were the base for my re-imaginings of old Manx stories in *Tales Told by Serendipity Wilson*. Jean Paul Sartre's classic first novel *Nausea* was the foundation of young Marina's belief system. And *Days and Memory* by Charlotte Delbo was an invaluable resource for trying to understand (although it's perhaps impossible to ever understand) the experience of holocaust survivors. The Freaks of Big Gen's book were all real people. I have tried, albeit briefly, to do justice to their real-life stories, which have been such an inspiration to me, in so many ways. I look down the passage of history and holler my thanks to them all.

I thank the Isle of Man, the landscape and the people, for giving me the stories that coloured my early life and fired my imagination. And finally, I thank my husband, Andy, to whom I dedicate this book. Thank you for your patience, your love and your unfaltering belief. This book is for you.